A **LIAM**

BLOOD RIDGE

NEW YORK TIMES #1 BESTSELLER **TONY LEE** WRITING AS

JACK GATLAND

Hooded Man MEDIA
INSPIRATION • PRODUCTION • PUBLICATION

Published by Hooded Man Media.

Cover design by L1graphics

First Edition: July 2025

PRAISE FOR JACK GATLAND

'Fast-paced and action packed, Jack Gatland's thrillers always deliver a punch.'

'This is one of those books that will keep you up past your bedtime, as each chapter lures you into reading just one more.'

'This book was excellent! A great plot which kept you guessing until the end.'

'Couldn't put it down, fast paced with twists and turns.'

'The story was captivating, good plot, twists you never saw and really likeable characters. Can't wait for the next one!'

'Totally addictive. Thoroughly recommend.'

'Moves at a fast pace and carries you along with it.'

'Just couldn't put this book down, from the first page to the last one it kept you wondering what would happen next.'

LIQUIDATE THE PROFITS

FOLDED HANDS

Declan Walsh. Ellie Reckless. Tom Marlowe. Liam Harper. Ryder Waites. Sebastian Silver & Laura Carlyle. Damian Lucas. Danny Charming.

Also by Jack Gatland

DI DECLAN WALSH BOOKS

LETTER FROM THE DEAD

MURDER OF ANGELS

HUNTER HUNTED

WHISPER FOR THE REAPER

TO HUNT A MAGPIE

A RITUAL FOR THE DYING

KILLING THE MUSIC

A DINNER TO DIE FOR

BEHIND THE WIRE

HEAVY IS THE CROWN

STALKING THE RIPPER

A QUIVER OF SORROWS

MURDER BY MISTLETOE

BENEATH THE BODIES

KILL YOUR DARLINGS

KISSING A KILLER

PRETEND TO BE DEAD

HARVEST FOR THE REAPER

CROOKED WAS HIS CANE

A POCKET FULL OF POSIES

CHEATING MY DESTINY

STAND AND DELIVER

WE PLAY WITH DEATH

TOM MARLOWE BOOKS

SLEEPING SOLDIERS

TARGET LOCKED

COVERT ACTION

COUNTER ATTACK

STEALTH STRIKE

BROAD SWORD

ROGUE SIGNAL

SNIPER ALLEY

SHADOW THREAT

SENTRY POINT

ELLIE RECKLESS BOOKS

PAINT THE DEAD

STEAL THE GOLD

HUNT THE PREY

FIND THE LADY

BURN THE DEBT

TAKE THE KING

LIAM HARPER BOOKS

FINAL STRIKE

BLOOD RIDGE

TRACK SHIFT

CARLYLE & SILVER BOOKS

SILVER AND THE SUNDAY CYPHER

DAMIAN LUCAS BOOKS

THE LIONHEART CURSE

STANDALONE BOOKS

THE BOARDROOM

As Tony Lee

STANDALONE

TWELVE TASKS

THE PLAYING CARD WAR

KNAVE OF SPADES

QUEEN OF BLADES

CHARMING

LAST PRINCE STANDING

For Mum, who inspired me to write.

For Tracy, who inspires me to write.

CONTENTS

1

PIT STOP

Liam Harper eased the Triumph Bonneville to a stop outside the rural petrol station, the engine's distinctive purr fading to silence. *Terry's Auto & Gas,* the weathered sign announced, though the illuminated letters had failed on the "Auto" part.

Harper's eyes scanned the property. Habit, not necessity. Older man in grease-stained overalls tinkering under a Chevy's hood. Young woman pacing beside a sedan, hood up, checking her phone with mounting frustration.

Harper swung his leg over the bike, removing his helmet and running a hand through his short dark-brown hair, flattened from hours on the road. The scar above his right eyebrow – a one-inch line that split it in two – caught the sunlight as he stretched.

Two months on the road and I still can't get comfortable on this bloody thing.

He reached into his satchel, fingers brushing against the smooth river stone he'd carried since childhood. Stupid superstition, but it had kept him alive this long.

'Need some fuel?' The mechanic straightened from the Chevy, wiping his hands on a rag that had seen better days.

'And your bay for about twenty minutes, if you don't mind,' Harper replied, his accent carrying traces of British inflection overlaid with American tones. 'Steering head bearing needs a quick adjustment.'

The mechanic – *Terry*, according to the name stitched on his coveralls – nodded appreciatively.

'You know your way around that Bonneville, then?'

'I'd hope so. We've been together long enough.' Harper unstrapped his compact toolkit from behind the seat and glanced towards the woman with the broken-down car. 'Problem over there?'

Terry followed his gaze and lowered his voice.

'Lady's alternator belt snapped. Simple fix, but she's waiting on the tow company. I offered to look at it, but...'

He shrugged.

'Warranty issues she said.'

Harper nodded. *Manufacturers and their service contracts.* The bloody stranglehold of the fine print.

The woman checked her phone again, frustration written across her face like neon.

'Bay's yours,' Terry said, gesturing towards the open garage door. 'I'll be inside if you need anything.'

Harper wheeled the Bonneville into the garage bay. It was a nice place with a well-organised tool wall, surprisingly clean for a middle-of-nowhere operation. Terry might run a small shop but he took pride in his work. These days, that seemed to be more and more a rarity.

He positioned the bike on its centre stand and began laying out his tools. The steering head bearing adjustment wasn't complex but required a touch of precision. Too tight and the steering would bind; too loose and it would develop a dangerous wobble at speed. Not that he hadn't driven through worse. *But why push your luck?*

As he worked, he kept one eye on the forecourt. The woman was still pacing, checking her watch now alongside her phone. She had somewhere to be, clearly. Something important, judging by her growing frustration.

Not your problem, he reminded himself. *Not everyone needs saving.*

Harper had just removed the top triple clamp when a pickup truck pulled into the station. Two men were inside, watching the woman with what Harper felt was a little too much predatory focus. They stepped out – country types in worn flannels and work boots, the driver had a knife clipped to his belt pocket.

Not unusual in these parts but Harper noted it anyway.

The passenger kept his hand in his jacket pocket.

Another knife maybe. Or something else.

They were a double act of a lanky driver in a yellow plaid shirt, beside a short, rotund passenger in a blue and white varsity jacket. For a moment Harper had an image of Laurel and Hardy with a nasty streak, or C3PO and R2D2 from *Star Wars* with switchblades instead of protocol programming.

They approached the woman who stiffened visibly.

'Car trouble?' the lanky one asked; loud enough for Harper to hear.

'I'm fine,' the woman replied, her tone clipped. 'Tow-truck's on its way.'

'Long wait out here. We could give you a ride into town,' the shorter guy said, flicking his tongue around his mouth like a frog as he moved slightly to the woman's left, blocking her path back to her car.

'No, thank you.' The woman stepped back, glancing towards the convenience store where Terry had disappeared.

Christ. This dance again.

Harper continued working on the Bonneville but his movements slowed, half his attention now on the developing situation outside.

Lanky moved closer.

'Come on now, don't be like that. Me and my buddy are just trying to help.'

'I said I'm fine.' The woman's voice took on an edge but, while she focused on Lanky, the man Harper now identified as "Frog" had circled around to the woman's car, peering through the windows.

'Nice ride. Lot of luggage in there. Going somewhere special?'

Harper set down his wrench. *Shit. This had just shifted from annoying to concerning.* The woman was travelling alone, vulnerable… and these arseholes weren't Good Samaritans.

Before Harper could decide whether to intervene, a tow-truck rumbled into the station, diesel engine announcing its arrival. The truck pulled up beside the stranded sedan, BRENDAN'S TOWING emblazoned on its side in garish red and yellow lettering.

The two men from the pickup exchanged glances, then retreated, climbing back into their truck… but not leaving. Instead they parked on the far side of the lot, engine idling, watching.

The tow-truck driver – a stocky bloke with a shaved head, his arms covered in faded tattoos – climbed down and approached the woman.

'You Nadine? Problem with the alternator belt, right?' the

driver's voice carried across the forecourt. 'That's what you said on the phone?'

'That's what I think,' the woman – Nadine – replied. 'It just stopped while I was driving. Battery light came on first.'

'Yeah, classic symptom,' the driver made a show of examining the engine. 'Problem is, with these models once the belt goes it usually damages the alternator too. Sometimes the water pump.'

Harper's hands paused on the wrench.

That was complete bullshit.

'But... it just stopped working. There wasn't any grinding or anything,' Nadine protested.

'That's how they fail in these cars,' the driver said with what felt like practised certainty. 'We're looking at parts and labour... probably eight hundred minimum. Plus the tow to our shop, which is—'

'Eight hundred dollars?' She sounded panicked now. 'I can't... I don't have that kind of money right now.'

'Credit card?' the driver suggested helpfully. 'Or we could work out a payment plan. Course, we'd need to hold onto the car until it's paid off...'

Screw this.

Harper wiped his hands on a shop rag, rose from his bike and walked over, toolkit in hand. Terry had emerged from the store, watching with a frown but keeping his distance.

'Sounds expensive,' Harper said, inserting himself into the conversation. 'Mind if I take a look?'

The driver's head swivelled towards him, eyes narrowing.

'You a mechanic?'

'Just someone who knows cars.' Harper placed his toolkit on the ground and leaned under the hood. Ten seconds was all it took to spot the issue. 'Serpentine belt's gone but the alternator looks fine. No damage to the pulleys either.'

'Listen, buddy—' the driver started.

'You got a replacement belt in your truck?' Harper asked, cutting him off. 'Should be a 6PK1740 for this model, if I remember right.'

The driver's face darkened.

'Look, I don't know who you think you are but this isn't your business. The lady called us.'

'I'm just offering a second opinion,' Harper straightened, meeting the driver's glare. 'Terry probably has the right belt in stock. Fifteen-minute fix tops.'

'And who's going to do the work? You?' The driver stepped closer, using his bulk to intimidate. Behind him, a second tow-truck pulled in, unmarked. Two men climbed out, watching the confrontation.

Harper also noticed the pickup truck was still there, both men now openly watching.

This wasn't random. Too coordinated. Not just opportunistic predators but a system.

'I could,' Harper shrugged. 'Or Terry could.'

'How about you mind your own business?' One of the newly arrived men approached, younger than the driver with a scraggly beard and too much confidence. 'This is our call.'

They were positioning themselves around him now; the driver slightly to the front, the others moving to cut off retreat. Practised. Coordinated. But Harper had seen this formation before in places a hell of a lot more dangerous than here.

'Ma'am,' Harper addressed Nadine without taking his eyes off the driver, 'would you prefer a fifteen-minute repair or an eight-hundred-dollar tow and overhaul?'

'I... the repair, obviously,' she replied. 'If that's really all it needs.'

The driver's jaw tightened.

'You're interfering with my business, pal.'

'Not intentionally,' Harper said. 'Just offering the lady options. Ones that aren't bullshit rip-off scams.'

The younger one with the beard moved first, reaching for Harper's shoulder.

'Time for you to leave—'

Harper sidestepped, using the man's momentum against him. Simple pivot and a subtle shift of weight. The man stumbled past, off-balance and confused.

The third man rushed in, swinging wildly; Harper threaded his forearm inside the punch and shifted his weight, throwing the aggressor off balance, then countered with a short vicious strike to the solar plexus – just enough to empty the lungs, put the guy on his knees, and build some room to work.

From the corner of his eye, Harper saw the pickup duo exit their vehicle, the shorter one reaching behind his back.

This was escalating way beyond a simple scam.

The driver pulled something from his back pocket – a collapsible baton that snapped open with a metallic click.

'You've made a big mistake, friend.'

Harper stood relaxed; hands loose at his sides.

'You sure? Because from my point of view, I haven't made any yet.'

The driver lunged, swinging the baton in a wide arc. Harper dropped under it, following with a Muay Thai sweep kick. As the driver stumbled backward, Harper twisted the baton from his grip with a sharp twist of the wrist.

The bearded guy had regained his footing and charged

again. Harper employed close quarters combat techniques, grappling and accelerating the now badly off-balance man face-first into the side of the tow truck. A deep metallic *thunk* was followed by the big man collapsing onto grease-stained pavement.

'You really need to learn from your mistakes, dipshit,' Harper said as he turned back to the others. The third man kept his distance now, reassessing.

The short guy from the pickup had drawn a battered pistol and was approaching fast, trying to keep it concealed at his side. Harper collapsed the baton and flicked it away with precision, sending it spinning at the armed man's face. The unexpected projectile made him flinch and raise his hands – gun momentarily exposed.

'He's got a gun!' Nadine shouted, diving behind her car. Terry ducked back inside – hopefully to call the police.

Harper glided towards the armed man. The glance toward the tall guy from the pickup showed him pulling something from the truck bed – a shotgun, from the look of things.

Bloody brilliant. Local welcoming committees pulling out all the stops.

Harper closed the distance to pistol guy before he could recover; a vicious elbow strike to the side of the head dropped him instantly, the gun clattered to the ground. Harper kicked it under a nearby car, then stomped a booted foot into the man's chest for good measure.

'That's what you get for waving a gun at me, asshole.'

The shotgun wielder was smarter, maintaining distance as he brought the weapon to bear.

'Freeze or I'll blow your head off!' he shouted, gesturing with the shotgun.

Harper froze; hands slightly raised. Fifteen feet – too far to close in before the man could fire. The barrel looked steady; he knew how to handle the weapon.

'Just walk away,' Harper said calmly. 'Nobody's been seriously hurt, yet.'

'You think this is a damn negotiation?' The man pumped the shotgun, chambering a round. 'On your knees, hands behind your head!'

Harper had been in worse situations. Kabul. Mosul. A particularly unpleasant night in Glasgow he preferred not to remember. But this was a petrol station in rural Pennsylvania. The stakes seemed disproportionate to a simple roadside scam.

What the hell was their game?

A sharp crack echoed across the forecourt and the shotgun wielder jerked backward, dropping his weapon. For a split second Harper thought someone had fired a shot – but then he saw Terry standing at the corner of the building, a compound bow in hand, another arrow nocked and ready.

'Next one won't just graze your arm,' Terry called out, voice steady. 'I suggest you boys clear out before the state police arrive. Called them five minutes ago.'

The shotgun wielder clutched his bleeding arm, looking from Terry to his fallen companions, then back to Harper.

'This ain't over,' he growled, backing towards the pickup.

'For today, it is,' Harper replied.

The remaining men gathered their injured, collecting the shotgun but leaving the pistol under the car. They piled into their vehicles – the tow-truck crews and the pickup duo – and peeled out of the station in a spray of gravel and exhaust.

Harper turned to Terry who was lowering the bow.

'Interesting choice of weapon.'

'Bow hunting's my retirement plan,' Terry said with a shrug. 'Gas station's just to pay the bills.'

Nadine emerged from behind her car, shaking.

'Who were those men? What did they want?'

'More than a tow job,' Harper said, scanning the area to make sure all threats had gone. 'You travelling alone?'

She hesitated, then nodded.

'I'm heading to my sister's place in Maryland. I've got... some things I need to sort out.'

Harper didn't press; everyone had their reasons for being on the road.

'Let's take a look at your car,' he suggested.

THIRTY MINUTES LATER, THE SEDAN'S ENGINE WAS RUNNING smoothly. Harper closed the hood as Nadine tried to press sixty dollars into his palm.

'Really, I can't thank you enough,' she said. 'They've done this before, haven't they? It wasn't just about my car.'

'Out here, you never know,' Harper replied, wiping his hands on a shop rag. 'Stranded motorists, local businesses. People like these guys? They create problems then charge to solve them.'

'The police don't do anything?'

'Hard to prove without witnesses willing to testify.' Terry had joined them, carrying a small paper bag. 'Most folks just pay to avoid trouble. I've called the cops before, but half of the guys around here gain a little "bonus" from people like these, if you get my drift, so it's better to either let it happen, or make it go away. Here, made you some sandwiches for the road.'

Nadine accepted the bag gratefully.

'I don't know what would have happened if you two hadn't been here.'

'Nothing good,' Harper said simply.

'Will they come back? For you, I mean?' she asked Terry.

The older man adjusted his cap.

'Probably. But I've made my bed now.' He patted the compound bow leaning against the wall. 'And I never miss twice.'

Harper had finished reassembling his Bonneville; the steering head bearing was now properly adjusted, the bike ready for the final leg of his journey.

'You should get going before it gets dark,' he told Nadine. 'Stay on the main highways the rest of the way.'

She nodded, climbing into her car.

'What about you?'

'I'll be right behind you until the Maryland state line,' Harper replied. 'Just to be sure.'

As Nadine prepared to pull out, Harper was securing his helmet when Terry approached.

'You military?' he asked. 'If you don't mind my asking.'

Harper paused, then nodded once.

'Something like that.'

'Thought so. My old man was 101st Airborne. Vietnam. He had that same way about him – seeing everything, moving like you do...' Terry hesitated. 'Taught me everything I know. Whatever you're heading towards, watch your back. Word gets around in these hills.'

'Appreciate the warning,' Harper said, meaning it. 'You?'

'I called my sons, they're in Hagerstown,' Terry grinned. 'One's a linebacker, the other's even bigger. Those guys come around here, they'll get a shock.'

He sighed, his face dropping.

'Shame neither of them can fix a car for shit,' he muttered sadly as he gave Harper a last nod and walked back to the garage. 'Heading out to see them once I close up shop. Got a hunting cabin near there we use; I'll be good there for a few days until things calm. And when we get back, if these damn fools want more? Then all three of us'll give it to them. You heading to Maryland for fun or business?'

'Neither, really. Old friend died a few weeks back,' Harper replied as he straddled the Bonneville. 'Funeral's tomorrow.'

'I'm sorry to hear that.'

Harper smiled at this and pulled out his phone, reading the text message he'd gained a few days back now.

> Mike Colton's dead. Accident at his garage two weeks back. Funeral next week. Be good if you could make it.

It was from a mutual friend from the forces. Harper stared at the screen, a memory flashing unbidden – desert heat, the crack of gunfire, Mike's voice shouting a warning that had saved his life.

A debt unpaid.

His hand slipped into his satchel, fingers finding the river stone, its smooth surface worn from years of similar moments.

And then the moment was over, and Harper put his phone away, nodded his thanks, then kicked the Bonneville to life. The engine roared, its distinctive note echoing off the mountains.

'If those men come back,' Harper shouted over the engine, 'use a shotgun next time, not the bow. And aim for centre mass.'

Terry's weathered face broke into a grim smile.

'Safe travels.'

Harper pulled onto the highway, quickly catching sight of Nadine's sedan ahead. He'd follow her to the state line as promised, make sure she reached safety. Then continue on to a small town named Blüdridge, Maryland.

To Mike.

To a debt long overdue.

The setting sun cast his shadow long on the asphalt ahead, stretching towards whatever waited for him at the end of this road.

Whatever it was, Liam Harper knew it'd likely end in a fight.

It always bloody did.

2

BLÜDRIDGE

BLÜDRIDGE, MARYLAND APPEARED LIKE MOST SMALL TOWNS AT dawn – deceptively peaceful.

Harper rolled the Bonneville slowly down Main Street as first light crept over the eastern ridge. He'd followed Nadine to the Maryland state line as promised, then he'd taken the scenic route through the night, arriving just as the town was waking.

Mist clung to the corners of buildings and hung in the narrow gaps between them – not quite fog, more like the town was exhaling slowly in its sleep.

Streetlamps still glowed against the early morning darkness. Shopkeepers unlocked doors, set out sandwich boards and prepared for the day. No one looked twice at the stranger on the motorcycle.

Not yet, anyway.

It was a small town with what looked to be one principal thoroughfare bisecting a collection of weathered buildings, Victorian architecture standing alongside utilitarian concrete blocks. As he rode past, he spotted signs of economic decline

– vacant storefronts, peeling paint – but also signs of money; security cameras at strategic locations, and a few high-end vehicles parked among worn pickup trucks and practical sedans. It gave off a feeling of old money living comfortably alongside new desperation.

Harper couldn't help noticing details others might miss; cameras covering the pharmacy had sight lines to the bank across the street. The hardware store's security system was newer than the electronics shop's. A black SUV with tinted windows idled at the kerb, driver watching the street with too much attention for this time of morning.

Someone's watching the watchers. Interesting.

A Greyhound bus ahead of him pulled away in a cloud of diesel exhaust, leaving Harper alone at the kerbside. Blüdridge seemed to hold its breath under the morning's grey October sky; the town felt watchful, contained, like a pressure system hung over it unrelated to the weather.

Harper adjusted his grip on his satchel, fingers briefly brushing his lucky stone through the fabric. He rode towards the town centre, where a small inn's sign swung in the intermittent breeze.

The Blüdridge Inn was exactly what he expected – dated furnishings, faded wallpaper and a front-desk clerk whose eyes lingered a moment too long on his face. *Outsider*. The scar above his eyebrow typically drew attention, but this was something else.

Small town suspicion.

Harper parked the Bonneville in the inn's lot around back, locked the bike well, paid cash for three nights, declined assistance with his bag and climbed the creaking stairs to room 204.

Inside, he dropped the duffel on the sagging bed and

moved straight to the window, surveying the street below. The funeral wouldn't start until afternoon and it was just past seven now. *Time for an hour's shuteye, get his bearings and find somewhere to rent a black suit.*

He laid on the bed, ignoring the sag in the middle and shut his eyes.

When he opened them, just under an hour had passed.

Feeling better for the power nap, he showered quickly, changed into fresh clothes and headed back downstairs.

Across the street stood a weathered clapboard building with a hand-painted sign:

Blood Ridge Retreat

Through steamed windows, Harper could see the warm glow of lights and the movements of the breakfast crowd, which meant it was likely the perfect place for local conversation.

Good, Harper thought to himself. *I'm in the mood for breakfast and gossip.*

The diner's bell chimed as Harper entered, momentarily drawing attention. Conversations didn't stop, but they dipped as eyes assessed the newcomer. Harper smiled at the counter and chose a booth with a clear view of both exits and the kitchen entrance. Civil War memorabilia covered the walls – faded photographs, framed letters, a glass case containing battlefield relics, and the smell of coffee and bacon wrapped around him like a blanket. Beneath it, he caught the sharper tang of disinfectant and the sweeter note of pancake batter, while the hiss of the grill punctuated the murmur of conversation.

A server – mid-sixties with silver-streaked hair pulled back in a neat bun and deep laugh lines – approached with a coffeepot.

'Morning, stranger,' she greeted, her voice carrying the distinctive lift of Appalachian roots. 'Can't recall seeing you before.'

She filled his cup without waiting for a response. Her name tag read *Joy*.

'Just arrived,' Harper replied. 'Here for a couple of days.'

Joy studied him with the shrewd assessment of someone who'd spent decades reading people across a counter.

'Mike Colton's funeral, I'd wager,' she said, her voice softening. 'Most new faces this week are here for that.'

'I won't take that wager,' Harper nodded, taking a sip. *Damn good coffee* – strong and fresh.

'Terrible thing,' Joy continued, pulling out her order pad. 'Known Mike since he was knee high to a grasshopper. His daddy before him too. Good people, the Coltons.'

She shook her head.

'Never did believe that nonsense about the lift failure.'

Harper's interest sharpened.

'No?'

'Mike checked his equipment daily. Meticulous, like his father.' Joy glanced around before leaning closer. 'But you didn't hear that from me. What can I get you?'

'Whatever's good,' Harper replied.

'Buckwheat pancakes and local sausage, then.' Joy made a note on her pad. 'Coffee's on the house for friends of Mike.'

As she walked away, Harper's gaze wandered to a framed map beside his booth, a detailed rendering of Blüdridge and the surrounding ridge lines dated 1864. Red markings indicated troop movements and battle positions. Comparing it to Google Maps on his phone, the terrain looked largely unchanged today.

Joy returned with a plate of steaming pancakes and sausage, nodding towards the map when she noticed his interest.

'The battle that gave this place its name,' she said, refilling his coffee. 'November 1864. Not in the history books like Antietam or Gettysburg but just as bloody for the folks who lived here.'

Harper took a bite of sausage.

'Confederate versus Union?'

'Well, that's complicated,' Joy gave a weak smile. 'We don't talk about it much but Maryland was a border state and also a slave state. Right before the Civil War kicked off, the whole place was pretty much split down the middle. People weren't exactly lining up to secede and the town was divided – some families wanted to join the Confederacy, like other southern states while their neighbours were Union sympathisers. Many had sons fighting on both sides.'

She gestured towards a faded photograph of soldiers.

'When a Confederate detachment retreated through here in 1864, pursued by Union forces, the townspeople turned on each other. Neighbour against neighbour. Brother against brother.'

She sighed, the sound carrying the weight of generations.

'By morning, the ridge ran red with blood, most of it spilled by people who'd known each other their whole lives.' Joy tapped the glass covering the map. 'Some say that's why trouble comes so natural to Blüdridge. Violence is in the soil.

And that was the day Blüdridge became known as "Blood Ridge."'

Charming. Nothing like a town with violence woven into its DNA.

Harper considered this as he took a bite of pancake. Excellent – light despite the hearty buckwheat with the subtle sweetness of real maple syrup.

'Town seems peaceful enough now,' he observed, testing for reaction.

Joy's smile didn't reach her eyes.

'Does it? Look closer, honey,' she nodded towards the other patrons. 'See how folks sit? Who talks to who?'

Harper had already noticed. Construction workers kept to themselves. An elderly couple by the window seemed relaxed but spoke in hushed tones. A group of men in one corner watched the door with too much attention, their conversation pausing whenever it opened.

'Same divide, different uniforms,' Joy whispered. 'Some folks work for Victor Daggett and his son Mitchell, some for Sean Brennan. The rest of us try to stay out of the crossfire.'

Before Harper could respond, the bell chimed as a sheriff's deputy entered – male, mid-thirties, sandy hair cut short, alert eyes in a careful face. The deputy nodded to Joy as he took a seat at the counter, his gaze lingering briefly on Harper before he unfolded a newspaper.

'Deputy Klein,' Joy explained, her voice pitched for Harper's ears alone. 'One of the few decent ones left in the department.'

Klein. Name to remember.

Harper nodded his thanks as Joy moved away to serve the deputy. He continued eating, observing the diner's dynamics. He couldn't have asked for a better crash course in how the town worked; the morning crowd gave him a perfect microcosm of Blüdridge's social structure – the workers, the watchers and the carefully neutral.

As he finished breakfast, the door chimed again. A tall man in an expensive overcoat entered, looking mid-to-late forties, followed by a younger associate who positioned himself near the entrance, scanning the room with professional attention.

Harper watched conversations falter as the older man moved to the counter, exchanging brief words with the deputy who straightened visibly.

'Mitchell Daggett,' Joy murmured as she returned to clear Harper's plate. 'Speak of the devil and he appears.'

Left alone again, Harper studied the man without appearing to focus on him. Mitchell Daggett wore tailored clothes and made deliberate movements, conveying authority without raising his voice or making overt gestures.

Not so much a businessman as a territory marker.

'The Daggetts control half the businesses in town,' Joy continued, appearing at his side again like a ghost, refilling Harper's coffee. 'The legitimate ones, anyway.'

'And the other half?' Harper asked.

'Sean Brennan. Irish fellow who moved in about five years back. Family used to be here for generations though. Different style, same game,' Joy's expression tightened. 'Mike got caught in the middle somehow. Started asking questions nobody wanted answered. Although I'm sure you'll hear about that later.'

She straightened as Mitchell concluded his conversation with the deputy and turned to leave, his gaze sweeping the diner in a final assessment. For a moment, his eyes met Harper's – and Harper felt a flicker of calculation cross the older man's features before he nodded to his associate and departed.

'St. Mary's Church,' Joy said after the door closed behind them. 'Service starts at one. Father Jonathan's good about not dragging things out, especially since it's still an open wound for everyone. I mean, it's been almost a month, but talk still happens.'

Harper nodded his thanks, leaving payment on the table with a generous tip.

'You don't know anywhere I can buy or rent a black suit?' he asked. 'Hard to keep a black suit packed away on a motorbike.'

'*Pennington's*, on Main,' Joy said. 'Tell them I sent you. They won't rip you off.'

'Appreciated,' Harper gathered his items.

'You watch yourself,' Joy added as he stood to leave. 'Strangers asking questions tend to find trouble in Blüdridge.'

'I appreciate the warning,' Harper replied, fingers briefly touching his satchel where the river stone rested.

'Not a warning, honey. History lesson,' she tapped the map again. 'Blood Ridge earned its name once. Some folks seem intent on keeping the tradition alive.'

OUTSIDE, THE MORNING HAD WARMED SLIGHTLY, THE OVERCAST sky occasionally broken by patches of pale autumn sunlight. Harper walked the town systematically – he couldn't help it, ingrained habit from his SRR days. *Streets and buildings. Security cameras. Foot traffic patterns. Distribution of businesses.*

The eastern section contained newer development and higher-end shops while the western edge showed greater economic strain – vacant storefronts and faded signage. It was while walking the town he found *Pennington's*, where an older couple, on hearing that he'd been sent by Joy and was a friend of Mike's, provided him with an off-the-peg black suit and tie, waving off offers to buy it, saying they'd simply rent it for the day.

'We do this for out-of-towners,' the old man said with a sad smile. 'Nobody needs to own a funeral suit they'll wear once.'

Harper wasn't going to argue but still bought a fresh white shirt and a pair of cheap black leather shoes. *It was the least he could do.*

Back in his room, he laid out his items and, full from breakfast with three hours before the funeral, decided to grab a couple more hours sleep.

St. Mary's Church stood on a gentle rise at the north end of town, its modest stone frontage and simple steeple a reminder of the German settlers who had originally established Blüdridge. The adjacent cemetery contained generations of residents with headstones dating back to the mid-1800s and a clear view of the ridge. At the side of the church, Harper noticed construction materials and equipment covered with tarps, apparently abandoned for some time based on the weather-worn coverings.

Renovation project that ran out of funding, probably.

By twelve-thirty, vehicles had arrived, forming a sombre procession along the narrow drive. Harper observed this from across the street, noting the attendees as they gathered in small groups on the steps or stood beside parked cars.

Local business owners, he guessed as he watched sheriff's department personnel arrive in dress uniforms, led by an older man with silver hair, likely the town Sheriff.

He also watched the others, the ones who didn't quite fit the small-town pattern – men standing too straight, eyes scanning too efficiently, postures suggesting concealed weapons. Security professionals dressed as civilians, maintaining a perimeter while pretending not to. Harper had seen such people before but hadn't expected to find them in a sleepy Maryland town.

At ten minutes to one, Harper crossed the street and approached the church. The sanctuary was filling quickly with mourners moving to the front but Harper slipped into a pew near the back – partly because he didn't know these people but mostly because his SRR instincts made him sit where he had clear sight lines to all entrances and most attendees.

A closed casket stood at the front, draped with an American flag – acknowledgement of Mike's military service. A man in his fifties with a carefully managed beard stood near the casket, directing who could approach and when. His posture and scanning gaze suggested authority or at least a desire to project it.

Harper didn't know who he was; Mike's father was long dead and he had no brothers. But this bearded man acted like he was in charge and that made him interesting. Harper watched as he repeatedly positioned himself between the casket and a slender woman with dark hair pulled back in a simple bun.

Harper had never met her but knew her from photos Mike had shown him. Sarah Colton, Mike's childhood sweetheart and wife. Mike's widow looked exhausted but composed, accepting condolences with quiet dignity.

A teenage boy beside her – Mike's son Jake, presumably – maintained a rigid posture that barely contained his anger. The boy's eyes moved constantly, watching the other mourners with suspicion beyond his years.

Harper leaned forward, focusing on the boy.

Something was wrong here.

Jake's fists were clenched as he glared across the church. Harper didn't have the right angle to see who he was staring at, but he recognised the expression. He'd had it himself at Jake's age.

The kid was angry. And from his posture and expression, it was going to boil over at any moment.

Harper's fingers found the smooth stone in his satchel, tracing its familiar contours.

Coming to pay his respects to a dead friend was one thing.

Getting caught in whatever storm was brewing here – *that* was something else entirely.

3

THE FUNERAL

THE SERVICE BEGAN WITH THE PRIEST STEPPING FORWARD, HIS measured tones echoing through the sanctuary. Harper watched Father Jonathan – a lean man with prematurely silver hair and deep-set eyes – wave for silence before speaking.

'We gather today not just to mourn our brother Michael Colton, but to celebrate a life of service – to country, to community, to family.'

Harper half-listened to the familiar funeral platitudes while observing the congregation's reactions. Older residents dabbed at tears with handkerchiefs. Men Harper guessed were fellow veterans sat stiff-backed, faces carefully blank. A cluster of mechanics in clean but worn shirts, presumably from Mike's garage, looked genuinely devastated.

More telling were the others – the carefully manufactured sympathy on the faces of men who seemed out of place in a church. The watchful gazes of security personnel positioned at the edges of the gathering, more focused on the living than honouring the dead.

Harper had been to enough military funerals to recognise the patterns, but something about this felt wrong. The tension in the air was too thick for a simple accident victim.

Father Jonathan's voice rose, capturing Harper's attention again.

'Cain and Abel were the first brothers to fight – but they weren't the last,' he announced loudly. 'We like to think blood should bring us together but too often pride drives us apart. And when brother turns on brother, it doesn't just scar the flesh, it wounds the soul of a family, a town, a nation.'

Murmurs rippled through the congregation. Harper thought of what Joy had mentioned about the town's history, the divided loyalties and blood spilled between neighbours.

Father Jonathan wasn't finished.

'Some say violence is strength. But I say it takes far more strength to forgive than to strike. So I ask you – before you raise your hand or your voice – ask yourself, is this justice... or is this just revenge wearing its Sunday best?'

Harper noted a few nods of agreement from the elder townsfolk but a definite tension in the air. For the first time, he realised the funeral had a visible split, with mourners clustered on opposite sides of a central aisle. The division wasn't complete, but it was unmistakable.

Same divide, different uniforms.

Midway through the eulogies, Harper sensed rather than saw movement at the side entrance. A well-dressed man in his mid-seventies entered, accompanied by two others who positioned themselves discreetly but strategically within the sanctuary.

The newcomer wasn't physically imposing, but with short, silver hair and cold eyes that surveyed the room with predatory assessment, Harper had the overwhelming impression the man was dangerous.

The man's gaze swept the congregation before settling on Sarah Colton. He made no move to offer condolences, simply watching Father Jonathan return to the pulpit.

From the tension in Sarah's shoulders, Harper could tell she was aware of his scrutiny even without turning to meet it.

There were hymns. There were tears. Harper tuned most of it out, trying to reconcile the Mike Colton in these eulogies – devoted husband, father, business owner – with the man he'd known in Helmand. The practical joker who'd rigged a fellow soldier's helmet to play "It's Raining Men" when tilted. The mechanical genius who could make a vehicle run on seemingly willpower alone.

Whatever was going on, Harper felt he owed it to Mike to look into it.

When the service concluded, Harper remained seated as others filed out towards the cemetery for the burial. He waited until the man with the beard led Sarah towards the door before rising to follow, and as he did so he heard the man's name as he spoke to Father Jonathan at the door.

'Look after her, Mister Halvorsen.'

'Ray, please, Father.'

Father Jonathan had nodded and then looked back to Harper, frowning. It passed almost instantly though; there were others from out of town and Harper knew he wasn't the only unfamiliar face.

Ray Halvorsen. Another name to remember.

At the graveside, Harper maintained a respectful distance, positioning himself where he could observe without drawing attention. The military honour guard performed the flag ceremony perfectly, presenting the folded triangle to Sarah who accepted it with trembling hands.

Harper was surprised to not recognise any of the honour guard. Although he knew Mike well, he'd still dealt with many others from Mike's unit – the SRR didn't announce their presence, and though Mike had been Corps of Engineers, their paths had crossed mainly during joint operations. One of them, Steve Gillette, had been the one to message him but Harper couldn't see him anywhere.

Not even bothering to show up for a mate's funeral. Typical Stevie. But why hadn't the others?

As the crowd dispersed following the final prayers, Harper noticed Sarah scanning the gathering, her eyes eventually finding his. Recognition flickered across her face – not of him personally but of what he represented.

Another soldier. One of Mike's buddies, perhaps.

She whispered something to Ray Halvorsen who frowned but stepped aside. Sarah approached Harper directly, her son following a step behind, still angry, his hooded eyes failing to hide his emotions.

'You served with Mike,' she said. It wasn't a question.

Harper nodded.

'Liam Harper. Special Reconnaissance Regiment. Mike and I worked together in Helmand.'

At Harper's name, relief softened her features momentarily.

'He mentioned you,' she said softly, recalling a conversation from possibly years ago. 'Said you saved his life once.'

'He returned the favour,' Harper replied simply. 'Twice, if I recall correctly. Surprised none of his unit turned up?'

Sarah nodded.

'Most are deployed abroad, couldn't get time off,' she explained. 'A couple of others called through the garage, and Ray told them the details. Looked like they decided not to come.'

As they spoke, Harper felt the weight of observation from across the churchyard. Ray Halvorsen watched from near the grave, his expression carefully neutral, giving nothing away. The silver-haired man from the church also observed them from beside a black SUV, speaking quietly into a phone while maintaining visual contact, and Harper wondered whether the army buddies who'd called the garage had really decided not to turn up, or had been either shut down or warned off by Ray. It would have been easy to claim "the widow wishes a small, family-only funeral", and nobody would have argued.

Jake Colton studied Harper with intense scrutiny; his jaw set in a way that reminded Harper painfully of Mike.

'My father wasn't careless,' the boy snapped. 'That lift didn't fail on its own.'

'Jake,' Sarah warned, her tone suggesting this was a recurring argument.

Harper's eyes met the teenager's.

'I knew your father. Careful doesn't begin to describe him. He was way past that, you understand?'

Something loosened in Jake's posture, like a spring unwinding slightly. Harper guessed this was the first validation he'd received from someone who understood.

'I'm sorry to hear of Mike's passing,' he returned his attention to Sarah now. 'I only found out about it last week. I actually don't know what happened.'

'Nobody does,' Jake muttered. 'Doesn't stop people from stating "facts" though.'

'Perhaps we could speak later,' Sarah said quietly, glancing towards Ray who was beginning to approach. 'Somewhere more private, where I can fill you in?'

'I'm staying at the Blüdridge Inn,' Harper replied, understanding her caution. 'Room 204.'

Sarah nodded almost imperceptibly as Ray reached them, placing a proprietary hand on her elbow.

'Sarah, the cars are waiting,' he said with a dismissive glance at Harper. 'Everyone's heading to the house.'

'Ray, this is Liam Harper, an old friend of Mike's—'

'Thanks for coming,' Ray said, nodding as he turned Sarah away.

'I'm passing through, staying a couple of days,' Harper decided to push the moment. 'Didn't realise Mike had brothers.'

'I'm a close friend of the family,' Ray muttered back, clearly having no time for the stranger talking to Sarah. 'You're old army, right? There's cash behind the bar for you to have a drink. You'll understand the rest of this is family only, right?'

Harper gave a smile.

'Of course,' he replied. 'And close friends.'

Ray frowned.

'What?'

'You're an old friend of the family. If it's family only and you're going, then you have to be allowing close friends.'

Ray's eyes narrowed.

'Look, buddy,' he hissed. 'Go get your free drink and then piss off, yeah? This town don't need any more macho swaggering bullshit artists. You knew Mike? Great. Then why haven't we ever seen you before?'

Harper couldn't answer that, not that he had a chance to, as Ray pulled at Sarah's arm, allowing herself to be guided away.

Jake lingered a moment longer, his eyes conveying a message Harper clearly understood.

We need to talk.

Harper watched them leave.

Charming bloke, that Ray. Puts the 'fun' in funeral.

As the crowd thinned, Harper noticed a balding, grey-haired man in an expensive suit standing apart from the other mourners. The man observed the proceedings with clinical detachment, checking his watch as if he had more important places to be. Several attendees nodded deferentially as they passed him, the kind of respect offered to authority rather than friendship.

Official? Mayor? Judge? Gangster even? He could be any of these.

After the mourners had departed, Harper remained at the gravesite, studying the temporary marker that would eventually be replaced with a permanent headstone. A memory surfaced, one of Mike pulling him to safety as gunfire erupted around their position, dragging him behind a crumbling wall seconds before an RPG hit where Harper had been standing.

'I owe you,' Harper said softly to the freshly turned earth. 'And that means I owe your family, whatever trouble they're in. I got your six, Colton. Don't you fret.'

His fingers touched the smooth stone in his pocket; an unconscious gesture of respect.

As he turned to leave, he noticed the silver-haired man

from before once more watching him from beside the black SUV, phone to his ear, posture casual yet alert. Their eyes met briefly before the man turned away, still speaking into the phone.

Bloody hell. I've been in town less than a day and already drawing attention.

Harper walked down the gravel path, a wry smile touching his lips. Ray Halvorsen hadn't even told him where the drink was waiting. Not that he planned to claim it. The man didn't want him around Sarah, which was precisely why Harper intended to speak with her again. That, and the way Jake had looked at him – desperate for someone to believe what seemed obvious to him. That his father hadn't died by accident.

Harper paused at the cemetery gates, looking back at the church and the ridge beyond it. He'd come to pay his respects, maybe have a drink in Mike's memory before moving on.

Now, he wasn't so sure.

The lift didn't fail on its own.

He'd seen enough to know Jake was likely right. And if Mike had been murdered, Harper owed it to him to find out who was responsible.

His debt just got considerably more expensive.

HARPER MADE HIS WAY BACK TO TOWN, FOLLOWING GROUPS OF mourners at a distance. Most headed towards a white Victorian house with blue shutters on Elm Street – likely the Colton residence where Ray had made it pretty clear Harper wasn't welcome. Harper continued past, filing away the location for later. He needed to establish patterns before making direct contact, start to understand the forces arrayed around Sarah and Jake Colton before potentially drawing those forces to them.

Bypassing the pub where the wake was presumably being held, Harper returned to the inn, his mind cataloguing the various players he'd observed.

Ray Halvorsen – overly protective of Sarah, hostile to outsiders, apparently a close family friend with unclear motives.

The silver-haired man watching from the black SUV – likely this "Victor Daggett" Joy had mentioned, as now, seeing him again, Harper could make out he had a loose resemblance to the man in the diner.

The well-dressed observer checking his watch – official capacity of some kind, seemingly bored with proceedings yet attending anyway.

And then there were the divisions in the town itself – the careful separation of mourners, the clusters of men with watchful eyes, the sense of a community under strain.

Back in his room, Harper retrieved his phone from where he'd left it hidden between the mattress and box spring, checking for messages.

> Sorry I couldn't make the funeral. Was told it was a small family affair. Hope you did.

Looked like Harper was right, and Ray had managed to warn off Stevie.

Harper replied in the affirmative and changed into less formal clothes, folding the rented suit and placing it on the sideboard. He'd take it back tomorrow when things were a little quieter. Evening would likely bring opportunity; the reception at the Colton house would occupy attention, creating space for Harper to move more freely as he poked into the dark corners of the town.

He settled by the window, watching the street while methodically reviewing what he'd observed and beneath it all the question that had plagued him since he arrived at Blüdridge.

What had Mike Colton discovered that was worth killing for, if it hadn't been an accident?

As daylight faded, Harper noticed a figure approaching the inn – Jake Colton, moving with the careful stride of someone who didn't want to be followed. The boy glanced over his shoulder twice before disappearing into the inn's entrance. Moments later there was a knock at Harper's door. Harper opened it to find Jake standing in the hallway, his face flushed from exertion or nervousness.

'I need to show you something,' the boy said without preamble. 'Mom doesn't know I found it.'

Harper waved the boy in, shutting the door behind them. As he did so Jake reached into his jacket pocket and withdrew a small metal key with an unusual cut; it wasn't a house key or car key but instead looked to be something more specialised.

'Look Mister Harper—'

'Just Harper.'

'Look, Harper, I don't remember much about dad's time in Helmand but he mentioned you more than once,' Jake stuttered nervously. 'He said you were a straight shooter, an honest man – even for a Brit.'

'Half Brit,' Harper smiled. 'My dad's American. Well, was. He died recently, like yours.'

It wasn't completely true; Harper's dad was dead, but he'd died in Harper's arms on a boat attacked by Myanmar rebels.

Jake didn't need to know that part.

Jake nodded at this, swallowing.

'Dad hid this in his work boots,' he explained, his voice low. 'The day before he died three weeks back, he told me if anything happened to him, I should find the spare key and give it to someone he trusted.'

He extended his hand, offering the key to Harper.

'I think he meant you.'

'You don't think he meant Ray?'

'I said trusted.'

There was enough venom in the boy's voice to drop a rhino. *Interesting.*

Harper took the key, examining its distinctive pattern.

'Did he say what it opens?'

Jake shook his head.

'Just that it was insurance. That it would "blow the lid off the whole operation."'

His eyes met Harper's; desperation barely contained.

'They killed him, Harper. They made it look like an accident but they killed him. And now they're watching mom all the time, telling her to keep the garage running, not to ask questions.'

'Who's watching?' Harper asked, though he suspected the answer.

'Daggett's people. Brennan's people. And Ray,' Jake's expression hardened. 'Mom trusts Ray because he worked for dad for years, but he's different now. Always at the house, always suggesting what mom should do about the garage, about the finances.'

Harper pocketed the key.

'I'll find out what it opens,' he promised. 'But Jake, you need to be careful. Don't let anyone know you came here. Don't tell anyone about the key.'

The boy nodded, looking both relieved and terrified to have passed the burden to someone else.

'Will you help us?' he asked, his voice suddenly younger than his years.

'I will,' Harper assured him. 'Your father saved my life more than once. I owe him this.'

After Jake departed – carefully checking the hallway before slipping out – Harper examined the key more closely under the room's lamp. The cut pattern suggested a specialised lock, possibly for a safe deposit box or secure storage unit. Whatever Mike had discovered, he'd been methodical enough to preserve the evidence and create contingencies for its discovery.

Harper's eyes drifted to the window where dusk had settled over Blüdridge. The town seemed to withdraw into itself as night fell, with streets emptying and businesses closing early. Only the Blood Ridge Retreat remained illuminated down the street.

Insurance that would "blow the lid off the whole operation." Mike's words, according to his son.

What had his friend stumbled into?

Tomorrow, Harper would begin his systematic investigation of what had happened to Mike Colton, find what the key opened and understand the "operation" Mike had discovered. But tonight, he would observe and prepare.

Across the street, Harper watched silently as a black SUV pulled to the kerb, engine running and the headlights off.

It was watching the inn. Watching for Harper.

His hand dipped into his pocket, fingers circling the river stone, its smooth surface cool against his skin.

For luck.

He'd need it.

Blüdridge was revealing itself hour by hour, awakening to the presence of a stranger asking questions no one wanted answered.

Harper had only come to pay his respects. It looked like leaving was off the table now.

But that was fine. He hadn't been looking forward to getting back on that bloody motorcycle and having another long ride anyway.

4

WIDOW'S DILEMMA

Morning arrived with a thin mist clinging to the valley, wreathing Blüdridge in spectral grey. Harper had risen before dawn, completing his daily exercise regimen in the limited space of his hotel room – a calisthenic discipline that had kept him alive in places far more dangerous than this small Maryland town, if only because it cleared his head.

As he worked through a series of movements, avoiding the sharp wooden corner of the bed (something he'd failed to do earlier, now sporting a bruised shin as proof), Harper mentally catalogued what he knew.

Mike Colton, former Army Corps of Engineers. Dead from an alleged equipment failure over three weeks back, that according to his son defied both probability and his meticulous nature.

His widow and son under surveillance.

A town divided between two power structures.

And a mysterious key delivered by a desperate teenage boy who needed proof his father had been murdered.

The pieces suggested a pattern though the picture remained unclear.

After a quick shower, Harper examined the key Jake had delivered. Whatever it opened likely contained evidence Mike considered important enough to protect and create contingencies for. Harper pocketed the key and picked up the black suit, now back in its garment bag, and left his room through the back entrance. He confirmed his Bonneville was still secure, then headed down the side alley and back onto the street.

The black SUV was still parked across the road, its occupant slumped slightly as if dozing but undoubtedly alert. Amateur enough to be visible but professional enough to be persistent.

Bloody surveillance basics, mate. If I can see you, you're doing it wrong.

Harper ignored the car and carried on southwards, away from the inn and the SUV.

AT THE BLOOD RIDGE RETREAT, THE MORNING CROWD WAS thinner than yesterday's. Joy nodded in recognition as Harper entered, gesturing towards the same booth he'd occupied before. The Civil War map on the wall now seemed more significant somehow, its battle lines reflecting current town divisions.

'You're still here,' Joy observed, pouring coffee without being asked. 'Funeral's over. Most out-of-towners have already left.'

'Unfinished business,' Harper replied.

'The suit? I can take it back to *Pennington's*, if you want.'

'More than that.'

Joy studied him with the same shrewd assessment as before.

'With Sarah Colton, I'd guess.'

Harper remained silent, watching Joy with the same careful assessment being directed at him.

'She could use a friend,' Joy continued as she realised Harper wasn't replying, lowering her voice. 'Especially one who isn't on somebody's payroll.'

'Daggett's?' Harper asked.

'His or Brennan's.'

Joy glanced towards the door as it opened, admitting two men in work clothes who took seats at the counter.

'Brennan's crew,' she murmured before raising her voice to normal levels. 'The usual this morning?'

Harper nodded, amused that one purchased meal now constituted a "usual" and Joy moved away to greet the newcomers. Through the window, he spotted a patrol car passing slowly; Deputy Klein from yesterday's funeral, scanning the street in that casual way officers do when they're not actively looking but staying prepared.

There was movement at the door, and a middle-aged man in a leather bomber jacket entered, walking over to the diner.

'Hey, Joy,' he said conversationally. 'Don't worry, just passing. Town fund payments are due in by end of the week.'

'I'm aware,' Joy said as she picked up a breakfast order, passing it across the diner counter. 'So come back at the end of the week, yeah?'

The man tipped a finger to his forehead, tipping an imaginary hat, and left the diner.

Looked like people lived hand to mouth here.

By the time Joy returned with his breakfast, Harper had planned his approach.

'I need to speak with Sarah Colton,' he said quietly. 'Preferably somewhere neither Daggett nor her garage foreman would expect.'

Joy considered this as she refilled his coffee.

'She teaches history at the high school. Planning period is second block, around ten. Faculty lounge in the administration building.'

'She's there the day after Mike's funeral?'

Joy nodded.

'They breed them tough around here,' she suggested. 'She was back at work the week after he died. Guess she needed to get out of the house.'

She wrote directions on her order pad, tearing it off and passing it over.

'Tell Marge at the front desk you're dropping off materials for Mrs. Colton's Civil War lessons. She won't question it.'

Harper nodded his thanks, impressed again by Joy's willingness to help.

'Mike was good people,' Joy said, answering the unasked question. 'Fixed my car for parts' cost when times were tight. Never talked down to me like some do.'

Her eyes hardened.

'Whatever happened to him wasn't right.'

Harper agreed. It was becoming clear something bad had happened and not by accident. He just needed to know who did it so he could gain recompense.

AFTER BREAKFAST, HARPER DROPPED THE SUIT OFF AT Pennington's, thanked them for helping him, then returned briefly to his room to collect his thoughts and check for surveillance.

The black SUV had moved to a different position with a new occupant – younger, alert and with narrow eyes that watched everyone passing. Harper opened his map app and worked out a route through town that would get him to the high school without being followed, using alleyways and side streets he'd noted during yesterday's reconnaissance. Plan formulated, he grabbed his jacket and left.

BLÜDRIDGE HIGH SCHOOL OCCUPIED A SPRAWLING CAMPUS AT the edge of town – brick buildings from the fifties with newer additions creating an architectural patchwork. Harper kept to his randomised route, losing the SUV down some side alleys and approached from the athletic fields, bypassing the main entrance.

The administration building stood separate from the classroom blocks, connected by a covered walkway. Harper entered through a side door, nodding to a passing teacher who barely glanced at him. Inside he located the front office where an older woman with steel-grey hair and reading glasses perched on her nose looked up.

'Can I help you?' she asked, her tone suggesting help was offered selectively.

'Dropping off materials for Mrs. Colton's Civil War lessons,' Harper replied, holding up a manila folder. There was nothing in it but hotel flyers but she wouldn't know unless she opened it.

The woman – Marge, presumably – assessed him over her glasses.

'I'll take them.'

'Precious family mementos,' Harper countered. 'Rather get them in the right hands. No offence.'

There didn't seem to be any given, as Marge simply sniffed and shrugged.

'She's in the faculty lounge. Down the hall, third door on the right.'

Harper thanked her and followed the directions, finding the lounge empty except for Sarah Colton who sat at a table grading papers, a half-finished cup of coffee beside her. She looked up at his entrance, surprise giving way to recognition, then cautious relief.

'Mister Harper,' she said, glancing towards the door as he closed it. 'This is unexpected.'

'Just Harper,' he corrected, taking a seat across from her. 'I thought we should talk somewhere away from watching eyes.'

Sarah's posture relaxed slightly as she set her pen down.

'So you've noticed, then?'

'Hard to miss. Also, Jake came to see me last night.'

Alarm flashed across Sarah's face.

'He shouldn't have—'

'He's worried about you,' Harper interrupted gently. 'And he's convinced his father's death wasn't accidental.'

'I know,' Sarah said, her voice tightening. 'He's been saying it since it happened but the sheriff's department, the insurance investigators – they all insist it was equipment failure.'

She met Harper's eyes directly.

'What do you think?'

'I think your son's correct. The Mike I knew was too careful for a catastrophic lift failure, especially some bullshit one claimed to be his own error,' Harper replied. 'And I think Jake was right to bring me this.'

He placed the key on the table between them. Sarah stared at it, recognition dawning.

'Where did he find it?'

'In Mike's work boots. Apparently, Mike told him if anything happened, he should find "the spare key" and give it to someone trusted.'

Sarah reached for the key, then hesitated.

'Do you know what it opens?'

'Not yet. But I intend to find out.' Harper studied her reaction. 'Jake said Mike mentioned something about "blowing the lid off an operation." Does that mean anything to you?'

Sarah glanced towards the window, likely gathering her thoughts.

'A few weeks before he died, Mike went up to Seneca Ridge in his Jeep. Something about checking an unusual installation for a potential customer.'

She shook her head.

'He came back different. Quiet. Started locking his office door at the garage, staying late.'

'Did he say what he found?'

'Not directly. Just that the people involved weren't who they claimed to be.' Sarah's fingers traced patterns on the table. 'The day after his trip to the ridge, Mitchell Daggett came to the garage personally. You heard of him or his dad yet?'

Harper nodded.

'Saw Mitchell at the diner. Not sure but I think I saw Daggett Senior too, at Mike's funeral.'

'Thought you might have. The locals don't keep secrets well,' Sarah continued. 'It was unusual – he normally sends one of his goons when vehicles need service. Mike was... unsettled after that visit.'

'And now Daggett's pressuring you about the garage,' Harper observed.

Sarah's eyes met his, sharper than her grief-worn appearance suggested.

'How did you know?'

'It's what I'd do if I needed to control a strategic location,' Harper replied. 'I checked the maps last night. The garage sits at the junction of Route 40 and Sawmill Road – the primary route in and out of Blüdridge. Perfect position for monitoring traffic as it passes.'

Sarah nodded slowly.

'Mike reckoned that was part of it. Yesterday, after the funeral reception, Victor made a direct offer to buy the garage – nearly double its appraised value.'

'Generous.'

'Suspiciously so,' Sarah agreed. 'Especially since Ray's been insisting I should maintain ownership, with him running operations.'

She paused.

'They're playing me on both sides, aren't they?'

'Seems that way,' Harper confirmed. 'Although I don't yet know what Ray's plan is. Perhaps he knows if you sell he doesn't make whatever he gets from this scheme.'

'He's a mechanic, a manager at best—'

'So he's skimming then,' Harper mused. 'You selling would stop that. He probably makes a fair penny too. What'll you do?'

'I told them both I needed time to consider options.' Sarah's jaw tightened with determination. 'But what I really want is to know what happened to Mike. What he found that was worth being killed for.'

'Don't worry, I intend to find out,' Harper assured her. 'But I'll need access to Mike's workspace – the garage, his office, anywhere he might have hidden information.'

Sarah considered this, tapping her pen against the table. In that moment, Harper could see the steel beneath her grief – a woman who'd held her family together while her husband served overseas, who now faced invisible threats with the same quiet resolve.

'Ray would be suspicious if I simply gave you access,' she said finally. 'But if you were working there temporarily, helping me sort out the business while I make decisions...'

'Providing a mechanical assessment of operations,' Harper suggested. 'Evaluating equipment, staff, workflow. Standard practice when considering a sale.'

'Ray couldn't reasonably object,' Sarah agreed. 'Though he won't like it.'

'Few people welcome scrutiny,' Harper observed.

Sarah pulled a small notepad from her bag and wrote briefly.

'This is the garage's address and alarm code. I'll tell Ray to expect you tomorrow morning.' She tore out the page and handed it to Harper. 'The rear left-side entrance has no security cameras. That was a requirement when Brennan started using Mike too.'

'Daggett and Brennan *both* used him?' Harper raised an eyebrow. 'Sounds like Ray was playing more than two sides.'

He didn't want to say the other option – *that Mike Colton had willingly sold out his services to two rival crime bosses.* Instead, Harper pocketed the information.

'There's something else,' Sarah added, her voice dropping

lower though they were alone. 'This morning I received a call from my bank. Someone attempted to access Mike's safe deposit box yesterday using an ID that didn't match authorised users.'

'Which bank?'

'Maryland Trust on Main Street.'

'Do you have access to the box?'

Sarah nodded.

'Joint account. I haven't checked it since before Mike died – there was so much to handle with the funeral arrangements. He seemed particularly anxious about it the last time we spoke. Said something about Judge Whitcomb asking too many questions about his business records.'

'We should look,' Harper suggested, noting the judge's name as he did so. 'Today, if possible.'

'I have classes until three,' Sarah replied. 'The bank closes at four.'

'I'll meet you there at three-fifteen,' Harper decided. 'Better if we're not seen together beforehand.'

The school bell rang, signalling the end of the period. Sarah gathered her papers, professional composure settling over her like armour.

'Thank you,' she said simply. 'For believing Jake. For helping us.'

'Mike would have done the same.'

Harper stood, preparing to leave as a thought struck him.

'One more thing – who has keys to your house?'

'Just Jake and me,' Sarah replied, then frowned. 'Though Ray has the spare set from when he used to watch the place if we were away.'

'Change the locks,' Harper advised. 'Today if possible. And check for cameras – inside and out.'

'You think they're watching that closely?' Sarah paled slightly.

'I think whatever Mike found was significant enough to warrant his murder,' Harper replied. 'Which means they'll be monitoring anyone who might have access to what he knew.'

As they prepared to part ways, Sarah asked the question Harper had been expecting.

'Why are you doing this? You could walk away, return to your life.'

'Mike saved my life in Helmand,' Harper replied. 'Pulled me clear seconds before an RPG hit my position.'

He met her eyes.

'I owe him.'

Sarah studied him, seeing beyond the simple explanation of the deeper code it represented.

'Debts should be paid,' she said finally. 'But be careful, Harper. I've already lost my husband to whatever this is. I don't want another death on my conscience.'

'I don't intend to die,' Harper gave the most reassuring smile he could. 'But that doesn't mean there won't be more deaths.'

He didn't mention whose.

5

THE BOSSES

HARPER LEFT THE HIGH SCHOOL VIA THE ATHLETIC FIELDS, retracing his approach path to avoid the main entrance where vehicles might be watching. Clouds had moved in while he was inside, turning the morning grey and threatening rain. The sudden chill felt appropriate – Blüdridge grew colder the more he learned about it.

As he'd expected, a dark sedan was parked across from the school, a figure inside monitoring the front doors with a telephoto lens. Not the SUV from earlier – an unfamiliar vehicle, a different surveillance team.

Not watching me. They're watching Sarah.

Harper made his way back to town the long way, stopping at a hardware store to purchase supplies – a small flashlight, multi-tool and other items that might prove useful but wouldn't draw attention. The clerk processed his purchase without interest, more focused on the television behind the counter showing a local news report.

'... authorities have closed the investigation into the accident at Colton's Auto Repair that claimed the life of owner Michael Colton

last month,' the reporter was saying. *'Official findings suggest equipment failure, though some community members have questioned the official narrative.'*

The screen showed footage of a garage exterior, police tape visible across the entrance, before cutting to a brief interview with a silver-haired man in an expensive suit, expressing condolences.

'A terrible tragedy,' the man said, his expression appropriately sombre. *'Mike Colton was a valued member of our business community. He will be deeply missed.'*

It was nothing more than the rehearsed sincerity of a practised liar; Harper had seen enough politicians to recognise the technique.

'Who's the guy?' Harper asked, keeping his tone casual.

'Victor Daggett. You must be from way out of town if you don't know that,' the clerk muttered, staring at the television.

So that *was* Daggett Senior. The resemblance to his son was unmistakable – same cold eyes, same calculating assessment beneath the public face. And Harper had been correct, as this was the same man who watched him, while on a phone, outside the church.

'I am,' Harper admitted. 'Only passing through.'

This gained interest and the clerk glanced at Harper as he handed over change.

'You knew Colton?'

'Passing acquaintance,' Harper replied neutrally.

'Shame what happened,' the clerk said, though his tone suggested there was limited personal investment. 'Good mechanic. Fair prices. I'm Jenkins. Let me know if you need anything.'

The same refrain Harper had heard repeatedly. *Good mechanic. Good man. A tragedy.* But no one asking the obvious questions except a teenager who knew his father too well to believe the official story.

'Harper. And thanks.' Harper pocketed his purchases and, after shaking Jenkins' outstretched hand, he exited the store, immediately spotting a familiar black SUV turning onto Main Street – obviously they'd tired of waiting at the school. He ducked into an alleyway, moving between buildings until he reached a narrow side street that led towards the western edge of town.

Four hours until the meeting with Sarah at the bank. Time to conduct preliminary reconnaissance.

AS MANY SMALL TOWNS DID, BLÜDRIDGE REVEALED ITSELF differently on foot, away from the major thoroughfares. For the second time since he'd arrived, Harper passed boarded storefronts with faded FOR LEASE signs, noting a playground that sat empty despite the reasonable weather. Three teenagers loitered on a corner, watching passersby with what Harper recognised as predatory attention. Their expressions changed as they saw Harper – not fear, but recognition of a fellow predator.

The economic divide Joy had mentioned became increasingly clear; prosperity concentrated near Victor Daggett's businesses on the eastern side of town, decay spreading from the western quarter, which Harper assumed was Brennan's territory.

After multiple trips now, a map was forming in Harper's mind; not just of streets and buildings, but of influence and control. Also, he could see movement since the last time he passed; the neutral zone between territories was narrowing, the businesses caught between struggling to remain independent.

He passed a construction site where the framework of a new building rose among the older structures. A sign proclaimed, "Future Home of the Daggett Enterprise Center," but the site appeared dormant, with construction equipment sitting idle. Two men in hard hats stood smoking beside a truck, their conversation falling silent as Harper walked by.

Their eyes followed him until he turned the corner.

Not construction workers, perhaps? Security dressed to blend in.

Harper wondered as he walked whether this was a fight between Brennan and Daggett or something more complex. *Was Mitchell happy with his father still running things? Was this a two-sided war, or a three-way power struggle with the son aiming to dethrone the father?* Either way, it was worth investigating.

Harper circled back towards Sawmill Road, approaching Colton's Auto Shop from the rear. The garage sat silent, broken strands of police tape still visible across the front entrance. Pausing to observe for a long moment, Harper saw no vehicles present and no signs of activity.

The strategic location of the garage was immediately apparent from this angle – positioned perfectly to monitor all traffic approaching from the west, including the road that presumably led towards Seneca Ridge.

Not just a chop shop. A checkpoint.

Moving on before his presence drew attention, Harper continued towards the north-eastern section of town where several higher-end businesses clustered around a small plaza. An artisan coffee shop, an art gallery, a boutique clothing store – all bearing discreet "Daggett Properties" markers on their signage. The clientele dressed better and drove newer cars, but it felt like an illusion of prosperity built on a foundation of corruption.

Harper ordered coffee at the upscale shop, choosing an outdoor table that afforded a view of the street. He pulled out his phone, appearing to check messages while observing patterns of movement. Two Blüdridge police cruisers passed in the last fifteen minutes, following what appeared to be a standard patrol route. They slowed beside certain vehicles – checking licence plates, but only for cars with out-of-town registrations.

Keeping track of strangers. Wonder where I rank on their watch list?

As he sipped his coffee, Harper noted another pattern. Every few minutes, someone from each business on the plaza stepped outside, ostensibly for a cigarette break or phone call. Their positions allowed collective surveillance of all approaches to the area – too regular to be random. Coordinated security disguised as routine activity.

Amateur but effective. The casual observer would never notice.

A sleek black sedan pulled to the kerb across the street and Harper watched as Mitchell Daggett climbed out of the passenger seat. The driver remained in the vehicle while Mitchell entered the building opposite, the signage reading "Daggett Financial Services".

Was anything in this half of town not owned by Daggett?

Harper almost chuckled to himself; usually when laundering money or legitimising a criminal empire, you tried to draw attention away from connections. Mitchell had gone the opposite way, announcing to the world the legitimate success that existed only on paper.

That said, this was still speculation. Harper knew nothing about Daggett or his father.

Yet.

Ten minutes later, Mitchell Daggett emerged with a slim leather portfolio under his arm, speaking intently into his phone as he returned to the sedan.

Harper memorised the vehicle's licence plate as it pulled away, then paid for his coffee and continued his circuit of the town.

THE WESTERN QUARTER OF BLÜDRIDGE PRESENTED A STARK contrast to the area he'd walked from. Buildings showed years of neglect with paint peeling and concrete crumbling. What businesses remained operated behind security screens and barred windows. Harper passed a pawnshop, a liquor store and more than one check-cashing service – predatory enterprises feeding on desperation.

The Rusted Nail bar stood as the apparent centre of Brennan's territory – more fortress than bar, giving the overall vibe of a former warehouse with reinforced doors and hastily installed windows.

Two men flanked the entrance, their bulky jackets failing to conceal the weapons beneath. They tracked Harper with hard eyes as he passed, one speaking quietly into a sleeve-mounted microphone.

Military-grade comms. Not your typical bar security.

Although so far, nothing seemed typical in Blüdridge.

By early afternoon, Harper had completed his circuit of Blüdridge, gathering intelligence while remaining inconspicuous. He grabbed a sandwich from a corner store as a walking lunch and returned to the inn briefly to organise his observations.

In his room, he found a local business directory, likely left by the staff for guests. Flipping through, he noticed businesses marked with either a 'D' or 'B' in pencil. At some point, someone else had mapped the town's divided loyalties.

A previous guest? Another outsider caught in Blüdridge's web? Or someone planning something more sinister? Harper sat back and studied it thoroughly.

At precisely two-thirty, Harper left the inn and made his way towards Maryland Trust Bank, finding a different cafe to the one he'd stopped in earlier, with outdoor seating across from the bank. Settling in, he ordered a coffee and positioned himself to observe the building while appearing to read news on his phone.

The bank occupied a corner building with classical architecture – columns flanking the entrance, tall windows, stone walls suggesting permanence. Two security cameras covered the main entrance while another monitored the ATM and a fourth was positioned to observe the small parking area to the side. Standard alarm system, a couple of security guards visible through the door. Nothing extraordinary but enough to make unauthorised access challenging.

At ten minutes past three, Sarah's Honda pulled into the bank's parking lot. She exited wearing the same clothes from the school but now carrying a leather satchel. Her movements were composed, casual even, but her eyes scanned her surroundings nervously.

Harper finished his coffee, settled the bill and crossed the street, timing his arrival to coincide with Sarah's entrance into the bank. They acknowledged each other with only slight nods, maintaining the appearance of casual acquaintances rather than collaborators.

'Mrs Colton,' the security guard greeted her as they entered. 'Sorry about Mike. He was a good man.'

'Thank you, Hector,' Sarah replied. 'I need to access our safe deposit box.'

The guard directed her to a teller who processed the request quickly, checking Sarah's ID and signature against bank records. Harper positioned himself nearby, filling out a deposit slip while keeping awareness of the bank's interior and the other customers.

'This way, Mrs Colton,' the teller said, leading Sarah towards the vault area. Sarah glanced at Harper, a subtle sign to follow. The teller hesitated, looking at Sarah for confirmation.

'Mister Harper was an old colleague of Mike's,' Sarah explained. 'I'd like him to witness the inventory of the box contents, if that's okay?'

'I'm helping Mrs Colton with her husband's affairs,' Harper explained as he approached.

The teller nodded and led them both into the secure area where rows of safe deposit boxes lined the walls. She located Box 473, inserted her key and then stepped back for Sarah to insert hers.

'I'll be just outside,' the teller said, providing them the customary privacy to examine the contents.

Sarah turned the key, the mechanism clicking open. She withdrew a rectangular metal container and carried it to a small table in the centre of the room. Inside were several neatly organised items – a small notebook with a black cover, a set of photographs and a sealed envelope with "Sarah" written on it in what Harper assumed was Mike's handwriting.

Sarah reached for the envelope first, her fingers trembling slightly as she broke the seal. Harper gave her space, instead focusing on the photographs – high-resolution images of what appeared to be construction activity on a ridgeline, showing unmarked trucks and heavy equipment at various access points and several men unloading crates from vehicles.

'It's a letter,' Sarah said, her voice tight with emotion as she read. 'Mike says he discovered an operation on Seneca Ridge that "doesn't align with permitted land usage or public records." Some kind of extensive network using old coal mining tunnels with heavy security but no official permits.'

She sighed.

'Goddamned fool,' she smiled faintly. 'You can take the man out of the military, but you can't take the military out of the man.'

Harper examined the notebook while she continued reading – inside were Mike's meticulous notes, including coordinates, observations, vehicle descriptions and names of individuals he'd identified. The handwriting grew increasingly urgent in later entries, the pressure of the pen on paper revealing Mike's growing concern.

The last pages detailed a discovery that explained everything.

Confirmed Brennan planning armed takeover of Victor Daggett's ridge operation within next two months. Multiple teams positioned. Schedule indicates coordinated strike when done. Garage targeted as strategic checkpoint. Ray actively facilitating both sides – preparing facility for Brennan's men while main-

taining Mitchell Daggett's smuggling operations. Evidence on USB encrypted but hidden. Meeting Klein when he gets back in three days to discuss immediate federal involvement. Unsure if Mitchell and Victor are allies here or on opposite sides.

Harper felt a chill run down his spine. *Klein*. The deputy from the diner, and apparently the man Mike had trusted with his discoveries.

'Mike was building a case,' Harper observed. 'Filling out methodical documentation before going to authorities.'

'But he never made it to that meeting,' Sarah said, finished with the letter, waving it as if to prove her point. 'According to this, he was going to meet Deputy Klein when he returned the day *after* he died.'

Her hands tightened on the paper.

'They killed him to stop him from talking to Klein.'

'And now they're pressuring you about the garage from both sides,' Harper concluded. 'Daggett wants to maintain his smuggling checkpoint while Brennan needs it as a tactical position for his planned takeover. The location is critical to both of them.'

Sarah nodded; her grief momentarily overtaken by anger.

'What do we do with this?'

Harper considered their options.

'We secure the evidence first,' he nodded towards the notebook and photographs. 'And these too. We need somewhere safe to examine everything in detail.'

Sarah gathered the items, returning the empty box to its slot.

'Not my house. If they're watching as closely as you suggested...'

'The inn isn't secure either,' Harper agreed. 'We need neutral ground.'

Sarah thought for a moment.

'There's a hunting cabin Mike kept. About five miles outside town, off Whispering Pines Road. Few people know about it – he used it mostly for storage and occasional fishing trips to the nearby creek.'

'Perfect,' Harper said. 'You have the key?'

'At home.'

'Get it but don't go to the cabin yet,' Harper instructed. 'Meet me at the Blood Ridge Retreat at seven. Once we know we're ready we can leave separately and approach from different directions, making sure we arrive around the same time.'

Sarah considered this, nodded and they exited the vault area, completing the necessary paperwork with the teller. As they walked towards the bank entrance, Harper noticed a familiar black sedan passing slowly outside, the driver watching the bank with too much interest for coincidence.

'Your three o'clock shadow is back,' he murmured to Sarah.

'How do you know it's not you?'

'They have an SUV on me,' Harper smiled. 'I saw the sedan near your school.'

'I've noticed them,' she replied quietly. 'Following at a distance, watching the house at night. Jake saw them first, put me onto them.'

'Act normal,' Harper advised as they reached the door. 'Continue your routine. Don't let them see anything has changed.'

Sarah nodded, squaring her shoulders.

'Seven o'clock, then. And don't forget – eight o'clock tomorrow morning at the garage. Ray'll be expecting you.'

They parted ways outside the bank, Sarah returning to

her Honda while Harper walked in the opposite direction, simply a man who'd left the bank at the same time. The sedan hesitated, then followed Sarah, confirming their primary interest.

But not for long.

They'd check with the bank, find out Sarah had accessed the safe deposit box with a stranger. Within hours, they'd know Harper had been there too.

Harper continued towards the inn, mind working through the implications of what they'd discovered. Mike had uncovered Daggett's smuggling network – whatever it was Daggett was smuggling – through old mining tunnels, but more critically, he'd discovered Brennan's imminent plans for a violent takeover. All pieces of a larger picture that had cost Mike his life.

Christ, I hope it's not all about bloody mining tunnels, Harper considered. *I had enough of them in Prosperity.*

As Harper approached the inn, he noted a patrol car parked across the street, Deputy Klein visible behind the wheel. Their eyes met briefly – acknowledgement rather than challenge – before Klein looked away, speaking into his radio.

The message was clear.

I know you're here and I'm watching too.

The question was whether Klein represented an ally or another threat in a town where allegiances were as complex as they were dangerous. Mike had planned to meet with him, to share his evidence. But Mike had died before that meeting could take place.

Harper entered the inn, his mind filled with questions. *Had Mike been killed to prevent him from meeting Klein? Or had*

Klein himself arranged for Mike's death to protect his involvement in whatever operation was happening on Seneca Ridge?

In a town with blood in its foundations, trust seemed to be a luxury Harper couldn't afford.

Once in his room, Harper saw that outside, the black SUV had returned to its position across from the inn, the watcher settling in for another evening of surveillance.

Let them watch, Harper thought, *because he was watching back.* They were looking for predictable behaviour while he was mapping their patterns and weaknesses. Sarah Colton's garage-selling dilemma had become a strategic opportunity.

And Harper intended to exploit it to uncover the truth about Mike Colton's death – and the operation that had made it necessary.

Whatever it was, it would be worth killing for.

Or dying to expose.

6

CABIN IN THE WOODS

THE FOREST CLOSED AROUND HIM LIKE A SHIELD, BRANCHES AND undergrowth providing cover as Harper guided the Bonneville down a narrow dirt track. The last traces of daylight had faded, leaving only the motorcycle's headlight cutting through the darkness as he navigated towards Mike's hunting cabin.

Sarah had followed his instructions precisely – meeting him at the diner at seven, leaving separately, then reconvening at a rural crossroads five miles outside town. She'd led the way since then, Harper following her Honda as it wound deeper into the woods.

Even though they'd seemed to be followed 24/7, right now Harper could see no signs of pursuit, but he remained vigilant; in a town where walls had eyes, it was safest to assume they'd been noticed.

The cabin materialised from the darkness – a simple silhouette against the night sky. Single-storey, weathered timber construction, set back beneath overhanging pines. No lights, no vehicles, no signs of recent occupancy.

'Mike bought it from an old hunting buddy ten years ago,' Sarah explained as they approached, the car and bike left where they could get to them quickly. 'No electricity connected, just a generator he'd run when necessary. Most people in town have forgotten it exists.'

'Perfect,' Harper replied. The isolation and anonymity were exactly what they needed.

Sarah unlocked the door, stepping inside and moving with the familiarity of someone who'd been there many times before. She found matches and lit an oil lamp, its warm glow revealing a spartan interior – main room with basic furniture, a small kitchenette in one corner, stone fireplace along the wall. A door opposite presumably led to a bedroom. The furnishings were basic but well-maintained – a worn leather sofa, sturdy wooden table with four chairs, bookshelves filled with fishing guides, survival manuals and military history. The air smelled of wood and dust and the lingering trace of gun oil.

But what caught Harper's attention were the details scattered around that spoke of Mike Colton's military background. The precise arrangement of firewood, a go-bag by the door, and the strategic positioning of the furniture providing simple lines to all entrances.

'Mike's sanctuary,' Sarah explained, following Harper's gaze. 'He came here when the town got too crowded, or when things at the garage became complicated, to centre himself.'

Sarah entered a code, and the door opened silently. From inside, she withdrew a Heckler & Koch MR762A1, the civilian version of the venerable HK417 battle rifle, with a Primary Arms SLx 5x36 prism scope mounted on it. She pulled the charging handle, confirming a clear chamber and no magazine before setting it on the table.

'You know how to handle that?' Harper asked, mildly surprised.

'Yup, Military wife - He put a two-stage AR-10 Triggertech Diamond trigger group on this, and that Precision Armament M41 Severe Duty muzzle brake – It shoots as light as a .223.' Sarah gave a tight smile. 'Mike insisted I learn. Said someday I might need to protect Jake if he couldn't.'

The statement hung in the air between them, its prophetic nature now painfully clear. She returned to the sideboard under the safe and continued extracting items: boxes of ammunition, an emergency radio, three compact trail cameras with motion sensors, a field medical kit that looked military-issue and a satellite phone.

'Mike was prepared,' Harper observed.

'More than I realised,' Sarah replied, her voice softer now. 'I thought this was just leftover habits from his deployment. Now I understand he was preparing for something specific. Look.'

Without explaining, she led Harper to what appeared to be a storage closet off the kitchenette. Inside, instead of shelves, there was a ladder descending through a trapdoor.

'Root cellar, supposedly,' Sarah explained. 'Actually an access point to an old mining tunnel. Mike discovered it when he bought the place. He sealed most of it off but kept it as an emergency exit.'

Harper examined the tunnel entrance with interest.

Bloody mining tunnels. I'm cursed.

'How far does it extend?'

'Miles, according to Mike. The whole ridge is honeycombed with old coal mines. Most collapsed or flooded decades ago but he told me last month he believes Daggett's people have been reopening and reinforcing sections.'

That explained the construction activity in Mike's photographs. Not building above ground but renovating below.

They returned to the main room where Sarah had spread the contents of Mike's safe deposit box across the table. Harper helped organise the materials, creating separate piles for photographs, financial records and Mike's handwritten notes.

'I've been meaning to ask,' he said as they worked. 'What's the story with Daggett and Brennan? Sounds like more than a simple territorial dispute.'

Sarah paused, sitting back in her chair.

'That's a complicated story and one that goes back generations. The short version? The Daggetts have been here since Blüdridge was created and have controlled it since Prohibition. Victor's grandfather ran bootlegging operations through these same tunnels, then diversified into drugs, prostitution, extortion, the usual sort of thing, I suppose. Victor inherited it all and legitimised portions but kept the criminal enterprises running across the county. Now his son wants what he believes is rightfully his.'

'And Brennan?'

'Sean Brennan showed up five years ago. Irish background, connected to some Belfast groups during The Troubles, if rumours are true. But he's not just another criminal looking for territory.' Sarah's expression darkened. 'His family were also founding fathers. Sided differently to the Daggetts during the Civil War, if you get my drift. Years later old Grandpappy Brennan owned half the bootlegging operation, holding a truce in the name of capitalism... until the Daggetts screwed them over, removing the Brennans once and for all before the Second World War. Well, until five years back, when Sean Brennan returned.

'So, it's personal,' Harper concluded.

'Very,' Sarah pushed a newspaper clipping towards him – a photo of two men facing off at what appeared to be a town council meeting, tension clear in their postures. 'Brennan's been public about his intentions to "reclaim his family's legacy". It started with small provocations – outbidding Daggett on property, opening competing businesses.'

'With money he made in Ireland, I'm guessing?'

'Maybe, it was never said. Then it escalated. Mitchell was assaulted outside The Rusted Nail, Brennan's bar – there'd been some altercation over a woman Mitchell has a thing for, who turned out to be Sean's cousin. She got sent home, Mitchell got a beating. A week later, one of Brennan's warehouses mysteriously burned down.'

'The town caught in the middle of a new civil war,' Harper mused.

'Exactly. Everyone's been forced to choose sides. Even Mike,' her voice caught. 'At first, he tried to stay neutral, but the garage's location made that impossible. Both wanted it as a monitoring point for the main road and they both had reasons for a solid mechanic who looked the other way when certain vehicles were... modified. Both pressured him.'

'I can see how a well-positioned chop-shop would work around here,' Harper stroked his chin. 'I just can't work out why if Brennan and Daggett are so equally matched, why half the town is in squalor while the other half is gentrified.'

'Victor Daggett has friends in high places, while Sean is scrabbling for what he can get,' Sarah shrugged. 'And Daggett's side might look pretty, but it's superficial, believe me.'

Accepting this, Harper examined a series of photographs showing various vehicles arriving at secluded mountain access points – unmarked trucks, SUVs with tinted windows, men unloading crates at night.

'Weapons shipments?' he guessed, holding it up.

Sarah shrugged.

'I don't know,' she replied. 'Mike tracked them for months. I think he once said that Daggett was moving drugs and cash through the ridge tunnels, but I can't be sure. According to Mike's notes, they're running distribution networks across three counties with protection and fentanyl rackets funding the entire operation.'

'Profitable business,' Harper commented, sorting through financial spreadsheets. A drug distribution network this extensive was dangerous enough, but with protection rackets added to the mix, Daggett had created a small empire.

'And protected,' Sarah added, pointing to a document bearing the county letterhead. 'Someone in local government is working with Victor and running interference, blocking investigations. That's why Mike was gathering evidence on his own.'

Harper pieced the story together as they worked. Mike had discovered Daggett's smuggling operation accidentally while servicing vehicles at a construction site on the ridge. Instead of looking away, the veteran in him had seen this as a red flag and he'd begun documenting shipments, photographing personnel, mapping the old coal mining tunnel network. Then he'd uncovered something worse: evidence that Brennan was trying to seize control of the entire operation.

'This is Brennan,' Sarah said, showing Harper a surveillance photo of a man in his fifties with silver-streaked black hair and the weathered complexion of someone who'd spent years outdoors. He had the compact, powerful build of a boxer and stood flanked by men with the hard eyes and tense postures of experienced enforcers.

Harper had seen many men looking like him during his various visits to Belfast.

'Former IRA enforcer, according to rumours,' Sarah continued. 'Moved his way up the chain, but was clever enough to never be visible, according to Mike. Definitely dangerous.'

'And Ray? Where does he fit?' Harper asked.

Sarah's jaw tightened as she pushed forward another set of photos – Ray Halvorsen meeting with men Harper recognised from outside Brennan's bar, exchanging envelopes in a parking lot.

'Playing both sides. Taking Daggett's money to maintain the garage as a checkpoint while secretly setting things up for Brennan's takeover,' her voice hardened. 'Mike confronted him two days before the "accident." They argued in Mike's office. I'd come by to visit, heard shouting but couldn't make out the words. When I walked in, they stopped.'

Harper studied financial records showing regular payments to Ray from shell companies, all of which were likely fronts for both crime bosses. In the margins were notes like "WHO IS THIS" and "WHAT FOR".

Mike had been so close.

'Anyone else at the garage involved?'

'I don't think so. The mechanics are just trying to make a living. But they know not to ask questions when certain vehicles come in for "special service."'

Harper studied a detailed map of the remains of the tunnel system, noting strategic chokepoints Mike had marked. Rather than simply gathering evidence, Mike had been thinking like a tactical analyst – identifying vulnerabilities, mapping escape routes, cataloguing security positions.

He was going to war.

'What about Deputy Klein?' Harper asked. 'Mike was supposed to meet him according to the notes we found at the bank. What's his story?'

'Klein's been building a case for years,' Sarah explained. 'Local interference kept blocking him but Mike's evidence provided what he needed – documentation that couldn't be explained away or buried by Daggett's connections.'

'You trust him?' Harper asked, observing her reaction.

'Mike did,' Sarah replied simply. 'Said Klein was one of the few honest cops left in the county. Klein was the one who suggested Mike document everything meticulously – timestamps, photographs, recordings. Said they needed to build an airtight case that couldn't be buried by local interference.'

As Harper continued to examine the map of the tunnel system, he noticed handwritten notations on the side, suggesting periodic flooding, structural weaknesses – information that could be tactically valuable if conflict erupted. Sarah had gone quiet, holding what appeared to be a personal letter. Her fingers traced Mike's handwriting, her expression a complex mixture of grief and pride.

'He knew the risks,' she said softly. 'Says here he was worried they'd discovered his investigation, that they might come after him.'

She looked up at Harper, eyes glistening but resolute.

'He didn't back down.'

'Mike never did,' Harper replied, a memory surfacing as he spoke. 'In Helmand, our unit got pinned down in a village. Taliban on three sides, no air support coming. Most men would've hunkered down, waited for help. Mike figured out a drainage route under the buildings, led us out right under their noses.'

He paused; the memory vivid.

'Saved twelve lives that day.'

Sarah managed a smile through her tears.

'That sounds like him. Always finding another way.'

'Yeah,' Harper smiled back. But all he could think about was that this time it'd be Harper, not Mike who'd have to find a way – and end this.

THEY CONTINUED WORKING THROUGH THE EVIDENCE FOR another hour, organising it by relevance and assembling a timeline of events leading to Mike's death. As they did, the picture became increasingly clear – Mike had been documenting both criminal operations while feeding information to Klein, hoping to build a solid case that couldn't be buried by local corruption. When his investigation threatened both Daggett's smuggling network and Brennan's planned takeover though, someone had decided he needed to be eliminated.

Harper laid out the garage schematic Sarah had brought, studying the layout.

'Tomorrow I'll need to check Mike's office,' he said. 'Find anything he might have hidden there that Ray hasn't discovered. Then inspect the service bays, especially any areas where "special service" happens.'

'The north-east bay is reserved for Daggett's vehicles,' Sarah replied.

'And what about Brennan's people? Do they come to the garage?'

'Not directly. Ray meets them off site,' Sarah showed locations on the map. 'But according to Mike's notes here, Brennan's considered using the garage as a staging area for his assault. The location gives them control of the main access road to the ridge.'

Harper was about to reply when a sound caught his attention – the distinctive crunch of tyres on gravel.

Sarah heard it too, her body tensing as she looked to Harper for direction. He signalled for silence, moving to the window and staying to the side as he peered through the blinds. Sarah doused the main lights, plunging the cabin into darkness except for the faint glow of the fireplace embers.

'Single vehicle. Headlight off,' Harper reported, seeing what seemed to be a trail bike or motorcycle arrive. 'You expecting anyone?'

Sarah shook her head, face pale in the dim light.

Harper positioned himself beside the door, hand moving to where he'd stowed his weapon. Footsteps approached the cabin – a lone person moving with what sounded like deliberate stealth.

But then came a gentle knock, followed by a voice Harper recognised.

'Mom? It's me.'

Sarah exhaled sharply, moving towards the door but Harper held up a hand, signalling caution. He peered through the peephole, confirming it was indeed Jake Colton standing alone on the porch, glancing nervously over his shoulder.

At Harper's nod, Sarah unlocked the door, pulling her son inside before securing it again.

'What the hell are you doing here?' she demanded, voice tight with fear and anger. 'You were supposed to stay at Lisa's!'

'I saw you packing the stuff from Dad's safe deposit box,' Jake replied defensively. 'I knew you were coming here. I wanted to help.'

'By putting yourself in danger?' Sarah's hands gripped his shoulders. 'Jake, these people killed your father!'

'I know! That's why I can't just sit around doing nothing!' The teenager's voice cracked with emotion. 'Dad was trying to stop them and now everyone's acting like it was just some accident!'

Harper noticed something in Jake's posture – the same determination he'd seen in Mike, the refusal to back down even when outnumbered and outgunned.

'How did you get here without being seen?' he asked.

Jake's expression shifted from defiant to cautiously proud.

'How did you both get here without being followed?' he asked in retaliation.

'We kept to the back roads,' Sarah explained 'Your father—'

'Taught me the back roads too,' Jake's chin came up defiantly now. 'And I've been watching the guys watching our house. They change shifts at nine. There's about three minutes when they're both in the car, talking. I went out the back, through the Mendez's yard and took Lisa's brother's dirt bike.'

Harper exchanged a glance with Sarah who looked torn between maternal fear and reluctant admiration.

'That was both smart and incredibly reckless,' Harper told Jake. 'But since you're here, you might as well make yourself useful.'

Jake moved to the table, taking in the spread of evidence.

'What did dad find?'

Sarah hesitated, then sighed.

'Everything. Drug trafficking, money laundering, corrupt officials, plans for an assault on the ridge.'

'I knew it,' Jake said, his jaw setting in a determined line that reminded Harper eerily of Mike. 'I told everyone the lift didn't just fail.'

Like father, like son.

'I've been documenting the surveillance cars if it helps,' Jake said after a while, pulling out his phone and showing Harper a series of photographs – different vehicles parked near their house, men changing shifts, close ups of licence plates. 'Three rotations, eight-hour shifts. The night crew is less careful – they leave blind spots on the east side of the house for about twenty minutes when they do their perimeter check.'

Harper raised an eyebrow.

'You've been busy.'

'Dad always said details matter,' Jake's face clouded. 'No one would listen to me about the lift. But I checked the maintenance log. Dad inspected it two days before... before it happened. Marked it in perfect condition.'

'Jake,' Sarah began carefully, 'I understand you want to help but this is dangerous. These people—'

'Already killed Dad,' Jake finished for her. 'I know. But they're watching us anyway. At least this way I can do something useful.'

Harper considered this for a long moment. There was no safe place in this situation – Jake was already a target by his relationship to Mike and Sarah. Excluding him completely might actually increase his risk if he continued his solo investigation.

Also, if Mike confronted Ray three days before he died, there was every reason for Ray to sabotage the lift. However, if Mike gave it a clean bill of health, this made it either a last-minute decision, or an actual accident.

He needed to see the maintenance logbook.

'How did you see the log?'

'I asked Ray and he showed it to me,' Jake shrugged. 'It was like there was no secret, nothing to be worried about.'

So Ray knew there was nothing there – whether genuine or planned.

'Okay then. Limited involvement,' Harper decided. 'You continue documenting the surveillance patterns, okay? That's genuinely valuable intelligence. But you stay away from direct confrontation and you follow security protocols exactly. No improvisation.'

'I can do that,' Jake nodded eagerly.

'And you tell no one – not your friends, not this Lisa, nobody – what you're doing or what we know,' Harper continued. 'As far as anyone's concerned, you're just a kid grieving his dad, trying to get through school.'

'Agreed.'

Sarah didn't look entirely convinced but seemed to recognise this was the best compromise available.

'If anything feels wrong – anything at all – you call me immediately,' she insisted.

Jake nodded and Harper could see the weight of responsibility settling on his young shoulders, and so after an hour more of research, Harper helped Sarah secure the evidence back in the gun safe.

'We should leave separately,' Harper said, checking his

watch. 'Jake first, then you, then me. Different routes back to town.'

Sarah agreed, but as Jake prepared to depart, Harper pulled him aside.

'Your father would be proud,' he said quietly. 'But he'd also want you to stay alive. That means being cunning, not brave. Understand?'

Jake nodded; his expression solemn.

'I won't let him down. Or you.'

Harper watched from the window as Jake disappeared into the darkness. Sarah left twenty minutes later, her Honda's lights remaining off until she reached the main road.

Harper used the next twenty minutes alone to familiarise himself with the cabin's layout and resources, mentally working out any likely defensive positions and escape routes. It'd make a good fallback position if things went sideways.

As he prepared to leave, Harper did a last sweep of the perimeter, checking for any signs they'd been observed. In the distance, just at the edge of his vision, something caught the moonlight briefly – a reflection where there should be none, gone almost as soon as it appeared.

Harper froze, focusing on the spot but saw nothing further. It could have been anything – an animal's eyes, dew on a leaf, or someone watching through binoculars. It was impossible to know for certain, and whatever it was would be gone long before Harper could investigate further. He filed the observation away as he mounted the Bonneville.

Tomorrow he would enter Colton's Auto Shop, ostensibly as a mechanic-turned-business-consultant evaluating operations, but actually hunting for anything that might connect Ray Halvorsen to Mike's death.

As he rode through the darkness towards Blüdridge,

Harper mentally prepared his approach. Ray would be watching, suspicious of this outsider suddenly inserted into his domain. Daggett's people would be alert to any change in the garage's routine. And somewhere, Brennan's forces were completing plans for an assault that would turn the simmering conflict into open warfare. Harper would need to navigate it all while finding the truth about what happened to Mike Colton. With each piece of evidence they uncovered, the stakes grew higher and the danger more immediate.

The moonlight cast his shadow long on the road ahead as he rode, stretching towards whatever waited for him at Colton's Auto Shop – and whatever price would be demanded for the answers he sought.

He just hoped it wasn't as high a price as the one demanded of Mike.

7

THE NEW GUY

Harper arrived at Colton's Auto Shop fifteen minutes before eight. The police tape that had once cordoned off the entrance was now removed, although fragments still clung to the door frame like tattered bunting. He'd deliberately chosen to arrive early – first impressions mattered, but he also wanted to observe the garage's morning routine before inserting himself into it.

The building was larger than it had appeared from a distance, a sprawling single-storey structure with three service bays, a small office area visible through front windows and a fenced lot and loading bay at the rear where several vehicles awaited attention, the woods of Blüdridge behind. Its position at the junction of Route 40 and Sawmill Road was even more significant now that Harper understood what moved through this intersection – and who controlled that movement.

He parked the Bonneville in full view, then leaned against it, watching as the first employees arrived. Two men in their thirties pulled up in separate trucks, eyeing Harper with the cautious assessment of small-town mechanics encountering a stranger on their turf. One nodded briefly before unlocking the side entrance while the other kept his distance, disappearing inside without acknowledgement.

At precisely eight, a blue sedan Harper recognised from the funeral – Ray Halvorsen's – pulled into the lot, parking in a spot marked "Management". Ray climbed out, spotted Harper immediately and approached with the same proprietary scowl he'd worn at the funeral.

'So, you actually showed up,' Ray said, extending his hand in a gesture that seemed more challenge than welcome. 'Sarah said her husband's old Army buddy would drop by but I didn't think you'd really come. Figured the cash behind the bar would've been enough for you to toast your buddy and then piss off.'

Harper shook the offered hand, noting the excessive pressure Ray applied – a small man's power play.

'Appreciate you letting me help out,' Harper replied neutrally, releasing the handshake first. 'Sarah's got enough on her plate without worrying about the garage operations.'

Ray's eyes narrowed slightly at the implication that Sarah might be worried.

'We've been managing fine,' he said. 'But I understand she wants a second opinion from someone with... experience.'

The pause suggested scepticism about Harper's qualifications.

'Mike and I worked on a lot of vehicles together while deployed,' Harper said, the lie coming easily, built on fragments of truth. 'He mentioned taking over this place from his dad when he got home. Seems like he did a solid job.'

'He did,' Ray agreed, gesturing towards the entrance.

'Let's get you inside. I assume Sarah briefed you on what we do here?'

'General mechanical work, specialising in fleet maintenance and custom installations,' Harper replied, recalling Sarah's description from the night before. 'Some high-end client work too, I hear.'

Ray led him through the side entrance, past a small break room where the two mechanics Harper had observed earlier were pouring coffee. The space opened into a large garage area with three service bays, two occupied by vehicles – a Jeep Cherokee with its hood up and a black Escalade elevated on a hydraulic lift.

'That's Chris and Darren,' Ray said, nodding towards the mechanics. 'Luis and Toby should be in shortly. We've been short-handed since... well, you know.'

Harper nodded, mentally cataloguing the staff while observing the garage layout. Standard garage equipment lined the walls – tool chests, diagnostic computers, parts inventories – nothing overtly suspicious, but Harper noted security cameras positioned to monitor all entrances and a keypad access system on a door marked "Private".

'Mike's office?' Harper asked, gesturing towards the door.

'Mine now,' Ray replied with a touch of too much satisfaction. 'We can use it to discuss operations.'

Ray made a point of shielding the keypad as he typed the code, but it didn't matter; his situational awareness was poor, shown by the mirror on the side wall Harper was able to watch while turning away – all four numbers, mirrored but readable. Sarah had given Harper the code anyway, but it wasn't the same as she'd said; Ray had obviously changed it... and not told his new boss.

Interesting.

The office beyond the door was small but organised with filing cabinets along one wall, a dated computer workstation and large windows overlooking the service area. A bulletin board displayed work schedules, service manuals and inspection certificates, but Harper noticed empty spaces where items had been removed, slight discolourations in the cork suggesting long-term postings recently taken down.

Ray settled behind the desk with the confidence of someone staking territory.

'So, what exactly are you hoping to accomplish here... Liam, isn't it?' he asked. 'Sarah wasn't entirely clear on your... role.'

'Call me Harper, everyone does.' Harper leaned against the filing cabinet, maintaining a relaxed posture while scanning the office for anything noteworthy. 'I'm just helping Sarah understand the operations. She knows the business side from handling the books but the technical aspects are outside her wheelhouse. She wants to make informed decisions about the garage's future.'

'Informed decisions,' Ray repeated flatly. 'Like whether to sell to Daggett?'

'That would be one option, I suppose,' Harper acknowledged. 'Is that what you'd recommend?'

Ray's expression hardened momentarily before he smoothed it back.

'I think Sarah should keep the garage,' he said carefully. 'It's a solid business, built by her husband and his father before him. Selling now when she's vulnerable and grieving would be a mistake.'

Harper noted the carefully constructed answer. Of *course* Ray wanted the garage to remain under Sarah's nominal control – with himself maintaining actual operations, collecting payments from both Daggett and Brennan.

'I'll need to familiarise myself with the entire operation,' Harper said. 'All service bays, equipment, special projects – get a complete picture for Sarah. I'll work my keep too, don't worry. As you said, you're shorthanded.'

'Of course,' Ray agreed too readily. 'Though some client work is confidential. High-end security installations, that sort of thing.'

'Like the north-east bay?' Harper asked casually, watching Ray's reaction.

The flash of suspicion was immediate but quickly masked.

'Sarah's been thorough in her briefing,' Ray said, his voice cooling. 'Yes, the north-east bay handles specialised work. We can review the basics but client confidentiality is something Mike always insisted on.'

Harper nodded as if accepting this limitation.

'Let's start with a general tour then. I'd like to meet the rest of the team.'

Ray led Harper back into the main garage area where all four mechanics were now present. The introductions were brief and professional though Harper detected undercurrents in each man's response.

Chris Mercer – early forties, the senior mechanic who'd nodded to Harper earlier, seemed genuinely grief-stricken over Mike's death and treated Harper with cautious respect.

Darren Wells – late-twenties, projected indifference, but watched Harper with subtle wariness when he thought himself unobserved.

Luis Vega – mid-thirties, was openly friendly, asking

about Harper's service and connection to Mike with what appeared to be genuine interest.

Toby Townsend – the youngest at perhaps twenty-five, remained distant, focusing on his work and responding to questions with minimal engagement.

As Ray guided him through the facility, Harper methodically stored details while appearing merely interested. The main area contained standard equipment and tools, used constantly on different projects though he noted everything was well-maintained and organised. The hydraulic lift in the centre bay – not the one that had allegedly failed – was currently supporting the Escalade as Chris worked underneath.

'And this is where it happened?' Harper asked as they approached the far bay where a newer hydraulic lift stood idle.

Ray's posture stiffened almost imperceptibly.

'Yeah,' he replied, and Harper caught a whiff of actual sincerity here. Either Ray genuinely mourned Mike or he hadn't been told it was happening, perhaps. 'The primary support gave way while Mike was underneath. It was... instantaneous.'

Harper moved closer, examining the equipment. The lift had been repaired or replaced – no signs of catastrophic failure remained visible – but Harper knelt beside it anyway, running his fingers along the hydraulic cylinder housing.

'Recent safety inspection?' he asked.

'Full certification after the accident,' Ray replied. 'Regional inspector signed off on it personally, and Mike had checked it off two days before. Freak accident. Poor bastard.'

Harper continued his examination, finding what he was looking for – almost invisible tool marks on the bleed valve housing, consistent with deliberate tampering rather than mechanical failure. The kind of sabotage that would cause a catastrophic pressure loss at the worst possible moment but might appear accidental to a cursory investigation. It wasn't accidental; in his time in the SRR, he'd seen similar on other occasions.

'This the secret client area?' Harper asked good-humouredly, moving towards the north-east bay which was currently empty but featured additional security – a separate keypad entry system. 'Mind if I take a look?'

'It's locked when not in use,' Ray said firmly. 'Company policy.'

Harper nodded, not pushing the issue yet.

'Fair enough. I'd like to check the equipment inventory next if that's all right. Sarah mentioned some recent purchases she wasn't familiar with.'

Ray's jawline tightened but he led Harper towards the parts room. As they passed Chris working on the Escalade, Harper paused.

'Beautiful vehicle,' he commented. 'Special client?'

Chris exchanged a quick glance with Ray before answering.

'Regular maintenance. Plus some... customisations.'

Harper nodded as if this explained everything but noted the vehicle's reinforced suspension, custom wiring harnesses extending beneath the dashboard and what appeared to be aftermarket compartments integrated into the floor panels. He'd seen the same in vehicles in Thailand a few years back – modifications consistent with vehicles designed to transport drugs and cash.

The parts room was exactly as he expected, and Harper could see Ray was tiring of this.

'Mind if I get my hands dirty?' he asked as they re-entered the workspace area. 'Best way to understand operations is to take part.'

Ray hesitated, clearly wanting to refuse but lacking a reasonable justification.

'Sure,' he finally agreed. 'Luis could use help with the transmission on the Ford pickup in bay two. Grab a cup of coffee, too. We have some solid Cuban blends I brew a few times a day. Better than the shit you drank in the army, I reckon.'

'Awesome,' Harper smiled. 'I'll get out of your hair, then.'

As he left, Harper felt Ray's eyes on him, but the manager said nothing.

LUIS PROVED TALKATIVE ONCE ENGAGED, AND OVER THE NEXT couple of hours he began sharing stories about the garage, the town and occasionally Mike.

'He was the best boss I ever had,' he said as they worked, voice lowered though Ray was in his office. 'Fair, you know? Never talked down to us, always shared credit for good work.'

'Sounds like Mike,' Harper agreed, using a torque wrench to secure a bolt. 'He'd wanted to have his own shop for years, even back when we served together.'

Luis handed him a gasket.

'He was different those last few weeks though. Tense. Staying late, locking his office – never did that before.'

'Any idea why?'

'Thought it might be financial troubles at first but then these fancy cars started coming in more often,' Luis shrugged. 'Ray would handle them personally. After hours, usually. Mike was sometimes involved, but Ray was the guiding force, if you get what I mean.'

Harper absorbed this, continuing to work while appearing casually interested.

'Ray seems to run a tight operation,' he observed.

'Different from Mike,' Luis said carefully. 'Last month or so now, Ray's all about procedures, restricted access. Mike believed in teaching us everything, making sure we all could handle any job.'

Their conversation was interrupted by the arrival of a black GMC Yukon with tinted windows that pulled directly into the north-east bay. Ray emerged immediately from his office, greeting the driver – a hard-faced man in his thirties. They spoke briefly before Ray pressed a code into the keypad, allowing the man access to the restricted bay.

Through the briefly open door, Harper glimpsed what appeared to be specialised tools and equipment unlike standard garage fare – tools designed for creating custom modifications.

'Happens a couple times a week,' Luis murmured, noticing Harper's interest. 'Always guys like that, always the same routine. Ray handles it personally, keeps the bay locked otherwise.'

'Special clients,' Harper said neutrally.

'That's what we're told.' Luis tightened a fitting. 'Mike used to handle those jobs himself. Said it was sensitive work, private clients who paid cash. There weren't many back then. But after he died, Ray took over and suddenly there were a lot more "special clients" turning up. Like three times the amount, you know?'

'Mike did them?'

'Yeah. I mean, he wasn't happy about it, probably because

they didn't pay as well as some of the others. But that doesn't seem to bother Ray.'

The bay door remained closed for nearly forty minutes before reopening. The driver emerged, exchanged a few words with Ray, then departed in the Yukon. Ray then spent several minutes in the bay alone before securing it and returning to his office.

Harper knew that at some point he'd need to look inside both the office and the bay.

Tonight, maybe.

He looked back at the office window to see Ray staring back at him. The face was unreadable, but Harper had seen it before.

Suspicion.

He'd made his way into the garage, but now he needed to survive long enough to get something *out* of the garage.

8

HAVING A WORD

By mid-afternoon, Harper had completed the transmission work with Luis and moved on to helping Chris with brake repairs on a local sheriff's cruiser.

'You knew Mike from the Army?' Chris asked as they worked.

'Special operations,' Harper replied, providing just enough truth to be convincing. 'Fixed a lot of vehicles in dangerous situations together.'

'He spoke highly of his service buddies,' Chris said. 'Never mentioned names but said they were the best men he'd known. Said we were his "new recruits" once.'

'You serve?'

'Just a stint in the ROTC. Most of us? We were "teenage delinquents" as the courts used to say,' Chris grinned. 'The Coltons? Either Mike or his pop? They took a chance on us.'

He looked away as his expression darkened.

'And we let them down.'

'How so?' Harper continued working, waiting for Chris to

reveal more. The senior mechanic seemed to weigh his words carefully.

'Look, I don't know what Mrs Colton told you,' Chris finally said, voice lowered, 'but that lift didn't fail on its own. Mike maintained everything in this garage personally. Double-checked all safety equipment weekly.'

'You think someone tampered with it?' Harper asked, matching Chris's hushed tone.

Chris glanced towards Ray's office.

'I think Mike was worried about something. Started documenting everything, taking photographs of vehicles that came through, kept a separate logbook in his desk. After the accident, I went to get it, see if he'd written anything but it had disappeared.'

I bet it did.

Harper nodded, allowing Chris to continue.

'Ray changed the lock code on the office the day after Mike died. Said it was standard procedure but nothing about how Ray runs things now is how Mike did it. We should have seen it coming, all these organisations sniffing around, but we hid, let Mike deal with it.'

A pause.

'And in the end it dealt with Mike.'

Their conversation halted as Ray emerged from his office, approaching with what appeared to be paperwork.

'Harper, got a minute?' he called. 'If you're working on these cars, I need you to complete some contractor forms for our records – and for insurance if you slice your hand open doing something stupid.'

Harper excused himself and followed Ray to the office where the forms waiting were exactly as he expected – standard liability releases and confidentiality agreements, contact numbers, that sort of thing. Harper reviewed them carefully, noting the unusually broad language regarding "specialised operations" and "proprietary client services".

'Pretty comprehensive for temporary help,' Harper observed.

'Just protecting the business,' Ray replied. 'Mike was always careful about documentation.'

'I'll bet he was,' Harper said, signing the forms with deliberate casualness, and adding the number of a new burner phone, more to see who'd now gain access to this than anything else. 'Sarah mentioned he kept detailed records of everything.'

Ray's expression flickered momentarily. The guy was definitely not a poker player.

'Mike was old school that way. Paper trails for everything.'

'Speaking of which,' Harper continued, 'Sarah asked me to locate some specific maintenance records. Recent equipment certifications, inspection reports – she's dealing with the insurance company.'

'I can handle the insurance,' Ray said quickly. 'No need to trouble Sarah with that.'

'She insists,' Harper replied with a shrug. 'You know how it is – she needs to stay occupied, feel like she's doing something. Where would those records be kept?'

Sighing as if it wasn't really that important to him, Ray gestured to the filing cabinet.

'Equipment records are in the third drawer. Help yourself.'

While Ray carried on with his duties, staying in the office to monitor the interloper at the filing cabinet, Harper spent the next thirty minutes methodically examining the files, finding exactly what he'd expected – the maintenance logs showed the hydraulic lift had been inspected and certified safe by Mike just two days before the "accident". However, he found the original inspection report had been modified, certain pages replaced by versions bearing the same dates but with different findings.

As he replaced the files, Harper accidentally dropped a folder. As he bent to retrieve it, his eye caught a small white business card that had fallen from the surface of the desk.

'You done?' Ray asked, amusement in his voice at Harper's clumsiness. 'All good?'

'All good, just dropped something.'

'Good,' Ray mocked. 'Now piss off out of my office, yeah?'

Harper did so, pocketing the card he'd picked up from the floor as he left.

Daggett Financial Services.

He didn't know why he'd taken it, but instinct said to hold on to it.

THE REST OF THE DAY PASSED SIMILARLY, WITH HARPER dividing his time between mechanical work and casual conversations with the staff. By closing time, he'd established himself as competent and helpful while gathering significant intelligence about the garage operations.

Ray approached as Harper prepared to leave.

'So, what will you tell Sarah?' he asked directly.

'That you're running a professional operation,' Harper replied honestly. 'The team's skilled, the equipment's well-maintained.'

'But?' Ray prompted, hearing the unspoken qualification.

'But there are questions about the specialised client work

that I'll need to understand better to give her a complete assessment.'

Ray's expression hardened slightly.

'Like I said, client confidentiality is non-negotiable. If Sarah has questions about that aspect of the business, she should speak with me directly.'

'I'll let her know,' Harper said, maintaining a neutral tone. 'I'll be back tomorrow to continue this if that works for you.'

'Sure,' Ray agreed, though his expression suggested otherwise. 'We appreciate the help.'

As Harper prepared to mount the Bonneville, he considered what he'd learnt about the man. Nothing Ray had said today suggested he was unaware of Mike's murder – it had either been his idea, or he'd been fully complicit in carrying it out.

Harper pulled onto Route 40, noting a black SUV parked across the intersection, watching the garage with the same disciplined attention he'd observed in Blüdridge for days now. It wasn't the same one he'd seen outside his inn, as the plates were different, but Harper was sure it was the same man giving orders.

Daggett's surveillance, monitoring his investment.

But as Harper continued down the road, something in his peripheral vision caught his attention – a dark-blue sedan pulling out from a side street to follow him. Not the SUV, not the car that had been following Sarah, either – this wasn't someone he'd noticed before. The car kept a precise distance, neither closing nor falling behind as Harper maintained a steady speed.

Amateur. If I can spot you that easily, you're doing it wrong.

Harper took a series of random turns, testing whether the

tail would continue. It did, maintaining the same distance through each manoeuvre. Whoever they were, they wanted Harper to know he was being followed.

A warning.

Or an invitation.

He circled back towards the main road, but as he approached an intersection, a second vehicle – a black pickup – pulled out directly in front of him, forcing Harper to brake sharply. The Bonneville skidded, nearly going down before Harper regained control.

Through the pickup's rear window, he glimpsed the driver – one of the men from outside The Rusted Nail.

Brennan's people.

The dark-blue sedan had closed the distance now, boxing Harper between the two vehicles. The pickup maintained a deliberately slow pace while the sedan remained close behind, leaving no room to manoeuvre.

Harper assessed his options. He could attempt to break free – accelerate around the pickup using the shoulder, but that would likely provoke a more aggressive response. Or he could play along, see what they wanted.

The pickup turned onto a gravel side road leading towards what appeared to be an abandoned industrial property. The sedan maintained position behind Harper, leaving him little choice but to follow.

Ahead, the pickup stopped in the centre of a weed-choked parking lot outside what looked like a defunct manufacturing facility. Two men emerged from the pickup – both tall, heavily built, with the hard expressions of experienced enforcers. The sedan pulled alongside Harper; the driver remaining inside with the engine idling.

'Mister Harper,' one of the men from the pickup called out. 'Boss would like a word.'

'Could have just called,' Harper replied, keeping the Bonneville's engine running.

'This way's more personal,' the man said with a humourless smile. 'Mister Brennan appreciates face-to-face conversation.'

Harper considered the situation. The men were armed – subtle bulges beneath jackets showing concealed weapons – but they hadn't drawn them. This wasn't an abduction, at least not yet. More likely an interview.

'Lead the way,' Harper said, killing the engine and dismounting.

The men escorted him to the sedan where the rear door opened. Inside sat a man Harper recognised from Sarah's photographs – Sean Brennan himself, silver-streaked dark hair and weathered features that suggested years of hard living.

'Mister Harper,' Brennan greeted him, his Irish accent distinct but slightly softened by a few years in America. 'Join me, if you would.'

Harper slid into the back seat beside Brennan, noting the driver watching through the rearview mirror and the two men from the pickup positioning themselves outside.

'Sorry for the theatrics,' Brennan continued, 'but I find conventional invitations lack a certain... immediacy.'

'What can I do for you, Mister Brennan?' Harper asked, maintaining a relaxed posture despite the circumstances.

'You can start by explaining your interest in Colton's Auto Shop,' Brennan replied. 'Beyond your stated role as Sarah Colton's advisor.'

Harper met the man's gaze directly.

'Mike Colton saved my life in Afghanistan. I'm helping his widow sort out his affairs.'

'Aye, that's admirable loyalty,' Brennan said, studying Harper with the shrewd assessment of someone accustomed to identifying lies. 'But you've been asking questions all over town. About Colton's death. About Daggett. About me. About things that don't concern a person simply helping a friend's widow.'

'When a friend dies under suspicious circumstances, those circumstances become my concern,' Harper replied. 'Especially when the official story doesn't add up.'

'Few official stories do in Blüdridge,' Brennan smiled without humour. 'But be careful which stones you turn over, Mister Harper. Some have scorpions beneath them.'

'I've handled scorpions before.'

'I'm sure you have,' Brennan's eyes narrowed slightly. 'Your military record suggests a man with... specialised skills. The kind that might be valuable in certain situations.'

Harper remained silent, waiting for Brennan to show his hand. *So, you know my record. That shows you know where to look, because it's not that easy to find. Belfast contacts, perhaps?*

'Events are unfolding in Blüdridge that'll change the balance of power,' Brennan continued. 'Daggett's time is ending. Those who position themselves appropriately now will find opportunities in what follows.'

'You're suggesting I choose a side,' Harper stated flatly.

'I'm suggesting that neutrality is a luxury few can afford in times of transition,' Brennan countered. 'Mike Colton learned that lesson too late.'

The implied admission of involvement in Mike's death hung in the air between them.

'What do you want, Mister Brennan?'

'Information,' Brennan replied simply. 'You've been inside the garage. Spoken with Ray. Examined the operations. Tell me what you've found.'

Harper contemplated his response. Brennan was offering an opening – provide information, establish value, potentially gain access to details about Mike's death. But it was a dangerous game, with Brennan clearly assessing Harper's potential usefulness versus the threat he represented.

'Ray's nervous,' Harper said finally. 'The north-east bay is highly secured, with specialised equipment for vehicle modifications. Client records are locked down tight.'

'And the staff?'

'Mixed loyalty. Chris was close to Mike, suspects foul play. Luis is talkative but keeps his head down. The others want a quiet life.'

Brennan nodded slightly, apparently satisfied with Harper's willingness to share.

'And what has Sarah Colton told you about the garage's... special operations?'

'Not much,' Harper lied. 'She handled the books but Mike kept the specialised work separate.'

Brennan studied Harper for a long moment, eyes calculating.

'You're an interesting man, Mister Harper. Skilled, observant, with connections to military and intelligence communities. You could be valuable to the right employer.'

'I'm not looking for employment.'

'Everybody works for somebody, even if only temporarily,' Brennan replied. 'Consider this a standing offer, even if I'm changing the world in a few days. Information for information. You tell me what you learn about Daggett's operations, I tell you what I know about Mike

Colton's death. The least I can do for someone from the Motherland.'

'My mother was English, my father American,' Harper smiled. 'I'm only Irish in name, Mister Brennan.'

'Feck, most of my men are that too,' Brennan gave a smile, but it didn't reach the eyes. 'Don't change anything.'

The proposal was almost certainly a trap, designed to compromise Harper while revealing how much he already knew. But it also offered potential access to Brennan's organisation – a way to gather intelligence from the inside.

'I'll consider it,' Harper said noncommittally.

Brennan reached into his jacket, producing a business card with only a phone number.

'When you're ready to continue our conversation,' he said, offering the card.

Harper took the card, pocketing it without comment.

'One piece of free information since you've been forthcoming,' Brennan added as Harper reached for the door handle. 'Ray Halvorsen isn't just Daggett's man, or even my man, for that matter. He answers to someone higher up the food chain.'

Harper paused, hand on the door.

'Who?'

'That,' Brennan smiled, 'would be part of our next exchange. Good evening, Mister Harper.'

The dismissal was clear. Harper exited the vehicle, maintaining awareness of the two men still watching him as he returned to his motorcycle. The pickup had already moved, clearing his path back to the main road.

As Harper started the Bonneville, he processed what had just occurred. Brennan had made a play to recruit him, or at least to compromise him. But he'd also revealed something potentially significant – Ray answered to someone above Daggett or Brennan, someone with broader influence. The question was whether Brennan was telling the truth or simply seeding disinformation to muddy the waters.

Harper rode back towards town, taking a circuitous route to ensure he wasn't followed again. The encounter with Brennan had been illuminating but dangerous – by engaging directly with one of Blüdridge's power players, he'd crossed a line that would make maintaining independence increasingly difficult.

And if Brennan had approached him, how long before Daggett did the same?

More concerning was the implication that forces beyond Blüdridge were involved – higher connections, broader influence. If true, it suggested Mike's death was part of something far larger than a local turf war.

Harper considered his next move as he pulled into the inn's parking lot. He needed to check the north-east bay, find what Ray was hiding and monitor Ray's conversations, see if he could catch him communicating with his mysterious superior. He must also warn Sarah that both Daggett and Brennan were likely to increase pressure on her as tensions escalated.

The sun was setting as Harper entered his room, casting long shadows across the floor. He placed Brennan's card on the bedside table alongside his newest acquisition – the Daggett Financial Services card from Ray's office. Two sides of Blüdridge's divide, both now reaching out to him.

A sharp knock at his door interrupted his thoughts. Harper moved cautiously to answer it, positioning himself to the side as he opened the door.

Jake Colton stood in the hallway; face pale with urgency.

'Mom just called,' he said without preamble. 'Someone broke into our house while she was at school. Her desk's been ransacked.'

'Is she all right?' Harper asked immediately.

'She's back at the school. Late faculty meeting. But she's afraid to go home.'

'I can see that,' Harper said. 'Tell her to stay where she is. Public place, witnesses. I'll meet her there in twenty minutes.'

Jake nodded, turning to leave, then paused.

'Harper... they took her laptop. And her phone's been acting weird all day. She thinks someone's listening.'

The implications were clear – whoever was watching Sarah had escalated from surveillance to active intervention. The timing, immediately after Harper's visit to the garage and encounter with Brennan, couldn't be coincidence.

'Somebody's getting nervous,' Harper said grimly. 'And it's not just Ray, and it's not just Brennan. This is bigger than we thought.'

The question was *how* much bigger.

9

THE INTRUDER

HARPER WAITED UNTIL NEARLY MIDNIGHT BEFORE APPROACHING Colton's Auto Shop again. The building sat dark and silent, its windows black against the moonless night, security lights casting harsh shadows across the empty parking lot.

After checking the Colton residence, a nervous Sarah beside him, he'd decided there was nothing to be worried about just yet, and it was likely a simple theft, but to keep a go-bag ready in case things changed. He'd then left as Sarah called Deputy Klein, the story being a simple break in – likely opportunistic teens, maybe even a student with a grudge. After going back to his room for another brief nap into the early evening, Harper had returned to the garage, spending the next few hours observing the property from various vantage points, confirming the patterns Sarah had described – no night security, a surprisingly basic alarm system and cameras covering only the main entrances.

He'd left the Bonneville hidden a quarter of a mile away, approaching on foot through the wooded area behind the property. The garage's rear fence offered minimal challenge;

eight feet of chain link Harper scaled in seconds, dropping silently onto the gravel on the other side. He paused there, crouching motionless in the shadow of a dumpster, listening for any sign his entry had been noticed.

Nothing but crickets and the distant hum of traffic on Route 40.

Harper moved to the service entrance at the rear left of the building, the one Sarah had mentioned was left unwatched for Brennan's people. The alarm keypad glowed faintly in the darkness – a basic model that many smaller businesses considered adequate. Sarah had provided the code but Harper hesitated, scanning for any sign the system had been upgraded since Mike's death. There didn't seem to be any evidence of tampering or additional security measures; Ray might be suspicious but he wasn't expecting a nocturnal visitor with military infiltration training.

More fool him then.

Harper entered the code and the keypad flashed green, the lock disengaging with a soft click. Once inside, Harper waited for his eyes to adjust to the darkness before using the small penlight he'd brought, keeping the beam low and shielded.

The main garage area looked different at night, the familiar tools and equipment transformed into looming shadows. Harper moved silently, making his way towards the north-east bay and the secured area that Ray had been so careful to keep off-limits during his tour.

The keypad on this internal door used a different code to the office. Sarah hadn't known this one but Harper had watched Ray enter it a couple of times during the day, noting the pattern of movement rather than the specific numbers. Six digits, entered in a particular rhythm; Harper mimicked it above the pad twice before feeling he had it nailed and then replicated the sequence.

Beep.

Wrong code.

Pausing and gathering his thoughts, Harper air-tapped a few more times, realised where he went wrong and tried again. This time he was rewarded with another green light and the soft click of the lock disengaging.

Inside, the north-east bay was larger than it had appeared from outside and was immediately distinctive from the rest of the garage. A rack of tools lined one wall but the opposite side contained equipment Harper had recognised from his quick view through the door earlier; tools designed for custom fabrication and installation.

A vehicle occupied the centre of the space – a black Ford Expedition, elevated on a hydraulic lift different from those in the main garage area. It hadn't been there when he left, so had likely arrived after the garage closed "officially" for the day. Harper approached it cautiously, noting the reinforced suspension and custom bumpers before focusing on what was happening underneath.

From the looks of things, the undercarriage had been modified extensively with hidden compartments built into the frame, accessible through cleverly disguised panels. One such compartment was currently open, revealing a space large enough to conceal substantial cargo – drugs, cash or other contraband. It was empty, but that didn't mean it had been when it arrived.

Harper examined the workbench beside the lift and, after rummaging through the drawers, he found schematics for similar modifications to various vehicle models, along with a logbook detailing appointments, vehicle identifications and a variety of scrawled cryptic notations that suggested inventory being moved rather than mechanical work performed.

He photographed these documents with his phone before continuing his search, opening cabinets and examining their contents carefully. In one, he found more tools designed for working on hidden compartments. In another, he discovered packaging materials and vacuum sealers typically used for drug distribution.

This wasn't simply a chop shop it seemed; Daggett – or was it Brennan? – was running a sophisticated smuggling operation through the garage.

Harper found Mike's hidden camera exactly where he'd suspected it might be – concealed within an air vent with a line of sight of the entire bay. The small device had been carefully installed with a separate power supply and large-capacity storage, allowing it to stay hidden and untouched for days, weeks even, at a time. Harper removed the memory card, pocketing it for later examination.

A locked file cabinet at the rear of the bay yielded quickly to Harper's skills, revealing folders organised by date and client code rather than name. He selected the most recent files, spreading them on the workbench to examine their contents. They were detailed records of shipments – quantities, destinations, payment confirmations... everything he needed right now.

Harper was photographing this evidence when he heard it – the soft scrape of a shoe on concrete, the sound of a subtle shift of weight; someone else had entered the garage. He extinguished his light immediately, sliding the files back into the cabinet and moving silently towards the doorway, positioning himself beside it rather than behind.

Footsteps approached – one person, moving with the deliberate stealth of someone who believed the building was empty, but wasn't 100 per cent sure of this. Harper controlled his breathing, listening as the intruder paused outside the north-east-bay door, then listened as he entered the code with a speed that showed knowledge of the numbers, the lock disengaging with the same soft click Harper had heard earlier.

The door opened slowly and a beam of light swept across the bay, illuminating the vehicle and workbench before continuing its arc. Harper remained motionless as the intruder stepped inside, closing the door behind him.

He was a man Harper didn't recognise – mid-thirties, compact build, wearing a dark jacket and carrying what appeared to be a small duffel bag. He moved towards the car with the confidence of someone familiar with the space.

Decision time.

Harper could attempt to retreat unnoticed but that meant leaving potential evidence behind. Or he could confront the intruder, risking exposure but potentially gaining information.

The decision was made for him when the man suddenly stiffened, his head turning towards where Harper stood in the shadows. Perhaps a sound or simply the instinct predators develop for other hunters alerted him.

'Who's there?' the man demanded, his accent carrying traces of Irish inflection. His right hand moved towards his jacket, suggesting a concealed weapon.

Harper stepped forward, keeping his hands visible, though not raised.

'Just looking around,' he said calmly. 'Same as you, I'd guess.'

The man's eyes narrowed, his hand still hovering near his concealed weapon.

'You're the one working with the widow,' he said, recognition dawning. 'Brennan's been wondering about you.'

That answered one question – this was one of Brennan's men, not Daggett's, but obviously not high enough in the food chain to know they'd spoken yet. Harper maintained his relaxed posture, mind calculating distances and angles.

'And you are?'

'Someone who's about to play about with this shiny car you were just looking at,' the man replied, nodding towards the cabinet. 'Step aside and there won't be trouble.'

'Is it your car?'

'Do you give a shite either way?' The man's expression hardened. 'That's not your concern. '

'Mike's death's my concern.'

'Colton got involved in something bigger than him. Made the wrong enemies.'

'Ray Halvorsen?' Harper suggested.

A flicker of surprise crossed the man's features.

'Ray's just a middleman. Taking money from both sides, playing everyone. But he's not calling the shots.'

'And who is? Brennan?'

The man smiled thinly.

'Above my pay grade. Now step aside so I can open up this beauty.'

Harper was understanding now why the car had been left overnight. Ray had obviously let Brennan know Daggett had left it there, and in the morning when it was gone, it'd be another thing to anger Daggett. Perhaps even aiming the theft at the new guy sniffing around.

'Not happening.' Harper shook his head.

The man's hand moved with unexpected speed, drawing a compact pistol from beneath his jacket. It was a Springfield Armory Hellcat, a micro-compact 9mm semi-automatic pistol but before it could fire Harper lunged forward, driving an elbow into the side of his attacker's face, while slamming a fist into the brachioradialis muscle just below the elbow on the man's gun arm. Thrown off target, the Hellcat fired with a deafening crack in the enclosed space.

Hot pain seared across Harper's upper arm – the round grazing rather than penetrating but drawing blood. The man recovered quickly though, driving his knee up into Harper's ribs with enough force to crack at least one. Harper's breath left him in a pained gasp but he clamped his hand around the wrist holding the Hellcat, slamming it repeatedly against the metal edge of the workbench until the weapon clattered to the floor.

The intruder's response was immediate and vicious – a head butt that connected with Harper's cheekbone, followed by a hook to the kidney that sent waves of nausea through him. This wasn't some amateur enforcer. The man moved with the brutality of someone who'd killed hand-to-hand before.

'Feckin' amateurs,' the man growled, his Irish accent thickening with exertion as he landed another blow to Harper's injured ribs. 'Think you can play in our league?'

Bugger this. Kill or be killed.

Harper dropped intentionally, seeming to buckle but concentrating his center of gravity while spinning a leg out, sweeping his attackers feet out from underneath him. Legs tangled, they both went down hard onto the concrete floor, rolling among scattered tools and debris, fighting for a dominant position. The Irishman grabbed a heavy end wrench, swinging it in a vicious arc that would have crushed Harper's skull had it connected. Harper twisted away, the tip of the tool grazing his temple and sending a shower of stars across his vision.

Blood streaming into his eye, Harper pinned his assailant's strong arm, but his weak side hand clamped onto Harper's throat. For a critical moment Harper felt himself weakening, the edges of his vision darkening as the man clamped down harder on his windpipe.

Memories flashed – a close-quarters fight in Kabul, an ambush in Croatia – moments where survival had come down to instinct rather than technique. Harper let his body go almost limp, a calculated surrender that caused the man to shift his weight, creating the fraction of space Harper needed.

The move was desperate – Harper's fingers finding the man's eyes and driving in with merciless pressure. The intruder howled, releasing his grip to protect his face and Harper seized the moment, smashing his forehead into the man's already damaged nose, then rolling them both over, reversing their positions.

The fight had moved them near the hydraulic lift controls. The man's hand found a long flat-head screwdriver, stabbing upward and Harper caught the wrist – but the tip still penetrated his shoulder, sinking an inch into muscle before he could stop it.

Harper twisted the arm with savage force, breaking the wrist and wrenching the screwdriver free. The man screamed as he bucked beneath him, still dangerous despite his injuries, catching Harper with an elbow that split his lip and loosened a tooth.

'They'll find you,' the man gasped, blood bubbling on his lips. 'Brennan don't forget—'

Harper silenced him by jamming the screwdriver upward through the soft tissue under the jaw, angling upward into the brain. The man's body went rigid, eyes widening in shock before a last spasm ran through him.

Then stillness.

Harper rolled off the body, collapsing onto his back beside it, chest heaving, gasping as he fought to regain his breath. Blood pounded in his ears as his body catalogued his growing list of injuries – cracked ribs, lacerated shoulder, gunshot graze and a possible concussion from the wrench impact. Survivable but debilitating. He allowed himself fifteen seconds of recovery, counting each one before forcing himself to his feet.

The garage remained silent – the struggle, though brutal, had been relatively contained. Harper wiped blood from his eyes, evaluating his condition with the clinical detachment and compartmentalisation his time in the SRR had taught him. He could function though his effectiveness was compromised. More concerning was the blood evidence – his blood – now splattered across the north-east bay.

First things first.

Harper moved slowly and carefully despite his injuries, leaving the bay and entering the main garage area, finding a first aid kit mounted on the wall near the exit. Military instincts took over as he treated the most dangerous wounds first. He stripped off his jacket and shirt, examining the bullet graze on his upper arm. The wound was messy but superficial – more blood than damage, luckily. The screwdriver puncture in his shoulder was more concerning though; a neat hole that leaked steady rivulets of blood down his chest.

Harper disinfected both wounds with antiseptic wipes from the kit, his face locked in a grimace as the alcohol burned his raw flesh. Next he packed the shoulder wound with gauze and bound it tightly with medical tape, creating enough pressure to slow the bleeding without restricting movement. The arm graze received similar treatment though it had already started to clot by this point.

His ribs were beyond immediate treatment – at least one was cracked, possibly two. Lacking proper bandages he found a pair of scissors and cut his T-shirt into strips – tearing was way too painful for this – and wrapped them around his torso, layering a clean mechanic's rag, still fresh from the plastic wrapping, beneath for padding. He held it all in place with duct tape, careful not to pull too tight as he needed to breathe, and binding broken ribs could do more harm than good. It wasn't perfect, but it steadied the pain into a dull, manageable throb.

The head wound had bled dramatically as scalp injuries tended to do but was already congealing. Harper cleaned it as best he could, applying a small butterfly closure to hold the edges together but knowing it'd likely not hold long. All it needed to do was hold on long enough to clot.

The emergency field treatment was complete and, after pocketing the 9mm Hellcat, Harper turned his attention to the blood evidence. The north-east-bay floor was concrete and non-porous thankfully; his blood had spattered in distinct droplets rather than soaking into absorbent material. Harper found cleaning supplies in a storage closet – bleach, industrial cleaner and paper towels. He worked quickly, using the bleach to destroy the DNA in his bloodstains, then the cleaner to remove all visible traces, before wiping clean the blood left on the concrete from the dead man on the floor. Where bleach – and more importantly the sickly, strong smell of it that now permeated the garage – might raise questions, he intentionally spilled motor oil or grease to mask the cleaned areas and provide a more familiar odour, even if it still gave a hint of bleach. A hint was better than full-on, after all.

His shirt was a loss, having been used as a bandage, so Harper found a mechanic's shirt hanging in a locker – not ideal but it would cover his bare, bandaged torso until he could reach clean clothes. The name "Luis" was stitched above the pocket and Harper made a mental note to return or replace it later, as Ray seemed the type of man to dock pay for lost uniforms.

Half an hour after the fight had brutally ended, Harper had completed the cleaning protocols; the dead man's body remained the only obvious evidence of violence, all traces of his and Harper's blood either eliminated or obscured and Harper's own wounds field-dressed to prevent further evidence from being left behind. The pain remained intense but manageable; Harper had operated under worse conditions during deployments.

He stood motionless after, controlling his breathing, listening for any sign the brief but violent struggle had been noticed.

The garage remained silent around him.

He knelt beside the body, searching through the man's pockets. There was an ID in the name of Patrick Doyle, and also cash, keys, a car fob and a burner phone, as well as a folded note with what appeared to be security codes, which explained the ease on how he entered the room. He didn't recognise the other codes, so guessing they might turn up handy at some point, Harper pocketed these items before checking the duffel bag the man had brought – empty, possibly intended to steal whatever had already been hidden in the secret compartments.

Idiot didn't know there wasn't anything to steal. Or was there?

Harper looked around. *Perhaps there were more items here he hadn't seen yet?* It'd have to wait though. Maybe the empty hidey-hole had something in it when it arrived and Ray had already removed it? Maybe Daggett's men had already been and the late Mister Doyle was, well, just *late?* Either way, the man's absence would be noted and questions would be asked. Harper had limited time before someone came looking.

He made a quick decision, returning to the file cabinet and retrieving the most damning evidence – the maintenance logs documenting the lift sabotage and records of recent shipments. These he secured in his stolen mechanic's shirt before considering his next move.

The man – Doyle – represented an unexpected opportunity. His body, if discovered here, would raise immediate questions about who had killed him and why. But if discovered elsewhere...

Harper's mind worked through the possibilities, recalling the territorial divisions of Blüdridge he'd mapped during his reconnaissance.

He returned his attention to the gathered car fob. Through the window in the main garage space, Harper spotted a dark sedan parked in the shadows across the street – positioned for a quick exit but concealed from casual observation. A plan formed; one born of necessity though, rather than moral consideration. Moving into Ray's office, using the code he saw typed in earlier, Harper worked quickly, deleting all security footage of the last hour, ensuring no digital evidence of his presence remained. He then returned to the north-east bay and quickly opened every secret compartment he could find on the vehicle before removing several of the Daggett vehicle files from the rear filing cabinet, and then after covering Doyle's bloody head in a cleaning rag to stop any further contamination, Harper checked he'd done everything he needed to remove all evidence of his, or Doyle's arrival, before cleaning away the blood under the body, placing everything into a bin bag that he secured tight, locking all doors once more and hoisting the body over his shoulder in a fireman's carry. This done, he moved cautiously through the garage towards the rear left exit, wiping the alarm keypad before stepping outside, closing the door behind him.

The night remained quiet as Harper carefully crossed over to where Doyle's sedan waited, noting it'd been parked in the Brennan "no camera" zone. The fob unlocked it with a soft chirp and Harper loaded the body and the bin bag filled with blood-stained cloths into the trunk. This done, he pulled on a pair of driving gloves that'd been discarded on the passenger seat, likely Doyle's own to hide his fingerprints before he made a point of driving past the front of the garage, making sure the car and the rear licence were seen on the actual, working cameras outside.

When Ray saw the filing cabinet missing Daggett files and the car in the bay had been ransacked, all he'd find was deleted video and footage of a Brennan man driving off.

That should muddy the waters a bit.

HARPER KEPT TO SIDE STREETS WHILE REVIEWING HIS MENTAL map of Blüdridge's territories. He recalled the eastern section

– Daggett's domain – contained a construction site, and after pausing on a back road beside a random business's dumpster, he secreted the bloodied bin bag near the bottom before replacing the others, holding his breath against the garbage smell. This done, he continued on, and as he approached the construction site he saw the half-finished "Daggett Enterprise Center" stood dark and empty, surrounded by construction equipment and materials.

Perfect.

Harper parked near the site but not too close, positioning the car to be discovered but not immediately obvious. He removed Doyle's body from the trunk, carrying it onto the construction site and arranging it among steel beams and building materials, giving the impression Doyle had been beaten, and then killed there during some clandestine meeting. The lack of blood would be a giveaway and the screwdriver was now missing, but there was still enough to give plausible deniability to this happening here. He placed the empty duffel bag nearby, suggesting Doyle had come to exchange something, maybe Daggett folders.

Then, most crucially, Harper removed the business card from Daggett Financial Services he'd picked up earlier that day, rubbing it between his gloved fingers to age it a little before placing it in Doyle's wallet – after taking the cash within of course – providing subtle but discoverable evidence pointing towards Daggett's involvement somehow, or a connection with Daggett that Brennan might not have been aware of.

A Brennan man who'd been turned by Daggett and then killed when his usefulness was over – but not without a fight.

The scene now set, Harper methodically wiped down the vehicle interior, removing any trace of his presence before locking the car and walking away. He circled the block to confirm no witnesses were present, then began the long walk back towards where he'd left the Bonneville.

THE NIGHT AIR WAS COOL AGAINST HIS SKIN AS HE MOVED through the sleeping town, his mind processing the implications of what he'd discovered and what he'd just done. The conflict that had been simmering in Blüdridge was about to boil over; Brennan would assume Daggett had eliminated one of his operatives, maybe after turning them. Daggett would recognise the attempt to frame him, assume this was Brennan playing games and respond accordingly. And somewhere in the chaos that followed, Harper would find the opportunity to expose the truth about Mike's death and the operation he'd uncovered.

By the time Harper reached the Bonneville, the eastern horizon was lightening. He secured the evidence in his pack, then rode back to the inn, watching for any sign of pursuit or surveillance.

In his room, Harper carefully peeled off the stolen mechanic's shirt, now stiff with dried blood despite his earlier first aid. He re-dressed his wounds properly now, using supplies from his own motorbike kit – the shoulder injury would need monitoring for infection, but for now, fresh bandages and antiseptic wipes would have to suffice.

Harper spread the documents on the bed, examining them more thoroughly now that time allowed. The maintenance logs didn't reveal any sabotage – but the notes made by "Mike" weren't an exact match to other notes, which gave Harper pause to consider that these were forgeries, hiding modifications to the hydraulic system that could cause catastrophic failure when sufficient weight was applied to the lift, all while "Mike" said it was in perfect working order.

Was this Ray, though?

The shipping records documented a pattern of likely contraband moving through the garage in the form of Daggett and Brennan vehicles, each likely unaware of the extent the other was moving – and there, in the most recent entries was evidence of heightened activity; increased shipments, new destinations and references to what appeared to be a timeline.

Brennan's planned assault was approaching, just as Mike had documented before his death.

Harper carefully washed away any trace evidence from the night's activities while keeping his new dressings dry, then changed into fresh clothes. Sleep would have to wait; at best, he could manage an hour or two. But that said, the adrenaline from the fight still ran through his system and, as dawn broke over Blüdridge, Harper watched from his window as the town stirred. Over time shops opened, people moved along sidewalks and patrol cars made their morning rounds – normal activities in a community unaware that the careful balance of power maintaining its uneasy peace had just been irrevocably disturbed.

The pain from his injuries had settled into a persistent throb, dulled somewhat by the over-the-counter medication he'd had in his bike's satchel. His mobility was limited but he could move without obvious impairment – crucial for maintaining his cover in the hours ahead. While across town, a body lay undiscovered among construction materials, evidence planted to direct suspicion towards a specific target. Soon it would be found, questions would be asked and accusations would be made. The carefully maintained territorial divisions of Blüdridge would begin to crumble and in the chaos that followed, Harper would place pressure at the exact point where tensions were already at their breaking point, watching as the whole damned thing collapsed, revealing what lay beneath.

'Let's go,' he muttered, turning from the window, walking to his laptop. He rummaged in his pockets, removing the SD card he'd found in the garage, connecting it through a USB C dongle, waiting for it to appear.

PASSWORD

Shit. Of course it'd be encrypted.

Harper tried a couple more common passwords; dates connected to Sarah or Jake that Harper already knew, but with no success. Eventually, after twenty minutes of trying, he leant back, shaking his head.

It seemed that, for the moment, some secrets would remain hidden.

10

CLICK THE RATCHET

HARPER ARRIVED AT THE BLOOD RIDGE RETREAT FIFTEEN minutes early, choosing a booth in the back corner with, as ever, clear views of all entrances. His body protested every movement, the night's injuries sending sharp reminders of how close he'd been to ending it all with each shift in position. The bandaged shoulder wound throbbed beneath his jacket and his cracked ribs made every breath a careful negotiation. He'd been meticulous about concealing the damage – new butterfly closures on his temple hidden by his hair, split lip manageable enough to pass for chapped lips in the cold weather and the bruised cheekbone minimal enough to escape casual observation. He was pretty sure he could get away with it as long as nobody asked him to take his shirt off.

Joy approached with coffee, her keen eyes studying him briefly.

'Long night?' she asked, setting the cup down.

'You could say that,' Harper replied, offering a tight smile that didn't quite reach his eyes. 'Lot on my mind.'

Joy's expression made it clear she didn't believe him for a

second but wouldn't press the issue. Harper nodded his thanks as Joy moved away to serve other customers. The diner was quieter than usual, he noticed, with several regulars missing and a definite undercurrent of tension among those present. Conversations were hushed; glances directed towards the window more frequently than normal.

Something had shifted in Blüdridge overnight, a subtle change in the atmosphere that raised Harper's already heightened awareness.

Through the window, he noticed increased patrol activity – two sheriff's vehicles passing within ten minutes, moving with purposeful speed rather than the usual casual surveillance. News travelled fast in small towns, but this suggested something specific had occurred.

Sarah arrived twenty minutes later, slipping into the booth across from him. Her eyes searched his face with concern.

'You okay?' she asked, her voice low. 'You look... tense.'

'Tense?'

'Well, more "had the hell smacked out of you".'

'Encountered some resistance at the garage last night,' Harper replied vaguely. 'Nothing I couldn't handle.'

Sarah studied him, clearly sensing more than he was revealing.

'Are you hurt?'

'I found what we needed,' Harper said, deliberately changing the subject. 'I think we can make a case that Ray sabotaged the lift.'

This redirected Sarah's focus as he'd intended. Her expression hardened, grief and anger briefly visible before being replaced by icy determination.

'You're certain?'

Harper nodded, wincing slightly as the movement aggravated his injuries.

'Maintenance logs in Mike's handwriting, but they're bad forgeries, likely ones Ray made. To a casual observer, it's just maintenance, but looking at it with the hindsight of what we now know, I can make out deliberate attempts to hide sabotage, designed to cause catastrophic failure when weight was applied.'

Harper neglected to add that specifically, he'd changed the bleed valve housing to cause pressure loss – nasty bit of work that would look like routine wear but was murder by machine.

Sarah's hands tightened around her coffee cup, knuckles whitening with pressure.

'I want him arrested,' she said, voice tight with controlled fury. 'Today. I want him in handcuffs by nightfall.'

'It's not that simple,' Harper cautioned. 'We can't prove it was Ray, it could have been anyone, even you. Also, this is all part of something bigger. The north-east bay is central to a smuggling operation – product and cash moving through those tunnels Mike documented. Some bookings had official credentials as cover.'

'All the more reason to go to the authorities.'

'Which authorities?' Harper asked quietly. 'Ray's been working for both Daggett and Brennan. Mike discovered it, started building a case and was killed for it – which means someone in law enforcement, not crime, outed him. We don't know how far the corruption reaches. And the maintenance logs alone wouldn't be enough for an arrest; they'd be circumstantial evidence at best without confirming Ray's intent. We'd need more. Much more.'

Sarah absorbed this and Harper could almost see her calculating angles and weighing options.

'Klein?' she suggested finally. 'Mike trusted him.'

'Possibly. But we need to be careful about how and when we approach him.' Harper leaned forward, ignoring the protest from his ribs. 'There's something else. The situation is accelerating. Brennan spoke with me, wanting to, well, recruit me, I think. And then last night I... had an encounter with one of Brennan's men at the garage. He won't be reporting back.'

Sarah's eyes narrowed slightly, reading between the carefully chosen words.

'So, someone did smack the hell out of you. But what exactly does "he won't be reporting back" mean?'

'It means Brennan'll be looking for him,' Harper replied, maintaining eye contact but offering no further detail. 'And when he does find him, assumptions will be made. It's better you don't know specifics.'

Better also not to mention that the specifics included a screwdriver through the man's throat and a staged crime scene at Daggett's construction site.

Sarah studied him for a long moment, understanding dawning in her expression – not the full truth but enough to recognise Harper had crossed lines she hadn't anticipated.

'You're protecting me from details that would make me complicit,' she stated rather than asked. 'Plausible deniability.'

Harper didn't confirm or deny, but his silence was answer enough.

Joy approached before Sarah could press further, refilling their coffee with unusual haste.

'You two might want to finish up,' she breathed. 'Something's happened at the Daggett construction site. Sheriff's department all over it.'

Through the window, Harper could see another patrol car speeding past, followed by what appeared to be a coroner's van.

'Body found,' Joy added, voice barely above a whisper, and Harper wasn't sure if she was targeting him personally with the information or whether the gossip was just too good to waste. 'Construction worker called it in.'

Right on schedule.

Sarah's eyes flicked to Harper, a question in them he deliberately didn't answer.

'Any details?' he asked Joy, his expression neutral.

'Not officially,' Joy replied. 'But Hector's nephew works dispatch. Said it was a man not from around here. Execution-style, from what they're saying. Maybe even tortured.'

"Tortured". And so the story was already starting to grow.

Harper nodded his thanks as Joy moved away, aware of Sarah's gaze across the table.

'We should go,' he said, placing cash beside his barely touched coffee. 'Too many eyes here.'

For once, Sarah didn't argue.

OUTSIDE, THE TOWN HUMMED WITH NERVOUS ENERGY. PEOPLE gathered in small groups on street corners, conversations halting when others approached. Harper noticed business owners watching from doorways, some making calls, others simply observing with wary attention.

'My car's around the corner,' Sarah said. 'We can talk more privately there.'

Harper followed her to the Honda; each step painful thanks to his injured body. Once inside, Sarah turned to him directly.

'How bad are you hurt? And don't lie to me.'

'Cracked ribs, shoulder wound, various contusions,' Harper admitted, seeing no point in further deception about his physical condition. 'Nothing that won't heal.'

Assuming infection doesn't set in from the screwdriver puncture, of course. God knows when it was cleaned last.

'You need medical attention.'

'What I need is to stay focused,' Harper countered. 'This situation's about to escalate rapidly. Brennan'll blame Daggett for his missing man. Daggett'll respond. The shipment Mike documented might be moved up as a result.'

'The garage will be central to whatever happens next,' Sarah replied, and Harper was impressed with the speed she shifted gear.

'Exactly,' Harper agreed. 'We need to—'

His words cut off as his phone vibrated with an incoming message. The text was from an unknown number, but the content made the sender clear:

> Need to talk. Alone. Quinn's Lookout. Noon.
> Klein

'Deputy Klein wants to meet,' Harper said, showing Sarah the message.

'That's not a coincidence,' she observed. 'Body found; Klein reaches out immediately?'

'But how did he get my number?' Harper frowned. 'Only you, Jake and the hotel have it.'

'Maybe he knocked on your door and you weren't there? Or maybe Jake gave it?'

Harper glanced at his watch.

'We have a few hours before the meeting. I need to check something at the garage first.'

'You're going back there? After what happened last night?' Sarah looked sceptical.

'Daylight hours, normal business operations,' Harper reasoned. 'Less risk, and I need to assess Ray's reaction to current events. Also, I need to make sure I'm seen.'

Sarah appeared unconvinced but didn't argue further.

'I have to get back to school – parent-teacher conferences this afternoon. Jake's staying with Lisa's family after school. I told him to remain there until I call.'

'Good,' Harper approved. 'Keep him away from the garage and your house for now.'

Sarah started the engine but hesitated before putting the car in drive.

'Harper,' she said quietly, 'whatever happened last night – whatever you did – was it necessary?'

'Yes,' Harper met her gaze directly. 'I don't kill for fun.'

She held his eyes for a moment longer, then nodded once, accepting his answer without requesting details she'd rather not know.

'Be careful at the garage,' she said as Harper opened the door. 'Ray's not stupid.'

'Neither am I,' Harper replied, stepping out onto the pavement.

As Sarah drove away, Harper walked back to his Bonneville and with deliberate casualness rode it towards Colton's Auto Shop, taking a winding and casual route that allowed him to observe some of the town's key locations with a fresh perspective.

The sheriff's department building showed unusual activity, deputies coming and going with purpose rather than routine. Outside The Rusted Nail – Brennan's territory – Harper noted several unfamiliar vehicles with out-of-state plates and men with the hard-edged alertness of security professionals loitering nearby, glaring at the helmeted man on the motorcycle as it rode past.

New muscle in town, it seems.

As he approached the eastern district – Daggett's domain – the pattern repeated: increased security presence, subtle but unmistakable to trained eyes like Harper's. Men in plain clothes but positioned to monitor approaches to Daggett's businesses. The construction site itself was cordoned off with police tape, multiple official vehicles still present, technicians in evidence-collection gear moving within the perimeter.

Colton's Auto Shop appeared normal from the outside – all three bay doors open, mechanics visible working on vehicles, no obvious security presence. Parking up, Harper entered through the main customer entrance, noting that Ray was in his office, on the phone, his expression tense as he spoke with animated gestures.

Luis looked up from the Jeep he was working on, offering a friendly nod.

'Morning,' he said, wiping his hands on a shop rag as he approached. 'Sarah call you in again today?'

'Just following up on a few things so I thought I'd give you all another hand since you needed me yesterday,' Harper gave a smile as he replied with a casual shrug that sent hidden pain lancing through his shoulder. 'Ray around?'

Luis nodded.

'In his office. Been in a mood all morning though, fair warning.'

'Any idea what?'

'Not specifically, but there's weird energy today,' Luis lowered his voice. 'Couple of guys showed up first thing, looking for Ray. Irish accents, if you get what I mean, and not the friendly type. Then Ray started making calls. There's a car in the north-east bay, but it's locked up tight again.'

Harper nodded his thanks, filing this information away.

Brennan's men looking for their missing colleague, Ray responding with increased security measures. Not surprising. Normal day in paradise.

'I'll check in with him,' Harper said, moving towards the office.

Ray ended his call abruptly as Harper entered, his expression shifting from surprise to suspicion to carefully manufactured welcome in rapid succession.

'Harper,' he greeted, gesturing to a chair. 'Was wondering when you'd show up today.'

Harper remained standing, using the higher position to maintain psychological advantage despite his injuries.

'Thought I'd continue the evaluation work for Sarah, finish helping Luis with the Jeep if that's okay,' he said casually. 'Unless there's a problem?'

Ray studied him closely, as if searching for something.

'Interesting timing,' he observed. 'Did you hear? There was a man found dead at Daggett's construction site this morning.'

Harper raised an eyebrow, saying nothing.

'Irish fellow apparently,' Ray continued, watching Harper closely. 'One of Brennan's people, from what I hear.'

'Blüdridge seems to get more dangerous by the day,' Harper observed neutrally.

'It certainly is,' Ray agreed, his gaze hardening. 'For everyone.'

The implied threat hung in the air between them, neither man backing down.

'The north-east bay is off-limits today,' Ray said finally. 'Special client work. Very hush-hush.'

'Sounds like every other day,' Harper replied.

'Yeah. Well, it's even more so today, right?'

'Seems like there's been a lot of that since Mike died.'

Ray's expression tightened at the deliberate mention of Mike's death.

'Business evolution,' he replied. 'We're just adapting to market demands.'

'Like hydraulic lift maintenance?' Harper suggested, the question pointed enough to register as the accusation it was.

Ray's eyes narrowed to slits, his posture shifting subtly to readiness rather than relaxation.

'Careful, Harper,' he warned softly. 'Accidents happen in garages all the time. Equipment failures, vehicles slipping off jacks.'

'They do,' Harper agreed. 'Especially when someone ensures they happen.'

Like when someone deliberately modifies a bleed valve housing to cause catastrophic failure.

The tension between them was broken by a commotion from the main garage area – raised voices and the sound of tools being dropped. Ray rose from his chair as Harper turned towards the noise.

Three men had entered through the main bay doors – hard-looking individuals with the unmistakable bearing of enforcers. Harper recognised the Irish contingent immediately – Brennan's men, searching for information about their dead colleague. Chris and Darren had backed away from their work areas while Luis stood frozen beside the Jeep, wrench still in hand.

'What the hell happened to Doyle?' the leader demanded, his accent confirming Harper's assessment. 'He came here last night, and then we found him dead in a construction site.'

Ray moved past Harper into the main area, hands raised in a placating gesture.

'Easy, gentlemen,' he said. 'There's been no one here except authorised personnel.'

'He was authorised,' the leader snapped. 'Had the codes and everything. Came to collect something for Mister Brennan.'

'Mister Brennan had nothing here last night and he never contacted me,' Ray insisted, though Harper noted the slight tells in his body language that indicated a lie. 'If he came here, it wasn't during business hours.'

Damn right, Harper thought to himself. Brennan would have been given the codes by Ray, but he couldn't state on the record he'd aimed them at Daggett's car.

The leader's gaze shifted to Harper, eyes narrowing as he noted the facial injuries.

'Who the feck is this?' he demanded.

'Temporary consultant,' Ray replied quickly. 'For Sarah Colton. Helping evaluate operations.'

The man studied Harper; eyes narrowed with suspicion.

'You new in town?' he asked Harper directly.

'Just passing through,' Harper replied, maintaining a relaxed posture despite his body's readiness for potential violence, regardless of the pain he tried to ignore.

'Funny coincidence,' the man said, echoing Ray's earlier observation. 'You showing up right when Doyle's found dead.'

Harper met his gaze without flinching.

'Lots of coincidences in small towns. And I turned up a few days back for Mike Colton's funeral. Not for whatever the hell this is.'

The leader took a step forward, but Harper held his ground as the other men flanked their leader, hands moving towards concealed weapons.

'Whoa, whoa!' Ray intervened, physically placing himself between Harper and the advancing men. 'Not in my garage! You want to talk to Harper, do it elsewhere. I've got a business to run.'

The leader hesitated, calculating risks and benefits before stepping back slightly.

'Harper?' he asked. 'You're the guy Sean spoke to?'

'I am.' Harper wondered where this was going.

The leader watched him carefully for a moment and then straightened.

'This isn't finished,' he said, went to move closer, thought better of it, and then the three men retreated, backing towards the exit rather than turning away – professionals who understood the tactical disadvantage of exposed backs. Once they'd departed, Ray rounded on Harper.

'What the hell was that?' he demanded. 'You trying to get us all killed?'

'They were looking for someone,' Harper observed. 'Someone who came here last night with authorisation codes.

The same, now dead, someone the police are checking out in a Daggett construction site.'

Ray's expression closed off.

'Nothing to do with me. Or you, supposedly.'

'Yet they seemed very interested in both of us.'

'And when were you going to tell me Sean Brennan spoke to you?'

'How about never?' Harper shrugged. 'It's none of your business. Class it as my own "north-east bay". No admittance.'

Ray glanced towards the mechanics who were watching the exchange with undisguised interest. He lowered his voice, stepping closer to Harper.

'Listen carefully,' he said, voice barely above a whisper. 'I don't know what game you're playing, but Blüdridge is about to become a war zone. Brennan's people are mobilising. Daggett's responding. And stuck right in the middle is this garage, which apparently you've taken a very special interest in.'

'Just helping Sarah understand her options,' Harper replied mildly.

'Here's an option,' Ray hissed. 'Tell her to sell. Today. Tell her to take Jake and leave town. Because, by tonight, this place is going to be a battlefield.'

'Tonight?' Harper noted the specificity of the timeline.

Ray realised he'd revealed more than intended, his expression closing further.

'Just friendly advice,' he said, stepping back. 'Now, if you'll excuse me, I have work to do.'

'I thought you didn't want her to sell?'

'That was before a goddamned war was sparked with a dead body in a construction site,' Ray snapped.

Harper watched as Ray returned to his office, closing the door with more force than necessary. The mechanics slowly resumed their tasks, though their movements were distracted, attention divided between their work and the lingering tension.

'You okay?' Luis asked, approaching Harper cautiously.

'Fine,' Harper assured him. 'Just business discussions getting heated.'

Luis glanced towards Ray's office, then back to Harper.

'Listen, man,' he whispered. 'Something big is happening. Ray's been moving equipment into the north-east bay all morning. Heavy stuff. And he's been on the phone non-stop. Ray told us all to take the next day or two off; said the garage would be closed for "inventory."'

'Appreciate the information,' Harper said. 'Any idea what's in the north-east bay now?'

'Can't say for sure,' Luis replied. 'But I heard metal cases being moved.'

Harper thanked him and left the garage, mind processing the new information as he walked towards Quinn's Lookout for his meeting with Klein. Tonight appeared to be the convergence point – the shipment Mike had documented, potentially sped up by the escalating tensions between Daggett and Brennan.

THE TOWN ITSELF SEEMED TO BE PROGRESSIVELY DIVIDING along territorial lines, residents instinctively staying within the boundaries of whichever faction they aligned with. Harper passed several businesses that were closing early, owners securing shutters and grates with unusual determination.

At the base of the trail leading up to the hiking path known as Quinn's Lookout, Harper assessed potential surveillance or ambush points. The location offered tons of advantages – an elevated position with limited approach vectors that could be easily monitored. Klein had chosen well for a private meeting.

Harper began the climb, each step sending fresh jabs of pain through his injured body. He wasn't sure what this was going to turn into; the deputy was Mike's contact with local authorities, ostensibly building a case against both Daggett and Brennan. But in a town divided by corruption and conflicting loyalties, trust was a luxury Harper couldn't afford, especially as the same authorities could have been the ones that killed Mike.

As he reached the summit, Harper saw Klein already waiting, leaning against the railing that overlooked Blüdridge, his expression grim as he surveyed the town below – a town that, unknown to most of its residents, stood on the brink of open warfare.

'Well, you've managed to stir everything to shit, Harper,' Klein said, his eyes still on the view. 'So, do I arrest you, work with you, or *shoot* you?'

11

DEPUTY DAWG

'Beautiful view,' Harper said, ignoring the question and stopping several paces away, maintaining a distance that allowed reaction time if needed.

'Used to be,' Klein replied, still facing outward. 'Now I just see territories and fault lines.'

Harper moved beside him, scanning the landscape. From this elevation, the divided nature of Blüdridge was even more apparent.

'No one followed you?' Klein asked, finally turning to face Harper.

'No one who succeeded,' Harper replied.

Klein studied him with the careful appraisal of a professional, his gaze lingering briefly on Harper's posture, the way he favoured his left side, likely noticing subtle indicators of injury that most people would miss. Not surprising. Good cops noticed things. Bad ones too, sometimes.

'You've been busy,' Klein observed.

'Just getting acquainted with the town.'

Klein's mouth tightened, a brief flicker of something like frustration… or amusement.

'Let's not waste time with games, Harper. I know who you are. Or at least what you were. Special Reconnaissance Regiment. Mike mentioned you several times.'

Harper didn't confirm or deny, simply waited for Klein to continue. No need to volunteer information to a man who might be clean… or might be as bent as a nine-bob note.

'I also know you're not here just to pay your respects at a funeral,' Klein added. 'You've been asking questions, exploring territories, spending time with Mike's widow – and now a body turns up at Daggett's construction site.'

'Sounds like you've been watching me,' Harper noted.

'Just as you've been watching this town.' Klein turned back towards the view. 'The question is why.'

'Mike saved my life. Twice. I owed him.'

A pair of hawks circled above the ridge, riding the thermals effortlessly. Both men watched them for a moment, the silence stretching between them. *Predators recognising each other.*

'Mike and I were building a case,' Klein said finally. 'The kind that would take down both Daggett and Brennan simultaneously. We were close – had documentation, financial records, witness statements.'

'What happened?'

Klein's expression hardened.

'Someone got to our evidence. Files missing, witnesses suddenly unreachable or changing stories. Then Mike died.'

'Ray Halvorsen,' Harper stated rather than asked.

Klein's eyes narrowed.

'You found proof?'

'Still working on that. But I have maintenance logs in

Mike's handwriting that look to be forged, and only Ray had access to them.'

Klein absorbed this with a nod that suggested confirmation rather than surprise.

'Ray's been playing both sides – taking Daggett's money for years while secretly preparing for Brennan's takeover. Mike caught him, confronted him and paid the price. But I'm guessing you knew that?'

Harper watched the deputy carefully, assessing trustworthiness.

'Why bring me here, Klein? Why now?'

Klein reached into his jacket, withdrawing a folded map which he spread against the railing. Harper recognised it immediately – it was a detailed topographical rendering of the ridge and surrounding areas, with markings indicating access points, roads and what appeared to be tunnel entrances that he'd seen in the cabin, give or take a few new markings.

'Because it's happening tonight,' Klein said, tapping a location on the map marked with a red X. 'Major shipment – largest yet. High-grade product coming in with a large cash transfer going out. Could be enough to fund their operations for months.'

Harper studied the map, noting the route highlighted in yellow – a county road approaching from the north, winding through the ridge before connecting with Route 40 near the garage.

'Daggett's operation?' he asked.

'Yes and no,' Klein replied. 'Daggett provides the distribution network but the product comes from higher up. Someone with serious connections, access to supply chains that most criminals can't touch. That's why I've been so interested.'

'How high?'

'Let's just say there's more than a few people in Washington who need a regular supply of "pick me ups" to get through the day, and coffee ain't cutting it.'

'And why Mike was documenting it.'

Klein nodded.

'We were building the case slowly and carefully. Needed everything rock solid before moving to the next step. These people have protection – interference that's blocked previous investigations.'

'Who's protecting them?'

'That's the million-dollar question,' Klein's jaw tightened. 'Someone in the county government, maybe even state level. Every time we got close to making a move, something happened. Evidence disappeared, witnesses changed stories, priorities shifted.'

'So what's changed now?' Harper asked. 'Why is tonight significant?'

Klein tapped another location on the map – an abandoned manufacturing complex, small but secure, halfway up the ridge.

'Because this shipment isn't just passing through. It's being stored here temporarily before distribution. And it's bigger than usual – higher grade product, more cash changing hands. Mike discovered it the week before he died. The kind of operation that brings serious heat.'

'Or for hired muscle involved in a takeover. That's what got him killed,' Harper concluded.

'Most likely,' Klein agreed. 'The shipment was originally scheduled for next week but with Brennan making moves and tensions rising after the body discovery this morning, they've accelerated the timeline.'

Harper nodded – this matched what Ray had said in the garage. *Tonight was definitely the night.*

He traced the route with his finger, noting choke points and potential ambush locations. The narrow passage two miles from the storage facility offered helpful terrain for intervention. Elevated positions for observation, limited escape routes, natural cover for approach.

'You're planning to intercept it?' he asked.

Klein's expression shifted; frustration clear.

'I've requested backup from the county. But, given the pattern of interference, I'm not optimistic about timely approval,' his hands tightened on the railing. 'Meanwhile, we've got a town about to erupt into open warfare, civilians caught in the middle and enough bad blood to turn this place into a bloodbath.'

'Who's blocking your requests?' Harper asked.

Klein's expression darkened.

'Judge Whitcomb reviews all significant operations. Man's never met a warrant request he couldn't find a reason to delay, especially when it involves certain properties in this town.'

Whitcomb. That name again.

'He an ally or an enemy?'

'A bit of both,' Klein admitted reluctantly. 'He blows whichever way the wind goes. You probably saw him at the funeral. Grey hair, suits that cost more than my salary, bored of everything. But don't worry about him, I'm pushing for some federal help there. I need you on point.'

Harper nodded; this matched the man he saw at the funeral, the one he thought could have been anything from official to gangster. And now possibly the one pulling strings above both crime bosses.

'You need options,' he stated.

'I need certainty,' Klein corrected. 'This shipment cannot reach its destination. If it does, whatever's coming next gets a lot worse than a turf war between local criminals. I need it stopped or at least delayed.'

Harper continued studying the map, mentally cataloguing details while considering Klein's position. The deputy was caught between institutional constraints and immediate threat – a dilemma familiar to anyone who'd operated within official channels while facing unofficial realities. Harper had found himself in similar situations – including on a container vessel, months earlier, his father dead in his arms.

'Tell me about the shipment specifics,' he said. 'Security, vehicles, personnel.'

Klein hesitated only briefly before responding.

'Three vehicles. Lead SUV with security team, middle vehicle – transport disguised as a commercial delivery truck – carrying the product and then a rear SUV with additional security. Total of eight to ten personnel, all solid players for the family. "Take a bullet" types.'

'Heavily armed?'

'Probably, but, from what we found, they rely on appearing unremarkable – just commercial vehicles on a routine delivery, near a couple of SUVs just happening to be sharing the road.'

'Route confirmed?' Harper asked.

Klein nodded.

'County Road 27 to the ridge access road, then down

through the old bridge path before connecting with Route 40. They avoid the main highway until the final approach.'

'Timeline?'

'Transport leaves the depot at twenty-one hundred hours. Estimated arrival at the facility around twenty-three thirty, depending on conditions.'

'You're remarkably well-informed,' Harper observed. 'Especially for someone investigating from the outside. These details seem like the kind that would change after Mike's death if they suspected he was building a case.'

Suspiciously well-informed, actually. Either Klein was extremely good at his job or he had sources that didn't align with his story.

Or he was playing both sides himself.

Klein's expression tightened.

'Mike wasn't their only security breach,' he admitted reluctantly. 'We cultivated multiple sources over months. One of Daggett's drivers has a daughter with a serious addiction problem. He feeds me information in exchange for keeping her out of jail.'

He paused before continuing.

'Another guy in Daggett's security detail has gambling debts to people even scarier than his boss. They change routes and times but my sources stay current.'

'And they don't suspect these leaks?'

'Operations this size can't function without compartmentalisation. The driver knows the route and schedule but not the cargo details. The security team knows defensive protocols but not the full distribution network. Mike was dangerous because he was piecing it all together.'

Harper considered this. The explanation made sense – criminal organisations typically operated on a need-to-know basis, avoiding vulnerabilities that law enforcement could exploit. Still, Klein's web of informants seemed too perfect, too convenient. *Could someone be playing Klein, knowing he was desperate to solve the case?*

'How reliable's your information?' he asked.

'As reliable as something like this can be,' Klein replied. 'And I've personally observed three previous shipments following the same basic pattern. They're creatures of habit despite the occasional variation.'

Harper turned back to the map, focusing now on the terrain surrounding the route. The ridge offered natural advantages for anyone planning to observe or intercept the convoy – elevated positions, limited approach vectors, predictable choke points where the road narrowed or curved sharply.

Was Brennan aware of the shipment too? Would he be on the ridge also, waiting to take what he believed was his?

'What's your play?' Harper asked finally.

'Official channels – I continue pushing for federal intervention, maintain normal patrols, avoid tipping our hand,' Klein folded the map carefully. 'Unofficially... I've been considering options.'

'Such as?'

Klein studied Harper for a long, awkwardly quiet, moment.

'That's where you come in. A man with your background sees possibilities others might miss.'

And there it was. The real reason for this little chat. *Someone to do the dirty work.*

'I'm just passing through,' Harper reminded him. 'Paying respects to an old friend.'

'Of course you are.' Klein's tone remained neutral despite

the implied accusations. 'Let's face it. You're more than a mourner, Harper. You're a man with particular skills and apparently a debt to repay.'

'What exactly are you suggesting, Deputy?'

'I'm not suggesting anything,' Klein replied carefully. 'I'm simply sharing information with a concerned citizen who might have insight into the situation. Whatever conclusions or actions result from that information are entirely independent of my official duties.'

The calculated deniability was familiar to Harper – the language of operations where official and unofficial realities maintained careful separation. Klein was offering an opening without making a direct request; in the process establishing distance that would protect both of them.

Or rather protect Klein if the shitstorm fell on Harper.

Before Harper could respond, though, Klein's radio crackled to life.

'Unit three to Klein.' The voice was tense, urgent.

'Klein here.' Klein unclipped the radio from his belt.

'Sir, we've got a situation at The Rusted Nail. Brennan's people and some of Daggett's crew. Weapons visible. Need backup immediately.'

'On my way,' Klein replied, clipping the radio back to his belt, fixing Harper with a steady gaze. 'Tensions escalating faster than expected. I need to handle this.'

'Of course,' Harper agreed.

Klein hesitated, then extended the folded map towards Harper.

'This might help your understanding of Blüdridge's geography,' he said, the pretence thin but necessary. 'You know, for a visitor unfamiliar with the area.'

Harper accepted the map with a nod, tucking it into his jacket.

'One more thing,' Klein added as he turned to leave. 'Mike kept equipment at a hunting cabin outside town. Might be worth looking into if you're interested in local hunting traditions.'

'I might do that,' Harper replied, understanding the subtext, but not mentioning he'd already been there. He also wondered if the line was deliberate – Klein saying he knew Harper had been there and was suggesting he go back, or he hadn't been able to follow him.

Klein nodded once more and headed down the trail at a brisk pace. Harper remained at the lookout after Klein's departure, unfolding the map again to study it more thoroughly now that he was alone.

The deputy had been forthcoming with information but careful about direct involvement – classic deniable operations protocol. He'd provided intelligence, suggested resources and established distance all in one conversation, but washed his hands on actual operational help. The question now, however, was how to proceed. Klein clearly hoped Harper would take action where official channels could not, but Harper had his own priorities – justice for Mike, safety for Sarah and Jake and resolution of his debt.

Preventing, rather than attacking the shipment aligned with those goals while offering additional advantages. If executed properly, the operation could disrupt both Daggett's and Brennan's plans while advancing Harper's personal mission, and it was easier for a lone man to push a deadline back than take on two armed SUVs, no matter how good Klein thought he was. And with the right evidence planted at the scene, it could speed up the conflict between the factions while directing suspicion away from himself.

Decision made, Harper folded the map and descended from Quinn's Lookout, his mind already planning the framework of a response. He'd need equipment, intelligence and preparation – and all within limited time constraints. But it could be done.

As Harper reached the base of the trail, his phone vibrated with an incoming message from Sarah.

> Garage being watched. Both sides. Ray acting strange. Be careful.

Harper checked his watch: it was past one in the afternoon; less than eight hours until the transport departed its origin point.

Enough time but barely.

Harper headed towards his motorcycle, already mentally cataloguing what he would need for the operation. Mike's hunting cabin would provide resources – the former soldier had been methodical in his preparations, creating stockpiles and contingencies that might now serve Harper's purposes.

He'd start there.

THE ROAD TO THE HUNTING CABIN WAS DESERTED, ALLOWING Harper to make good time despite his injuries. The cabin itself appeared undisturbed when he arrived though Harper approached with caution, conducting a thorough perimeter check before entering.

Inside, the space remained as they had left it earlier –

evidence secured, equipment organised, the hidden entrance to the mining tunnel still concealed within the closet.

Harper moved directly to the gun safe, entering the code Sarah had provided during their previous visit. Inside, the HK .308 battle rifle remained in its case, alongside ammunition and a half dozen 25 round magazines, plus the radio and other equipment Mike had accumulated during his investigation. But Harper's attention focused on the trail cameras and motion sensors he'd seen the previous time – technology that could be repurposed for his needs.

He gathered items, placing them on the table and assessing each for utility in the operation he was planning: the trail cameras for surveillance, the radio for monitoring communications, and basic explosive components Mike had documented finding in the tunnels for... well... blowing shit up.

Most importantly, he located items from the garage, left behind from the various visits over the years – a work rag with the Colton's Auto Shop logo, a set of tools with the garage's distinctive marking system, elements that could implicate someone from the garage – likely Ray – when strategically placed.

As Harper collected these materials, he considered for a moment the ethical calculations of what he was planning. The shipment represented a genuine threat – drugs and money destined for criminal use, protected by corruption at local levels. Preventing it served a greater good. But using the opportunity to frame Ray, to speed up the conflict between Daggett and Brennan... those were moral grey areas Harper was a little concerned about. One reason he was travelling across America was to right the wrongs his father had committed before he died… and he had a full on notebook's worth of his father's sins to atone for.

But his father, Dominic Kane, had been down the same route as his son now walked, having created his own security firm, *Aegis*, to do the things he couldn't do officially.

And in doing so, he'd "scorched earthed" his soul.

Harper wasn't going to follow that route willingly but he was no stranger to death. Even aside from Doyle the previous night, he had killed before – in war zones, in self-defence, and now in Blüdridge. Each time carried weight and consequences he accepted as necessary.

Ray had murdered Mike, sabotaging equipment in a calculated act – tampering with that bleed valve housing to create catastrophic failure – that demanded response, and justice rarely arrived through official channels for men like Ray Halvorsen.

Sometimes it required individuals willing to operate in the shadows.

BY LATE AFTERNOON, HARPER HAD COMPILED WHAT HE NEEDED and secured it on the Bonneville. The plan taking shape in his mind was straightforward in concept but complex in execution – intercept the shipment at a vulnerable point, turn back the vehicles, and plant evidence implicating Ray before disappearing.

Usually when planning an op, he'd have used a team but here he was alone. Success required precision timing, adaptability and accepting significant personal risk, particularly given his already compromised physical condition.

Harper conducted a last check of the cabin, ensuring no

trace of his activities remained visible, then secured the location and departed. The sun was beginning its descent towards the western ridge, casting long shadows across the landscape.

In less than four hours, the transport would begin its journey and, by then, Harper needed to be in position, preparations complete, ready to execute an operation that would alter the trajectory of Blüdridge's simmering conflict.

As he rode back towards town, Harper's mind settled into the familiar calm of pre-operation focus – objectives clear, contingencies considered, risks accepted. Whatever happened tonight would create ripples extending beyond the immediate outcome, potentially placing him in greater danger.

But that calculation had been made the moment he arrived in Blüdridge seeking answers about Mike's death.

Some debts could only be paid in equal recompense.

12

SETTING THE BOARD

Harper drove the Bonneville well past the Blüdridge town limits, following the narrow ridge road that wound through dense pine forest. The motorcycle's engine echoed against the trees, its distinctive engine sound fading as he slowed at a particular bend where the foliage thickened. Unlike his previous journey, this time he wasn't just gathering intelligence, he was preparing to make his first moves in a carefully orchestrated and violent one-man campaign. The town's criminal equilibrium had been maintained for years by mutual suspicion between Daggett and Brennan, and now Harper intended to transform that suspicion into open conflict.

The wind had picked up, sending fallen leaves scattering across the road surface; perfect conditions for what he had planned. The wind would erase some signs of his presence, cover any sounds and the rustling foliage would provide natural camouflage for his movements.

Nature conspiring to aid his mission.

His first stop was a derelict hunting shelter half a mile off the main road, the kind of place locals had forgotten existed, but marked on one of Mike's maps. Harper navigated the Bonneville down an overgrown trail, the suspension protesting against exposed roots and weather-carved ruts. He parked the motorcycle behind a fallen oak, taking time to brush away tyre tracks and disturbed vegetation. Even here, miles from town, Harper operated with the assumption of being watched.

He approached the shelter on foot, moving cautiously despite the persistent ache in his ribs and shoulder from his encounter with Doyle. Every few yards he paused, listening to the forest, scanning for any signs of human presence. His injuries complicated matters – the cracked ribs sent sharp reminders with each uneven step while the puncture wound in his shoulder had begun a dull, insistent throbbing that had worsened throughout the day, making him wonder if he *had* got it infected. Inside the shelter – little more than four walls, a roof and a stone firepit that hadn't seen flame in years – Harper laid out the supplies he'd collected from Mike's cabin. Trail cameras with motion sensors positioned for surveillance radius, a small radio scanner with freshly charged batteries for monitoring frequencies used by both criminal organisations, lock picks and tension wrenches for accessing secured locations and most crucially, items that would implicate Ray in betrayals to both sides.

From Colton's Auto Shop, he had a couple of distinctive tools with the garage's marking system – each modified with slight scratches and marks added over years of use, making them as identifiable as fingerprints to those who knew what to look for. An invoice book with the garage letterhead showed Ray's characteristic method of notation – abbreviations and shorthand that he'd developed for tracking work orders. Shop rags with the garage logo still carried traces of the degreaser Mike, and then likely Ray, ordered from a supplier in Baltimore, according to Luis when he showed it off. These would be his signature, left at strategic locations to suggest Ray was playing both sides, maybe spilling from a rucksack as he pulled items out – something that wasn't far from the truth but Harper would amplify it into something that couldn't be ignored or explained away. Mike and Ray's prints would be clear on several surfaces – exactly what Harper needed, as Mike couldn't be accused of what was about to happen any more, which left only Ray.

He paused – there was a chance the mechanics themselves could become targets here, but he hoped the book with Ray's handwriting would push that aside. Either way, he'd have to keep an eye on the four mechanics once this went to hell.

He carefully preserved the items, being sure not to wipe off or smudge any fingerprints – after all, he didn't know how detailed the teams Daggett and Brennan used were – while adding his own touches, handling each object with latex gloves after confirming the existing evidence.

He spent an hour preparing the first set of evidence – doctoring paperwork showing Daggett's delivery schedules with Ray's handwriting in the margins, creating what looked like information being prepared for Brennan's crew. Harper had studied Ray's writing from the garage records, spending time getting familiar with the pressure patterns, the slight leftward slant, the way certain letters connected while others remained deliberately separated. His forgery was basic but convincing – nowhere near perfect under forensic examination but more than good enough to raise suspicions among paranoid criminals operating on limited information and heightened instincts for self-preservation, and definitely better than Ray's half-assed attempt at Mike's.

Harper created the documents with the same inconsistent pressure that he'd seen in Ray's writing – pressing harder at the beginnings of words, lighter towards the ends, with occasional heavy full-stops and commas when emphasis was intended. He even replicated the slight smudging that appeared when Ray, who was right-handed, dragged his hand across fresh ink, as opposed to the left-handed Mike.

Details mattered.

As his fingers worked, Harper's mind drifted unexpectedly to another time, another place. Myanmar. The container ship. His father's last operation.

Get down!

The phantom voice echoed in his head – his father's last warning before taking the rounds meant for Harper. The memory came unbidden, vivid enough that Harper could almost smell the salt air and gun smoke.

Make it right. Make it right.

His father's dying words, spoken through blood-flecked lips as Harper had cradled him.

Harper's hand stilled momentarily. He reached into his pocket, fingers finding the river stone he'd picked up during basic training, from the River Wye in Herefordshire, its smooth surface cool against his skin. He rolled it between his fingers, centring himself as he'd done countless times before when the memories threatened to overwhelm him.

The irony wasn't lost on him. He'd left the SRR after the Myanmar incident and hadn't looked to work in the corporate military sector to avoid becoming like his father – a man who operated in shadows, manipulating events, creating chaos to achieve his ends. Yet here he was, employing precisely the same methods.

His father would have been proud. And that thought disturbed him more than he cared to admit.

Harper returned to his work, pushing the discomfort aside. In his experience, the most effective deceptions weren't elaborate fabrications but carefully constructed variations of truth with enough familiar elements to be instantly recognisable.

Next, he created a similar package appearing to reveal Brennan's operations to Daggett – pickup locations, security rotations and a crude map marking vulnerable points in Brennan's territory. For this set, he used different paper – slightly yellowed with minor water damage in one corner, taken from papers he'd picked up after the fight with Doyle, and kept in the garage's filing cabinet where Ray stored sensitive information. Again with Ray's handwriting, complete with the distinctive way he wrote numbers – Harper had even added a coffee stain from the garage's distinctive dark roast – the Cuban blend Ray had special-ordered and brewed four times daily since he'd started there, its unique aroma and colour immediately identifiable to anyone who'd spent time at Colton's Auto Shop.

Harper worked systematically and with purpose. On some, he included information that only Ray would know – details about vehicle modifications done for Brennan's people, specific payment amounts, meeting locations – establishing a pattern of deep involvement that went beyond casual betrayal. On others, he suggested financial motivations, creating the impression that Ray was selling information to finance some unknown obligation or ambition.

Setting trip wires, Harper thought as he worked. Each

piece of evidence was designed to be discovered, to create doubt, to make each side suspect betrayal not just from Ray but potentially from within their own organisations. The planted evidence wouldn't just suggest Ray's betrayal – it would imply the existence of other informants, creating paranoia within each group about who else might be compromised. There was a moment of concern on this, though; Klein had mentioned real informants, so Harper had deliberately aimed at different areas.

But then if they worked for Brennan and Daggett, they'd made their own beds.

Harper felt bad for even thinking that.

It didn't stop him from continuing, though.

THE AFTERNOON WAS SPENT SCOUTING LOCATIONS.

Despite his injuries slowing his movement, Harper covered significant ground, moving through the woodlands with care, identifying three sites that were potentially critical to his plan, and mentioned in Mike's paperwork – a storage shed used by Daggett's crew for holding product before distribution, a nondescript building with minimal security but a definite strategic importance; a long-ago abandoned petrol station where Brennan's men conducted money counts away from their primary operations, its isolation providing privacy while its multiple access points offered escape options; and the county road intersection that both organisations used for transport, a natural choke point where territories converged and security protocols often relaxed because of the transitional nature of the location.

At each location, Harper moved carefully, understanding

the importance of not leaving traces of his own presence. The trail cameras were positioned to capture any activity and left visible to anyone looking – not for Harper's use primarily but to make both sides paranoid about who might be watching.

At the storage shed, Harper picked the padlock with surprising ease for what was inside, entering the dim space where stacked crates from prior drops contained packaged drugs ready for street distribution. He didn't tamper with the product – that wasn't his goal. Instead, he planted the first set of doctored papers, dropping them carelessly beside a crate where they might be discovered during a routine inventory. Along with them, he left one of Ray's tools, a wrench, positioned as if accidentally forgotten, perhaps even used to open a crate. To enhance this, he even used the wrench to force open one, making sure if anyone checked, they could see what it was used for, and why it could have been dropped. He also took a couple of packages with him; enough to show someone had taken some, but small enough to be considered an oversight – just like someone who was skimming would do. Before leaving, he reset the lock, ensuring no signs of entry remained visible.

He then dug a hole and buried the drugs where nobody could find them.

The petrol station required similar care. Harper accessed the back office through a window, planting evidence suggesting Ray had been documenting the location's security vulnerabilities for Daggett. A discarded disposable coffee cup on the floor with the garage's logo completed the scene, carelessly left behind by a man supposedly in Brennan's confidence.

Whoops. Must have dropped it, Ray. How clumsy of you.

The road intersection was his final and most ambitious

setup. Both Daggett and Brennan used this crossing for transport, carefully scheduling to avoid confrontation. Harper placed one of his trail cameras overlooking the approach, then systematically created what appeared to be a planned ambush site – subtle markers on trees showing firing positions, disturbances in the ground cover suggesting recent preparations. Nothing obvious but enough to trigger alarm in security-conscious criminals.

Here, he planted the most damning evidence – a "discarded" leather knapsack from the cabin, unfortunately dropped in a rush, the strap torn and snapped, and within it paperwork in Ray's handwriting detailing the schedule of Daggett's next major shipment, suggesting Ray was helping Brennan plan a major hit on Daggett's operation.

By early evening, with the groundwork laid, Harper's next task was to ensure certain evidence would be discovered quickly. Information couldn't just be planted – it needed to be found by the right people at the right time to maximise impact. For this, he needed to create circumstances that would draw attention to the locations he'd prepared. He pulled out a brand new burner phone to call the number he'd memorised from the card found in the office – at this time of night it'd likely be monitored by a low-level member of Daggett's crew.

'Daggett Industries,' a cautious voice answered, using the established cover.

'I need to speak with Victor,' Harper said, adopting the nervous energy of an informant. 'It's about the storage on Willow Creek.'

A pause.

'Who's this?'

'Someone who doesn't want to see his operation hit

tonight.' Harper let tension fill his voice. 'I overheard two of Brennan's guys this afternoon. They were talking about your storage shed, man. Someone gave them the location.'

Another longer pause.

'Why are you telling me this?'

'Because I owe you guys from way back. Just tell him to check the place, alright? Tell him someone's been in there.'

Harper hung up before further questions could be asked. The call would achieve several objectives – prompt an immediate inventory check where his first evidence was planted, create initial suspicion about a security breach and establish the first whispers of a traitor within Daggett's organisation. Similar calls to Brennan's operation would follow, carefully timed to escalate tensions gradually rather than all at once.

Harper moved to a different location for his second call, this one to Brennan's warehouse-looking bar, The Rusted Nail.

'Yeah?' The greeting was terse, impatient.

'The petrol station on Old Mill Road,' Harper said without preamble. 'Daggett's people know about it. I saw them taking pictures earlier today. Thought someone should know.'

'Who the fe—'

Harper cut the connection. *The seed was planted.* Brennan's people would investigate, find the planted evidence and draw the intended conclusions.

He made one final call, this time anonymously to Deputy Klein's direct line. It'd be crucial to have law enforcement positioned to witness – but not prevent – the initial confrontations that would follow.

'Blüdridge Sheriff's Department, Deputy Klein speaking.'

'Unusual activity at the county road intersection tonight,'

Harper said, disguising his voice slightly, but not so much Klein wouldn't work it out. 'Lots of traffic expected. Might want to have someone watch it.'

He disconnected before Klein could respond and then dismantled and tossed aside the burner phone. With the triggers set, Harper rode back towards the outskirts of town, and the woodlands that surrounded it. The last component of his plan required visual confirmation of the players' positions – he needed to understand exactly who'd respond to his manufactured crisis.

From a wooded ridge overlooking Daggett's compound, Harper settled into a concealed observation position, using natural features to break up his silhouette. Through Steiner Military-Marine 8x30 binoculars picked up from the cabin, Harper observed increased activity in Daggett's compound. Men were checking weapons and vehicles were being positioned for rapid deployment, fuelled and staged for immediate response. Harper recognised the distinctive patterns of security personnel responding to a potential threat – perimeter checks conducted at shortened intervals, communications more frequent, weapons hanging from tactical slings rather than secured.

Through the powerful lenses, Harper spotted Mitchell Daggett himself in the compound's central courtyard, engaged in intense conversation with his security chief. Daggett's body language told its own story – the emphatic hand gestures, the frequent pointing towards the eastern sector of town, the way he repeatedly consulted his phone, likely his father, before resuming the discussion. Whatever information Daggett had received, it had triggered immediate concern at the highest level, exactly as Harper had intended.

Harper maintained his position for nearly an hour, marking down personnel movements, identifying key officers and noting which areas received heightened attention. The compound had transitioned from standard evening operations to what appeared to be pre-combat preparation. Individual behaviours also revealed additional intelligence – which men checked their weapons repeatedly (the inexperienced ones), which maintained calm efficiency (the veterans), and which seemed uncertain about protocols (the newest recruits). All information that might prove useful in upcoming phases of his operation.

Carefully withdrawing from his observation post, Harper repositioned across the town to a secondary location overlooking Brennan's headquarters at The Rusted Nail. The movements aggravated his injuries, a sharp reminder in his ribs as he navigated a steep embankment. He paused halfway to his destination, taking shallow breaths until the pain subsided to manageable levels, but from his new vantage point, Harper noted similar preparations underway at Brennan's operation. Men were loading into vehicles while comms were distributed and weapons issued from what appeared to be a secure room accessed through the bar's rear entrance.

His anonymous calls had achieved precisely the desired effect – both organisations mobilising, each believing they were responding to intelligence about the other's plans, falling back on established security protocols that, while effective against conventional threats, created recognisable patterns that could be exploited by someone with Harper's training.

The beauty of his approach was its simplicity. He hadn't

created elaborate fabrications – just positioned information in ways that suggested betrayal, then provided the minimal nudge required for each side to discover it. The evidence itself was largely authentic but contextualised to imply betrayal. Their existing paranoia and territorial instincts would do the rest, transforming reasonable caution into escalating suspicion that would inevitably lead to conflict.

Good. Let them fight each other in the woods. As long as the town stays out of the firing line for the moment. I'll work out a way to stop it permanently later.

Now past nine, Harper continued his surveillance from a variety of vantage points around Blüdridge, wondering if Daggett had allowed the shipment to continue, or had wisely delayed it a day – after all, he had no idea what was waiting for it. Both criminal organisations had dispatched teams to investigate the locations Harper had compromised, and through his scope he observed Daggett's men discovering the planted evidence at the storage shed – their body language shifting from routine inspection to heightened alert as they examined the paperwork and discovered Ray's tool.

Across town, and watched through a Wi-Fi trail camera connected to *Starlink*, Harper saw a similar scene unfold at the abandoned petrol station, with Brennan's men securing the location and evidence Harper had left behind. The coffee cup was bagged as if it were forensic evidence, exactly as he'd expected.

Harper's phone vibrated – a text from Sarah.

Jake says Brennan's people are watching our house. Not even trying to hide.

Expected. They're looking for Ray. Keep lights on, doors locked. Don't engage.

Why Ray?

Harper didn't answer. Ray would soon be contacted by both Daggett and Brennan, each demanding explanations about the discovered evidence. His denials would seem hollow given the physical proof – his apparent handwriting, his tools, items from the garage he managed. By morning, Ray would be desperately attempting to explain himself to two increasingly suspicious criminal organisations. By afternoon, he would be under surveillance from both sides. By evening, he would be fighting for his life – or running. And, in the chaos that followed, Harper would find the space to manoeuvre, to apply pressure at key points, to eventually extract the truth about Mike's death and ensure those responsible faced consequences.

HARPER RETURNED TO THE INN SHORTLY BEFORE MIDNIGHT, avoiding the increased patrols now circulating through Blüdridge. No convoy had been spotted on the route, Daggett wisely choosing to stand down, it seemed. That said, even for this time of night, the town appeared unnaturally tense, vehicles moving with purpose, men positioned at street corners with the watchful stillness of sentries rather than loiterers.

In his room, Harper quietly cleaned and secured his remaining equipment. He disassembled his small toolkit, and the Wi-Fi trail camera monitors were reset to factory settings, erasing any operational data, no longer connected to any satellite links. The burner phone had already had the SIM card and battery removed, components separated to prevent tracking, and every item that could connect him to the night's activities was either sanitised or prepared for disposal.

Next, he attended to his injuries with the same detachment – checking the shoulder wound for signs of infection, probing the edges for excessive tenderness that might show complications. The puncture was healing slowly, the surrounding tissue still inflamed, and still sore as hell. He applied a fresh antiseptic solution that burned with reassuring intensity before replacing the bandages.

His ribs presented a more persistent problem. The day's activities had aggravated the fractures, evident in the darkening bruise pattern spreading across his left side. Harper performed a careful self-assessment, testing range of motion and pain response. The discomfort was significant but not debilitating – he'd operated under worse conditions in Afghanistan and Yemen. He applied a new compression wrap to provide stability without restricting breathing, a compromise between medical ideal and operational necessity.

As he wrapped the bandage around his ribs, Harper caught a glimpse of himself in the bathroom mirror. The man staring back was haggard, determined, but focused.

He looked like his father.

Harper's hand paused midway through securing the bandage. The parallel was undeniable. His father had built *Aegis* similarly, creating systems that manipulated events to achieve specific outcomes. His father had operated in the shadows, turning factions against each other when necessary, all in service of what he'd believed was right.

"Make it right," Harper muttered to his reflection, remembering his father's final words. *Was that what he was doing here? Making things right for Mike? Or was he simply following in his father's footsteps, unable to escape the patterns ingrained in his DNA?*

The river stone was cool in his hand – he didn't remember taking it out but rolled it between his fingers as he considered the question. He'd created charitable trusts with his father's fortune, directed resources to veterans' organisations, and lived on a modest allowance while giving away more than he used to make in a year in a single payment. All attempts to atone, to distance himself from his father's legacy.

Yet here he was, implementing the same playbook, becoming what he'd once judged his father for being.

His phone vibrated with an incoming call from a blocked number. Interest, rather than surprise, flickered across his features, and he answered without speaking, simply waiting for the caller to identify themselves.

'What the hell did you do?' Klein's voice was tense, controlled anger clear beneath the professional tone. The background noise suggested he was in his vehicle.

'Nothing that wasn't already in motion,' Harper replied calmly, moving to the window to scan the street below while they spoke. The deputy's reaction was predictable – law enforcement instinctively resisted circumstances they couldn't control, even when those circumstances might serve their ultimate objectives.

'Bullshit.' Klein's response was immediate, the single word carrying more emotion than his usual measured demeanour. 'I've got reports of both Daggett and Brennan's crews mobilising. Armed men at three locations. This town's about to explode.'

'Or reveal itself,' Harper countered. 'Sometimes pressure exposes what's hidden.'

He kept his tone measured, reasonable – presenting the

situation as an opportunity rather than crisis, but Klein wasn't biting.

'You're playing with people's lives,' he warned, his voice dropping lower, more intense. 'Civilians could get caught in the crossfire.'

'That's why you're watching the intersections tonight,' Harper said. 'To ensure they don't.'

A pause followed, stretching several seconds as Klein presumably weighed his options, his responsibilities, his own place in the unfolding scenario. Harper waited, patient, knowing that silence often revealed more than words.

'This conversation never happened,' Klein finally said, his tone suggesting reluctant acceptance rather than approval.

'What conversation?' Harper replied before ending the call, the professional courtesy of deniability extended and accepted.

He continued to watch out of the window, observing the town from his elevated vantage point. The neutral territory between factions had narrowed overnight, the balance of power shifting with each hour. By morning, accusations would fly. By afternoon, demands for explanation. By tomorrow night, probably the first blood spilled.

The board was set. The players positioned. The opening moves made.

And Harper was ready for what came next.

13

LIGHT THE TOUCHPAPER

Morning broke over Blüdridge with the unmistakable tension of a town on edge.

Harper stood at his window, watching the activity below. The evidence he'd planted during the night was already having its intended effect, ripples of suspicion and accusation spreading outward from the initial discoveries.

He'd spent the night monitoring police frequencies and tracking the inevitable aftermath of his operation. His body demanded rest, but he ignored it – the situation would speed up rapidly now, and he'd require all his attention to ensure the next phase unfolded correctly. Around four he'd finally tried sleep, but had spent a few hours dozing, wincing and groaning, his cracked ribs protesting every time he shifted position, finally giving up when his phone vibrated with an incoming message from Sarah:

> Something's happening. Daggett's men at the north end of town. Ray hasn't shown up at garage, entire place is closed up. What did you do?

He replied with deliberate vagueness:

> Setting things in motion. Keep distance from Ray if he appears.

Once up, Harper showered, the hot water temporarily easing his aching muscles while reopening a small section of the knife wound on his shoulder. Fresh blood trickled down his arm, a crimson reminder of his vulnerability. He reapplied antiseptic and a clean bandage, the sting a welcome distraction from deeper discomfort.

He dressed and consumed a protein bar with a strong coffee while continuing to watch the street below. Down Main Street, the Blood Ridge Retreat was open, and Harper could almost imagine Joy moving between tables, less a server than an information broker this morning as she carried both coffee and news.

Harper left the inn shortly after eight, walking towards the diner. The morning air carried a chill that penetrated his jacket, finding the bruised ribs beneath. Arriving inside the diner, the atmosphere crackled with tension, conversations dropping to whispers as he entered before resuming with renewed intensity.

He paused in the doorway, scanning the room. In the corner booth sat a familiar, grey-haired man in an expensive suit; Judge Whitcomb, county judge and, according to Klein, someone who changed alliances like the wind, likely protecting criminal operations through his judicial authority.

Was he the one who outed Mike? Who gave the order that killed him?

The judge was reading a newspaper casually, though his eyes tracked movement across the diner with too much precision for genuine disinterest. Harper noted the expensive watch peeking from beneath a crisp shirt cuff, the too-perfect Windsor knot of his tie, the manicured fingernails – a man who attended to details and appearances with obsessive care.

Harper chose his usual booth while appearing casual. As he settled in, he noticed Whitcomb looking up from his paper, their eyes meeting briefly across the room. Recognition flickered in the judge's gaze, followed by something colder and more calculating.

He knew who Harper was.

Joy approached, coffeepot in hand, her expression knowingly neutral.

'Quite the morning,' she said, filling his cup without asking. 'Daggett's people found someone going through their storage shed. Evidence of tampering.'

'Anyone hurt?' Harper asked conversationally, fingers wrapping around the warm mug.

'Not yet,' Joy's eyes held a warning. 'But they're saying someone from the garage was involved. Found tools with the shop marking. And the Brennans had similar, apparently.'

Harper sipped his coffee, neither confirming nor denying, but wondering where the hell Joy got her intel from. Joy studied him briefly before continuing.

'Deputy Klein picked up Ray Halvorsen this morning,' she added, voice lowered almost to a whisper. 'Said it was for his own protection after evidence connecting him to both Daggett and Brennan turned up. But Hector's nephew at the station says they're questioning him about Mike's accident too.'

'Interesting timing,' Harper commented neutrally.

Before Joy could respond, Judge Whitcomb appeared beside their table, perfectly tailored suit making him seem out of place among the diner's working-class clientele.

'Ms Williams,' he said to Joy, his tone pleasant but authoritative. 'Sheriff Mills is looking for you. Something about your nephew's parole hearing next week.'

Joy's expression tightened almost imperceptibly.

'I'll stop by the station later today.'

'I'm sure he'd appreciate that,' Whitcomb replied with a thin smile that didn't reach his eyes. As Joy moved away, he turned his attention to Harper. 'Mind if I join you?'

Without waiting for a response, he slid into the booth opposite Harper, placing his folded newspaper precisely on the table between them. The movement was smooth, practised – a man accustomed to taking without asking.

Harper's hand slipped into his jacket pocket, fingers finding the river stone, its smooth surface cool against his skin. Not for comfort this time, but for focus – the same grounding technique he'd used before high-risk operations.

Don't give yourself away, Liam.

Don't be like Dad, Liam.

'Eventful morning,' the judge commented, his posture relaxed but eyes watchful. 'For a town that typically values its routines.'

'Small towns,' Harper replied. 'Always something happening beneath the surface.'

Whitcomb studied him carefully for a long moment. His cologne was subtle but expensive, another layer of carefully constructed appearance.

'You seem remarkably comfortable with chaos, Mister Harper. Most visitors find Blüdridge's... complexities... overwhelming.'

'I adapt quickly.'

'Indeed.' The judge's fingers tapped once against the newspaper. 'A useful skill, adaptation. Though sometimes outsiders misinterpret what they observe, lacking context for local dynamics.'

Harper briefly wondered if his father had encountered men like Whitcomb during his *Aegis* operations – powerful men who believed their influence made them untouchable. Puppet masters who rarely faced consequences for the strings they pulled.

'Such as Ray Halvorsen's connection to both Daggett and Brennan?' Harper asked, tiring of the back and forth verbal jousting and deciding to cut to the chase.

Something flickered in Whitcomb's eyes – surprise quickly masked by control. A corner of his mouth tightened, the momentary tell of a man unused to being caught off-guard.

'I wouldn't know about private business arrangements. My concern is maintaining judicial order in this community.'

'Even when that order protects criminal operations?'

Whitcomb's smile remained fixed, but his voice dropped slightly.

'That's quite an accusation from someone who's been in town less than a week.'

'Not an accusation. An observation.'

'Observations without proper context can lead to unfortunate conclusions,' the judge replied, leaning forward slightly. 'And actions based on those conclusions can have... consequences.'

Harper held the judge's gaze, fingers still wrapped around the river stone in his pocket, forcing himself to not pull it out and slam it into Judge Whitcomb's smug face.

'Like what happened to Mike Colton?' he asked instead.

This time Whitcomb's reaction was more controlled, but Harper caught the slight constriction of his pupils – a physiological response impossible to fully suppress. Then a deliberate blink and an equally deliberate smoothing of his expression.

'Mike's death was a tragic accident,' Whitcomb said, his tone suggesting the matter was closed. 'Though I understand Deputy Klein has taken a renewed interest in the case. An interesting coincidence, given your arrival in town.'

'I'm just helping Sarah Colton understand her options.'

'A noble purpose.' Whitcomb stood, straightening his jacket. 'Though I wonder if she fully appreciates the complexities her husband was involved in. Mechanical aptitude doesn't always translate to understanding more nuanced systems.'

He placed his hand flat on the table, leaning slightly closer.

'Blüdridge maintains balance through established channels, Mister Harper. Those who disturb that balance rarely find their stay here comfortable. Or lengthy.'

With a slight nod that somehow contained both courtesy and warning, Whitcomb departed, stopping briefly to exchange words with two men in suits near the door who'd been watching their conversation with obvious interest. Harper watched him leave, taking note of the way Whitcomb spoke to the men – giving instructions rather than exchanging information. This wasn't a consultation; it was a command. The judge had just put a target on Harper's back, using the same careful, implied language with which he likely ordered Mike's death.

Joy returned with Harper's breakfast; her expression troubled as she glanced towards the departing judge.

'Whatever game you're playing with him,' she breathed,

'be careful. Whitcomb doesn't lose often, and he doesn't forget.'

Harper nodded his thanks. The judge's interest confirmed his suspicion that Whitcomb represented another layer of protection for those responsible for Mike's death – and another obstacle to removing them.

'I'll keep that in mind,' he replied, not mentioning that Whitcomb had just moved to the top of his priority list.

As Harper ate, he continued observing the diner's dynamics. The usual social divisions of Blüdridge had intensified overnight. Patrons clustered according to allegiance – Daggett's associates near the front, Brennan's people towards the rear, neutral parties squeezed uncomfortably between. Conversations remained hushed but Harper could make out undercurrents of accusation and speculation.

The diner's small television behind the counter was showing the local morning news, the volume turned low but still audible. The anchor was reporting on increased police activity in Blüdridge.

'... Sheriff's Department has confirmed increased patrols in response to what they're calling "community tensions". While no official statement has been made regarding specific incidents, sources indicate items connecting multiple businesses were discovered overnight, prompting an ongoing investigation...'

A ripple passed through the diner – shifting postures, exchanged glances, the subtle realignment of alliances as the gossip already spreading was seemingly confirmed. Near the front, two men Harper recognised as Daggett's employees finished their meals quickly, leaving cash on the table before departing. At the rear, a group associated with Brennan's interests huddled closer, conversation intensifying while glances tracked the departing men.

Harper's phone vibrated again. Sarah.

Ray taken in by Deputy Klein. Mechanics saying it's for "protection" but they're searching the garage. What should I do?

Nothing. Let them search. You have nothing to hide.

After a moment's consideration, he added:

Can we meet?

Meet me at high school. 10:30. Faculty lounge.

Harper finished his coffee, left payment on the table and exited the diner. As much as he needed the rest the diner gave him, he needed to observe the town's response directly, to gauge how effectively his planted evidence was dividing the criminal organisations.

Outside, Harper strolled in no hurry towards the eastern section of town: Daggett's territory. The streets felt different this morning – shopkeepers watching from doorways instead of greeting customers, civilians moving quickly with heads down, tension visible in the set of shoulders and wary glances.

The Daggett Financial Services building showed obvious signs of heightened security, and as Harper passed the front door opened and Mitchell Daggett emerged, flanked by two security men. In person, Mitchell presented a study in controlled tension – expensive suit concealing an athletic physique, handsome features hardened by what appeared to be genuine military experience rather than civilian security training. Harper wondered if he'd done time in the military, reminding himself to check into this, as Mitchell moved with the balanced awareness of someone who had operated in genuinely dangerous environments, not merely simulated ones.

His men continued to scan the street, identifying Harper as a potential concern. Mitchell followed their assessment, eyes locking briefly with Harper's in mutual recognition – operators recognising one another across opposing sides of a developing situation.

Harper continued walking without alteration of pace or direction but mentally filed the encounter for future reference. Mitchell Daggett possessed training and experience beyond typical criminal organisation standards – a factor that would influence him moving forward.

BY MID-MORNING, HARPER HAD COMPLETED A FRESH CIRCUIT OF the town's key locations, gathering intelligence through direct observation rather than reliance on rumours. Daggett's operations showed more clear signs of defensive posturing: increased security, restricted access, preparation for potential conflict. Brennan's territory displayed similar patterns but with a more aggressive stance; offensive action rather than purely defensive measures.

The neutral zone between factions had narrowed to the thinnest of strips, civilian presence diminishing as residents recognised the approaching conflict and withdrew accordingly. Meanwhile, the garage remained cordoned off, with sheriff's department vehicles still present, the investigation continuing under official auspices.

At the hardware store on Main Street, Harper observed Jenkins hastily boarding up his display windows; a man preparing for violence rather than merely reacting to rumours.

'Expecting trouble?' Harper asked, pausing beside him.

The old man glanced up, hammer pausing mid-strike.

'Been through this before, back in '89. When things get tense between Daggett and whoever he's having a pissing contest with, best to protect what's yours.'

'Happens often?'

'Every decade or so.' Jenkins drove another nail in. 'Someone gets ideas about changing the order of things. Usually ends with buildings burning and people disappearing.'

'Brennan?'

'Just the latest in a long line of pretenders to the throne. Just so happens this one has a claim he reckons is genuine.'

'And the sheriff doesn't stop it?'

Jenkins gave Harper a look that suggested the question itself revealed naivety.

'Sheriff's part of the arrangement, son. Always has been.'

Harper nodded, filing away one more piece of the puzzle that was Blüdridge's corrupt ecosystem. Not just criminal factions with corrupt officials on payroll, but a generational system of control with its own cycles and patterns.

Harper arrived at the high school campus at ten-twenty, once more approaching via the athletic fields to avoid being observed. His shoulder wound had bled again during his circuit of the town, the bandage beneath his shirt now stained with a warm wetness he could feel against his skin. Nothing critical, but a reminder of his physical vulnerability in what was rapidly becoming a war zone.

Sarah was already waiting in the faculty lounge when Harper entered, pacing near the windows with barely contained tension. She turned at his approach, relief and concern warring in her expression.

'What's happening?' she demanded without preamble. 'Klein's got Ray at the station, supposedly for his protection and deputies are going through the garage. They took his computer, files, started questioning the mechanics, asking why they were told to take today off.'

She paused.

'Why were they told to take the day off?'

'That's a question for Ray.'

'Yeah, well Ray's not contactable right now. What did you do?'

'The evidence I planted at Daggett's storage facility and Brennan's counting house was discovered,' Harper replied. 'Both sides believe Ray is playing them against each other.'

'You planted evidence?' Sarah's voice held both surprise and understanding. 'That's why they found tools and garage paperwork?'

'Ray's been working both sides for months,' Harper explained. 'I simply provided evidence that made it impossible to ignore; placed where both Daggett and Brennan would discover it simultaneously.'

Sarah processed this, her intelligence filling the gaps.

'And now both sides think he's betraying them.' It wasn't a question.

'Exactly. Ray's position at the garage gave him access to both operations. Now each side believes he's been selling information to the other.' Harper moved to the window, scanning the campus. 'Klein already suspected Ray's role in Mike's death. This gives him leverage to apply pressure during questioning.'

'Chris says Klein told Ray it was for his own protection,' Sarah added. 'But everyone in town thinks he's talking to the police about Daggett and Brennan. The mechanics said deputies found shop rags with our logo and marked tools at multiple locations. Ray's claiming he's being framed. Is he wrong?'

'In essence? No. In substance?' Harper met her gaze directly. 'As I said, Ray was betraying both sides. Already working angles for his own benefit. I just made it visible. And if the evidence convinces Sheriff Mills to press harder about Mike's death? Then all the better.'

Sarah held his gaze steadily.

'I don't disapprove,' she said finally. 'But frame or not, Ray was involved in the sabotage that killed Mike. That's what matters to me.'

Harper nodded, respecting her decision. Sarah had more resilience than he'd initially given her credit for; not surprising given she'd been married to a man like Mike.

'What's happening at the garage now?' he asked.

'Chris and Luis have come in and are handling customers outside while deputies finish searching Ray's office. They're focused on his records, client files, anything that might confirm relationships with both Daggett and Brennan.' Sarah leant back on the chair, looking up at the ceiling.

'Jake's been documenting everything. Taking photos on his phone of who's coming and going, noting times and activities.'

Harper frowned.

'Where is he now?'

'I told him to stay in school today but...' Sarah shrugged slightly. 'He's Mike's son. Following orders wasn't exactly Mike's strength either.'

'No, it wasn't,' Harper felt a reluctant smile form, memories of Mike's stubborn independence surfacing briefly.

Sarah turned back to him.

'With Ray in custody and both Daggett and Brennan thinking he's informing to the police and each other, they're going to be looking for answers.'

'The situation will escalate,' Harper confirmed. 'Each side suspects betrayal at multiple levels now. Ray's become the focal point but that won't last. They'll want to establish who else might be compromised, who knew what, who's working with whom.'

'And we're caught in the middle,' Sarah noted bitterly.

'Strategic location,' Harper agreed. 'The garage remains valuable to both sides regardless of Ray's status.'

'I've been thinking about that,' Sarah considered this. 'If the garage is so important to both of them, maybe I can use that. They both want it but neither can move openly against me without creating problems with the townsfolk. Mike was respected here. If either Daggett or Brennan tried to force me out directly, they'd lose support they can't afford to lose.'

Harper nodded, acknowledging her reasoning.

'That gives you some protection, at least in the short term,' he observed.

'I've decided to make it clear I'm considering offers from

both sides,' Sarah continued. 'Playing for time while this situation develops.'

'A practical approach.'

'There's something else,' Sarah added, reaching into her purse and pulling out a sheet of folded paper. 'Jake found some more notes taped behind a drawer in Mike's desk at home. He took one of them in case they helped, left the rest hidden.'

Harper unfolded the paper – a handwritten list of names, dates and locations. Some he recognised from Mike's previous documentation but others were new. Most significantly, it detailed connections between Daggett, Brennan and several county officials, including Sheriff Mills and Judge Whitcomb. As Harper studied the document, however, he began wondering if Daggett and Brennan weren't the bitter enemies they portrayed themselves to be, at least, not in all aspects of their operations.

Well, until right now, anyway.

The patterns reminded Harper of operations he'd observed in Eastern Europe; rival factions maintaining the appearance of conflict while secretly coordinating when profitable. His father had exploited similar arrangements during his *Aegis* work, turning managed competition into genuine conflict by targeting the connections that maintained the balance.

Harper was following the same playbook, whether he'd intended to or not.

On the other side, Harper found lists of number and random letters – *possibly passwords?* He wasn't sure, and right now wasn't the time to start deep diving.

Their conversation was interrupted by Sarah's phone

vibrating with an incoming call. She checked the screen, frowning slightly.

'It's Chris from the garage,' she explained before answering. 'Yes?'

Harper watched as Sarah's expression shifted from concern to alarm.

'When?' she demanded. 'How many?... No, tell everyone to leave. Lock up and go home... No, Chris, this isn't a discussion. Get everyone out now.'

She ended the call, turning to Harper with renewed urgency.

'The deputies left.'

'Surely that's a good thing?'

'It would have been, but five minutes after they went, Brennan's men just showed up at the garage. Six of them, armed, asking about Ray and his connections to Daggett. Chris says they're searching the place, looking for evidence. Also, Daggett's people were spotted heading that direction as well. Chris thinks they're about to walk into each other.'

Harper moved immediately towards the door.

'You stay here,' he instructed. 'I'll handle it.'

'No,' Sarah countered firmly. 'It's my garage. My responsibility. I don't have classes until this afternoon; I'll go.'

Harper paused, calculating. Normally he'd prefer to handle this alone, but Sarah's presence might actually defuse the immediate situation. Both Daggett and Brennan's men would hesitate to start violence with Mike's widow present – at least long enough for Harper to assess and potentially control the situation.

'It's about to become a confrontation point between armed factions,' he warned, making sure she understood the risk.

'All the more reason I should be there,' Sarah insisted, grabbing her car keys. 'Without me, it's just territory to fight over.'

Harper nodded; decision made.

'We'll take your car. Less conspicuous than my motorcycle.'

They exited through the side entrance, moving quickly towards the faculty parking lot. Harper kept his senses alert as they drove, scanning for surveillance or pursuers, seeing the familiar sedan following him – or was it Sarah – while his hand reached into his pocket, fingers finding the 9mm Hellcat. He didn't want to reveal it in case he scared Sarah, but he sure as hell wasn't going in unarmed.

As they approached the garage, the situation's volatility became immediately apparent – Brennan's vehicles parked haphazardly in the lot, Daggett's approaching from the east, townsfolk and customers hurriedly evacuating the area. Harper could see armed men taking positions, their body language communicating readiness for violence.

'Stop here,' Harper instructed as they reached the block before the garage. 'We assess before entering.'

Sarah complied, pulling to the kerb. Through the windscreen, they could see the confrontation developing – Brennan's men had established positions near the garage entrances while Daggett's people approached with deliberate caution, weapons not yet drawn but clearly available.

An incredibly violent *pissing contest* was about to begin.

14

ACCUSATIONS

HARPER PRESSED HIS BACK AGAINST THE COLD METAL OF THE tool cabinet, angling his position to observe the confrontation unfolding in the garage's main service bay through a polished chrome inspection mirror mounted on the adjacent wall. Sarah crouched beside him; her breathing controlled but rapid. They'd slipped in through the side service entrance less than two minutes ago, just before Brennan's men had established positions at the building's front and after Daggett's crew had arrived from the east.

Now they were witnessing the inevitable collision Harper had engineered.

'Find everything that connects Ray to us,' a voice with distinctive Belfast inflection was saying – one of Brennan's lieutenants, a compact man with greying temples and predator's eyes. 'Logs, invoices, anything with his handwriting.'

'This is private property,' countered someone from Daggett's group – younger, trying to project authority he didn't fully possess. 'You've got no right to be here at all. You want to talk to Ray, go to the sheriff's station.'

'Where your boss has already got his hooks in him?' The Irishman laughed without humour. 'Not bloody likely.'

Harper counted eight men in total – five from Brennan's organisation, positioned near the main entrance and office, and three more representing Daggett's interests by the north-east bay. All armed, though weapons remained holstered or tucked beneath jackets. Chris and Luis had wisely evacuated, leaving tools abandoned mid-task and a Chevy still elevated on the hydraulic lift.

Sarah leaned closer; her voice barely audible.

'What now?'

'We wait,' Harper murmured. 'Let them establish positions and intentions before we reveal ourselves.'

Through the polished metal surface, Harper watched as Brennan's lieutenant crossed to Ray's office door. Finding it locked, he gestured to one of his men, who produced a crowbar from beneath his jacket.

'That's private property, McSorley,' Daggett's man protested, his hand drifting towards his waistband. 'You damage anything, there'll be consequences.'

'There already are consequences,' McSorley replied, eyes hardening. 'Your boss's pet mechanic sold us out to you, then you to us. Now we're finding out what else he's been hiding.'

The crowbar bit into the doorframe with a splintering crack that echoed through the garage. Tension visibly ratcheted upward – hands moved closer to weapons, postures shifted towards combat readiness.

Harper assessed options, calculating risks against potential intelligence gain. The situation was deteriorating faster than expected. If gunfire erupted with Sarah present, the tactical complexity would increase exponentially.

'I'm going to create a distraction,' he whispered. 'When I move, stay here unless I signal otherwise.'

Sarah nodded, but before Harper could implement his plan, the external dynamics shifted. Through the garage's front entrance, he spotted two black SUVs pulling into the lot – reinforcements for Daggett's side, evening the numerical odds. The approaching vehicles triggered an immediate response from Brennan's men, who abandoned the office door to take defensive positions behind toolboxes and support columns.

McSorley barked orders in clipped, urgent tones.

'Secure that entrance. Weapons ready but not visible. Let's not start what we can't finish.'

The garage's atmosphere transformed in seconds – from tense standoff to imminent violence, and in that moment Harper reached his decision point. Allowing the confrontation to escalate further risked a firefight that would endanger Sarah and destroy potential evidence. Intervention now might defuse immediate tensions while positioning him to gather critical intelligence.

'Change of plan,' he told Sarah. 'Follow my lead. Project authority but say as little as possible.'

Without waiting for response, Harper stepped from concealment, keeping his movements deliberate and hands clearly visible. Sarah followed a half-step behind.

'Gentlemen,' Harper's voice carried across the garage with calm authority. 'This has gone far enough.'

Eight heads snapped in his direction, hands instinctively moving weapons before recognition dawned on some faces.

'Who the hell are you?' demanded one of Daggett's newly arrived men, hand inside his jacket.

'Liam Harper,' Harper replied evenly. 'And this is Sarah

Colton, who owns this establishment you're all so eager to destroy.'

McSorley's eyes narrowed with recognition.

'The SAS mate of Colton's. Heard you were asking questions.'

'You'll find that's *SRR*, mate. Get it right,' Harper replied, maintaining eye contact while positioning himself to keep all parties in his field of vision. 'And I'd rather you didn't turn this garage into a war zone.'

Sarah stepped forward; her composure remarkable under the circumstances.

'This is my property, gentlemen. Whatever grievances exist between your employers; they don't justify destroying my business.'

A momentary pause as both factions recalculated. Harper watched their eyes – calculating risks, evaluating the new variables he and Sarah represented. McSorley seemed to communicate silently with his team, subtle hand gestures suggesting positioning adjustments. Harper caught the motion, recognising tactical signals from his own military days.

They weren't standing down; they were repositioning.

The situation deteriorated in a heartbeat. The side entrance door crashed open as Mitchell Daggett himself entered, flanked by two guards whose bearing screamed retired military. Unlike his men, Mitchell moved with the controlled precision of someone comfortable in conflict zones.

'Mrs Colton,' Mitchell acknowledged Sarah with a respectful nod before his gaze locked onto Harper. 'And Mister Harper, I believe. Interesting company you're keeping these days.'

'Just trying to prevent bloodshed in a civilian business,' Harper replied, mind racing through revised options. Mitchell's presence complicated everything; he wasn't just another enforcer, but a strategic player with his own agenda.

'Noble,' Mitchell replied, though his tone suggested scepticism. 'Though one might wonder why you're here at all, given this isn't your fight.'

'It became my fight when these gentlemen decided to destroy private property,' Harper countered, watching as Mitchell's security took positions that gave them clear firing lines. 'After Mike Colton was murdered.'

The accusation landed with calculated impact. Ripples of reaction passed through both factions – shifted stances, exchanged glances, subtle positioning adjustments. Mitchell's expression remained controlled, but his eyes hardened.

'Careful with accusations, Mr Harper,' he warned. 'My father and I respected Mike Colton. His death was unfortunate but accidental.'

'Was it?' Harper challenged. 'Or was it connected to what Mike discovered about cooperation between supposedly rival operations? Was it you who broke into his *grieving widow's house?*'

That struck a nerve. Mitchell's guards exchanged glances, while Brennan's men seemed suddenly more interested in Harper than their immediate adversaries.

'I think we should continue this conversation elsewhere,' Mitchell suggested, his tone deceptively casual. 'Perhaps my office—'

'Not happening,' McSorley interrupted. 'Sounds like Harper here might have interesting theories about Ray

Halvorsen's extracurricular activities. Before anyone leaves, we'd like to hear more.'

'He can chat to his buddy Brennan later,' Mitchell snapped. 'It's not the first time, I hear.'

'All you had to do was ask,' Harper gave a smile. 'My dance card's not full.'

Tension crystallised as both factions redirected focus towards Harper as he now found himself the focal point of dangerous scrutiny.

'Ray worked both sides,' Harper stated flatly. 'Taking Daggett's money while feeding information to Brennan, and vice versa. But that's not what got Mike killed.'

'Enlighten us,' Mitchell suggested, the dangerous edge in his voice barely concealed.

Harper met his gaze directly.

'Mike discovered something bigger. Something involving Judge Whitcomb and connections beyond Blüdridge. Something worth killing to protect.'

The garage fell silent save for the soft ticking of a cooling engine. Harper had just played his highest-value card; revealing knowledge he shouldn't possess to gauge reactions. The calculated risk exposed his own position but might yield something through their responses.

McSorley recovered first.

'That's quite a theory. Got any evidence to back it up?'

'Enough to concern certain parties,' Harper replied. 'Which is why deputies have collected Ray's computers and files from this very building.'

It was a bluff, but it was plausible. Mitchell's eyes narrowed slightly; his team had subtly adjusted positions, creating clearer firing lanes towards both Harper and Brennan's people.

'Interesting as this conversation is,' Mitchell said, 'it doesn't resolve our immediate situation. Mrs Colton's property is being damaged, and Brennan's people are the ones doing the damaging.'

'While your people prepare for armed confrontation on private property,' Harper countered. 'Neither faction has a legitimate claim to be here.'

'Actually,' McSorley interjected, 'we have a business arrangement with the garage. Authorised by Ray Halvorsen himself.'

'Who's an employee of Mrs Colton here, and is currently enjoying Sheriff Mills' hospitality,' Harper noted. 'Makes one wonder what he's sharing with law enforcement.'

The implication hit its mark.

Mitchell broke the silence, addressing Sarah directly.

'Mrs Colton, my condolences again for your loss. My father and I respected Mike greatly. I can promise you; we never broke into your house.'

'Neither did we!' McSorley blustered.

Mitchell, however, ignored him, continuing to speak to Sarah.

'Perhaps we could discuss appropriate compensation for today's... inconvenience?'

It was a transparent attempt to establish control of the narrative, but before Sarah could respond, events transcended diplomatic resolution. The rear service door opened as two more of Brennan's men entered, weapons already drawn. Seeing Mitchell and his men, they reacted instinctively, raising firearms towards perceived threats.

Mitchell's men responded with professional efficiency; the lead man shoving his principal towards cover while raising his own weapon, the second moving laterally to create distance between targets.

McSorley dropped to one knee, pistol materialising in his hand, barking orders to his team that were lost in the cacophony that followed.

Harper had Sarah on the ground in the same instant, using a heavy toolbox as cover, his body positioned to shield hers. He'd identified the nearest exit – the short hallway leading to the parts department – and calculated the three seconds they'd be exposed while moving to it.

The first shot came from one of Brennan's new arrivals, a panicked reaction rather than deliberate targeting. The round struck a metal cabinet with a hollow clang, ricocheting into the ceiling tiles and sending dust cascading down.

Then discipline disintegrated entirely.

Gunfire erupted from multiple positions – muzzle flashes strobing in the garage's fluorescent lighting, brass casings tinkling against concrete, the distinctive sound patterns of different calibres creating a chaotic percussion.

'Stay down,' Harper ordered Sarah, his voice pitched to carry through the chaos. 'When I move, follow directly behind me. Three seconds to the hallway, then right into the parts room.'

She nodded, fear clear but controlled. Harper counted shots, tracking firing patterns through sound. One of Mitchell's team was providing covering fire – three-round bursts, professional rather than panicked. Most others were firing reactively, creating more noise than effective suppression.

'Now!' Harper ordered, timing their movement during a momentary lull.

They covered the distance to the hallway entrance in two

seconds, Harper keeping his body between Sarah and the main firing positions. As they reached the doorway, a burning line scored across Harper's left bicep – not deep but enough to draw blood as a round grazed him.

Another bloody bullet to the same arm. This was taking the piss now.

Inside the hallway, relative quiet descended, the gunfire now muffled by walls and distance. Harper guided Sarah towards the parts department, checking the wound as they moved. Just a graze, adding to his collection of recent injuries but nothing debilitating.

'You're hit,' Sarah said, noticing the spreading red stain on his sleeve.

'It's nothing,' Harper dismissed. 'We need to get out through the loading dock.'

The parts department was mercifully empty, its rows of shelving offering concealment as they navigated towards the rear exit. Through a small window, Harper confirmed the loading dock remained clear – the fighting had drawn everyone towards the main garage area.

'This wasn't supposed to happen,' Sarah whispered as they reached the exit. 'Not like this.'

'No plan survives contact with reality,' Harper replied, checking her for injuries. 'Are you hurt?'

She shook her head.

'Just scared. And angry. They're destroying Mike's business.'

'The business can be rebuilt,' Harper said. 'Let's focus on getting clear. Can you make it to your car?'

Before Sarah could answer, the distinctive wail of police sirens penetrated the chaos. Multiple vehicles, approaching rapidly. The confrontation had escalated beyond containment.

Harper made a split-second decision.

'Change of plan. Find somewhere safe to wait this out. I need to get back in there.'

'What? Why?'

'Intelligence opportunity,' Harper explained tersely. 'Mitchell Daggett, Brennan's lieutenant, and potentially valuable evidence, all in one location? I won't get a better chance.'

'It's too dangerous,' Sarah protested. 'They're shooting in there!'

'Which means they're distracted,' Harper countered. 'The loading dock connects to the woods behind the garage. Stay there until I get you.'

Sarah clearly wanted to argue further, but years with Mike had taught her to recognise when military determination had engaged. She nodded reluctantly.

'Be careful.'

'Always am,' Harper replied, the lie coming easily as he turned and moved quickly back into the garage.

15

DANGER ZONE

THE GARAGE HAD TRANSFORMED INTO A COMBAT ZONE – shattered glass scattered across the floor, toolboxes overturned for improvised cover, the acrid smell of gunpowder hanging in the air. However, the gunfire had diminished to occasional single shots rather than continuous exchange, suggesting positional fighting rather than active advance.

From his limited vantage point, Harper counted four men down – two from Brennan's group, one of Daggett's originals, and someone he couldn't immediately identify. The others had established defensive positions behind vehicles and structural elements, maintaining standoff while sirens grew louder. Most critically, Harper spotted Mitchell Daggett and one of his guards retreating towards Ray's office – likely seeking the same documentation Brennan's people had been attempting to access earlier but likely taken by the deputies.

Unless they'd not known where to look.

The distance between Harper's position and the office was approximately twenty feet of exposed space. Under normal circumstances, an unacceptable risk. But with attention focused on opposing factions rather than peripheral areas, it was a calculated gamble, and so Harper waited; when Brennan's remaining men concentrated fire on Daggett's other men's position near the front entrance, he moved – swift, staying low while covering the distance to the office.

Inside, Mitchell was methodically searching Ray's desk while his man was under it, pressing at what was likely some kind of hidden compartment. Harper had a momentary thought of whether this was where Daggett's card had fallen from, but this probably wasn't the moment to ask as he slipped through the splintered doorframe, positioning himself against the wall beside a filing cabinet.

'Nothing here,' Mitchell muttered, frustration visible. 'The deputies must have taken everything—'

He paused when he finally registered Harper's presence. His guard's hand raised his gun, but Harper had expected the reaction.

'I wouldn't,' Harper advised quietly. 'You can't afford another casualty when police are seconds away.'

Mitchell turned sharply; surprise quickly masked by calculated assessment. There was noise outside; it seemed both sides had left before the cops appeared. Now it was just Harper, Mitchell, and his armed friend.

'Mister Harper. I thought you'd left with Mrs Colton.'

'And miss this opportunity? Never underestimate the value of chaos,' Harper kept his voice calm despite his heightened awareness of the other man's trigger finger and the dwindling seconds before police arrival. 'You're looking in the wrong place. The evidence you're looking for isn't here. It's already secured elsewhere.'

'And you know this how?'

'Because I've seen it,' Harper stated simply. 'Financial records. Meeting minutes. Names, dates, locations. Everything connecting you, Brennan, and Whitcomb in your little triumvirate of corruption.'

Something flickered in Mitchell's eyes; a momentary tell quickly suppressed.

'Quite a theory. Rather elaborate conspiracy.'

'Not a theory. Documented fact,' Harper bluffed as he maintained direct eye contact, watching for micro-expressions that might reveal useful information. 'Including the order for Mike's death.'

Mitchell held up a restraining hand.

'I think you have the wrong member of the family here,' he said. 'And, as interesting as this conversation is, we have more immediate concerns. Law enforcement will secure this location momentarily.'

'Which creates opportunity,' Harper suggested. 'For those with mutual interests. You want something Ray hid. I want the truth about Mike's death. Perhaps we could help each other, unless you're the killer.'

The wail of sirens reached a crescendo as police vehicles surrounded the building. The time had run out for extended negotiation. Mitchell studied Harper for a calculated moment before reaching a decision.

'I suggest we all find more appropriate locations and discuss this at a time for quieter heads,' he said. 'You know, before Sheriff Mills begins asking uncomfortable questions.'

This said, Mitchell Daggett decided the conversation was over and moved to the door, pausing as he gave Harper a final assessing look.

'I underestimated you, Mister Harper. I won't make that mistake again.'

'Most don't get a second chance,' Harper replied evenly.

WITH MITCHELL AND HIS LONE GUARD HEADING OFF TOWARDS a nearby car with the knowledge of someone who, even stopped by deputies, wouldn't be held for long, Harper headed into the woodlands behind the garage, checking his left arm wound as he did so. The new bullet graze had mostly stopped bleeding, though his sleeve was soaked. Nothing requiring immediate medical attention, but it was yet another reminder of his physical vulnerability in an increasingly dangerous environment – and now with two wounds in different areas, his arm *really* bloody hurt.

Looking back through the trees, he paused to assess the widening impact. Multiple police vehicles had converged on the garage. Two ambulances stood with rear doors open, paramedics checking what Harper assumed were the casualties he'd observed. In the distance, smoke rose from what appeared to be a warehouse in Brennan's territory – the conflict already spreading beyond its initial flashpoint.

The town was being dismantled by war.

'Sometimes old structures need to collapse before truth can emerge.'

His father had said that once, Harper recalled. After an operation in Sarajevo that had destabilised entrenched power networks to expose evidence of war crimes, back when he wasn't purely working for himself, and Harper was still a boy, hoping for a father's attention. The methodology was identical – apply pressure at strategic points, create controlled chaos, exploit the resulting opportunities.

Like father, like son.

There was a rustle to the side and Harper spun, the 9mm Hellcat in his hand, but he stopped, lowering it as he saw the terrified face of Sarah Colton.

'I thought you were dead,' she said.

'Not yet,' he smiled, putting the gun away and pulling out his phone, texting Klein.

> Daggett interested in Mike's desk. Possible secret compartment. Best you check it first.

This done, he looked back at Sarah.

'Right then,' he said, keeping his voice as relaxed as he could. 'Shall we get out of here?'

ONCE IN THE CAR, SARAH SLAMMED THE ACCELERATOR DOWN AS they sped away from the garage crime scene, far enough to not be watched by the deputies, but close enough to see the chaos caused.

'We need to get Jake,' she said as they travelled. 'If the situation's escalating this quickly, I want him somewhere secure.'

Harper nodded agreement. She was right, but at the same time it wasn't just Jake who needed to be secure. Sarah had shown herself to be a piece on the board now, and any of the other players could try to take her off.

As they approached the high school, Harper spotted a familiar figure on the periphery of campus – Jake Colton, phone in hand. Harper noted Jake's expression as he reached the car – excited rather than frightened, engaged rather than intimidated.

Mike's son indeed, it seemed.

'Mom,' Jake greeted as he climbed into the backseat. 'You heard about the garage? Brennan's people and Daggett's almost shot each other.'

'We know,' Sarah replied tersely. 'We were there.'

Jake's eyes widened briefly before narrowing.

'You went inside? What happened?'

Sarah glanced at Harper, silently delegating the explanation while she navigated away from the school.

'First direct confrontation,' Harper informed Jake. 'Accusations about Ray working both sides. But Brennan's men suggested there are more informants in Daggett's organisation.'

'Is that true?' Jake asked.

'Doesn't matter if it's true,' Harper replied. 'What matters is that Daggett believes it might be. He'll start looking for traitors in his ranks. That creates opportunities.'

'Opportunities for what?' Jake pressed.

'For escalation,' Harper said simply. 'For turning controlled conflict into open warfare.'

'And that gets us justice for dad how, exactly?'

'When systems are stable, secrets stay buried,' Harper explained. 'But when organisations are fighting for survival, protecting secrets becomes secondary to immediate threats. Evidence emerges. People talk. Truth surfaces.'

Jake nodded slowly, understanding dawning.

'You're using their paranoia against them.'

'Precisely.'

Sarah's hands tightened on the steering wheel.

'We can't go home or back to the cabin,' she announced. 'Both places are too obvious. After what just happened at the garage, they'll be watching everywhere connected to us.'

She glanced at Harper.

'We need somewhere they wouldn't think to look.'

Harper considered their options.

'We need to get you out of town,' Harper nodded. 'Now that Brennan and Daggett are pointing fingers, we need to understand exactly what Mike discovered about their relationship. The supposed rivalry might not be as complete as it appears.'

There was a jerk however, as Sarah slammed the brakes on. The road was empty, there wasn't anything to cause this, but she turned to face Harper.

'We need to go home first,' she said.

'You can't,' Harper shook his head. 'If either side feels they need to retaliate, they'll look at you. Also, I don't know if you picked up on it, but both sides said they didn't break into your house, which means that if they're telling the truth, there's a third party out there, too. If they think you're connected to Ray, they'll look at you. If they think Mike had information—'

'I know, they'll look at me,' Sarah snapped. 'But let's be serious for a moment. You want us out of town? I get that. But what happens if someone burns down the house while we're away?'

'They won't—'

'Can you guarantee that?' Sarah snapped. 'Because you're all about justice for Mike, but you don't seem to give a crap about the town and the people in it!'

Harper went to reply but then stopped.

She was right.

He'd been too hyper focused on the events to look too hard at the surrounding—

No. He'd known. He'd not cared.

Like father, like son.

'Okay,' he said softly. 'What do you need?'

'I need to grab some things from the house,' Sarah replied. 'The closest mall's thirty miles away, and I'll be damned if we're going to go clothes shopping somewhere public, when I can grab a suitcase and load it up in five minutes. Also, there are some family things I need to keep safe, and let's face it, it's not the first time they've gone through my stuff. They hear we're gone? They'll take their time.'

Harper understood that. Some items from her life with Mike were priceless. She couldn't leave them behind.

'And dad has some more notes there,' Jake added. 'The ones in the desk.'

Harper sighed.

'Then that's where we go first,' he replied. 'But carefully. There's a good chance everyone's watching your house by now.'

SARAH STOPPED THE HONDA A LITTLE WAY DOWN FROM HER house, eyes scanning the quiet street. The late morning sun cast short shadows across the lawn.

'Wait here,' Harper said, checking for watchers. 'I'll make sure it's clear.'

Moving as quick as he could despite the pain, he circled the property once, moving through the side yard, checking potential observation points. There was nothing obvious, but something felt off.

Back at the car, he nodded to Sarah and Jake.

'Quick in and out. Five minutes.'

Inside the house, Jake went straight to his room, likely

grabbing a bag of his own things, but after a couple of minutes he returned down the stairs, heading over to Mike's desk in the den, shifting a panel Harper wouldn't have noticed without being shown. He extracted several folded papers; likely the ones Jake had found earlier as they matched the sheet he'd already passed across.

'Everything dad documented,' he said, voice tight. 'Dates, names, connections.'

Harper took the papers but stopped.

This wasn't everything, and he didn't just use paper notes.

He pulled out the SD card, the one he'd not been able to get into, as if remembering it for the first time.

'Your dad had this,' he said. 'It's encrypted. There has to be a password somewhere...'

Password.

Harper pulled out the sheet of notepaper Sarah had given him. On the back were the same varying letters and numbers. He turned the papers and saw that there were even more here.

Jake, watching this, understood.

'You think one of these opens that?' he asked. Before Harper could answer, however, movement outside caught his attention. He slid over to the window, staying to the side.

A black SUV crawled past the house, moving slower than casual traffic would.

'Company,' he said, watching as the vehicle reached the end of the street and turned around.

'Who?' Sarah asked, walking back into the room.

'Can't tell yet, but they're watching the house.'

The SUV made another pass, confirming Harper's suspicion.

This wasn't random.

Jake appeared beside him at the window, staring out before Harper gently but forcefully nudged him to the side as outside, the SUV finally pulled up outside the house.

'What do we do?' he asked.

Harper gestured them both away from the windows.

'Hide. Now.'

He moved them to the kitchen as car doors slammed outside. Footsteps approached the house – multiple sets, moving with purpose. Sarah and Jake crouched behind the counter while Harper positioned himself beside the back door, pulling out the 9mm Hellcat, ignoring Jake's surprise at the weapon. Through the window, he counted three men approaching, while two more remained with the vehicle.

Shit.

The lead man spoke into a radio.

'Her car's out front, down the road,' he said, his accent hinting an Irish accent. *Brennan's men.* 'They're definitely here, as it wasn't there ten minutes back.'

They paused at the foot of the porch steps as he looked at the others.

'Remember, we want the woman and the kid alive,' the leader said. 'The boss wants to know what they know.'

The second man checked his weapon.

'What about the Brit if he's with them?'

'No orders given, so kill the limey prick.'

'The boss is fine with this? He seemed chummy in the car.'

'That was before his men were killed and the fires started,' the leader snapped. 'Now it's eye for an eye time.'

Harper looked at Sarah, their eyes meeting across the kitchen. There was no need for words. The stakes were clear now. He looked around for a kitchen knife, something else he could use—

There was a buzzing sound on the other side of the door – the men were halfway up the steps when the leader's phone rang.

The leader answered, listening for several seconds.

'You sure?' he asked, tension clear in his voice. 'When?'

The man glanced back at the Honda, then at his companions.

'Change of plans. They're pulling us to the ridge. Boss wants us all together so we can't be picked off.'

He hesitated, clearly unhappy as he continued the call.

'Yes, boss. Understood.'

'What about the woman and the kid?' one of the men almost whined.

'We'll deal with them later,' the leader growled. 'While we skin the feckin' Brit alive.'

They retreated to the SUV; the leader casting one last look at the house before climbing in. The vehicle pulled away, moving with new urgency.

Harper waited two full minutes after they left, releasing the breath he didn't realise he'd held.

'We need to move,' he said as he shook himself into action. 'They'll be back.'

'Where to?' Sarah asked. 'They'll hunt everywhere for us.'

'We split up. You two need to leave town,' Harper said, decision made. 'They're looking for both of you specifically now.'

'We're in this together,' Sarah protested.

'I get that,' Harper cut her off. 'But they know the car. They'll be watching all the roads. I can move alone without drawing attention. You need to get Jake somewhere safe.'

Sarah hesitated, then nodded reluctantly.

'Interstate 70 motel?'

'Too obvious,' Harper replied. 'Head east, past Cumberland. Find a new location, one you've not been to before. Pay cash, use different names.'

'And then what?' Jake asked.

'I finish what Mike started,' Harper replied.

AFTER PACKING A COUPLE MORE BAGS WITH ESSENTIALS, THEY slipped out the back door, cutting through neighbouring yards until they reached a parallel street. Harper hot-wired a nondescript Chevy from a neighbour while Sarah kept watch.

'Three days,' Harper said as they prepared to separate. 'If you haven't heard from me by then, contact this number.'

He handed her a piece of paper with digits scrawled on it.

'Former colleague. He'll help you disappear if needed.'

'I'd rather not disappear,' Sarah said.

'Nor would I,' Harper replied. 'So, let's make sure that doesn't happen.'

He turned to Jake, passing him the SD memory card and the sheets of paper.

'See if any of these random numbers open that,' he smiled. 'I took photos of the other sides, so I'll check through those while you're away.'

Jake watched him suspiciously, and Harper knew he was aware this was something Harper himself could have done, but was giving to Jake to make him feel part of this.

'Thanks, Harper,' he said simply, sticking the sheets and the card into his bag. 'I'll tell you if I find anything.'

Harper watched them drive away, hoping they'd follow his advice of keeping to side streets until they were clear of town. Then he turned and moved in the opposite direction, already planning his next move.

Alone was how he preferred to operate when things got messy, anyway.

16

THE PUPPET MASTER

Late afternoon found Harper on a wooded hillside overlooking Daggett's compound again. After speaking to Mitchell at the garage, and with Brennan's men hunting Sarah now, he'd wondered what would happen next in the Daggett family, especially with the son's cryptic message about the father. So, he'd headed here and had been there for nearly an hour, observing the security protocols implemented since the gunfight.

Through his binoculars, Harper studied the compound's vulnerable points – blind spots in the camera coverage, guard rotation patterns, access routes that might be exploited. His injuries from the encounter with Doyle, now added to with more recent bullet grazes and bruises, protested the extended stillness of surveillance.

Bloody uncomfortable, this surveillance lark.

The compound itself was a study in criminal pragmatism – a central residence converted from a colonial-era farmhouse, surrounded by outbuildings repurposed for security, storage and operations.

Harper noted the pattern of patrols – clockwise rotations with overlapping fields of vision, yet still containing exploitable gaps where attention naturally waned at shift changes.

'Amateurs,' he muttered to himself. 'Always leave the same gaps.'

With Sarah and Jake safely away and hopefully hidden, Harper was free to speed up his campaign against both criminal organisations without concern for collateral damage to Mike's family.

The phone in his pocket vibrated. Klein.

> Ray's still insisting he's been framed. Both Daggett and Brennan have people watching the station. Where are you?

Harper considered his response.

> Working. Stay visible. Let them think you're focused on Ray.

The deputy's involvement represented both opportunity and complication. Klein wanted justice for Mike, which aligned with Harper's objectives, but his methods were constrained by law enforcement protocols and ethical boundaries Harper wasn't obligated to respect.

Harper shifted position, easing the pressure on his injured side while maintaining his view of Daggett's compound. The front gates opened, admitting a black Lincoln with tinted windows.

Victor Daggett, patriarch of the family emerged from the main house to greet the vehicle's occupant – a man in his sixties, silver-haired, with the bearing of someone accustomed to authority.

Harper recognised him immediately from the funeral, though the sheriff's demeanour had changed considerably – gone was the public servant's professional reserve, replaced by the relaxed familiarity of longstanding alliance. The men embraced briefly before disappearing inside the main house.

The timing was perfect. From the moment the car pulled up, Harper had raised his phone, snapping a couple of shots, documenting the meeting before sending a message to Klein.

Who's the silver-haired Sheriff that was at the funeral?

The message came back swiftly.

You mean Sheriff Mills? Why?

Harper decided not to send the photo until he had more information, but it looked very much like he'd found the mole in the Sheriff's department.

After thirty minutes, Mills departed. Harper allowed him a five-minute head start before descending the hillside to his Bonneville, concealed beneath camouflage netting in a dry creek bed.

As he prepared to mount the motorcycle though, Harper paused, noticing disturbances in the surrounding vegetation – broken stems, displaced leaves, subtle impressions on the soft ground nearby. Someone had been here, examining his hiding spot... and recently.

Well, shit. That's inconvenient.

Harper crouched, examining the footprints more closely. Boots, or shoes. Not trainers. Whoever it was had circled the bike completely, studying it from all angles.

'Sloppy tradecraft, Liam,' he muttered to himself. 'Getting careless.'

He filed this information away as he started the motorcycle. It hadn't been touched, so maybe they'd just walked past? Unlikely though. And Harper had a pretty distinctive motorcycle.

Oh well.

He'd consider what this meant later. Right now, it was time for the next phase.

THE BLÜDRIDGE COUNTY SHERIFF'S DEPARTMENT OCCUPIED A brick building at the edge of town, its architecture suggesting 1970s municipal pragmatism rather than nostalgic small-town Americana.

Harper approached from the adjacent public library parking lot, his bearing casual yet purposeful – someone with legitimate business rather than covert intent. His hand touched the river stone in his pocket, a moment of focus before the infiltration began.

Inside, a civilian administrator whose nameplate identified her as *Doris Fletcher* staffed the front desk. She glanced up as Harper entered, her expression the professional neutrality of someone who dealt with public inquiries routinely.

'Can I help you?' she asked, eyes taking in Harper's appearance with subtle assessment.

'I hope so,' Harper replied with practised politeness. 'I need to speak with Deputy Klein regarding a statement.'

'Regarding?' Her tone sharpened slightly, likely protective of her department's resources.

'The incident at Colton's Auto Shop,' Harper replied. 'I'm a friend of the family. Deputy Klein said he needed additional details about what I witnessed.'

'You were there when it happened?' A hint of curiosity crept into her professional demeanour.

'Aftermath,' Harper replied, keeping it vague. 'Saw things that might help the investigation.'

Doris consulted a computer screen, frowning slightly.

'He's interviewing a suspect right now and can't be interrupted. I can take a message.'

Ray Halvorsen. Had to be.

'Actually, I was also hoping to provide some documentation for the file,' Harper indicated a manila envelope he carried. 'Deputy Klein specifically asked for it. Is there somewhere I could leave it for him?'

Doris considered this, her expression suggesting internal debate between procedure and convenience.

'You can leave it in his inbox,' she finally decided. 'Through that door, third desk on the left. Just don't touch anything else.'

'Appreciate it,' Harper smiled, projecting as much harmless gratitude as he could show while she buzzed him through the security door.

Second time a manila envelope had allowed him past gatekeepers, he thought. *I should use these more often.*

The bullpen contained six desks, with only two currently occupied by deputies engrossed in paperwork. Harper moved to Klein's desk; it was meticulously organised, with case files stacked precisely, pens arranged by type, and the computer screen showing a password-protected lock screen.

The bloke's got military-grade OCD with his desk organisation. Interesting character trait for a small-town lawman.

Harper placed his envelope in the wooden inbox, then casually dropped a small flash drive behind the desk. The movement appeared accidental to casual observation – a man adjusting his jacket, unknowingly dislodging an item from his pocket. In reality, the drive contained the photo he'd taken of Daggett and Mills, but also fabricated notes he'd created on his phone an hour earlier, suggesting Sheriff Mills had been taking payoffs from both Daggett and Brennan simultaneously – hinting at potential financial records on Mills' own computer, creating an interesting narrative of corruption and betrayal.

Time to see who's honest or not.

He could see one deputy had noticed this, but said nothing, likely intending to pick it up once Harper was gone. He wasn't sure, but Harper guessed that if Klein was worried about moles in the department, there were likely more than one, and this was someone looking to gain a good word with his "real" boss.

Good boy. You go pass that up the chain.

Committing the inquisitive deputy's face and badge to memory, Harper exited the building, nodding to Doris on his way out.

'Find everything you needed?' she asked, a slightly suspicious edge to her tone.

'All sorted,' Harper replied with a calm smile. 'Please tell Deputy Klein I stopped by.'

'I'll make a note,' she said, already turning back to her computer. 'Name?'

But Harper was already out of the door. Phase one was now complete – evidence planted that would eventually reach either Brennan, Daggett, or both, creating additional pressure against Mills while suggesting new connections between the criminal organisations.

Now to spread some *more* love.

By eight that evening, Harper had completed similar operations at two additional locations – a storage facility used by Daggett's crew and the county records office where building permits were filed, an after hours visit through door locks that were as bad as any he'd seen before.

The last part of his plan required a different approach.

St. Mary's Church stood quiet in the evening light, its modest stone frontage and simple steeple silhouetted against the darkening sky. The German heritage of Blüdridge's founders showed in the practical design – solid construction without ornate flourishes, a testament to function over form.

Harper approached the side entrance, noting the construction materials still covered with tarps – evidence of renovation work abandoned months ago. The door was unlocked, giving way to a simple, austere interior. Wooden pews lined a central aisle leading to a plain altar. Unlike Catholic churches with their ornate decorations, St. Mary's reflected its Lutheran roots – modest and unadorned.

Father Jonathan was arranging pamphlets when Harper entered, the priest's movement pausing as he recognised his visitor.

'Mister... Harper? Friend of Mike's, right?' Father Jonathan acknowledged, straightening. 'I didn't expect to see you back in our church so soon. I heard you'd stayed around to help Mrs Colton. Very Christian of you.'

'Sorry for the interruption, I needed some quiet,' Harper replied, moving down the aisle. 'Hope I'm not intruding.'

'The Lord's house is open to all seekers,' Father Jonathan said, though his expression suggested he doubted Harper had come seeking spiritual guidance. 'Though I suspect you're looking for something other than prayer.'

Harper smiled slightly. *The priest was perceptive.*

'Information,' he admitted, stopping a few feet from Father Jonathan. 'About Ray Halvorsen.'

Father Jonathan's expression tightened almost imperceptibly.

'You know I cannot share what's told to me in confidence.'

'I'm not asking for confessions or anything given in trust,' Harper clarified. 'Just your observations, as someone who sees more than most in this town.'

The priest studied Harper for a long moment, then gestured towards the front pew.

'Sit with me,' he said. 'These old knees prefer not to stand longer than necessary.'

They sat side by side, facing the altar.

'Ray was here yesterday,' Father Jonathan said finally. 'Not for confession – he's never been much for that – but to help with our electrical issues. The renovation was his project, before...' He gestured towards the covered scaffolding.

'Before things got complicated?' Harper suggested.

'Before Mike died,' Father Jonathan corrected, his tone sharpening slightly. 'Something changed in Ray after that. He became... withdrawn. Nervous. Started checking over his shoulder even in church, took over more duties in the garage.'

'The actions of a guilty man,' Harper observed. 'The nerves, that is. Not the duties.'

'Or a frightened one,' Father Jonathan countered. 'Fear and guilt can look remarkably similar from the outside.'

'Is that what you believe? That Ray's afraid rather than guilty?'

Father Jonathan sighed, folding his hands in his lap.

'In this town, Mister Harper, it's possible to be both victim *and* perpetrator. No one's hands stay clean for long.'

'Even yours?' Harper asked.

'Even mine,' the priest acknowledged. 'I've maintained my position by knowing when to speak and when to remain silent. It's a complicated form of complicity.'

A complicated form of complicity. The phrase carried weight beyond its immediate context.

'Have you heard about Ray's current situation?' Harper asked.

'That he's being held by the sheriff's department? Yes. The town talks of little else.' Father Jonathan glanced towards Harper. 'They're saying he betrayed both Daggett and Brennan. That evidence has been found connecting him to both organisations.'

'And what do you think?'

'I think someone wants very badly for that to be the narrative,' Father Jonathan replied carefully. 'Whether it's true or not seems almost beside the point now.'

Harper smiled inwardly. The priest was sharper than he'd given him credit for.

'People are saying strange things about you as well, Mister Harper,' Father Jonathan continued. 'That you're not simply Mike's friend paying respects, but something more... purposeful. An Angel of Vengeance, even.'

'People talk,' Harper dismissed.

'Yes, they do,' Father Jonathan agreed. 'Especially to their priest. Sheriff Mills was here this morning, lighting a candle for what he called "coming difficulties". Mitchell Daggett made a substantial donation to our restoration fund yesterday, asking for prayers for his father's health. Sean Brennan attended early service, something he hasn't done in months, especially as he's a good Catholic, and has his own places of worship.'

'Catholics not allowed here?'

'Oh, we allow all,' Father Jonathan smiled. 'We're just not usually "bells and smells" enough for God fearing Irish Catholics.'

Harper considered the information.

'The powerful seeking divine protection,' he observed.

'Or absolution,' Father Jonathan suggested. 'The kind that comes before significant action, not after.'

The implication was clear – the town's major players were preparing for something imminent.

'The town feels different tonight,' Father Jonathan said, staring towards the stained glass window behind the altar, where the last light of day filtered through a simple cross design. 'There's a tension in the air, like before a thunderstorm. People are afraid, though most couldn't tell you exactly what they fear.'

'Change,' Harper suggested. 'The unknown.'

'Justice, perhaps,' Father Jonathan countered. 'For those who've avoided it for too long.'

He turned to face Harper directly.

'Whatever you're doing – and I won't ask for details I don't wish to know – be careful. This town has survived on its careful balance of power for generations. When such balances shift suddenly...'

'People get hurt,' Harper finished.

'People *die*,' Father Jonathan corrected. 'As Mike did. As others will before this is finished.'

His words hung in the air between them.

'I should continue my preparations for tomorrow's service,' Father Jonathan said, rising from the pew. 'You're welcome to stay as long as you need.'

'Thank you, Father,' Harper replied, remaining seated. 'For the conversation.'

Father Jonathan nodded, turning away before pausing.

'One last thing, Mr. Harper. Deputy Klein has been asking questions about you – your background, your relationship with Mike, your movements since arriving in Blüdridge. Just this afternoon, in fact.'

'Has he indeed?' Harper kept his tone neutral, though this information was significant.

'I thought you might find that relevant, that for all your believed assistance, even your allies don't trust you,' Father Jonathan said before walking towards the sacristy, leaving Harper alone in the quiet church.

Harper sat for several minutes, processing what he'd learned. The priest's information about Klein was troubling – the deputy had presented himself as an ally but now appeared to be conducting his own investigation into Harper's activities. Although that was understandable, Harper was an unknown quantity here. Still, it felt like Klein was another player with hidden motives.

This town was full of them.

As darkness fell, Harper returned to his hotel room, securing the door before laying out the day's gathered intelligence. Most interesting were the building permits and property records from the county office. They revealed a pattern Harper hadn't initially recognised – both criminal organisations were acquiring properties along the ridgeline, creating a network of seemingly unrelated holdings that collectively controlled access to areas on the edge of the ridgeline and Quinn's Lookout that, when overlaid to a map, could link to the old mining tunnels. However, the aggregated view suggested coordination rather than competition in certain areas, despite the public appearance of rivalry.

Brennan and Daggett *were* working together. *But which Daggett?*

Harper organised this information, identifying patterns and connections that would form the basis for his next actions. Tomorrow, he'd begin targeting specific individuals within both organisations.

A phone vibrated with an incoming message from an unknown number; it threw Harper for a moment until he realised it was the burner number he'd given Ray on the documentation. Locating it and checking the display, he saw a text containing an image – a surveillance photograph of Harper entering the sheriff's department earlier that day. Beneath it, a single line of text:

> You're playing a dangerous game. Not everyone is who they appear to be – D

D for Daggett. Mitchell Daggett perhaps, breaking radio silence to deliver what could be interpreted as either warning or threat? Or could it be Victor, the patriarch, wanting this stopped before his son was hurt? Either way, it was an interesting development, especially as the only way Daggett could have got it was from Ray.

No, that wasn't true. It could have been on the desk when Mitchell Daggett checked through Ray's papers.

Harper stored the information without immediate response. Daggett's awareness of his activities gave confirmation that his actions were having the desired effect.

A second message arrived moments later, this one on his normal phone, and from Klein:

> Found your package, deputy picked it up for me. Contents concerning. Need to meet. Old logging road, mile marker 7. Midnight.

Harper considered the request; meeting Klein presented both opportunity and risk – the deputy could provide valuable information about the sheriff's department's involvement but also represented a potential vulnerability if Harper's more extreme methods came to light. There was also the question of whether the meeting request originated from Klein himself or represented a trap set by Mills or another player. After all, the deputy that passed it to him could have checked or even altered the contents before passing across.

After deliberate consideration, Harper sent a single word reply:

> Acknowledged.

The pieces were moving faster now, the careful equilibrium of Blüdridge's criminal ecosystem destabilising exactly as Harper had intended. Both organisations were turning inward, searching for betrayal within their ranks and, in that growing chaos, Harper would find the specific thread that led to Mike Colton's death – and pull it until the entire structure unravelled.

Harper studied the street below, noting the black SUV now parked across from the inn – Daggett's surveillance team maintaining their watch.

Let them watch, he thought. *Let them believe they understood what they were seeing.* He glanced around, wondering why they hadn't checked his hotel room when he left, but then there was always the possibility they had, and he simply hadn't realised.

No. He was better than they were. They'd never find the steps he took to show if someone had been in.

A final line from his father, given in passing to someone else while an almost-teenage Liam Harper was in the room, came to mind.

'The best manipulations occurred in plain sight, with targets believing they maintain control even as the ground shifts beneath them.'

Harper stared down at the SUV.

He had to end this soon – not to save the people of Blüdridge, but to stop himself from becoming his father.

17

MIDNIGHT MEETING

THE OLD LOGGING ROAD STRETCHED LIKE A DARK RIBBON through the forest, rutted from decades of heavy trucks and persistent neglect. Harper positioned himself among the shadows at the edge of a small clearing, the worn mile marker seven barely visible in the moonlight. He'd arrived twenty minutes early – standard protocol for uncertain rendezvous. Time enough to secure approach routes, identify potential ambush points, establish fallback positions.

Something moved in the underbrush fifty yards east – too large for a fox, too deliberate for deer. Harper's hand moved towards his weapon before the creature revealed itself – a raccoon, ambling along its nocturnal route, oblivious to human concerns.

Not every shadow hides a threat. Though in Blüdridge, that was becoming less certain by the hour.

At precisely midnight, the distinctive cadence of a Crown Victoria's engine broke the silence. Harper recognised the particular sound – American police cruiser, well-maintained but with slight valve tick on cylinder three.

Details that could save your life in the wrong circumstances.

The vehicle approached with headlights extinguished, moving slowly along the logging road before coming to a stop twenty yards from the mile marker, engine idling, lights still dark. The driver's door opened, and Klein emerged alone, his silhouette unmistakable against the deeper shadows of the forest.

The deputy surveyed the area, hand resting casually near his sidearm as he approached the mile marker. Standard procedure for an officer entering uncertain territory. Harper allowed him to wait, watching Klein's body language for thirty seconds before speaking.

'You came alone.'

Klein turned towards Harper's voice, not startled but clearly unable to pinpoint his location precisely.

'Of course I did,' the deputy replied. 'Though I've got a feeling you'd know if I hadn't.'

Harper stepped from the shadows, moving deliberately.

'Standard precaution.'

Klein nodded, understanding. In his left hand, he held a manila envelope that Harper recognised from his earlier visit to the sheriff's office – the one he'd placed in Klein's inbox as cover for the flash drive.

'You've been busy,' Klein said, tapping the folder for emphasis. 'Ray Halvorsen's been receiving payments from both sides for at least eight months, according to these records. Comprehensive documentation, and it almost looks authentic.'

'Almost?' Harper replied mildly.

'The dates align perfectly with case files I've been tracking. The payment amounts correspond with specific events we've documented. The signatures match samples we have on record.' Klein met Harper's gaze directly. 'If I didn't know better, I'd swear these documents were genuine evidence rather than carefully manufactured deception.'

Harper studied Klein's face, noting the subtle tells – slight tension around the eyes, the controlled cadence of his speech. *Professional scepticism or something more personal?*

'What makes you think they're not genuine?'

'Because I've been investigating these operations for two years and while Ray's dirty, he wasn't playing both sides until the last few months. Someone wants very badly to make it look like he's been a double agent much longer than he actually has.'

Harper maintained his impassive expression, revealing nothing while noting Klein's timeline. Two years of investigation with apparently little progress until Mike got involved.

Coincidence or convenience?

'Does it matter?' he asked. 'If the evidence leads to the truth about Mike's death either way?'

Klein considered this, his silence revealing internal conflict. The deputy stared into the darkness for a moment, his expression suggesting genuine moral wrestling.

'That's the question I've been wrestling with since finding your little gift,' he finally said. 'Ray's guilty – of Mike's death, of betraying the town, of working with both criminal enterprises. But falsified evidence, even against guilty parties…'

'Compromises the case,' Harper finished for him. 'Creates vulnerability to legal challenges, procedural dismissals.'

'Exactly.'

'Unless the evidence leads to legitimate discoveries that can stand on their own merit.'

At this, Klein studied Harper with new interest.

'You've worked with law enforcement before.'

'Adjacent to,' Harper corrected. 'Close enough to understand the constraints.'

A smile flickered across Klein's face.

'It's already working,' he said after a moment. 'Whatever you did. Brennan brought three of his men to the station today, demanding protection – claims Daggett's planning to eliminate his entire operation. Meanwhile, Victor Daggett has doubled security at all his properties, convinced Brennan's preparing an assault.'

Harper nodded, a slight feeling of satisfaction at the accelerating chaos having precisely the intended effect.

'And the photo?'

At this though, Klein paused.

'What photo?'

'The one on the flash drive?'

Klein shook his head.

'Empty,' he replied. 'I'm guessing it wasn't?'

Harper's instincts sharpened. The flash drive had been found, passed to Klein, but stripped of its most incriminating content. Someone between drop and delivery had made a deliberate choice.

'I think we've narrowed down your mole,' he said. 'Whoever picked up the flash drive and passed it to you must have deleted it first.'

'What was on it?'

'Image I took of Mills and Daggett getting cosy,' he replied. 'I could show you it—'

'I don't need to see it, I already know he's on the take,' Klein literally spat the words out, genuine disgust colouring his tone. 'But you should be careful. If someone's taken interest in the photo you took, they'll take more interest in you.'

Klein's visceral reaction to Mills seemed authentic – either the deputy truly despised corruption, or he was an exceptional actor. Harper filed the observation away, neither committed to trust nor distrust.

'Let them try,' Harper shrugged. 'I've fought bigger and scarier in my time.'

'Any idea who could have taken it?'

'You've got a deputy named Santos, right?' Harper asked. 'Short guy, black side fade? He seemed very interested in what I was doing.'

Klein nodded, and his expression wasn't one of surprise.

'Although you already suspected that,' Harper realised. 'What about Ray?'

'That's another interesting development.' Klein changed tack now. 'I questioned him for six hours about Mike's death. He maintained his innocence until I showed him selective portions of the documentation you provided. The financial records, specifically – seeing those, he assumed Daggett had framed him to cover their connection.'

'He started talking?'

'Like a man drowning, but not the things I want to hear,' Klein sighed, frustration evident. 'He knows something about the lift failure, hinted at details only the saboteur would know. But he's playing it close – dangling just enough to suggest he has valuable information without actually confessing to anything.'

Harper recognised the tactic – he'd seen it in interrogation rooms from Belfast to Baghdad.

'A bargaining chip,' Harper observed.

'Exactly. Kept saying things like "I could tell you how

someone might have modified those specific fittings", or "If I wanted to make a lift fail, I'd know exactly which backup systems to disable". Classic guilty knowledge without admitting guilt.'

'And the orders? Any mention of who wanted Mike dead?'

Klein's expression darkened.

'Even vaguer there. Just cryptic references to "people who don't like questions" and "orders that come down from places you don't expect". When I pushed, he shut down completely. Without hard evidence connecting him directly to the sabotage, we couldn't hold him.'

'You let him go?' Harper asked, surprised.

'That's the complication. Came down from above – and by that I mean Mills. Ray had an out-of-town lawyer turn up. Smarmy bastard tore us to shreds. Ray got a free pass and left the station three hours ago.'

Harper's mind worked through the implications. A lawyer of that calibre didn't come cheap – Ray couldn't afford such representation on a garage manager's salary. Someone with resources was protecting him, someone concerned about what Ray might reveal under pressure.

Klein's expression hardened.

'He was picked up by Brennan's people less than two blocks from the station,' he continued. 'My sources say they're convinced he's betrayed them to Daggett.'

'While Daggett believes the opposite.'

'Exactly. Neither side trusts him any more, both think he's working with the other and he's likely being questioned very thoroughly by Brennan's people as we speak.'

An owl called somewhere in the darkness, the sound carrying across the clearing. Harper glanced towards it automatically – not just an owl's call, but territorial marking, a warning to others to stay clear. Fitting, under the circumstances.

'You think he'll survive until morning?' Harper asked, turning his attention back to Klein.

'Fifty-fifty. Brennan might keep him alive to extract information about Daggett's operations. Or he might make an example of him,' Klein shrugged. 'Either way, I've got a murder case with solid evidence but potentially no defendant to prosecute.'

'Unless you find him tonight,' Harper suggested, watching Klein's reaction carefully.

Klein's eyes registered interest, but caution moderated his response.

'What exactly are you proposing?'

Harper chose his next words carefully.

'Ray knows who ordered Mike's death. That information dies with him if Brennan decides he's outlived his usefulness.'

'I've got a general idea where Brennan might hold him but insufficient cause for a warrant. And no backup – Sheriff Mills has made it clear this is a "low priority" situation that can wait until morning.'

The subtext was clear – Klein was isolated within his department, any official action blocked by compromised leadership. And Mills probably saw Ray as a thread to cut as well.

'Mills is compromised.' Harper stated it as fact rather than a question.

'Has been for years,' Klein confirmed. 'Takes money from both sides though primarily loyal to Daggett, as you saw with the photo you sent me, which someone then deleted.'

Klein's apparent hatred for Mills was either sincere or masterfully performed. Either way, it created common ground between them – a shared enemy, a foundation for limited trust.

'Would you say the situation in town is deteriorating?'

Klein laughed without humour.

'That's an understatement. There's been three separate confrontations between Daggett and Brennan's people since this afternoon. Nothing fatal following the garage attack, but escalating – fistfight outside the hardware store, shots fired behind The Rusted Nail, one of Daggett's delivery trucks run off the road on the east side. But there's something else. After questioning Ray, I searched the drawer in the office, like you suggested. Found documentation suggesting both Daggett and Brennan receive protection from someone at the state level – a political connection shielding their operations from serious investigation.'

'Name?'

'Nothing concrete, just reference to "The Judge" in several notations. Likely candidate is Whitcomb, but there's nothing solid we can progress on yet, and even if I did, it'd get closed down by Mills. But whoever it is, they've been instrumental in keeping federal agencies away from Blüdridge, redirecting investigations, ensuring certain evidence disappears.'

The Judge. Whitcomb. The connection Father Jonathan had hinted at. Another piece sliding into place.

Harper weighed his options. Ray was a murderer who deserved justice, but he also possessed crucial information. If he died tonight, the chain of evidence leading to those who ordered Mike's death might be severed permanently.

Ray needed to survive – for now.

'You've got a decision to make, deputy,' Harper said. 'Ray Halvorsen murdered your friend or at least arranged for the death of a man you respected. He's currently being held somewhere in Brennan's territory, possibly experiencing similar treatment to what Mike would have received if he was caught. Official channels are compromised; backup unavailable.'

'You're suggesting I operate outside official channels.'

'I'm not suggesting anything,' Harper replied carefully. 'I'm stating facts. What you do with them is your decision. Just like you did for me when we first met.'

Klein considered this, the internal struggle between his life in the police and his sense of personal justice clear in his expression.

'I can't officially ask for help locating a suspect being held by known criminals without proper warrants and department authorisation,' Klein said finally, his phrasing deliberate.

'Understood.'

'But if I was conducting routine patrol near Brennan's warehouse on Sawmill Road around two a.m. tonight, and witnessed something requiring immediate intervention...'

'Purely coincidental,' Harper agreed.

'Exactly,' Klein checked his watch. 'I should continue my patrol route. Wouldn't want dispatch noting an extended unexplained stop.'

As the deputy turned to leave, he paused and asked one last question.

'Sarah and Jake Colton – they're out of town?'

The question came too casually, raising a flag in Harper's mind. Had Klein been monitoring Sarah and Jake? If so, for protection or surveillance? Was there something more here, a protective nature born from failure to save Mike?

'Gone since the shooting at the garage, according to neighbours,' Harper said, keeping the answer vague, revealing nothing about their actual location. 'I think there's an out-of-town friend they're visiting.'

'Smart move, getting them clear before things escalate further,' Klein replied, appearing satisfied with the non-answer.

'Be careful, deputy. The situation's becoming unpredictable.'

'That's putting it mildly,' Klein replied before walking back to his cruiser.

Harper maintained his position, watching until the deputy's tail-lights disappeared around a bend in the road. He listened for engine sounds, confirming Klein had actually departed rather than circling back, before moving to retrieve his motorcycle concealed beneath brush nearby.

His shoulder protested as he uncovered the Bonneville, the wound reopening slightly with the exertion. Harper catalogued the pain, acknowledged it, then set it aside.

The engine started smoothly and, as he rode towards Blüdridge, Harper evaluated what he'd learned. The mysterious "Judge" – likely Whitcomb – represented a higher level of corruption, someone with reach beyond the town limits. Mills was compromised; Klein apparently isolated within the department.

But Klein himself... Harper wasn't certain. The deputy's hatred for Mills seemed genuine, his commitment to finding Mike's killers plausible. But something in his manner – perhaps the too-precise questioning about Sarah and Jake – suggested layers Harper couldn't yet fully see.

Trust was a luxury Harper couldn't afford. But strategic alliances? Those were simply operational necessity.

He'd work with Klein to extract Ray, not because Ray deserved saving, but because the information he carried was too valuable to lose. Justice would come, but in Harper's time, not Brennan's or Klein's.

And if Klein proved to be playing his own game? Harper would adapt accordingly.

Another player on the board, another set of motivations to map. Someone else to identify and neutralise before justice for Mike was complete.

18

EXTRACTION

The Sawmill Road warehouse occupied a decaying industrial zone at the western edge of town. Harper approached on foot, having left the Bonneville concealed behind an abandoned manufacturing plant a quarter of a mile back. He circled the perimeter, staying within the shadows of adjacent buildings, cataloguing security. Eight visible personnel – suggesting at least that many again inside the structure. Predictable patrol patterns, overlapping fields of vision, but with exploitable gaps during rotation changes.

Amateurs playing at professionalism. Dangerous, but predictable.

Most telling was the ambulance parked at the rear entrance – not a formal emergency vehicle but a repurposed van with medical insignia. Preparation for transportation rather than on-site treatment, suggesting they expected moving Ray tonight.

Harper identified three potential entry points – the main entrance (heavily guarded), the loading dock (moderate security), and a maintenance access at the north-eastern corner.

The maintenance door showed signs of infrequent use but appeared connected to the building's utility systems. The lock was commercial-grade, nothing Harper couldn't bypass given appropriate tools and time. It was the perfect approach vector. Minimal security, maximum access.

As Harper completed his reconnaissance, a vehicle approached from the direction of town; a sheriff's department cruiser moving at normal patrol speed.

Klein, right on schedule.

Harper watched from concealment as the cruiser slowed near the warehouse entrance, the deputy visibly noting the security presence before continuing along his route. Klein would complete his circuit, then likely establish an observation position with a clear view of the warehouse entrances, waiting for a sign to trigger his completely unconnected return.

Harper considered his options. Direct confrontation would create unnecessary risk. Better to manipulate the environment, create confusion that could be exploited. His military training provided multiple approaches for a lone operator to disrupt organised security with minimal resources; the communication system presented a vulnerability – standard commercial equipment likely susceptible to basic interference. The electrical supply provided another opportunity – the building drew power from a commercial transformer at the property's edge, with no visible backup generator. And the ambulance itself? Well, its presence suggested imminent transport, creating a potential diversion if properly leveraged.

Harper moved through the abandoned industrial area surrounding the warehouse, scavenging materials from the detritus of forgotten businesses, amused at the fact that, for an organisation that loved to spend most of their time in SUVs following strangers, their own surveillance was worth crap. From a collapsed maintenance shed, he recovered a length of copper wire, likely stripped from the building during its abandonment. Behind a rusted dumpster, he found a discarded car battery – not ideal, but sufficient for what he needed. His trusty *MacGyver* pocketknife provided the means to fashion these components into something useful.

Dad would have appreciated the improvisation, Harper thought. *Making something from nothing is the essence of field craft.*

His father's face flickered briefly in memory – that focused expression when crafting impromptu solutions during Harper's early childhood lessons in adaptability. The legacy of a complicated man who had prepared his son for a complicated world.

And who was never there. Don't forget that.

With materials gathered, Harper returned to the perimeter, selecting a position that combined concealment with access to the facility's communications and electrical infrastructure. The wind had picked up, bringing the scent of rain – useful cover for sound, but potentially complicating electronics.

Just before one-thirty in the morning, as the security patrol moved towards the opposite corner of the property, Harper advanced to the utility pole near the communications box. Working quickly, he jury-rigged a simple but effective disruption setup – stripped wires positioned to create a controlled short circuit in the junction box where the security team's communication lines connected. Nothing sophisticated, just fundamental electrical principles applied carefully.

For the power, he identified the main circuit breaker on the exterior wall – older model, minimal security, standard commercial installation. Harper created a simple remote trigger using one of Mike's burner phones, copper wire, and the salvaged battery – basic electronics he'd learned in field training, and similar to setups he'd used in Afghanistan when proper equipment wasn't available.

Amusingly, Mike had taught him part of this technique during a particularly difficult extraction. The memory brought a grim smile – *using his dead friend's lessons to save the man who'd murdered him.* Life's ironies never ceased.

Both setups complete, Harper withdrew to his observation position. From his jacket pocket, he pulled a small radio scanner – a basic civilian model he'd had with him in his Bonneville's pack. Most security operations used standard frequencies; finding the right channel was simply a matter of patience and methodical testing.

'... perimeter secure, no activity on the north side,' one voice reported.

'Acknowledged. East side clear,' another responded.

'Medical update?' a third voice inquired, the accent suggesting supervisory authority.

'He's stable but uncooperative. Doc says another session risks permanent damage.'

'Brennan wants results tonight, not excuses.'

'Understood. We'll proceed with alternative measures.'

Harper processed this information with clinical detachment. "Alternative measures" suggested escalation in interrogation techniques – torture – likely increasing risk to Ray's survival. As much as Ray deserved punishment for Mike's death, this wasn't justice – just different criminals extracting information through brutal methods.

Not that Harper's hands were clean. His operations in the SRR had sometimes required measures that wouldn't withstand public scrutiny. The difference was purpose – national security versus criminal enterprise. A distinction that sometimes felt thinner than he cared to admit.

Focus on the mission. Philosophical debates could wait.

As he considered next steps, a new vehicle approached from the east – another sheriff's department vehicle but not Klein's cruiser. This one proceeded directly to the warehouse entrance where security personnel admitted it without inspection or hesitation.

Harper shifted position for better visibility, recognising the silver-haired figure emerging from the vehicle. Sheriff Mills, greeted with deference by Brennan's security team. Not a surprise visit then – expected, welcomed even.

Looks like Mills definitely plays for both sides.

The sheriff entered the warehouse without hesitation, suggesting prior arrangement rather than spontaneous response. This development altered the tactical landscape significantly. If the sheriff was personally participating in an extrajudicial interrogation...

Bloody hell. Our esteemed sheriff just upgraded this from local corruption to a federal case.

Harper wondered if Klein had seen this, but didn't need to wait long for confirmation. Within minutes, the deputy's cruiser appeared at the far end of Sawmill Road, lights extinguished, moving with deliberate caution towards an observation position near an abandoned loading dock.

Through the radio scanner, Harper monitored internal communications:

'Sheriff's with the prisoner now. Says he wants ten minutes alone.'

'Understood. We'll maintain perimeter security.'

Harper moved silently to a position where he could observe Klein's vehicle. The deputy had established surveillance, his department-issued camera likely documenting arrivals and departures – creating an official record that could potentially implicate Mills. Klein's apparent commitment to documenting his superior's misconduct seemed genuine. Another point suggesting the deputy's vendetta against Mills wasn't merely performance.

Time to accelerate events and give him a reason to enter.

Harper activated the home-made communications disruptor, the small device creating a controlled short circuit in the junction box. A massive shower of sparks erupted, visible even from his position, as cascading technical failures rippled through Brennan's security system. Radio communications dissolved into static screeches, surveillance cameras flickered off, and the patrol patterns immediately deteriorated as guards attempted to compensate for lost awareness.

Even with the power back up, until they found the source of the problem, they weren't speaking to each other any time soon.

'Comms down,' a crackled voice reported through Harper's scanner as he hurried from the location, the signal breaking up. *'Possible... interference... check backup systems...'*

The resulting confusion provided Klein with the pretence he needed – a law enforcement officer observing what appeared to be a security incident, potentially a fire hazard at a facility where he happened to be passing, conducting his nightly routine patrol.

Perfect justification for official intervention.

Harper watched as the deputy activated his cruiser's emergency lights, approaching the main entrance with official purpose rather than covert observation. Klein's timing was impeccable, and exactly what the situation demanded. The deputy knew his role and played it well. Harper couldn't help but appreciate competence, regardless of underlying motivations.

As the confrontation unfolded at the main entrance, Harper circled to the north-eastern utility door. The security disruption had created opportunity – personnel focused on the deputy's unexpected arrival, communication systems compromised, attention divided. The lock yielded to Harper's pick with minimal resistance, allowing silent entry to what proved to be a maintenance corridor. The subdued lighting provided just enough illumination to navigate, casting sharp shadows across exposed piping and electrical conduits. Harper moved quietly, following the sounds of agitated conversation, shouting now the radios weren't working.

'... deputy insisting on interior inspection... possible gas leak reported, saw sparks and an explosion as he was driving past...'

'Stall him. Get Mercer out here to handle it.'

'Sheriff wants to know what's happening.'

'Tell him we've got a situation at the front. Keep him and the package secure until we sort this out.'

Harper followed the voices down the corridor until he reached a junction opening onto the main warehouse floor. From this vantage point, he could observe most of the interior – stacked crates creating a maze of temporary walls, a central area cleared for operational purposes and at the far end, a partitioned section with portable lighting suggesting temporary interrogation setup.

The electrical disruptor was Harper's next play – activating it would plunge the facility into darkness except for emergency backup lighting, creating maximum confusion while preserving minimum visibility for those who anticipated the effect.

Harper waited for the optimal moment, watching until Klein's voice became audible from the main entrance, the deputy now inside the warehouse perimeter. Harper activated the electrical disruptor, dialling the number that triggered the remote device burner.

Instantly, the warehouse plunged into near-darkness, emergency lights casting pale blue illumination across the concrete floor. Security personnel reacted with predictable confusion – weapons drawn, positions compromised, discipline deteriorating as conflicting orders were shouted across the space.

From his position, Harper could see Klein now, using the disruption exactly as intended – maintaining official composure while pushing to advance deeper into the facility under the pretence of safety concerns, his badge and uniform providing authority that the confused security personnel hesitated to challenge directly.

Harper advanced ahead of Klein's path, using the stacked crates as concealment, maintaining position to intervene if necessary. Through gaps in the makeshift walls, he caught glimpses of the interrogation area – medical equipment, restraint chair and Sheriff Mills standing over what appeared to be Ray Halvorsen's slumped form.

The scene confirmed Harper's worst suspicions – Mills actively participating in Ray's interrogation, far beyond what any legitimate law enforcement procedure would permit and probably telling him what to say to save his life. The evidence was damning, especially with Klein's body camera presumably recording everything, creating an evidence chain that would be difficult to suppress, even for someone with Whitcomb's connections.

'Sheriff?' Klein's voice carried across the warehouse floor; professional surprise evident in his tone. 'Wasn't expecting to find you here, sir.'

Mills turned sharply, his expression shifting from irritation to calculated control as he recognised his deputy.

'Klein. What the hell are you doing here?'

'Responding to reports of suspicious activity, sir. Saw an explosion of sparks as I was passing, which necessitated full facility search for public safety protocols,' Klein's explanation was flawless, his presence now officially justified through multiple procedural requirements.

'This is a private matter,' Mills replied, gesturing towards Ray's battered form. 'Department business.'

'In an unsecured facility, without backup, and with no medical personnel present?' Klein's tone remained respectful but his implications were clear. 'Interesting approach to official interrogation, sir.'

The confrontation unfolded exactly as expected – Klein establishing jurisdictional authority while documenting Mills' involvement, the sheriff attempting to maintain control of a rapidly deteriorating situation.

'Ray Halvorsen,' Klein continued, approaching the restraint chair. 'Subject of an active murder investigation. I've been looking for him since his release earlier today.'

'I'm handling that investigation personally now,' Mills countered, his authority increasingly undermined by the circumstances.

'With respect, sir, he was released through due process. I'd need to see official paperwork to explain why he's here... and in such a state.'

Mills hesitated; calculations visible in his expression as he weighed increasingly limited options.

'I have no idea of the state,' Mills said, his tone suggesting he was already constructing plausible deniability. 'Brennan's men found him here. They called me in, knowing I'm unbiased in the matter. Someone has been torturing Ray Halvorsen – maybe that newcomer friend of Sarah Colton, as he's been sniffing around the garage. Maybe he brought Halvorsen here, and then ran when Brennan's men found him?'

'And you didn't call it in because…'

'Because like you, I'm worried about snitches in the department,' the sheriff finally said, stepping aside to allow Klein access to Ray. 'But this remains department business, Klein. I called the ambulance outside to get him somewhere safe, and Brennan's men are assisting.'

Harper had to admire the sheriff's quick thinking – constructing a narrative that, while implausible under scrutiny, provided just enough cover to maintain appearances, blaming the outsider for the actions of Brennan's men. Mills was attempting to reframe his participation as investigation rather than collaboration, a distinction that might not hold up legally but could create enough doubt to complicate prosecution.

Mills straightened, adjusting his uniform with authority.

'I expect a full briefing on your investigation first thing tomorrow. You can deal with this now.'

'Of course, sir. By the book.' Klein's emphasis on procedure carried subtle weight as he moved to secure Ray, mindful of the prisoner's obvious injuries.

Harper withdrew as the scenario resolved, retracing his path through the maintenance corridor while security personnel remained focused on the central confrontation. His direct involvement was no longer necessary – Klein had established legal custody of Ray, documented Mills' questionable presence and created an evidence chain that would withstand initial scrutiny.

Though Harper noted Mills hadn't actually been seen actively interrogating Ray – a small but potentially significant gap in the evidence. The sheriff had room to claim he'd just arrived, was assessing the situation.

Outside, Harper moved to his observation position, watching as Klein emerged from the warehouse with Ray supported between himself and a reluctant security officer. The deputy secured his prisoner in the ambulance before exchanging last words with the facility supervisor – maintaining the official narrative of responding to a potential safety hazard.

As Klein's cruiser and the ambulance departed, Harper noted the arrival of additional vehicles at the warehouse perimeter – reinforcements responding to the security breach, but too late to prevent the extraction of their prisoner.

Harper moved with increased caution back to the Bonneville. The night had grown colder; the wind carrying the scent of approaching rain. His injuries protested each movement, the reopened shoulder wound a persistent reminder of physical vulnerability despite tactical success.

The motorcycle started silently as Harper navigated back roads away from Brennan's territory, monitoring for pursuit that never materialised. By three in the morning, Harper had returned to his hotel room, secured his equipment and treated the minor abrasions reopened during the operation.

His phone vibrated with an incoming message from Klein:

> Package secured. Official custody, medical treatment documented. Evidence chain intact. Mills potentially compromised beyond recovery. Meeting tomorrow?

Harper replied with a single word:

> Affirmative

Justice for Mike Colton was proceeding. Ray would face legal consequences for his actions and, seeing his options outside of this involved torture and death, would likely be screaming for witness relocation right now. Mills would find his authority undermined by documented misconduct. Both criminal organisations were destabilising as planned, their previously secure operations compromised by manufactured suspicion and escalating conflict.

Harper checked his weapon and secured his equipment, mind already mapping tomorrow's approach. Blüdridge's criminal equilibrium was collapsing precisely as designed.

He just couldn't shake the feeling he was missing something.

19

FIRST BLOOD

HARPER STOOD AT HIS HOTEL WINDOW, WATCHING TENSIONS boil over in Blüdridge. A plume of smoke rose from the eastern edge of town where a storage shed had caught fire. Near the main square, a crowd had gathered, their raised voices carrying even at this distance. On the western approach, flashing lights marked where deputies had established a roadblock.

The inevitable result. Pressure with purpose.

His coffee grew cold as he catalogued his injuries. The shoulder wound had finally stopped bleeding, but the bruised ribs protested with each deep breath, the graze on his arm bandaged and throbbing silently.

The price of progress, he supposed.

Harper tucked the 9mm Hellcat into his waistband, hiding it under his shirt, and headed downstairs.

THE MORNING STREETS HUMMED WITH NERVOUS ENERGY – people hurried with heads down, no lingering, no casual conversation. At the Blood Ridge Retreat, the usual morning crowd had thinned, but those present sat in tight clusters, voices low but heated. Harper noticed several tables where customers were comparing notes and marking locations on town maps – not frightened refugees but citizens planning.

Joy moved between these gatherings; her efficiency tempered by purpose. She wasn't just serving breakfast but connecting people.

'The Mendez family needs help boarding windows if anyone's heading west,' she told one table, before turning to another. 'Tom's offering his truck to move supplies to Father Jonathan's church. He's opened it as a shelter.'

She spotted Harper and approached, coffeepot in hand.

'Your usual booth's open,' she said, nodding towards the back. 'Though nothing else is usual today.'

Harper slid into the booth, accepting the coffee, noting the glares that came his way as he did so. It was expected; they knew much of this was because of his actions. *He'd have to fix that.*

'Looks bad out there.'

'Bad is relative,' Joy replied, glancing towards a table where the hardware store owner was deep in conversation with three other men. 'Some folks are finally remembering this town belongs to them, not Daggett or Brennan. Most of them, including us, pay into the "town fund".'

'Protection?'

'As I said, it's a "town fund",' Joy said humourlessly. 'We wouldn't dare call it anything else.'

Harper remembered back to the man who arrived earlier

that morning, realising how wrong he'd been the first time he'd seen his conversation with Joy.

You can't live hand to mouth when someone takes it before your hand reaches your mouth.

'You should consider closing,' Harper suggested. 'Things might get worse before they improve.'

Joy's eyes hardened.

'This diner's fed this town through floods, blizzards, and the riots in '89,' she snapped. 'These gangsters don't scare me, and from what I'm hearing, they're not scaring a lot of others any more either.'

As she spoke, the door opened and the man Harper recognised from earlier that week entered, still wearing the leather bomber jacket. The conversation died as heads turned. Joy straightened; coffee pot held like a weapon.

'We're closed to your type, Mister Wilson,' she said, voice carrying through the silence. 'Take your business elsewhere.'

The man's hand drifted towards his jacket, but he froze as every customer in the diner shifted – subtle movements that collectively signalled clear warning.

Outnumbered and suddenly uncertain, he backed towards the door.

'Town fund payment's due tomorrow, Joy,' he said with more than a little bravado, trying to maintain authority. 'The boss won't forget.'

'Neither will we,' called the hardware store owner, standing now. 'You go tell Victor Daggett his payments are finished. All of them.'

Wilson's face darkened, but he left without further comment. As the door closed behind him, the diner remained quiet for a moment before conversation resumed with fresh energy. Harper caught fragments – "neighbourhood watch" and "safe houses" and "time to push back".

Joy returned to his table.

'See what I mean? Town's finally waking up.'

'Dangerous time to pick a fight,' Harper observed,

'More dangerous to keep taking it,' Joy countered. 'Mike Colton wasn't the first to die in this town. He was just the one that finally made people question why.'

Harper nodded and sipped at his coffee as Deputy Klein's cruiser pulled up outside, the deputy looking grim as he entered, scanning the diner before spotting Harper. Conversation quieted again, but with less hostility than for Wilson – more cautious assessment than outright rejection.

Klein slid into the booth across from Harper.

'Ray's talking, but hedging. Says he was following orders when he sabotaged the lift but won't name names.'

'He's playing for a deal,' Harper suggested, studying Klein's face. The deputy looked genuinely frustrated, but something about his eyes – too focused, too deliberate in their avoidance of certain tables – raised Harper's instincts.

'Exactly,' Klein agreed. 'Sheriff Mills is handling it personally now, which makes me wonder if Ray knows something about him too.'

'You think Mills is involved.'

'I think everyone with power in this town has dirt on their hands,' Klein replied, voice lowered. 'Including the sheriff. No... *especially* the sheriff.'

Outside, raised voices drew their attention. Through the window, Harper could see a confrontation developing – Brennan's men at one end of the street, Daggett's at the other, townsfolk caught between.

'Damn it,' Klein muttered, already standing. 'This is exactly what we don't need.'

Harper, aware the comment was more an accusation at his tactics than a statement of the current state of affairs kept quiet and followed him outside, where the situation was deteriorating rapidly. Six men from each faction faced off across Main Street, hands near concealed weapons. A woman with a stroller found herself in the middle, frozen in fear.

Klein moved immediately, positioning himself between the groups, badge visible.

'Come on guys, this ends now,' he called, voice carrying authority. 'Take your personal beefs somewhere else.'

'This ain't personal, deputy,' one of Brennan's men replied. 'This is business. That side of the street belongs to Mister Brennan now.'

'Like hell it does,' challenged a Daggett enforcer. 'Your boss knows the boundaries.'

'Boundaries have changed, or haven't you been paying attention?'

As the men argued, the woman with the stroller tried to move, drawing attention from both sides. Klein motioned to Harper, who understood immediately – *get the civilian clear while Klein maintained the buffer.*

Harper moved casually but purposefully, reaching for the woman and guiding her towards the diner, maintaining his body as a shield. As they reached safety, a bottle shattered in the street behind them, thrown from one side or the other.

Klein's hand moved to his weapon.

'Next person who throws anything gets arrested. Everyone else gets five seconds to disperse before I call for backup.'

The tension held; a rubber band stretched to breaking. Then, surprisingly, from behind Harper, Jenkins, the hardware store owner emerged from the diner, followed by several others.

'You heard the deputy,' he called, standing beside Klein. 'This is our street. All of you – Daggett's men, Brennan's – you're not welcome here any more, and you can all piss right off back to where you came from.'

More townspeople appeared from neighbouring shops. Nothing coordinated, nothing planned, just individuals making individual choices that collectively became something more. Outgunned by this unexpected resistance, both factions retreated – Daggett's men east, Brennan's west – leaving an uneasy peace in their wake.

Klein exhaled slowly as the street cleared.

'That could have gone differently.'

'Town's changing,' Harper observed.

'For better or worse remains to be seen,' Klein replied, watching the hardware store owner organising the impromptu civilian patrol. 'Listen, I'm headed back to the station to press Ray harder. You want to meet later? Compare notes?'

'Call me when you're free,' Harper agreed, noticing how Klein seemed genuinely relieved by the peaceful resolution.

Harper returned to the diner, more to observe the surrounding people than eat, but paused as his burner phone vibrated with a text. Unknown number, but the content identified the sender:

> Need to talk. Warehouse at Sawmill Road.
> One hour. Come alone. – MD

Harper considered the invitation. Mitchell hadn't been with his father's men in the street confrontation – interesting in itself. A meeting carried obvious risks, but also potential information value.

He finished his coffee, left payment on the table, and walked back to the inn and his motorcycle, noting how the town had transformed overnight. Townsfolk stood at corners where thugs had previously loitered. Shops remained open despite tensions. Minor acts of resistance rippling outward.

This wasn't part of Harper's plan, but it might work to his advantage.

The Bonneville roared to life, and Harper rode towards the eastern edge of town, taking note of the altered landscape. Two more roadblocks manned by citizens rather than criminals. The church with doors open, people carrying supplies inside. The mechanics from Colton's garage – Luis and Chris – helping board windows at the pharmacy.

These weren't organised resistance fighters, they were simply ordinary people finally pushed too far. But that made them unpredictable – to both the criminals and to Harper himself.

He reached the warehouse on Sawmill Road forty minutes later, approaching cautiously. The building stood alone in an industrial zone, windows dark, no vehicles visible except a black Audi parked near the loading dock. Harper circled once, checking for surveillance or ambush points before approaching the side entrance.

The door opened before he reached it, a Daggett guard gesturing him inside.

Inside, Mitchell Daggett waited in what had once been a manager's office, now serving as an improvised and off-grid command centre, from the looks of things. Maps covered one wall, surveillance photos another. Mitchell himself stood studying a laptop screen, looking up as Harper entered.

'Harper,' he greeted, voice neutral. 'Appreciate you coming.'

'Your invitation was compelling,' Harper replied, remaining near the door. 'Have to ask though, who gave you my number?'

Mitchell smiled but said nothing. Sighing, Harper looked around.

'What's so urgent?'

Mitchell gestured towards the window, where smoke from the morning's confrontation was still visible on the horizon.

'This situation is escalating beyond anyone's control,' he said. 'My father's lost perspective. Brennan's pushing into territories he's never challenged before. And the townspeople are becoming unpredictable. Almost like someone's deliberately destabilising the careful balance of power.'

Mitchell smiled thinly.

'Someone with tactical training and a personal vendetta, perhaps?'

'I'm just here for justice for Mike Colton.'

'And creating chaos to expose his killers.' Mitchell turned from the window. 'I understand the approach. It's effective. But there are factors you may not have considered.'

'Such as?'

'Judge Whitcomb,' Mitchell replied, retrieving a folder from his desk. 'The man behind both my father and Brennan. The one who's been using their rivalry to maintain his own power for almost five years.'

Harper studied Mitchell's face, looking for deception but finding only calculated assessment.

'Whitcomb's just a county judge,' he said.

'A county judge with federal connections,' Mitchell corrected, opening the folder to reveal photographs of Whitcomb with men in expensive suits. 'His brother-in-law sits on the appropriations committee overseeing Justice Department funding. His nephew works for the DEA's eastern operations.'

Harper examined the photographs, recognising the implications immediately.

'He ensures certain investigations never gain traction,' Mitchell continued. 'In return, his family prospers. Let's call it a "consultancy fee". The arrangement has worked smoothly for years.'

'Until Mike discovered something that threatened it.'

'Precisely.' Mitchell spread additional documents across the desk: meeting minutes, financial records, surveillance photos. 'Mike found evidence connecting Whitcomb to operations beyond Blüdridge. Specifically, military-grade hardware moving east, high-grade fentanyl moving west. The kind of operation that attracts federal attention regardless of political connections.'

Harper considered this information. It aligned with what he'd pieced together himself, but the weapons aspect was new... and concerning.

'How did you get this?'

'Off Mike's laptop, in his house—' Mitchell held a hand up. 'I wasn't lying when I said we didn't break in. But whoever did, wanted us to have this. Wanted me to see what my father was doing, and which bastards he was playing with.'

'Whitcomb?'

'I don't give a damn about the judge!' Mitchell snapped back. 'I mean that snake Sean Brennan. I've wanted him dead since he arrived, but no, I'm told to "stand down" and be a good goddamned soldier for my daddy.'

'Why the hatred?' Harper asked. 'Surely this isn't about the history?'

'It's about bloody Moira!' Mitchell snapped. 'We loved each other. Kept it secret for a year. Then her cousin Sean, he finds out when one of her friends accidentally gives it up, beats the living shit out of her and sends her away to Ireland. I don't even know if she's alive or not, nobody's been able to find her.'

'I can't see Brennan killing family...' Harper trailed off. 'What don't I know?'

'Moira was working for me, too,' Mitchell admitted. 'An asset. She hated the family, wanted out. I was that escape. She'd given us a ton of intel on his business dealings, and we were using it to break him down.'

Harper said nothing, but now he understood. If Moira Brennan had been giving Sean's biggest rival the keys to his kingdom while sleeping with him, this wasn't as *Romeo And Juliet* as first imagined. And Moira was likely missing because she was in a shallow grave somewhere.

'Sounds like whoever sent you the information knew this, and wanted you and Brennan at each other's throats,' Harper mused. 'Any idea who?'

'Unknown,' Mitchell shrugged. 'Dead drop, middle of the night. Never asked, either. Why demand the name of your guardian angel when they're doing their job so well?'

Harper stretched, regretting it instantly.

'Why tell me this?' he asked. 'What's your angle?'

Mitchell met his gaze directly.

'My father's response to the current situation has been...

disproportionate. Burning his own town to maintain control. I prefer more surgical approaches.'

'You want to replace him.'

'I want to modernise operations,' Mitchell corrected. 'My father's methods belong to another era. Violence attracts attention. Attention brings investigations. Investigations threaten everything. I mean, come on, guns? You can get them on the internet now, bigger and badder than the shit my father peddles.'

'So, drugs are okay, but guns are a no-no.'

'You say it like I'm still killing people.'

'Just saying how noble of you to consider the town's welfare,' Harper said, sarcasm obvious.

'Business pragmatism,' Mitchell replied without offence. 'Destroying your own market is a poor strategy. But that's beside the point. What matters now is Whitcomb. He's planning to escape while everyone else burns.'

This caught Harper's interest.

'Escape?'

'He's in court today, cleaning up his shit, but once he ties up loose ends like Halvorsen, he'll be off until we kill each other, use the war as a way to "scorch earth" the whole damn place. Heard there's a helicopter extraction from the courthouse roof tonight at eleven. Mills will go with him, as Whitcomb needs his sycophants. They're destroying evidence as we speak – anything connecting them to operations here.'

Harper processed this. If true, it represented a critical timeline. Whitcomb escaping would mean justice for Mike slipping away permanently. And that Whitcomb saw Ray as a "loose end" meant Ray Halvorsen, and anyone near him... was a target.

'Why should I believe you?' he asked.

'Because I'm offering proof,' Mitchell replied, handing over the folder. 'Everything connecting Whitcomb to the operation on the ridge, including his role in ordering Mike's death.'

Harper took the folder, scepticism evident. 'Your own involvement conveniently absent, I assume?'

'I play the long game, Harper. Unlike my father, and unlike that scumbag Brennan, I understand adaptation. The town's changing. I intend to change with it.'

'Into what? A legitimate business owner?' Harper scoffed. 'I just watched as your own man was hounded out of the diner. Something about "town funds".'

'My father's man, not mine. And my father's bullshit small-time-thinking extortion.'

'Fair point,' Harper conceded.

'The line between legitimate and illegitimate is thinner than most realise,' Mitchell continued. 'Just ask the bankers who launder billions but never see the inside of a cell.'

He raised his wrist, showing what looked to be a Rolex.

'All watches have the same time, no matter how expensive,' he said. 'People always need the time but will always covet richer items. It's just human nature.'

Harper resisted the urge to comment on this flawed anecdote as he tucked the folder into his jacket.

'What happened downtown this morning wasn't planned by either my father or Brennan. The townspeople forcing both sides to retreat? That's new. Unexpected. It changes calculations.' Mitchell moved to the window again, watching as a patrol car passed on the main road. 'My father sees only threats to eliminate and product to move. Brennan sees only territory to claim. Neither recognises the actual danger – a community finally deciding it's had enough.'

Harper couldn't argue with this assessment.

'What do you want from me?' he asked directly.

'Focus your considerable disruptive talents on Whitcomb,' Mitchell replied. 'That serves both our interests. Justice for your friend, and a power vacuum I can manage more effectively, and more peacefully, than my father. All I ask is you give him the day, let him plait the rope you hang him with.'

'And if I refuse?'

'Then we each proceed according to our own priorities,' Mitchell said with a shrug. 'But consider this – in the conflict to come, you'll need allies. My father and Sean Brennan are accelerating towards mutual destruction – Sean faster if I get my hands on him. I'm offering a third option.'

Harper nodded once; decision made.

'I'll consider it. One thing, though. Sarah Colton and her son. Whatever happens next, they remain untouched. Agreed?'

'They were never targets,' Mitchell said. 'But they could become collateral damage when institutions collapse. I've given orders they're to be protected if necessary.'

Harper nodded again, understanding the unexpected gesture from a man whose business usually disregarded such distinctions.

And with that, the meeting was over.

OUTSIDE, HARPER MOUNTED THE BONNEVILLE AND RODE BACK towards town. It was now early afternoon, and the pattern of resistance he'd noticed earlier had spread. Nothing coordinated yet, nothing powerful enough to truly challenge either

Daggett or Brennan individually but collectively creating a third force neither crime boss had expected.

Mike would have been proud, Harper thought. *His death becoming the catalyst for the town's awakening.*

A complete picture was forming, but with pieces still missing. The SD card from the garage remained inaccessible now with Jake and Sarah, who were safely away from Blüdridge. But if Whitcomb escaped tonight, with evidence destroyed and Mills covering his tracks, even that card might not be enough to bring justice.

His phone vibrated with a text from Klein:

Ray lawyered up. Release pending. Need to talk. Meet me at the station in an hour.

Harper replied.

On my way.

Distant sirens suggested another confrontation somewhere in town. The pressure he'd applied was creating unpredictable results now, forces moving beyond anyone's control – not Daggett's, not Brennan's, and perhaps not even his own.

Harper felt the first drops of rain against his face as storm clouds gathered above Blüdridge. *Appropriate weather,* he thought, for a town caught between what it had been and what it might become.

The endgame had begun.

20

HOMECOMING

HARPER ARRIVED AT THE SHERIFF'S STATION TEN MINUTES early, deliberately allowing himself time to assess the situation before meeting Klein. The building stood as an island of relative calm amidst Blüdridge's growing chaos – but inside it was a different story; three deputies manned the front desk, phones ringing constantly as reports of disturbances flooded in. Through the front windows, Harper could see smoke rising from somewhere on the town's eastern side, marking where confrontations had erupted into open violence.

Inside, he approached the front desk, where Doris – the heavyset receptionist he'd met during his previous visit – greeted him with a nod of recognition.

'Back again, Mister Harper,' she said. 'Here for Deputy Klein, I expect?'

'Right on the money,' Harper replied with an amiable smile. 'He's expecting me.'

'He's just finishing some paperwork,' she said, reaching for the phone. 'I'll let him know you're here. Coffee while you wait? You look like you could use it.'

'Wouldn't say no,' Harper admitted.

As Doris made the call, Harper noted the subtly increased security throughout the station – deputies checking weapons, bulletproof vests stacked near the rear exit, preparations for what everyone now recognised as inevitable escalation.

'Deputy Patterson will take you to a waiting room,' she said, walking over with a cup of coffee. Harper took it and nodded to a young woman waiting patiently by a door.

Lead the way,' he said, taking a sip.

THE WAITING ROOM WAS STANDARD SMALL-TOWN FARE OF BEIGE walls, a metal table, two chairs, and wallpaper that likely hadn't been upgraded since the nineties. Frowning, Harper took a seat, his cracked ribs protesting with a dull throb that had become his constant companion.

'Why here?' he asked.

'Deputy Klein said he needed you away from others,' Patterson shrugged. 'Sorry, all I know. But if you're to blame for the chaos outside, it's best you're in here anyway, for your own good.'

With this said, she left Harper alone. But, to prove it wasn't as bad as he thought, she left the door open.

Klein entered a few minutes later, shortly before three in the afternoon according to the clock on the wall, carrying a manila folder and two coffee mugs, sliding one towards Harper as he settled into the chair opposite.

'Sorry to keep you waiting,' Klein said, his expression showing the strain of the day's events. 'Town's coming apart at the seams.'

'So I've noticed,' Harper replied, nodding his thanks for the coffee but leaving it untouched. Klein looked up, saw Harper's already half-drunk cup and nodded to himself as he opened the folder, spreading photographs across the table – images of the garage's north-east bay, the modified vehicles, documentation of customisations.

'Look, I'm going to be blunt, Harper. Outside? It's a shit-storm. I'm trying to build a legitimate case here. One that'll stand up in court when this is all over.'

'And I'm trying to get justice for Mike,' Harper replied, unsure where this was going. 'Sometimes that means working outside official channels.'

'That creates problems for me,' Klein said, leaning forward. 'I can't use illegally obtained evidence.'

Harper studied Klein, reconsidering their relationship.

'Are you planning to arrest me, deputy?'

'No. But I needed you to understand the position you're putting me in,' Klein sighed, rubbing his face. 'We want the same thing, but we're going about it very differently.'

'Ray's situation?' Harper asked.

'Complicated,' Klein spoke slowly. 'He lawyered up faster than expected. Started making noises about illegal detention, procedural violations.'

'Mills intervened?'

'Eventually,' Klein confirmed. 'Ordered Ray's release despite my objections. Said we didn't have enough to hold him. Just like before.'

'Convenient.'

'Isn't it?' Klein's tone carried genuine frustration. 'He'll be back on the streets within hours.'

Harper maintained a neutral expression despite the information's significance. If Ray was being released, it suggested the power structure was closing ranks, protecting its assets.

'And the evidence from the garage? The logs showing the lift maintenance?'

'Officially logged into evidence, but we'd need a handwriting expert to confirm if it's a forgery or not.'

'Ray forged them,' Harper replied coldly. 'You know that, I know that.'

'What I know is that Ray was playing both sides, scheduling their work to avoid overlap. Smart system until someone caught on.'

'Mike,' Harper said, pausing as his phone vibrated in his pocket. He checked the display – it was Sarah's number. He showed it to Klein.

'I should take this,' he said, rising from his chair.

'Speakerphone,' Klein nodded, gathering the photographs back into the folder. 'She might need police help, rather than a vigilante.'

Harper answered, immediately setting the phone to speaker so Klein could help if needed.

'Sarah?'

'Harper,' Sarah's voice carried unmistakable tension even through the phone's small speaker. 'It's Jake. He's gone.'

'Gone where?' Harper asked, meeting Klein's concerned gaze across the table.

'I don't know,' Sarah replied, her voice tight with controlled fear. 'He said he was going to try more password combinations on the SD card. I fell asleep, and when I woke up, he'd left a note saying he was going back to the house to look for more of Mike's papers.'

'How long has he been gone?' Harper asked, checking his watch.

'At least two hours. I've been trying his phone, but it's going straight to voicemail.'

'What SD card?' Klein asked, frowning at this fresh development.

'One from the garage, a camera hidden in the north-east bay,' Harper explained. 'It's recorded everything in there, possibly for weeks – but it's encrypted. Jake was trying to get into it.'

'Christ, that'd break this whole damn thing wide open,' Klein was already on his feet, concern clear in his expression as he leaned closer to the speaker.

'Mrs. Colton, it's Deputy Klein,' he said. 'We'll find Jake. Where are you staying? I can send officers to your location while Harper looks for your son.'

'Ridgeline Motel outside Cumberland, towards Hagerstown, Room twelve,' Sarah replied. 'But Jake's the priority right now, not me.'

Klein immediately spoke into his radio, ordering a patrol car to the motel. His efficiency was reassuring – whatever else was happening in Blüdridge, at least Sarah would have protection.

'I'll handle Jake,' Harper said, already moving towards the door. 'Keep your men back from the house. Any official presence will just attract attention we don't need.'

'Be careful,' Klein called after him. 'And Harper – we're not done with this conversation. When you've got the boy, we need to finish what we started. Get me that SD card. We can provide better cyber-experts at a state level than a teenage boy.'

Harper acknowledged with a nod, then left the station, moving quickly towards where he'd parked the Bonneville. Jake had gone back to the house looking for password hints, which was a brave but dangerous move given the tensions now gripping Blüdridge.

As he started the engine, Harper recalled Jake's determination to crack the SD card's protection. The password sheets they already had contained multiple combinations – lines of letters, numbers and symbols that Jake had been systematically testing.

But what if the answer had been there all along, hiding in plain sight?

HE PARKED THE BONNEVILLE TWO BLOCKS FROM THE COLTON house, approaching on foot through neighbouring yards and side passages. From a position of concealment, Harper observed the residence carefully. No vehicles visible on the street, no obvious watchers, but that meant little. Professional surveillance would maintain distance and disguise.

The house appeared undisturbed – curtains drawn as they'd left them, doors presumably locked. Harper circled the property once, checking for signs of forced entry or surveillance equipment. Finding none, he approached the rear door, the one they'd used during their hasty departure earlier.

He was about to attempt entry when he detected movement inside – a shadow passing behind the kitchen curtain. Harper withdrew to cover, waiting. Moments later, the rear door cracked, and Jake peered out, checking the yard with caution before stepping outside with a backpack slung over one shoulder.

Harper moved quickly, covering the distance between

them in seconds. Jake started as Harper's hand caught his shoulder, then relaxed upon recognition.

'Goddamn, Harper,' he whispered, fear giving way to relief. 'You scared the hell out of me.'

'Inside,' Harper directed, guiding the boy back into the house. 'Now.'

Once the door was secured behind them, Harper turned to Jake, keeping his voice low despite the apparent absence of watchers.

'Your mother's worried sick. What the hell were you thinking?'

Jake's expression hardened.

'I need to crack the password. I needed to check Dad's office for more notes.'

'You risked your life for that?' Harper's tone was neutral but carried underlying tension. 'After everything we've done to keep you safe?'

'It's the only way to prove what happened to him,' Jake countered. 'I just need the right combination.'

'Show me what you've got,' Harper replied, relenting slightly.

Jake led him to the table and laid out the papers.

'These are all the codes dad left. I've tried dozens of combinations from these sheets. Nothing works.'

Harper examined the papers – on one, he saw lines of letters, numbers and symbols arranged in random patterns across multiple lines. Some were clearly passwords or access codes.

'What's the password format requirement?' Harper asked, studying the patterns.

'Sixteen characters,' Jake replied. 'The SD card reader

gives an error message after three failed attempts, then resets after thirty seconds. I've been trying for hours.'

'Insanity,' Harper said, looking at them.

'What?'

'Insanity is doing the same thing over and over again and expecting different results.'

'Einstein,' Jake smiled.

'No,' Harper looked up. 'It's attributed to him, but he never said it. Civil rights campaigner and writer Rita Mae Brown put it in a novel in the eighties. But what it means is that rather than trying the same thing time and time again, we need to look at the pages from a different perspective. Not individual codes or passwords, but the overall pattern.'

He continued to stare at the codes, almost begging the answer to reveal itself. His SRR training had included both cryptography and counter-intelligence – recognising when information was hidden in plain sight—

The sheet contained approximately sixteen separate lines of code when looked at together.

'Jake,' Harper said slowly, studying the patterns, 'what if it's not any one of these codes? What if it's all of them?'

Jake frowned. 'What do you mean?'

'Military technique,' Harper explained, showing the first line on each sheet. 'Your dad always believed in strength in numbers. When you need to remember a complex password but can't write it down directly, you create a key using the first letter of each line. It's called an acrostic password. First letter of each line, creating a sixteen-character sequence.'

Jake quickly grabbed a pencil, writing the first letter of each line from the first sheet.

H7D3r9#5plL6@8F1

'Let's try it,' Jake said, reaching for his laptop, but Harper placed a restraining hand on Jake's arm.

'Not here. We don't know what it'd open. If it links to a server and someone's monitoring us? We could be caught before we even read what's on it. We need to move to a more secure location, where we can see anyone coming.'

Jake hesitated, clearly eager to test the solution immediately, but nodded his agreement.

'Where?'

Harper considered their options. They needed somewhere isolated but defensible, offering privacy to examine the SD card's contents without interruption...

'The fire tower,' Jake suddenly decided. 'It's isolated, good visibility in all directions. We can see anyone approaching long before they reach us.'

Harper hadn't really spent time checking the fire tower – which meant the others spent little time there, or else he would have. So, they gathered the papers quickly, Jake stuffing them into his backpack alongside the laptop and SD card reader. Harper led the way out through the rear door, checking for watchers before guiding Jake through neighbouring yards towards where he'd left the Bonneville.

As they mounted the motorcycle, Harper felt Jake's tension – anticipation mingled with fear, the boy's grasp on Harper's jacket unconsciously tight as they rode away from the house.

HARPER TOOK A WINDING ROUTE TOWARDS THE FIRE TOWER, avoiding anywhere Daggett or Brennan's patrols might stop them. The tower stood on a wooded rise two miles outside town – a steel structure reaching above the treeline, offering unobstructed views of the surrounding countryside. Jake explained, shouting as they rode, that it had been abandoned by the forestry service years earlier, but remained structurally sound despite its neglect. By the time they arrived, with the cautious route and the constant stopping, it was almost seven in the evening.

Harper didn't ask how Jake knew this; all he remembered was his own love of climbing dangerous things as a teenager.

They climbed the metal staircase to the observation platform near the top; Harper positioned himself where he could monitor the approach path while Jake set up the laptop on a weathered desk that had once held radio equipment. With hands steadier than Harper would have expected from a teenager in these circumstances, Jake connected the SD card reader, entered the new sixteen-character sequence, and waited with visible tension as the system processed.

The screen flashed once, then after a moment of scrolling decryption code opened a directory containing video files.

'It worked,' Jake whispered, his voice catching between triumph and trepidation.

Harper moved closer, studying the file listing. Dozens of videos, each labelled with dates and locations, were organised chronologically across the past three months. Mike's documentation of whatever operation had ultimately cost him his life, taken from a hidden camera in the north-east bay.

'Look,' Harper pointed at the information. 'The files were revised up to here, which means Mike watched them. Each batch is dated on a Sunday.'

'So dad would take out the camera, check the videos and

then put the camera back up,' Jake nodded. 'But why haven't we found these on his own computer?'

'Probably because he hid them,' Harper said. 'He was probably copying them to a backup drive every Sunday and keeping that safe. But here—'

He pointed to a date approximately two weeks earlier.

'This is three days before his death,' he said. 'Chances are he never saw these. The camera was motion detected, so there's a chance whatever killed him was shown here.'

He tapped on the screen.

'That one,' he said. 'Two days before his death. Six in the evening. That has to be something off books.'

Jake selected it, and the video began playing – the timestamp indicated what Harper had suspected; early evening a couple of days before Mike's death, the garage closed for normal business.

On the screen, and slightly blocked by the ventilation grille that hid the camera, the always-locked bay door opened, and Ray entered, followed by Sheriff Mills.

'Problem?' Ray asked, moving behind his desk.

'Change of schedule,' Mills replied, remaining standing. 'Judge wants the operation accelerated. Too many variables in play.'

Ray's posture stiffened.

'What kind of acceleration?'

'Two shipments consolidated into one. Bigger payload, higher risk, bigger reward.'

'That creates logistical issues,' Ray objected, moving to the side toolbox. 'We'd need more vehicles, more drivers—'

'Already arranged,' Mills cut him off. 'Not your concern. Your job is ensuring the checkpoint remains secure.'

Ray hesitated, then nodded his acceptance.

'And Colton?'

Mills's expression hardened.

'That's why I'm here. Klein's confirmed he's been gathering evidence, taking photographs of shipments, documenting vehicle modifications for weeks now. We've been heading him off at the pass, but there's only so many passes you can head off.'

The mention of Klein sent a visible shock through Jake. Harper placed a steadying hand on the boy's shoulder, feeling the trembling beneath his palm as they continued watching.

Bastard.

'How much does he know?' Ray asked on the screen.

'Enough to create problems,' Mills replied. 'Klein says he's preparing to take everything to the FBI's field office in Baltimore. Bypass local channels entirely.'

Ray rubbed his face.

'Christ. What does the judge want done?'

There was a sound off camera, likely the door to the north-east bay opening again, and Harper tensed as on the screen Deputy Klein entered, his manner entirely different from the professional law enforcement officer Harper had come to know – colder, more calculated, without the pretence of integrity.

'The judge wants it handled clean,' Klein said, joining the conversation as if his arrival had been expected. 'Accident, not murder. Nothing that raises questions.'

Jake's breathing quickened, hands clenching into fists as he watched the conspiracy unfold on screen.

'The hydraulic lift in bay three,' Klein continued. 'You've stated it's already showing signs of stress. Catastrophic failure during routine maintenance would raise few eyebrows.'

Ray looked visibly uncomfortable.

'Mike's already logged it as faulty.'

'So, change his logs and mark it as okay,' Mills muttered. 'I'm sure you can forge more than a signature. You've been skimming long enough using his name.'

'There'd be an investigation.'

'Which Sheriff Mills here will oversee personally,' Klein assured him. 'With my assistance to ensure findings align with the official narrative.'

As Harper and Jake watched, they heard every aspect planned, and every contingency considered by Ray Halvorsen, Sheriff Mills and Deputy Klein. As the video ended, Jake remained motionless, face pale, eyes fixed on the screen where the men who'd orchestrated his father's murder had just revealed their guilt beyond any question. Harper allowed him this moment to process, respecting the weight of what they'd witnessed.

'He trusted Klein,' Jake said finally, his voice barely audible. 'Dad said he was one of the few honest cops left.'

'That made him the perfect person to betray your father,' Harper replied gently. 'The one Mike wouldn't suspect until it was too late. Mills probably set it up so all roads led to Klein *as* the only honest cop. They led him along from the start. Confirmation bias at its best.'

Jake looked up at Harper, eyes shifting from bitter anger to horror.

'Klein knows where mom is. The motel. Room twelve.'

Harper nodded, already pacing.

'Klein wanted to know what the SD card held when you mentioned it, but he probably already suspected. Chances are he's already checked everywhere else... he could even have been the one who broke into your house. Or it was Ray, realising the locks had been changed. If he thinks we have these videos, he'll make a move – either sending legitimate protection or something else. Either way, it confirms what we need to know.'

'And Mom?' Jake asked, fear returning.

'We warn her,' Harper replied, already reaching for his phone.

Jake nodded, gathering his equipment while Harper scanned the surrounding forest for any sign they'd been followed. The revelation of Klein's involvement changed everything – not just confirming a conspiracy Harper had already suspected, but revealing the deputy as an active, calculating participant in Mike's murder. But, with this, the stakes had escalated again.

Sarah's phone rang six times as they headed down the fire tower before switching to voicemail. With nothing else to do, Harper left a voicemail.

'Sarah, it's Harper. Klein's involved – he helped plan Mike's murder. Deputies at the motel aren't protection, they're containment. Don't trust them. Find a way out without being seen. We're coming.'

He tried twice more with the same result, each unanswered ring increasing his concern. He looked back at Jake but paused as he saw the knife in the boy's hand.

'What the hell?'

Jake looked up from the blade, reddening as if caught with something he shouldn't have.

'It was Dad's,' he said, holding it up, and Harper saw it was a Gerber StrongArm – compact and solid, with a stonewashed blade and a straight spine. Its handle was rubberised and textured, moulded to fit the hand, and capped with a steel pommel. The sheath was matte-black polymer, angular and utilitarian in design. The Gerbers were favoured by mechanics and engineers for their toughness, easy maintenance, and the fact they could pry, cut, or hammer without complaint.

It was also one Harper had seen clipped to Mike's hip on several occasions.

'I recognise it,' Harper said, placing it back into the sheath and returning it to Jake. 'Keep it safe for now, yeah?'

Jake nodded, placing it away in his rucksack.

'What do we do now?' he asked, his voice steadier than Harper might have expected given the circumstances.

'We do what your father would have done,' Harper replied. 'We use their system against them. Every secret, every connection, every vulnerability. We make them pay for what they've done.'

He didn't say what he truly worried for.

That Sarah Colton was now in Klein's control, and only the SD card they had would get her back, but at the cost of revealing the truth.

21

THE LONG GAME

HARPER AND JAKE STOOD AT THE BASE OF THE FIRE TOWER, Harper planning scenarios to a play he hadn't seen coming.

Bloody amateur. How did you miss this?

'Jesus,' Jake whispered, his face pale, still going over what he'd seen. 'He sat in our house. Had dinner with us. The whole time...'

Harper was already moving towards the Bonneville, his cracked ribs protesting as he mounted the motorcycle, the wound in his shoulder throbbing in time with his pulse. The injuries from his fight with Doyle were far from healed, but physical discomfort ranked low on his priorities now. He pocketed the phone, already calculating options. The Ridgeline Motel was at least an hour away by direct route, longer if they avoided main roads, which they'd need to do if Klein had alerted his deputies.

Jake climbed on behind him, clutching the backpack containing the laptop and SD card. The autumn chill had intensified with nightfall, mist gathering in low spots between the trees. Overhead, clouds obscured most stars, promising rain by morning. Harper went to kickstart the engine but then paused.

'We need help,' he said. 'Someone outside Blüdridge's system.'

'She's alone!' Jake muttered. 'We need to—'

'Klein sent deputies before I even found you, and that was over three hours back,' Harper checked his watch. 'They're likely there by now or setting up damn close. We need to think clever. What's nearby?'

'Hagerstown's about half an hour away, maybe we can call the police—'

Hagerstown.

Harper thought back to the confrontation at Terry's Auto & Gas; Terry had mentioned heading to Hagerstown to visit his sons. If he was there already, then Sarah and the approaching deputies were perhaps thirty minutes from Terry's location.

'I know someone,' Harper said, pulling his phone back out. 'Not connected to Blüdridge. Might be near your mother already.'

'Who?' The scepticism in Jake's voice was fair – trust had become a rare commodity.

'Someone who stood up against armed men to protect a woman he'd never met,' Harper replied. 'Right now, that's recommendation enough.'

Harper searched for Terry's Auto & Gas on his phone's browser, finding a business number. The answering machine provided a mobile contact.

'You've reached Terry's Auto & Gas. We're closed until next week. For emergencies, call Terry's cell at...'

Harper dialled immediately. After three rings, it was answered.

'Terry speaking.'

'Terry, it's Liam Harper. We met at your gas station last week – helped with the woman's car trouble.'

'British guy with the Triumph,' Terry replied without hesitation. 'What can I do for you?'

'Where are you?'

'I'm with my sons in Hagerstown. Why?'

'Look, I'm real sorry about this, but I need someone to check on a friend staying at the Ridgeline Motel outside Cumberland,' Harper continued. 'Room twelve. Local law enforcement is there, but they're not protecting her.'

A brief pause.

'How not-protecting are we talking?'

'The kind where they killed her husband and made it look like an accident.'

Terry's tone shifted, becoming clipped and precise.

'I can be at the motel in thirty minutes. What do you need?'

'Eyes on it, nothing more for the moment. Verify law enforcement presence and behaviour. No engagement unless absolutely necessary.' Harper kept his instructions clear and direct. 'My friend might be in immediate danger.'

'We'll head out now,' Terry replied. 'Call you when we have a visual.'

'We?'

'My sons aren't gonna let me go off and have all the fun on my own, now are they?' Terry laughed.

Harper ended the call, turning to Jake.

'Terry and his sons are on their way. We need somewhere secure for the evidence while we figure out next steps.'

Jake considered this.

'Why not stay here?'

Harper waved his phone.

'I've made four calls from it,' he said. 'If Klein's looking for us, he'll use the triangulation. Maybe we can find better coverage...'

He trailed off.

'Klein won't have *started* looking for us,' he said coldly. 'He's been playing the game since I arrived. He'll have made sure he can always find me.'

Motioning for Jake to get off the bike, he knelt beside it, carefully checking the engine, the support struts...

There.

Inconspicuous, but doing its job well, was a small tracker.

'Shit,' he said, pulling it off and holding it up to the light.

'Is that...'

'Yeah,' Harper said, mentally chiding himself. He'd known someone had been near his Bonneville when he'd been in the woods, but he hadn't considered being tracked.

All those texts asking where he was, and Klein always knew.

Bastard.

'They'll be coming fast,' he said, tossing it into the undergrowth. 'We need a new place.'

'The cabin?'

'Somewhere they won't look. Remember, Klein knows your father well.'

'Oh, yeah, right,' Jake looked sheepish at this. 'Okay, there's an abandoned forecast station on the western ridge. Dad showed it to me once. It's Government property, but since they got the new weather satellites, it's been pretty much empty. Has back access through the forest.'

'Did he ever talk about it with Klein?'

'I don't think so,' Jake shook his head. 'It was only a passing comment once.'

'Okay then,' Harper nodded. 'Show me.'

THEY RODE THROUGH BACK ROADS TOWARDS THE FORECAST station, avoiding primary routes where Klein's deputies might patrol. At one crossroads, they passed a local church where Father Jonathan directed volunteers unloading supplies from pickup trucks. The priest nodded solemnly at Harper as they passed, his expression conveying both recognition and resolve.

'People are fighting back,' Jake observed, his grip on Harper's jacket tightening slightly.

'Your father's death changed things,' Harper replied. 'Put a face on what they've been living with. Made it personal rather than abstract.'

After ten more minutes of riding, the forecast station appeared ahead – a solid concrete building perched on the ridge's western face. Its weathered exterior showed decades of neglect, but the structure remained sound, and the cold air inside smelled of dust and abandonment.

Good enough for the moment.

Hiding the Bonneville, Harper checked around the property while Jake set up the laptop on a desk that had once held radio equipment. Rain had started falling outside, drops tapping against the windows in an irregular rhythm as Jake copied the video files to a flash drive.

'Dad knew about places like this,' Jake said, working efficiently. 'Said the government never really closes anything, just puts it on standby for future use...'

He trailed off as a video appeared on the screen. It was one of the earlier videos, and it showed Mike, hard at work in the north-east bay, the motion alerting the camera. But that wasn't what stopped him; the video was Mike customising a car, making sure the secret compartment opened while one of Daggett's men, the one Harper had seen the first day at the funeral beside Victor himself, watched on.

'Don't be hard on him,' Harper said softly. 'He was in a tough situation.'

Jake, silently and with no visible expression, nodded. The boy had changed in the days since Harper had arrived for Mike's funeral. The initial shock and grief remained, but beneath it, something hardened had formed – determination, purpose, a focused anger that reminded Harper of Mike's response to injustice.

Harper examined the station's interior over the next few minutes, if only for something to do while waiting. The main room offered good visibility through windows facing all directions. A small generator in a side room might provide power if needed. Communications equipment was outdated but potentially useful in emergency and remained intact under dust covers.

'Storage lockers still have emergency supplies,' Jake called from a back room. 'First aid kits, water purification tablets. Dad was right – they kept everything ready.'

Harper's phone rang – Terry's number.

'Go ahead,' he answered without preamble.

'We have eyes on the motel,' Terry reported. Rain was audible in the background, suggesting he was positioned outside. 'Two deputies in a cruiser across the lot watching the room.'

'Any visual on my friend inside?'

'Lights on, curtains drawn. Can't confirm occupancy.

We're positioned on the hillside behind with limited visual through the curtain gaps.'

Harper processed this information, scenarios branching in his mind.

'Any chance of approaching without being spotted?'

'Motel's built against the hill. Service corridor at the back connects to all rooms. My younger son's checking it now. Might be a way in without crossing their line of sight.'

'Can you maintain position?'

'I've got the compound bow if things get dicey. Older son's positioned with a clear view of both deputies.'

Harper checked his watch – it was heading into evening now. If Klein planned to move against Sarah, it would likely be soon, while darkness provided cover but before civilian traffic increased as bars closed.

'Hold position but don't engage. I'll call with next steps. If something changes before then, use your judgment.'

'Will do,' Terry replied. 'One more thing – when we walked past, pretending to check out the vending machines, we overheard radio chatter from the deputies. Mentioned something about an "extraction" being on schedule. Referenced someone called "The Judge" leaving.'

Bollocks. Whitcomb's escape plan at eleven. He'd been so busy sorting out Jake and Sarah, he'd forgotten what Mitchell Daggett had told him. The window for stopping him was closing faster than expected.

'Thanks. Be careful.'

Harper ended the call, looking towards Jake who watched expectantly from the computer.

'They're definitely watching your mother. Not standard protection – looks like surveillance waiting for something. Or someone.'

Jake paled slightly.

'Us?'

'Possibly,' Harper admitted. 'Or waiting for orders from Klein about what to do with her. Either way, we need to move her before they decide.'

'Is Terry reliable?'

'Three armed men against two deputies who don't know they're being watched. Good odds,' Harper replied. 'Also, Klein will want her contained but not taken. Not until he knows he's compromised. They won't hassle her until he tells them to. But we need to coordinate.'

'What about this?' Jake gestured towards the computer and the evidence they'd collected. 'If Klein's involved, who do we take it to?'

'That's our other problem,' Harper said. 'Whitcomb's looking to fly out in the next couple of hours and find a bolt-hole to hide until this blows over. We need to split up; your mother needs immediate extraction, and Whitcomb needs to be stopped before he disappears.'

'I'm going for Mom,' Jake stated without hesitation. 'They don't know her, and maybe if the deputies see me, I could lead them away while your friend gets her out. I'll use the dirt bike I rode here on. I hid it near the Mendez house.'

'Keep to the back roads,' Harper replied. 'I'll handle Whitcomb.'

'Alone? Against the sheriff, Klein, and whoever else is protecting the judge?'

'Not alone,' Harper said, moving to the window where distant fires marked growing conflict in Blüdridge. 'Look at what's happening. The town's waking up. Father Jonathan at the church. The mechanics from your father's garage. The hardware store owner. Ordinary people who've had enough.'

'You're going to use the town.'

'The conspiracy worked because people were isolated and afraid,' Harper explained. 'Your father started breaking that when he began collecting evidence. Now we finish it.'

Harper checked his watch again, making calculations.

'We need the evidence uploaded and sent to the feds. But we need someone we can trust.'

'There was a name in the notes. An FBI agent named Davis.'

'Fine, get in touch with him and get the information across,' Harper nodded while outside, the rain had intensified, drumming against the roof and windows. Lightning flashed in the distance, followed seconds later by rolling thunder.

Appropriate weather for the storm about to break over Blüdridge.

Harper's phone vibrated with a text from Terry.

> Deputy just checked in with someone. Mentioned "package secure" and "timeline confirmed." Seemed agitated after call.

Harper showed the message to Jake.

'They're coordinating something. We need to move fast. You'll meet Terry two miles south of the motel. I'll drop him a message on how to recognise you. His sons will create a diversion to draw the deputies away while you and Terry extract your mother. Then get clear of the area – minimum thirty miles – before contacting this FBI guy and State Police.'

'What about you?'

'I'll gather allies in town, then move on to the courthouse before Whitcomb can escape. Klein will watch for us, but he won't expect a coordinated effort from townspeople.'

Outside, a fresh lightning strike illuminated the valley below, the flash revealing Blüdridge in stark relief – a town divided against itself, the careful balance of power finally collapsing under its own corruption.

'Dad'd be proud of you,' Jake said suddenly, securing the backpack. 'Taking on all this for him.'

'Your father would have done the same for me,' Harper replied simply. 'You're the one he'd be proud of.'

THE RAIN HAD EASED SLIGHTLY AS THEY PREPARED TO DEPART, moving gear onto the Bonneville. Harper checked his watch; less than two hours until Whitcomb left.

'I'll drop you at the Mendez house. Ready?' he asked Jake.

'Ready,' the boy confirmed, a new steadiness in his voice.

Harper started the motorcycle, headlight cutting through the darkness as they began their descent from the ridge. Behind them, the forecast station stood silent against the night sky.

The game had changed. By morning, nothing in Blüdridge would remain the same.

22

TWO TRIBES

RAIN DRUMMED AGAINST THE METAL ROOF OF THE BUS STOP AS Harper watched the courthouse. Jake had left half an hour ago, heading to meet Terry. The plan was simple in theory – create a diversion to draw away the deputies watching Sarah, then extract her through the motel's rear maintenance corridor. In practice, though, Harper knew such operations rarely unfolded without complications.

He checked his watch. Just past ten. Whitcomb's extraction was happening in less than an hour.

His phone vibrated – Terry.

> Meeting the kid now. Deputies still at position. Will update when things happen

Good. The first phase was proceeding as planned. Harper returned to the courthouse and its surroundings. The building dated from the 1920s, with multiple access points and a flat roof suitable for a helicopter landing. According to Mitchell Daggett, Whitcomb planned to escape via helicopter from that roof. Stopping him meant controlling those access points.

Harper gathered his equipment – the 9mm Hellcat gained from Doyle, a small tactical kit, and an evidence flash drive, copied from the SD card. As he zipped his jacket against the rain, his phone vibrated again. Terry.

Deputies moving. One leaving, replacement arriving. 20 minute window between transition.

Take advantage if possible. Maintain caution.

The extraction window had presented itself earlier than expected. Good for Sarah, but it meant Harper needed to speed up his own timeline, as the moment he made a move, Klein would retaliate.

Lightning periodically illuminated the landscape, thunder following close behind. The weather system was directly overhead now, unleashing its full force on the town below.

Harper left the safety of the bus stop, deciding that getting wet was better than having the whole thing struck by a lightning bolt, and stopped at the hardware store, now apparently serving as an impromptu community centre. Inside, two dozen people gathered around a table where Jenkins looked to be directing operations with the steady composure of a man discovering capabilities he hadn't known he possessed.

Conversations halted as Harper entered, water streaming from his jacket onto the worn floorboards. Jenkins straightened, recognition flashing across his weathered features.

'Harper,' he said, not a question but an acknowledgement. 'Been wondering when you'd show up.'

'Situation's accelerated,' Harper replied, running a hand through his wet hair, moving to the table. 'Judge Whitcomb is planning to leave town in the hour. Helicopter from the courthouse roof.'

'In this weather?'

'Apparently so.'

Jenkins's expression hardened.

'After everything that's happened, he thinks he can just fly away?'

'That's the plan,' Harper confirmed, glancing at the others gathered around the table. He recognised several faces – the pharmacist from Main Street, Chris and Luis from Colton's garage, the local doctor, Father Jonathan from the church, and perhaps a dozen others. Ordinary people drawn together by extraordinary circumstances.

'What's your interest in this?' Jenkins asked, though his tone suggested he already suspected the answer.

'Justice for Mike Colton,' Harper replied simply. 'He was murdered for what he discovered about Whitcomb's operation.'

'We know,' Luis spoke up. 'Word's spread since this evening. Whitcomb's been protecting both Daggett and Brennan for years. Taking cuts from their operations while blocking any proper investigation.'

Harper nodded, somewhat surprised by how quickly the information had circulated.

'I have evidence confirming it. Video of Klein, Mills and Ray Halvorsen planning Mike's murder on Whitcomb's orders. Dozens more on an SD card.'

The room fell silent, the impact of concrete confirmation

washing over the gathered townspeople. Father Jonathan stepped forward; his clerical collar incongruous against the hunting jacket he wore.

'What do you propose, Mister Harper?'

'Citizen's arrest,' Harper replied. 'Secure the courthouse, prevent Whitcomb's escape, and hold him until state police can take custody.'

Jenkins snorted.

'You make it sound simple. Mills has deputies patrolling the building, and Klein's been mobilising reinforcements all day.'

'That's why I need your help,' Harper said, meeting each person's gaze. 'Not to fight, but to contain. Control access points, document everything, create logjams and choke-points, peaceful situations where Whitcomb can't disappear without answering for what he's done.'

'And why should we risk our lives?' someone asked from the back.

Harper had expected the question.

'Because Mike Colton wasn't the first victim of this system, just the most recent. If Whitcomb escapes, the cycle continues. Different names, same corruption, same "town fund", but this time it'll be bigger. And with worse penalties for not paying.'

Father Jonathan nodded slowly.

'The man speaks truth. We've endured this situation for generations. Sons inheriting their fathers' fears, mothers teaching daughters which streets to avoid. This storm…' he gestured towards the windows where rain lashed against glass, 'it was inevitable. The only question is what we build after it passes.'

The room fell silent again, each person weighing

personal risk against collective responsibility. Harper didn't press – forced allegiance was worthless in situations like this.

Finally, Jenkins spoke.

'I'm in. Been watching Daggett's people intimidate my customers for fifteen years. Time to finish it.'

'For Mike,' Luis nodded.

One by one, several others showed their support. It wasn't universal, but sufficient.

Harper leant against the table, as his ribs reminded him he still wasn't getting enough rest.

'Okay, so looking at maps, there's what, five access points, including the roof?'

'Six,' Father Jonathan corrected. 'We'll need eyes on each, plus communication to coordinate.'

Jenkins produced a box of walkie-talkies from beneath the counter.

'Police scanner bands. Been using them to track deputy movements since this morning.'

He looked around as a hiss of surprise came from the group.

'They're not illegal,' he protested. 'I don't sell hot or illegal items.'

'Shame,' Chris said to a smattering of laughter.

'We could use the floodlights?' Father Jonathan suggested. 'The ones we light the tree up at Christmas? It'd light up the roof, show them for what they are.'

'Both are good ideas,' Harper said as his phone vibrated – Terry again.

Diversion created. Deputies responding to alarm at adjacent building. Moving in now.

Acknowledged. Maintain communications.

He checked his watch again. If Whitcomb's escape was imminent, they had minutes, rather than hours to prepare.

'So, where are these lights?' he asked.

THEY DIVIDED INTO TEAMS, EACH ASSIGNED TO A SPECIFIC access point with simple instructions – observe and report, document everything, maintain distance. Father Jonathan would coordinate from the church, which offered an excellent view of the courthouse roof. Jenkins and four others would monitor the main entrance, while the remaining teams covered side access points. Finally, two of the floodlights would be hefted up to the bell tower and the fire station, ready to light up the roof, potentially scaring off the helicopter if needed – although the storm itself was likely to do that, while Harper would approach through an old bootlegger's passage connecting the courthouse basement to a building across the square. The tunnel's existence had been almost forgotten, but the town's amateur historian Jenkins had discovered it while tracing water damage in the county records office a few years back.

'Questions?' Harper asked, surveying the determined faces around him.

'What if Klein or Mills resists?' Jenkins asked.

'Document everything,' Harper replied. 'The evidence on my drive proves their involvement in Mike's murder. Their actions tonight will only strengthen the case.'

Jenkins nodded, satisfied with the answer. As the teams prepared to depart, Harper's phone vibrated again.

Mom secured. Heading to extraction point.
Deputies still diverted.

'You okay?' Luis observed Harper.

'Jake,' Harper showed the message. 'We just rescued his mother from Klein's deputies.'

There was a moment of silence, and Harper realised he hadn't mentioned this part.

'Okay,' Luis muttered. 'Let's go give that son of a bitch some hell.'

OUTSIDE, THE RAIN HAD EASED SLIGHTLY, THOUGH LIGHTNING still split the sky at irregular intervals. Harper moved through side streets towards the courthouse square, staying close to buildings where shadows provided concealment. His right hand remained near the Hellcat, though he hoped the weapon would prove unnecessary. The courthouse loomed ahead; its neoclassical frontage illuminated by security lights. Two sheriff's department cruisers were parked at the main entrance where deputies stood watch, rainwater streaming from their uniform hats. Harper counted four men visible, but suspected others inside the building.

He continued past, circling towards the antique shop through whose basement he would access the bootlegger tunnel. Once there, the lock to the basement yielded silently to his usual skills, allowing Harper to slip inside without alerting anyone. Finding the entrance to the tunnel, Harper located the latch, triggering the mechanism that swung the wall section outward to reveal a low, narrow passage extending into darkness.

The air inside carried the musty scent of decades past – a reminder of Blüdridge's Prohibition-era history when bootleggers, likely named Brennan or Daggett, had constructed these passages to move product without detection. Harper switched on his small torch, revealing rough stone walls and a dirt floor worn smooth by years of use.

He moved carefully; water dripped from the ceiling in places where the storm had saturated the ground above, forming muddy puddles that Harper skirted to avoid leaving tracks.

His phone vibrated – Father Jonathan.

> Activity on roof. Two men inspecting landing zone.

So Whitcomb was indeed planning departure tonight. Harper quickened his pace through the tunnel. The passage ended at a similar false wall in the courthouse basement, and Harper located the interior release mechanism and triggered it cautiously. The wall swung inward with a faint scraping sound, revealing a storage room filled with archived court records. Harper paused, listening for any sign the noise had been detected. Hearing nothing, he stepped through, easing the false wall closed behind him.

His phone vibrated again – Jenkins.

> Four more deputies arrived main entrance. Mills with them.

The sheriff's presence confirmed the operation's significance. Looked like Mills was personally overseeing Whitcomb's extraction, ensuring nothing interfered with the judge's escape.

Harper navigated through the basement. He didn't need

to know the full layout; most court houses were the same, and the central stairwell would lead up to the main floor, then to the upper levels and finally roof access. His goal was to reach the judge's chambers on the second floor, the only thing he'd gained confirmation of in the hardware store, where Whitcomb would likely prepare for departure.

A text – this time from Klein.

You've gone quiet on me. All okay? Jake secure? Worried?

I bet you are, Harper thought as he typed a reply.

All good. Trying to decrypt SD card.

A moment later, a reply.

I said to leave that to us. I'll come to you. Where are you?

Harper paused, considering his next moves. Klein suspected but didn't know for sure if his cover was blown. They had to be careful here.

Fire Tower. No idea where it is, Jake brought me here.

You sure?

Yes. Why?

Harper watched the three dots that showed Klein was replying. The tracker would still show them there; with luck the storm wouldn't allow them to find that it'd been discarded. Chances were he'd sent someone there to look, but they'd found nothing.

Taking a calculated risk, he typed again.

Hiding at the top – I think we saw Mills come by. Definitely a police cruiser.

The three dots disappeared – Klein deleting, maybe revising his answer. If he did send someone, this would have confirmed Harper and Jake were still on site.

Could be. Stay hidden. I'll send help.

Come yourself. I don't trust anyone else.

Can't. Being watched.

More "getting the hell out of here", Harper thought.

Fine. Hurry though. Worried about Sarah.

This done, Harper continued on. There was every chance they could check his phone signal, but with the storm blowing, it might cause enough variance to hold for a few more minutes.

And that was all he needed.

As Harper approached the stairwell, a deputy rounded the corner, nearly colliding with him. Harper reacted instantly, a thunderclap strike against an ear while sliding behind to wrap the man's neck in a blood choke hold. The deputy didn't have time to struggle before steady pressure to the carotid arteries left him unconscious in less than ten seconds. He dragged the man into a storage closet, securing him with his own handcuffs and using the deputy's necktie as a gag. One problem handled, but the encounter confirmed increased security throughout the building. Harper would need to adjust his approach.

The service elevator in the building's eastern wing offered a possibility. Used primarily for maintenance staff, it likely connected all floors, including roof access. If operational, it would bypass the guarded stairwell.

Harper circled around to approach the elevator from behind. As he rounded the last corner, he nearly collided with two men in suits – security personnel rather than deputies, based on their bearing and equipment.

Private contractors, likely hired specifically for tonight's operation.

Harper reacted instinctively, stepping back into a recessed doorway as the men passed. Their conversation carried clearly in the empty corridor.

'... helicopter confirmed for twenty-three-hundred hours,' one was saying. 'Weather's still marginal but pilot says it's doable.'

'Judge isn't happy about this,' the other replied. 'Said his arrangements at the new location aren't finalised, and he wants to wait until tomorrow.'

'Better unfinalised arrangements than a cell at Cumberland County,' the first man said with a short laugh. 'After what happened to those Brennan guys this afternoon, the entire operation's compromised. I'm stunned Whitcomb's managed to keep everyone away for so long.'

They continued past without noticing Harper, turning towards the central stairwell. Their conversation confirmed the timeline, giving Harper less than thirty minutes to intercept Whitcomb before extraction.

He continued to the service elevator, and on pressing the button the elevator hummed to life, doors sliding open to reveal an empty car. Harper stepped inside, selecting the second floor where the judge's chambers were located. After a nervous few seconds – Harper knew very well that an elevator car could easily become a kill-box if things went wrong – the elevator doors opened onto the second-floor corridor, and Harper moved quickly but carefully. The judge's chambers should likely be at the end of the eastern corridor; probably a corner office with exterior windows and a private bathroom.

Voices ahead caused Harper to pause. Through the frosted glass panel of a door, he made out the silhouettes of two people in conversation – one tall and straight-backed, the other shorter. Their voices carried, though individual words remained indistinct.

Harper considered his options. Direct confrontation risked compromising the operation, but continued observation might yield something useful. He needed to get closer, to hear what they were saying.

He moved to an adjacent office, finding it unlocked. Inside, he quickly located a ceiling vent that likely connected to the room where the conversation was taking place. Standing on a desk, Harper could make out their words clearly.

'... taken care of,' one figure, the voice sounding like Sheriff Mills, spoke. 'Deputies reported the room is empty. She's gone.'

'And the boy?'

'No sign, but we're tracking Harper's movements. Last seen at the Fire Tower an hour ago.'

'Heh. Prick didn't even realise we'd tracked his bike.'

Harper recognised Klein's voice and gritted his teeth, forcing himself not to give away his position.

'I want them found,' Klein's voice now. 'Both of them. The evidence the kid has would create problems for all of us.'

'My men are searching the Tower area,' Mills replied. 'But the town situation is complicating things. Jenkins and his people are screwing around on the streets, slowing us down. The hardware store has become a rallying point.'

'Handle it,' Klein snapped. 'The judge leaves in thirty minutes. I want this contained before then.'

Mills replied in the affirmative, and Harper considered the new dynamics here; *Mills took orders from Klein.* So who exactly *was* the deputy Mike had classed as a friend?

Harper waited until the sheriff's footsteps faded down the corridor before exiting the office and moving towards the judge's chambers where Klein remained, weighing his options. Direct confrontation with Klein alone might succeed, but Whitcomb would likely have additional security. He needed to create leverage, force a situation where the evidence he possessed became the dominant factor.

Inside the chambers, he could hear Klein speaking urgently, presumably on the phone.

'Accelerate the timeline. Mills reports townspeople gathering. No, I don't care what they're doing. If they get in your way, goddamned *shoot* them!'

Yeah. Screw this. Harper drew the Hellcat, checked the chamber, and made his decision. He pushed through the door, weapon raised and aimed at Klein.

'Evening, Deputy,' Harper said, keeping his voice steady. 'Hands where I can see them.'

Klein froze, phone still pressed to his ear, his expression shifting from shock to calculation in seconds. He raised his free hand slowly, eyes never leaving Harper's.

'I'll call back,' he said into the phone before setting it down carefully on the desk. 'Harper. I thought you were at the Fire Tower.'

'Only my friends and people I trust who didn't kill my friend get to call me that,' Harper snapped. 'You don't get to call me anything any more.'

'Oh yeah? And why's that?' Klein snarled.

'On account of my shooting you in the throat,' Harper said as he made sure his Hellcat was aimed directly at Klein's neck. 'But before that, let's have a little chat.'

23

FACE OFF

'WHERE'S WHITCOMB?' HARPER DEMANDED, SCANNING THE room; the judge was conspicuously absent.

'Preparing for departure,' Klein replied, his composure returning. 'Though I expect you've already figured that out.'

'Hands on your head, turn around,' Harper instructed, advancing into the room. 'We're going to have a conversation about Mike Colton.'

Klein complied, turning slowly with his hands raised.

'There's nothing to discuss. Accidents happen in small towns.'

'Not accidents involving hydraulic lifts that were deliberately sabotaged,' Harper countered, removing Klein's service weapon from its holster and stepping back. 'Not accidents discussed and planned by you, Mills, and Ray.'

Klein's expression remained neutral, but his eyes hardened.

'You have no idea what you're involving yourself in, Harper. This goes far beyond a local mechanic's death.'

'I know exactly what I'm involving myself in,' Harper

replied. 'Drug shipments. Federal protection. Mike found it all, documented it all.'

For the first time, genuine concern flickered across Klein's features.

'Where's the evidence?'

'With Sarah and Jake, who you'll never find now.'

The distant sound of helicopter rotors penetrated the room's heavy windows. Klein's eyes flickered towards the ceiling momentarily.

'Your ride's here,' Harper observed. 'But you won't be on it.'

Klein assessed Harper for a moment before speaking again.

'What exactly do you think happens next, Harper? You turn me over to Mills? The same Sheriff who helped plan Mike's death? You present your evidence to a judge in this county? The same judicial system that's been protecting this operation for years?'

'FBI, maybe state police,' Harper replied. 'Federal authorities not compromised by Whitcomb's connections.'

Klein actually laughed.

'You really don't understand the scope of this, do you? There are no "uncompromised authorities" within three hundred miles of Blüdridge. We provide Washington's elite with everything they need! This operation has protection at levels you can't imagine!'

The helicopter was louder now, nearly overhead. Harper kept his weapon steady, his mind working through options. He needed to get Klein to the roof, use him as leverage to prevent Whitcomb's escape. But the deputy was right about one thing – simply turning him over to local authorities would achieve nothing.

'Move,' Harper ordered, gesturing towards the door. 'We're going to the roof. You're going to help me stop Whitcomb's departure.'

Klein began moving towards the door, but his compliance felt too easy, too calculated. Harper maintained distance, watching for any sign of resistance or deception. In the corridor outside, they could hear voices, footsteps approaching from the stairwell.

Klein's backup, likely Mills with additional deputies.

Harper needed to change course.

'Where's the maintenance access to the roof?'

'Stairs.'

'No, the real one.' Harper cocked the Hellcat, pressing it against Klein. 'If we get caught, or if I see one person before we get up there, you die instantly.'

Klein tensed; probably unsure how serious Harper was.

'In the janitor's closet,' he said.

They hurried down the corridor, the approaching footsteps growing louder behind them. Inside the closet, Harper guided Klein towards the roof access ladder.

'Up,' he instructed, keeping the Hellcat trained on the deputy. Klein began climbing, Harper following close behind, maintaining his weapon despite the awkward angle and the strain on his ribs. The hatch at the top opened onto the roof itself, rain and wind immediately lashing against them as they emerged.

The helicopter was hovering above the designated landing zone, its powerful searchlight scanning the rooftop. At the centre of the illuminated area stood Judge Whitcomb, soaked and angry, surrounded by four security contractors.

'About bloody time—' Whitcomb said, but paused in horror.

Harper kept Klein in front of him as they moved towards the group, using the deputy as both shield and leverage. The helicopter pilot spotted them, the searchlight swinging to illuminate their approach. The security team immediately raised weapons, forming a protective circle around Whitcomb.

'That's far enough,' one of the team called. 'Release the deputy or we will fire.'

'Lower your weapons or I put a bullet in Klein's spine,' Harper countered, pressing the Hellcat against Klein's back for emphasis.

A standoff developed, rain cascading around them as the helicopter maintained position overhead, unable to land while the confrontation continued below.

Suddenly, brilliant light flooded the rooftop from multiple sources – two powerful floodlights positioned around the courthouse square, activated simultaneously.

Father Jonathan had found the power of God, apparently.

The helicopter pilot, clearly startled by the unexpected illumination, banked slightly away from the rooftop, maintaining hover but increasing altitude to assess the situation.

'What the hell?' one of the security contractors muttered, momentarily distracted by the sudden light. Harper seized the moment, shoving Klein forward while diving to the side, finding cover behind a rooftop ventilation unit. The security team's attention divided between Klein's stumbling form and Harper's new position as the stairwell door crashed open and Sheriff Mills emerged onto the roof, breathing heavily, his uniform soaked within seconds by the driving rain.

'We've got trouble,' he called to the group. 'Victor Daggett just arrived with a security team. They've secured the main entrance.'

Klein turned sharply.

'What? Daggett wasn't supposed to be involved until Baltimore.'

'Well, he's here now,' Mills replied, moving closer. 'And he's not alone. Brought at least a dozen men, professional types. They've locked down the building.'

As if confirming his words, the helicopter suddenly veered away, banking sharply as the pilot aborted the landing approach.

'What the hell is going on?' Whitcomb demanded, his judicial composure cracking. 'This wasn't the arrangement!'

The rooftop door opened again; this time, Victor Daggett himself emerged, flanked by four men in tactical gear – not his usual enforcers, but professionals with military bearing and discipline.

'Judge Whitcomb,' Daggett said, his voice carrying clearly despite the rain and helicopter noise. 'Leaving so soon? Without saying goodbye?'

Klein moved protectively towards Whitcomb, retrieving his backup weapon from an ankle holster.

'This is a secure operation, Daggett. Your presence wasn't requested or required.'

Victor Daggett smiled thinly.

'On the contrary, deputy. My presence is essential. Or did you think the Judge would leave his most valuable partner behind?'

Whitcomb's expression shifted – surprise giving way to calculation.

'Victor. This is... unexpected.'

'Necessary adjustments,' Daggett replied, advancing across the roof with his security team fanning out around him. 'The situation has developed.'

Harper remained in cover, assessing the rapidly changing situation. This wasn't part of the plan. Daggett's arrival had completely altered the dynamic – not preventing Whitcomb's escape but securing it with greater force. Daggett, meanwhile, regarded the sheriff with casual dismissal.

'Plans change, Sheriff. As does your usefulness.'

At a subtle gesture from Daggett, two of his security team moved towards Mills, their intentions unmistakable.

'Now wait a minute,' Mills protested, backing away. 'I've done everything asked of me. Contained the investigation, managed the deputies, kept the feds out of Blüdridge—'

'And we appreciate your service,' Daggett interrupted smoothly. 'But transitions require… streamlining.'

Understanding dawned in Mills' expression.

'You're cutting me loose? After everything I've done for this operation?'

'Not cutting loose,' Whitcomb interjected, obviously deciding to side with Daggett now. 'Simply leaving you to manage the situation here while we establish the new operational base. Someone needs to remain to oversee the transition.'

The lie was transparent even to Mills, whose face hardened with sudden comprehension.

'You're hanging me out to dry. Setting me up to take the fall when this all comes down.'

He looked over to Klein, as if hoping he'd have an ally against this additional complication. However, Klein's expression remained neutral while his silence confirmed Mills' accusation. The sheriff had served his purpose and was now expendable – a sacrificial piece in a game where loyalty flowed only upward.

'You backstabbing son of a bitch,' Mills said, turning to

Klein. 'I trusted you. Followed your lead on everything, including Colton.'

'This isn't personal, Mills,' Klein replied, his tone matter-of-fact. 'Someone has to manage the aftermath. Isn't that right, Mister Harper?'

It was shouted out; Klein wasn't sure where Harper was hiding, but at the mention of his name, all the security on the roof now spun to look for him again.

Great. This was going well.

'Aftermath?' Mills repeated, voice rising. 'You mean the goddamn mess you're leaving me to clean up while you disappear with new identities and offshore accounts!'

A new sound reached them – the distinctive beat of helicopter rotors, but not from the aircraft that had retreated moments earlier. A second helicopter was approaching from the west, its lights visible against the storm clouds.

'*My* ride is here,' Daggett announced, checking his watch. 'Right on schedule. My security team will escort us to a revised extraction point.'

Reluctantly, aware he had no choice, Whitcomb nodded, turning to Klein.

'Secure Mills. We can't afford complications at this stage.'

Klein aimed his G26 at the sheriff's head.

'Don't make this difficult, Mills. It's nothing personal.'

'Nothing personal?' Mills laughed bitterly. 'You had me set up Ray to take the fall for Mike's murder. You knew Colton was recording everything in that shop.'

Daggett's expression sharpened.

'What recording?'

'The video,' Klein muttered, aware of where the conversation was going. 'Mike had cameras hidden in the garage. Recorded everything – including Ray, Mills and me planning the sabotage with Ray. His kid has the footage, probably gave it to Harper.'

Whitcomb's carefully maintained composure cracked.

'You told me all evidence was contained!'

'It is,' Klein insisted, though uncertainty had entered his voice. 'Mills is bluffing, and Harper's hiding on this very roof, probably contemplating incredibly bad life choices.'

'It's all contained, is it?' Mills challenged. 'Then why were townspeople surrounding the courthouse? Why are they shining floodlights at us? They know, Klein. They all know!'

Mills reached for his belt – not for a weapon, but for his radio. The sheriff was making a final desperate attempt to call for backup, to alert someone to the betrayal unfolding on the courthouse roof.

Klein noticed it too. His reaction was immediate and decisive – a single shot that caught Mills square in the chest, the impact driving the sheriff backward. Mills collapsed, blood spreading from the single wound, the radio falling from his hand unused.

'Problem solved,' Klein said calmly, lowering his weapon.

Daggett nodded approval. The second helicopter was approaching rapidly now, descending towards the rooftop with greater confidence than its predecessor. The pilot clearly identified their group as the intended passengers, the spotlight illuminating the landing zone.

Harper knew he had seconds to act before the situation became completely untenable. He emerged from cover, weapon raised, targeting Klein as the most immediate threat.

'Federal agent!' Harper shouted, adopting the most authoritative identity he could improvise. 'Weapons down! All of you!'

The gambit created momentary confusion – security

personnel hesitating, uncertain how to respond to this fresh development, and blinded by the spotlight. Even Klein paused, apparently calculating the possibility that Harper might *actually be* federal law enforcement. The momentary hesitation gave Harper the opening he needed. He fired twice – shots that caught two of Daggett's security men in the shoulders, dropping them to the roof's surface. But, with this, chaos erupted. The security team returned fire, forcing Harper back into cover. Klein grabbed Whitcomb, dragging him towards the approaching helicopter while Daggett's remaining men did the same. Harper made a desperate attempt to circle around, to get a clear shot at Klein before he reached the helicopter, but the wall of security created an effective barrier, their coordinated fire keeping him pinned behind the ventilation equipment.

From his position, Harper could see Klein shoving Whitcomb into the helicopter's open door before climbing in himself, Daggett already in the cockpit and yelling to the pilot to get the hell out of there. The helicopter immediately began gaining altitude, banking away from the courthouse with its high-value cargo secured.

On the roof, Daggett's security team had been reinforced by men emerging from the stairwell. Harper's position had deteriorated rapidly; outgunned and outnumbered, with his primary targets now escaped, he needed to extract himself before Daggett's men, now without their boss to temper them, could close in.

The sheriff's body lay where he had fallen, blood pooling around him. Harper waited for a momentary lull in the gunfire, then made a desperate dash across the open space, sliding the final distance to reach Mills.

The sheriff was still alive, but barely. Blood bubbled at his lips as he struggled to breathe, the chest wound clearly fatal.

'Harper,' he gasped, recognition and something like relief in his expression, the sound turning into a wet cough. 'Don't let them get away with it. Any of them...'

His eyes lost focus, his grip relaxing as consciousness faded. Harper continued applying pressure to the wound, but the sheriff's breathing was becoming increasingly laboured. Without immediate medical attention, he wouldn't survive.

Harper's phone vibrated – Jake.

> Hearing on the radio state police intercepted at county line. Turned back by federal agents. Something's wrong.

The implications were clear and disturbing. The operation extended beyond Blüdridge, beyond even Whitcomb's connections. Someone with federal authority was ensuring no official law enforcement reached the courthouse.

A shout from across the roof drew Harper's attention.

'He's over there! With the sheriff!'

Harper looked up to see two deputies – one he recognised as Santos – emerging from the stairwell, weapons drawn.

'Don't move!' Santos shouted, advancing cautiously. 'Hands where I can see them!'

Harper raised his hands slowly, calculating options. He could run, but there were half a dozen guards up there who wanted him dead. Santos was corrupt, most likely, but he still had to keep the lie that this was legitimate, which gave Harper a little more time... although not that much.

The other deputy moved to check Mills, fingers pressing against the sheriff's neck to check for a pulse.

'He's dead,' the deputy reported, looking up at Santos. 'Sheriff's gone.'

Santos's expression hardened as he trained his weapon on Harper, calling into his radio.

'This is Deputy Santos! Officer down! Rooftop! The Brit has killed Sheriff Mills!'

'I didn't shoot him,' Harper said evenly. 'Klein did. You can check the ballistics.'

'Save it,' Santos snarled, advancing cautiously. 'On your knees, hands behind your head. Now!'

Harper complied slowly, mind racing through options. Surrender meant certain death – either "shot while resisting arrest" or quietly eliminated in a cell. But fighting his way out meant becoming a fugitive, hunted by both law enforcement and Daggett's organisation.

As Santos approached to apply handcuffs, Harper dropped fully to the ground, pivoting his body around one hand, sweeping a leg in a powerful arc that caught Santos behind the knees. The deputy crashed down, his duty weapon skittering across the wet rooftop.

The second deputy, the one who'd made him the coffee hours earlier fired, the shot going wide as Harper rolled behind Mills's body for momentary cover. He came up with the Hellcat in hand, firing a single round that caught her in the thigh, dropping her with a howl of pain.

Sorry. You made good coffee.

Santos was scrambling for his weapon. Harper lunged forward, driving his boot down on the deputy's wrist before he could reach it. He grabbed Santos by the collar, hauling him up.

'Tell them Harper says he's coming for them,' he growled before delivering a vicious right cross to the point of the deputy's chin, rendering him unconscious, probably with a nasty concussion.

Better than being dead, like Mills.

Shouts from the stairwell indicated more deputies arriving in the confused chaos above. Harper moved quickly to the roof edge, looking for an escape route. The fire escape offered his only option – a rusted metal structure descending the building's eastern face.

As gunfire erupted behind him, Harper swung over the parapet onto the fire escape, descending rapidly despite the slippery metal. Bullets pinged off the surrounding structure, none finding their mark.

He reached the ground level, dropping – well, more falling – the final distance to the alley below. Sirens wailed nearby; every available deputy was now converging on the courthouse. Harper moved through back alleys, avoiding principal streets where he would be immediately spotted.

His situation had transformed entirely. Whitcomb had escaped with Klein. Harper was now wanted for killing the sheriff, with only Victor Daggett's men as witnesses to the truth – and they weren't helping him anytime soon. Within hours, his description would circulate to every law enforcement agency in the state, whether they worked for Whitcomb and Klein... or not.

Idiot, idiot man. How could you get this so wrong? You thought this was local. You thought you were better.

Mason Carrick and your father would be appalled.

Deciding that surviving was better than berating himself, Harper now moved through the shadows, avoiding the increasing patrol activity. The inn was no longer safe – it would be the first place they'd check. The cabin might offer temporary sanctuary, but they would eventually find it too.

As Harper reached a momentary haven in an abandoned building, his phone vibrated once more.

Harper, it's Mitchell Daggett. We need to talk.
Temporary alliance?

Harper read the message twice, considering implications. Mitchell reaching out suggested desperation – his plan to stop Klein and Whitcomb had partially failed, his position now compromised with his father. The power struggle within the Daggett organisation had become open warfare.

An unexpected development, but one that created opportunities. Mitchell's knowledge of his father's operation would be valuable, his resources useful in tracking Klein.

There was no trust between them, but trust wasn't necessary – only aligned interests for as long as they served both parties.

Harper replied with a single word:

Where?

The night was far from over, and Blüdridge's power structure was collapsing into something new and unpredictable. Two tribes had developed into multiple factions, alliances shifting like quicksand beneath their feet. And somewhere in the darkness, Deputy Klein was still alive, still dangerous, and still the last obstacle between Harper and justice for Mike Colton.

24

OUTLAW

RAIN HAMMERED AGAINST THE ABANDONED WAREHOUSE ROOF as Harper crouched behind a stack of rotting shipping pallets. His soaked clothes clung to his body, the chill reaching through to his bones. The warehouse – an old textile storage facility on the outskirts of Blüdridge – stood silent and empty, save for the persistent drumming of rain-water against corrugated metal.

Harper checked his watch – 2:17 a.m., Mitchell Daggett was late.

The Hellcat rested in his hand, its weight reassuring against his palm. Outside, the storm continued unabated, providing cover for movement but masking the sounds of potential approach. Which was good, because within hours, his face would be broadcast across every law enforcement channel in the tri-state area – wanted for the murder of Sheriff Mills.

A scrape against concrete drew Harper's attention to the warehouse's rear entrance. He shifted position, keeping the

Hellcat trained on the sound's origin as a figure emerged from the darkness – Mitchell Daggett, alone and moving with the cautious precision of a hunted man.

'I know you're here, Harper,' Mitchell called softly, his voice barely carrying above the rain. 'I came alone, as agreed.'

Harper waited three more seconds before revealing his position.

'Over here,' he said, stepping partially into view while maintaining tactical advantage.

Mitchell turned, eyes finding Harper in the gloom. Gone was the expensive suit and careful grooming, replaced by tactical clothing and a functional utility vest. A pistol was holstered at his hip, though his hands remained carefully away from it.

'Interesting night,' Mitchell said, approaching slowly.

'That's one word for it,' Harper replied, Hellcat still ready. 'I can think of more colourful ones.'

A hint of a smile crossed Mitchell's face.

'Fair assessment. Though not entirely unproductive from certain perspectives.'

'Yours, for instance?'

'In some ways.' Mitchell stopped, maintaining a respectful distance. 'Though not according to plan. Klein's betrayal complicated matters.'

'He murdered the sheriff, framed me for it, and escaped with your dad and Whitcomb,' Harper said flatly. 'I'd call that more than a complication.'

'Hence our current situation,' Mitchell gestured towards two weathered crates nearby. 'May I?'

Harper nodded once, and they both sat, maintaining the careful distance of men who recognised mutual danger.

'I'd expected to secure Whitcomb myself,' Mitchell explained, genuine frustration clear in his tone. 'The judge has information – account numbers, contact protocols, distribution networks – that I need to establish independent operations. Klein was supposed to facilitate the handover.'

'And the second helicopter?' Harper asked.

'My father's,' Mitchell shrugged. 'He didn't trust the Judge, so he's taken them to his ridge facility. He'd have landed there and taken them into "protection" approximately forty minutes ago.'

Harper's mind fitted this into the evolving power dynamics of Blüdridge.

'You're moving against your father directly now. No more pretence.'

'My father intends to liquidate assets and transfer operations. The ridge facility – nothing more than an old coal mining plant, but he does love his exciting terms – contains everything: weapons, cash reserves, documentation. He'll offer his services to Whitcomb and Klein, and by "offer" I mean "force them to take the option", and once they move those resources, the opportunity is lost.'

'And why should I care about your family succession plan?'

Mitchell met his gaze directly.

'Because Klein is with them. The man who framed you. The man who orchestrated Mike Colton's murder. And because I can get you inside where they're hiding.'

Harper considered this, searching for deception. Mitchell wanted control of his father's operation and needed Harper's skills to breach the likely fortified facility. Self-interest rather than alliance, but potentially useful. And Mitchell wanted

Sean Brennan dead, if only to get justice for the probably-dead love of his life.

'And Brennan?' Harper asked. 'Where does he stand in all this?'

Mitchell's expression shifted subtly.

'Gone to ground. My sources say he withdrew from The Rusted Nail when the shooting started. Not seen for hours.'

'Tactical retreat or strategic repositioning?'

'Unclear,' Mitchell admitted. 'Brennan's never been predictable. His Belfast background taught him when to fight and when to disappear. What concerns me is his organisation hasn't dissolved – just gone quiet. That suggests coordination rather than abandonment.'

'You think he's planning something.'

'I think absence during conflict rarely means surrender,' Mitchell replied. 'Particularly for someone with Brennan's history. Don't get me wrong; if he turns up, I'm going for him. The man's a cockroach and needs to die for what he did. But until then...'

Harper understood far too well.

'What exactly is this ridge facility?'

'Former coal mining operation, repurposed years ago,' Mitchell explained. 'Multiple levels, reinforced access points, independent power and communication systems. Dad always wanted a fortress, and this is as close as you can get here.'

'And security?'

'Unknown, as my father's likely changed up everything,' Mitchell admitted. 'Used to be minimal. With recent events, he's probably upped that considerably.'

Lightning split the sky, momentarily illuminating the warehouse interior. Harper caught the tension in Mitchell's posture.

'You're in a hurry,' he observed.

'We both should be,' Mitchell replied. 'Once it's all complete, they disappear – new identities, offshore accounts, protected extraction. Whitcomb has already initiated the manhunt for you, broadcasting your description to every law enforcement agency within five hundred miles. Sure, they'll eventually stop once the truth catches up with the story, but "shoot to kill" is still an unofficial code for cop killers. By the time the truth comes out, you'll be dead.'

As if confirming his words, distant sirens wailed, drawing closer to the warehouse district. Mitchell glanced towards the sound before continuing.

'The news will get out,' he said.

At this, though, Mitchell Daggett laughed.

'Will it?' he asked. 'Have you checked your phone recently?'

Harper did so – *no signal.*

'Storm hit hard just after midnight, according to the news. Power lines down, trees everywhere. Then at one a.m., like clockwork, the whole town went dark – no cell, no internet, nothing. Turns out the fibre junction flooded – happens fast in low-lying ground like that – and the crew flagged it as a weather-related outage.'

'Let me guess, a crew provided by Whitcomb?'

'Meanwhile the cell tower was "taken offline for safety checks",' Mitchell almost chuckled as he relayed the news, likely at the ludicrousness of it. 'That wasn't nature. That was Whitcomb. The junction didn't flood – someone opened the access hatch and dumped a drum of saltwater on the cables. And that tower? It wasn't taken offline. It was shut down by someone who knew the codes. This wasn't weather. It was a blackout. Whitcomb wanted a night where no one could scream, and nobody outside the county can prove otherwise until morning.'

Harper weighed his options. Working with Mitchell meant alliance with a criminal, but the alternative was attempting to reach the ridge facility alone, against superior forces and without inside knowledge.

'Lucky your text came through,' he said.

'It was before they decided it was better to blackout the town,' Mitchell shrugged. 'Be grateful. If it'd been before we wouldn't be here.'

'I need to contact Sarah and Jake,' Harper decided. 'Warn them and coordinate our approach.'

'Did you not hear what I said?'

'There has to be ways to communicate,' Harper argued. 'Whitcomb won't have blinded himself when blinding the town.'

Mitchell went to speak but then simply nodded, agreeing.

'Okay, so we need to work out how to punch through this. Your resources?'

'Limited,' Mitchell admitted. 'My father kept control of most operational assets. I've got nothing but minimal equipment and compromised communication channels. Maybe a few loyal soldiers, but no way to get them.'

Harper checked his watch – nearly three now, with dawn perhaps four hours away. The storm continued unabated, providing concealment but complicating movement.

'We need transportation that won't attract attention,' Harper said. 'And we need to get to the coal plant.'

'I have vehicles staged at a maintenance building two miles from here,' Mitchell offered. 'Nondescript service vans, used by repair crews throughout the county. GPS tracking disabled, registration untraceable.'

Harper nodded; decision made.

'Let's move. But understand this – first sign of betrayal, I put a bullet in your head. Nothing personal.'

'Likewise,' Mitchell replied with a grim smile. 'Professional courtesy between operational assets.'

They moved towards the warehouse exit, Harper maintaining spacing as Mitchell led the way. Outside, the rain had slackened slightly. They advanced through industrial shadows, avoiding main roads and streetlights, and as they reached the edge of the warehouse district, Mitchell gestured towards a chain-link fence marking the boundary of a municipal maintenance yard.

'Through there,' he whispered. 'Vehicles in the covered parking area.'

Harper scanned the surroundings, noting a police cruiser passing two blocks east – but it felt more like a standard patrol pattern rather than active search. They crossed quickly during the gap in coverage, scaling the fence and dropping silently into the maintenance yard.

The service vans – three white Ford E-Series with county water department logos – were parked beneath a metal awning, keys secured in a lockbox that Mitchell opened with the familiarity of doing this before.

'Take this one,' he said, pointing at the middle vehicle. 'I'll follow in the other.'

He smiled as Harper paused.

'I can take the other? I haven't set anything up. You're not going to explode or anything while you're useful to me.'

Harper nodded, accepting the keys.

'Checkpoint locations?'

'Main routes only for now,' Mitchell replied. 'Deputies don't have manpower for comprehensive coverage. Primary focus is on the eastern approaches where they believe you'd exit towards Cumberland.'

'Your source being?'

'Deputy Santos,' Mitchell answered with a thin smile. 'I know, he's not your friend, but he's financially motivated to provide accurate intelligence.'

Financially motivated was a hell of a term.

'Rendezvous point?' Harper asked, opening the van door.

'Storage shed near Whispering Pine Road,' Mitchell replied. 'It'll be familiar to you, as you left incriminating evidence there, remember?'

Harper smiled.

'Fun times.'

THEY SEPARATED, EACH TAKING A VAN AND EXITING THE maintenance yard through the rear gate. Harper drove cautiously, maintaining speed limits, presenting the appearance of a legitimate utility worker despite the early hour. In his mirror, he could see Mitchell following at an appropriate distance.

Harper navigated carefully, the van's suspension protesting as they left paved surfaces for uneven terrain; the track wound through dense woodland before connecting with Whispering Pines Road, approximately a mile from the main highway. No checkpoints visible here – the deputies focusing on major arteries rather than rarely used forest routes.

The storage shed appeared in the darkness, and Harper had a distinct sense of déjà vu. Its doors stood closed, windows dark, the appearance suggesting years rather than months of abandonment – something Harper had used to his advantage but days earlier.

Harper parked behind the building, Mitchell joining him moments later. They secured the vehicles out of sight from the road before approaching the shed's rear entrance, Mitchell producing a key for the padlocked door.

He paused.

'Oh, do you want to do the honours?' he asked. 'I mean, you did so well last time.'

Harper waved him on, ignoring the barbed comment.

Inside, the shed was the same as before, but Mitchell carried on through, into a section Harper hadn't bothered entering the last time he was here, a side-linked garage. It kept the functional simplicity of its original purpose – vehicle bays now empty, equipment racks bare, but the structure itself sound and secure. Most importantly, it offered isolation from Blüdridge's manhunt and a base from which to plan.

'A few weeks before he died, Mike went up to Seneca Ridge in his Jeep. Something about checking an unusual installation for a potential customer.'

Harper wondered whether this was where Mike had travelled to when he first realised that something was rotten on the ridge.

'Communications?' Harper asked.

Mitchell moved to a storage cabinet, retrieving a satellite phone.

'Secure channel, independent of local networks. My team uses it for coordination when we know the police are listening in, but it's a coin toss if anyone's on it right now.'

Harper took the phone, considering his next call carefully. Sarah and Jake needed warning, but providing their location risked compromising their security if the communication was intercepted.

He dialled Terry; the number locked in his memory. The connection was established after three rings.

'Who?' Terry's voice, tense but controlled.

'Harper. Status?'

'Secure for now,' Terry replied, relief clear in his voice.

'Package location?'

'Coming to you,' Terry said after a moment's hesitation. 'Jake insisted on making direct contact. Says he should be stepping up.'

'And you agreed?'

'Christ no! I have sons. They always make bad decisions.'

There was a pause.

'Look, I said no. I really did. But then he ran off anyway before I could stop him.'

Harper frowned.

'Dammit. It's too risky with the current situation. Also, I'm not in the town.'

'Yeah, we heard, but it's too late – we're already in motion,' Terry replied, his tone suggesting the decision had been made. 'ETA approximately forty minutes.'

Harper muted the phone, turning to Mitchell.

'They're coming to Blüdridge. Sarah, Jake and Terry.'

'Who the hell's Terry?'

'Someone who has my back,' Harper smiled darkly. 'In case you betray me.'

Mitchell tensed visibly.

'Too late to change it. If they hit town, they'll be taken in, used as hostages,' Harper continued before unmuting the call. 'Confirmed. Approach with extreme caution.'

He gave the GPS numbers for the storage shed and then turned back to Mitchell.

'Right then,' he said. 'As half the world wants me, and probably you, dead, what security do you have here? Because the last time I was here, it was abysmal.'

'We might have upgraded since a couple of days back,' Mitchell smiled. 'Let me show you around.'

25

UNDERGROUND

As they finished securing the vehicle bay, Harper detected movement outside – not Terry's approach, but something more cautious, deliberate. He signalled silently to Mitchell, who immediately moved to a defensive position as Harper drew the Hellcat.

The sound came again – movement attempting stealth but hampered by the wet ground.

Amateur rather than professional.

Harper positioned himself beside a window, using shadow for concealment. A figure emerged from the treeline – alone, moving with the awkward determination of someone unused to field craft.

The figure resolved into clearer detail – Joy from the diner. The last person Harper had expected.

He signalled to Mitchell, indicating non-threat status before moving to the rear door. Joy had nearly reached it, determination outweighing caution.

Harper opened the door just as she raised her hand to knock, startling her momentarily before recognition replaced fear.

'Thank God,' she whispered, exhaustion clear in her voice. 'I've been walking for hours trying to find this place.'

'Joy?' Harper frowned, pulling her inside quickly. 'How did you find us?'

'Honestly, it was more a Hail Mary,' Joy explained. 'When the deputies started arresting people, I ran. And then I remembered this place.'

'You know this?'

'Who do you think showed Mike?' Joy straightened, hands on hips. 'My nephew—'

'Used to work for us before he was arrested,' Mitchell sighed. 'Of course.'

Harper smiled, remembering Whitcomb's comment to Joy in the diner.

'Ms Williams, Sheriff Mills is looking for you. Something about your nephew's parole hearing next week.'

'Hold on,' Harper exchanged glances with Mitchell as his brain caught up with what was said. 'Arresting people?'

'Started around midnight,' Joy explained. 'Deputies going door to door, taking anyone who'd spoken against Daggett or Brennan. Father Jonathan, Jenkins from the hardware store – maybe twenty people so far.'

'Klein and my father consolidating control,' Mitchell observed. 'Removing potential resistance while he hunts for you.'

Joy nodded.

'They came to the hardware store, where we were hiding, around one in the morning. I slipped out the back when I heard their vehicle approach. Been moving through the woods since. Communications are down. You can't get a bar in the town – rumours are the storm, or you, took everything out during the night's chaos.'

'And the townsfolk?'

'Most of them don't care, or they're too scared to show it,' Joy muttered. 'It's the middle of the night, Harper. They went to bed, hoping it'll all be okay in the morning. When it isn't and there's some bullshit reason likely involving you, Mister Daggett here and the Brennans? They'll just wait until afternoon. And then evening.'

Harper got the idea.

'I thought more would step up,' he said.

'This ain't the Civil War,' Joy replied tersely. 'Folk here might have divisions, but most haven't picked a weapon up or had to fight for their comforts in years. Too many elderly folk are happy to just let things be, hoping it'll all blow over.'

'Brennan?' Mitchell asked casually, but it was forced.

'Brennan's men cleared out of The Rusted Nail a few hours back. Loaded up trucks and disappeared. Smart money's on a tactical retreat, that they're planning something big and bad.'

'Brennan himself?'

'Wasn't with them. Some say he's cut a deal with Whitcomb and left already, leaving his men to blow everything standing to hell.'

'A deal against Daggett?' Harper was surprised at this.

'Blood feud runs deep,' Joy replied. 'Their families were enemies since this town had its first mayor. Some rivalries outlast reasons.'

She glanced at Mitchell.

'And some rivalries have reasons in spades.'

'But working with Whitcomb?' Harper shook his head. 'That's something else.'

'Survival makes strange bedfellows,' Joy concluded, her expression grim. 'Though I'd not trust any of them further than I could throw either of you.'

A distant engine sound interrupted her – the distinctive note of a pickup. Mitchell took position covering the approach while Harper motioned for Joy to take cover and stepped outside; it could be Terry, or it could be others, looking for sanctuary.

Or, it's someone coming to kill you.

The pickup appeared through the trees, moving without lights along the overgrown access road, and Harper saw Terry at the wheel, Sarah beside him, Jake and two other figures in the back – Terry's sons, Harper guessed.

The vehicle stopped at the edge of the clearing. Terry exited first, approaching on foot.

'Damn glad to see you in one piece,' he said as he reached Harper. 'When you ask for help, you *really* need help, don't you?'

'So I've heard,' Harper replied, clasping the older man's hand briefly. Sarah approached from the pickup; Jake close behind her. Exhaustion lined their faces, but determination burned in their eyes.

'Inside,' Harper directed, gesturing towards the storage shed and side garage. As the group moved inside, Harper performed a final perimeter check, ensuring no pursuit had followed. Within hours, Klein's stooges would intensify the manhunt, expand the roadblocks, and continue eliminating potential opposition. Victor Daggett and Judge Whitcomb would accelerate their liquidation of evidence and assets.

Harper secured the door behind him, joining the others.

'So,' Terry smiled. 'Wanna get us up to speed?'

It didn't take long to update the situation, and for everyone to introduce themselves, including Terry's linebacker son Zach and his brother Connor; they'd heard some of the revisionist news from the radio in the pickup, so had a vague idea that things had gone to hell. But once finished, Harper rested his hands on the table, watching them all.

'We have hours before they leave the coal plant,' Harper explained. 'We need to get the evidence we have to authorities who aren't compromised, stop Klein from consolidating control, and prevent Whitcomb from destroying operational records.'

'And clear your name,' Sarah added, meeting his gaze. 'They're calling you a cop-killer on every channel, using it to justify the crackdown.'

'My name's secondary to the truth,' Harper replied. 'Mike deserves justice. The town deserves freedom from this system.'

Jake nodded, his young features hardening into something resembling his father's resolve.

'Dad always said chains of command exist for a reason – you follow them until they break, then go outside them. We uploaded the videos and sent them to the local FBI field office, so they'll...'

He trailed off as Mitchell shook his head.

'FBI's compromised at the supervisory level. Whitcomb's connections extend throughout regional law enforcement. Chances are, they've been intercepted. Who were you sending to?'

'Davis.'

'Straight arrow, but probably still in the dark,' Mitchell

said. 'Satellite phone should punch through to him, tell him to go hunting before Whitcomb's guys delete it all, but they'll triangulate the call fast. Better do it right before we leave for the coal plant. I'm guessing you want to end this whole thing?'

'You'd help expose this operation?' Joy asked sceptically. 'When your family built it?'

'My interests align temporarily with yours,' Mitchell replied simply. 'My concern is controlling the fallout, not preventing it entirely.'

Harper almost laughed at this. *Mitchell was positioning himself for the aftermath, ensuring distance from his father's collapsing empire.*

'We need to move, and fast,' Harper decided. 'Joy? Get back to the town. Go to the church, let the people know what's going on.'

'And do what?'

'Keep them safe,' Harper replied. 'Take Sarah and Jake—'

'The hell we are,' Sarah snapped. 'Mike was my husband. I'm seeing this through.'

'Klein killed Dad. I'm not sitting this one out,' Jake added. However, at this, Sarah looked back at him.

'This isn't your fault—'

'I didn't protect him,' Jake said. 'He didn't bring me in because I'm just a kid. Well, I won't let Klein underestimate me either.'

'This isn't the time for vengeance,' Harper said. 'But if you're going, then your mum's returning to town.'

Sarah went to reply but then shut her mouth.

'Are you sure the way back's safe?' Joy asked nervously.

'Sure,' Jake smiled, pleased he'd been accepted. 'A mile south you'll reach a shallow stream. Follow it downstream for three hundred yards, and then there's a smuggler's path straight to the town.'

'Great, wet and muddy,' Joy muttered.

'Better wet than caught,' Terry replied almost jovially, as if he was enjoying this. 'I'll come with you and Mrs Colton part of the way, if you want... Mrs Williams, isn't it?'

'*Ms* Williams,' Joy smiled coyly.

Harper couldn't help it; a smile broke out on his face too. Even in the depths of utter despair, certain things always shone through.

He turned to Mitchell.

'Layout?'

'Three main access points. But there's a maintenance tunnel on the eastern perimeter. dad uses it for discreet movement when he doesn't want to be seen using main entrances.'

'Security?'

'Should be minimal. It's more about privacy than defence.'

Harper made his decision.

'Terry, you up for this?'

'Absolutely,' Terry agreed, Zach and Connor beside him. 'Although this'll make all future father-son days tame.'

'I get that. You and your sons will create diversions at the coal plant entrance, but don't engage unless necessar—'

'No, son, I'm coming with you.'

'Fine. But your sons still create the distractions with Jake.'

At this, Jake's expression darkened.

'I said—'

'I know what you said, Jake. And you'll have your chance for revenge,' Harper replied calmly. 'But to get it, we have to take them down first. Mitchell? The two of us and Terry go through the maintenance tunnel.'

'What's your target once inside?' Sarah asked.

'Stop Whitcomb, Klein and Daggett senior from leaving. By whatever means necessary. Questions?'

'Yeah,' Terry held a hand up. 'Why didn't you just pop them all when you were on the roof?'

Harper didn't have an answer.

As the group dispersed, Sarah approached, medical supplies in hand.

'You should change those bandages,' she said, nodding towards the dark stain spreading across his shoulder. Harper accepted without argument, following her to a quieter corner. As she removed the old dressing, he winced involuntarily.

'Looks worse than it is,' he said.

'Liar,' her hands were steady as she cleaned the wound. Up close, Harper could see the exhaustion in her eyes, the strain of recent days etched in subtle lines across her face.

'Jake shouldn't be here,' he whispered.

Sarah's hands paused momentarily.

'Do you think I don't know that?' She resumed her work, applying antiseptic. 'He's Mike's son. Stubborn as his father and twice as determined. He won't stay behind.'

'We'll finish this together,' Harper said.

Sarah met his gaze directly.

'Don't make promises you can't keep,' she replied without hostility. 'Just make sure they pay for what they did to Mike. That's enough.'

Harper moved to the window, scanning the forest approaches.

'We're running out of options, Harper,' Sarah breathed. 'Klein, Daggett and Whitcomb control the roads, the communications, the town itself. We're effectively on our own, no matter how good you are.'

'Not the first time I've operated with limited resources in hostile territory,' Harper replied. 'We adapt, improvise, persevere. You mentioned the town being controlled? I'm not so sure.'

He glanced over at Mitchell, who was talking to Terry, examining the compound bow.

'You think the town's an asset here?' Sarah asked.

'I do,' Harper nodded. 'More than you might think.'

'You don't know them,' Sarah continued. 'You don't know the history.'

'Actually, I think I know the history quite well,' Harper replied softly. 'Every time I've been in the diner, Joy's had me in the same booth, right beside the map, the story, the resolution... I've read it multiple times. And now, with war in the streets, this is the perfect time to capitalise.'

'You want to contact the town?' Sarah frowned.

'Not just that,' Harper smiled. 'I want to *weaponise* it.'

He turned to face her, lowering his voice.

'Here's what we do next,' Harper began. 'And why I want you back in Blüdridge before we even start.'

26

RESISTANCE

THE ABANDONED COAL PROCESSING STATION REEKED OF RUST and stagnant water. Harper crouched by a shattered window, observing. Unlike military installations he'd breached in the past, this looked more like a converted manufacturing plant with hastily added security – chain-link fencing with razor wire, scattered floodlights, and what appeared to be five or six guards wandering between buildings in uncoordinated patterns.

Which, he supposed, *it was.*

'Looks like six guards,' Harper muttered. 'Maybe seven. One of them's checking his phone every five minutes. Another's using the main building porch to smoke. Security's there but it's basic – civilian guards, not mercenaries.'

Mitchell pointed to some trucks, just about visible to the right where motion could be seen.

'They're speeding up,' he said. 'First transports being loaded now. A couple of hours until departure, maybe less.'

'What exactly are they moving?'

'Everything,' Mitchell replied. 'Weapons, financial

records, money, documentation. Once it's gone, we have nothing.'

'Joy – I mean *Ms Williams* – said your man Brennan's regrouping at a property twenty miles north,' Terry said, checking his compound bow. 'Said she saw a convoy heading that way yesterday with armed men and supply trucks. Like he's preparing for something big.'

'Phase two of the war, perhaps,' Harper replied, deciding not to mention the suspicion he'd had of Daggett Senior and Brennan working together to buy up land, which meant Brennan could be working as Whitcomb's backup here.

Mitchell's expression revealed nothing, but Harper caught the slight tension in his shoulders. Brennan's absence from visible conflict didn't mean absence from strategic considerations, and Harper knew he'd risk everything if it meant grabbing hands around Sean Brennan's throat.

'You reckon the women got back okay?' Terry asked.

'You worried about Joy?' Harper smiled. 'Don't worry. She's probably taken more care of Sarah, than Sarah's taken of her.'

'Good move, getting her out of danger,' Mitchell muttered. 'Women shouldn't be involved in war.'

'She wasn't happy about going back, but she understood the risks,' Harper replied. ' Of course, it'd be better if Jake had gone with her.'

'Kid wants to avenge his father, I get that,' Mitchell shrugged. 'I was younger than he is when I saw my first taste of war. Not your army war, I mean *street* wars.'

'Still doesn't fill me with optimism,' Harper said as he checked his watch; eight minutes until Connor, Zach and Jake started the first diversion.

He glanced back at Mitchell, currently checking his

weapon; the assault rifle looked like a standard M4 at first, but it was heavier, sharper. Harper recognised it as a HK416 — military issue, piston-driven, built to keep firing through sand or blood.

Exactly what someone like Mitchell Daggett would use.

Through his binoculars, Harper observed a security patrol passing twenty yards from their intended breach point. Two guards with hunting rifles and civilian jackets, one lighting a cigarette while the other yawned. They moved more like night watchmen than trained security.

'Remember,' Harper said quietly, 'once we breach the perimeter, we'll have minutes before they recognise the diversions are coordinated rather than isolated incidents.'

They began their approach, using the forest's natural shadows for concealment. They reached the fence unseen, positioning themselves fifty yards from a maintenance tunnel entrance. Harper watched as security continued normal operations, unaware of what approached. He was about to make a comment when an explosion erupted at the northern perimeter – the diversion executing perfectly. Fire blossomed from storage containers, black smoke billowing into the night sky as guards sprinted towards the disturbance.

'Moving now,' Harper ordered, leading the others towards the fence. Terry produced bolt cutters, slicing through the chain link, and they slipped through the gap, staying low as they approached the maintenance tunnel entrance. Unlike Mitchell had suggested, the access point wasn't merely secured – it was concealed behind construction materials and deliberately camouflaged.

'They've upgraded security since you last visited,' Harper told Mitchell who, unable to argue this, simply shrugged as Harper examined the electronic lock securing the access door. 'Different system than expected. Commercial-grade, not military.'

'Meaning?' Terry pressed.

'I can work with it,' Harper replied, examining the lock. 'Although it might take a while to get through.'

'Nah, I'll sort this one,' Terry said, and Harper wasn't sure if the older man had the technical skills, but this proved to be irrelevant as Terry stepped back and loosed an arrow from his compound bow into the lock, shorting it out in a spectacular array of sparks and the lock disengaged with a soft click.

'Never underestimate the power of a mechanic,' Terry smiled, as if this was the most obvious answer to the problem.

'Well, either way, we're in,' Harper announced, shaking his head at the smiling Terry, currently taking back his spent arrow while Harper was drawing the Hellcat as he moved into the dimly lit tunnel beyond.

THE PASSAGE EXTENDED APPROXIMATELY ONE HUNDRED YARDS, eventually ending at a service door connecting to the complex. Unlike the tunnel itself, this inner door featured only basic security – a standard commercial keypad, the kind used in office buildings, and Mitchell removed a small crowbar from his pack, making quick work of the lock. This done, they entered the facility proper – utilitarian corridors with commercial-grade construction rather than hardened fortification. The layout suggested conversion of existing buildings rather than purpose-built security architecture; emergency lighting pulsed in response to the ongoing security alert, casting alternating patterns of light and shadow.

'Where now?' Harper asked.

'This way,' Mitchell now took charge, which was logical considering he was the only one who'd been here before.

They moved through the compound, encountering minimal resistance initially. Most security personnel were responding to the perimeter diversions, leaving internal corridors temporarily understaffed. However, at an intersection, voices approached – security personnel returning from outside. Harper signalled the others into an adjacent storage room, holding position as the guards passed.

'They're implementing lock-down protocols,' Mitchell whispered. 'Recognising the diversions as coordinated rather than isolated.'

The window was narrowing faster than expected.

As they continued to the administrative section, Harper found it suddenly transitioning from utilitarian basement to actual conference centre level with carpet, corporate furniture, and meeting rooms. Victor Daggett obviously didn't mind his men working in dull, utilitarian corridors, but drew the line when it came to his own comfort.

'Whitcomb will have established temporary headquarters in the main conference room,' Mitchell said, directing them towards a set of double doors at the corridor's end.

Harper signalled for silence as they approached. Inside, voices were audible – urgent conversation punctuated by occasional commands.

'Security will confirm perimeter containment first,' Victor Daggett spoke, his tone suggesting impatience.

'They're diversions,' Klein's voice joined the discussion. 'We need to get the fu—'

Harper pushed through the door, weapon raised and

aimed at Klein. Mitchell followed, his weapon covering his father.

Inside, the scene confirmed what Harper had expected – Whitcomb and Daggett surrounded by documentation being prepared for transport, Klein using a laptop. Two Daggett security guards stood near the windows, looking more like bouncers than professionals, weapons visible in shoulder holsters.

All five looked up in shock as Harper, Terry, and Mitchell entered.

'Gentlemen,' Harper said, the Hellcat's barrel unwavering as it targeted Klein, 'I believe we need to discuss Mike Colton.'

Klein's hand moved towards his weapon.

'I wouldn't,' Harper warned. 'Not after what happened to Sheriff Mills.'

'You're making a serious mistake,' Victor Daggett said, his voice calm despite the circumstances. 'Whatever you believe you understand about this operation is wrong.'

'Enlighten me,' Harper replied, maintaining aim on Klein while Mitchell covered the room. 'Starting with why Mike Colton needed to die.'

One of the bodyguards moved slightly, hand drifting towards his weapon. Harper shifted his aim instantly.

'I think everyone should keep their hands where we can see them,' he said, voice carrying dangerous certainty.

'I'd rather show than tell. Bring them out,' Klein called towards a side door.

Two more of Daggett's men appeared from what looked like a converted office space, pushing forward a pair of battered figures with hands secured behind their backs. Ray Halvorsen stumbled into view, his face barely recognisable beneath bruises and dried blood. Behind him came Sean Brennan – the Irish crime boss looking considerably less imposing without his usual entourage, his expensive clothes torn and stained.

Mitchell Daggett straightened at the revelation, his HK416 now aimed at Brennan.

'So, you never released Ray then,' Harper nodded. 'Thought as much after we never saw him released. Why all the cloak and dagger at Brennan's?'

'Insurance policies,' Klein explained with satisfaction. 'Mister Brennan thought he could negotiate separate terms with Judge Whitcomb by gaining information from Mister Halvorsen. Unfortunately for him, loyalty is a precondition of our arrangement. Brennan needed to be stopped, and Ray needed to be removed. You helped admirably.'

Ray's bloodshot eyes found Harper's.

'I didn't want Mike dead,' he mumbled through swollen lips. 'Just the lift adjusted... *hurt* him, not kill him—'

The shot echoed through the room before Harper could react.

Ray collapsed, a neat hole between his eyes, his last confession hanging in the air.

'One loose end resolved,' Klein said calmly, turning his weapon towards Brennan. 'Care to negotiate now?'

Brennan showed no fear, his bloody face twisting into a bitter smile.

'You think killing me solves your problems? The moment you pull that trigger every one of my men follows standing orders – *kill all of you in fiery, bloody vengeance.*'

'If they ever find out,' Klein smiled. 'Right now, they think you've gone into hiding.'

'You might think that, but you'd be making a terrible mistake.'

Klein hesitated; weapon still trained on Brennan's forehead.

'You're bluffing.'

'Try me,' Brennan replied. 'I've survived Belfast, lad. You think I didn't prepare for betrayal?'

At this, he now winked theatrically at Mitchell.

'After all, I learned about betrayal from my own family, didn't I?'

'This is bullshit!' Mitchell now spoke, stepping closer. 'If you're not killing this piece of crap, then I am!'

Victor Daggett stepped forward.

'Stand down.'

'But Dad—'

'You want him dead? I'll let you take the role of executioner, but only if I can trust you,' Victor snapped back. 'And right now you're not proving anything to me!'

Harper looked across at Mitchell and saw a man conflicted.

Shit.

Klein lowered his weapon reluctantly.

'Secure the Mick for transport. We'll sort this out on the road.'

Harper watched impotently, weapon in hand but useless as security personnel dragged Brennan back towards the holding area. Brennan's presence suggested complications beyond simple corruption. The blood feud between Daggett and Brennan ran deeper than territory or profit, as shown by the anger on Mitchell's own face as he watched his nemesis dragged off.

'So, this is what you murdered Mike Colton for,' Harper

concluded, looking around, trying to work out his next option, hoping Mitchell was still on his side here 'Don't think much of it.'

'We protected essential interests,' Whitcomb countered, judicial authority entering his tone despite his compromised position. 'This operation serves strategic necessities beyond local concerns.'

'By creating a personal empire funded by trafficking?'

Victor Daggett smiled thinly.

'You have no idea what you're involved in, Harper. This facility is one node in a network. Functions your government approves while maintaining plausible deniability.'

The implications settled heavily. Not just local corruption or organised crime, but systematic operation with tacit federal approval. The scale explained the resources deployed to protect it – and why Klein operated with such impunity.

'Corruption with a patriotic letterhead is still corruption,' Harper replied. 'And murder is still murder regardless of the justification. The video evidence we have has reached people who still believe in accountability. Real federal authorities, not compromised local assets. The videos of you that Mike had, the letters we found, everything.'

Klein and Victor Daggett exchanged glances clearly calculating odds and options. The momentary silent communication confirmed another detail from Mitchell's intelligence – neither fully trusted the other, their alliance one of necessity rather than loyalty.

And then Klein smiled.

'If you sent it to Agent Davis, then you've already closed your own casket,' he said. 'We own his department.'

'But not Davis?' Harper countered.

'Davis is irrelevant and powerless,' Whitcomb finally

seemed to grow a backbone now. 'We still control enough people to keep things smooth.'

'Sure, with a town in communications blackout and under federal law,' Terry, who'd been standing silently at the back now spoke. 'How long do you think it'll stay that way before others wonder why it's taken so long to fix storm damage?'

'Who the hell is this?' Victor asked, looking at Terry.

'Someone who doesn't like bullies,' Terry replied coldly.

'Oh, so a nobody then,' Daggett looked over at Klein. 'Ensure they're alone.'

As Klein reached for his radio however, Harper's aim centred between his eyes.

'That would be unwise.'

The standoff intensified, neither side willing to concede advantage.

'Whatever you believe you're accomplishing here will be temporary at best,' Whitcomb said. 'This operation has contingencies for every scenario.'

'Including betrayal from your own family?' Harper asked, glancing meaningfully at Mitchell.

Victor Daggett's expression hardened as he turned towards his son.

'I wondered when you'd make your move.'

'Someone had to,' Mitchell replied evenly. 'You've lost perspective. Turned an efficient operation into a personal empire at unacceptable risk.'

'Risk I managed successfully until your interference,' Victor countered.

Klein tensed, clearly weighing options despite the weapon trained on him.

'Don't,' Harper warned him. 'You're already facing

murder charges for Sheriff Mills and Ray Halvorsen. Don't add stupidity to the list.'

Victor Daggett's eyes met Harper's directly.

'You don't know what forces you're challenging, Harper. This isn't a simple matter of local justice or personal vendetta. The system you're attacking extends far beyond Blüdridge.'

'I don't care how far it extends,' Harper replied, the Hellcat unwavering. 'Mike Colton deserves justice. And this operation ends tonight.'

'Does it?' Victor looked at his son. 'Family... it matters, doesn't it? Do you think you can honestly take over my role, knowing *you never gained vengeance on the man who killed your secret fiancée?*'

'Bring him back out, I'll do it right now.'

'No, I don't think so,' Victor smiled. 'Only allies get to ask requests.'

Mitchell laughed, and Harper hoped it was at the incredulity of the situation, but then he sighed, straightened, and turned his HK416 onto Harper.

'Sorry, man,' he said. 'But I *really* want to kill Sean Brennan. And if my father has Brennan, then I'm with him.'

27

WAR ZONE

THE WORDS HUNG IN THE AIR BETWEEN THEM, MITCHELL'S weapon now directed at Harper's chest. The sudden shift left Terry and Harper momentarily frozen, caught between betrayal and the immediacy of danger.

'Your father?' Harper kept his voice level despite the weapon trained on him.

'Blood runs deeper than ambition,' Mitchell replied, his eyes cold. 'Three generations of Daggetts have waited for this moment. Brennan's family took everything from mine during Prohibition. My grandfather died in prison because of their betrayal.'

Mitchell's finger tensed on the trigger, his focus absolute.

'My father was right about one thing – some debts can only be paid in blood.'

Harper shook his head.

'Bullshit. This isn't about family. This is about Moira.'

'You're damn right it is!' Mitchell replied angrily. 'Because to me, Moira *was* family!'

'Don't fall into this hole,' Harper said carefully. 'Be your own man. The last thing you want is to be controlled by your father.'

'Sounds like you have personal experience in this,' Victor Daggett raised an eyebrow.

'I do,' Harper replied. 'And now I'm travelling across America with a notebook of his sins, fixing them before I can finish.'

'Sounds like a loser,' Victor shrugged as, from behind, guards came rushing into the room with weapons drawn. 'Shame you won't be continuing that mission. Well done, Mitchell, I knew you'd make the right choice eventually.'

Mitchell nodded; a hint of tension visible only to Harper.

'Family first, Father. At least until you let me kill that bastard Brennan.'

The guards surrounded them, disarming Terry and Harper, but he maintained eye contact with Mitchell, searching for any sign that this was strategic betrayal rather than genuine defection.

He found none.

'Search them,' Klein ordered, approaching with the cautious respect a hunter gives dangerous prey. 'Harper's resourceful.'

As guards patted them down, Victor studied Harper.

'I must admit, your interference has been unexpectedly persistent, Mister Harper. Though I suppose I should thank you for delivering my son back to the fold.'

The guards found Harper's pocketknife, tossing it onto a nearby table alongside Terry's compound bow, and the Hellcat he'd taken from Doyle.

'Where are the others?' Victor demanded.

'Maintenance shed, quarter of a mile west,' Mitchell

answered without hesitation. 'Jake Colton and the old guy's sons are trying to cause distractions.'

Harper kept his expression neutral. Watching Harper, Klein smiled.

'Sucks to be you, right now, eh?'

Harper kept silent, refusing to give Klein any satisfaction. Victor now stood beside Mitchell, the family resemblance between father and son suddenly striking. Same calculating eyes, same careful composure, same underlying coldness. The only difference was Mitchell burned with personal vendetta while Victor maintained professional distance.

'Your associates will soon be secured,' Victor said. 'Now we discuss terms.'

'Terms?' Harper raised an eyebrow.

'You've created considerable disruption, Mister Harper. You compromised our security and forced us to fall into backup plans. All quite impressive for one man with limited resources,' Victor studied him with something that almost resembled professional respect. 'In different circumstances, I might have recruited you.'

'I'm quite selective about my employment.'

'Clearly,' Victor smiled thinly. 'Your allegiance to a dead man speaks to your dedication.'

Harper maintained eye contact, refusing to react to the deliberate provocation.

'So what, you're all packing for a holiday? Won't last long until they catch up to you.'

'You think so?' Victor leant back, shaking his head. 'They won't "catch up" because nobody knows the truth. Sure, they suspect, but we still control the narrative. Once the disruptors see there's no hope, they'll step back in line. Give it a week or two, and your antics will be nothing more than another campfire story to tell about Blüdridge, another "legend", And everything will go back to normal.'

'So no running away, then?'

'Oh, there'll be a strategic withdrawal, but only until we make sure the story *we* want to tell is told.'

'Mills and Halvorsen will take the blame for everything, both murdered by you,' Whitcomb added. 'Klein will become Sheriff until he gets bored with playing cops.'

'And Brennan?'

The question triggered visible tension in Mitchell, who had positioned himself beside his father. Victor glanced at his son before responding.

'Awaiting appropriate justice, and yet another footnote in the town's story. His men will be exterminated, a fake war keeping everyone's head down.'

Mitchell stepped forward, control slipping.

'I want to see him, Father.'

'You've seen him before, son. All in good time,' Victor replied, his tone suggesting the matter was closed. 'First, we address our current situation.'

'I *want* Brennan,' Mitchell insisted, surprising both Harper and Victor with his intensity. 'That was the agreement if I sided with you. He's mine.'

'Containment first, personal matters later,' Victor countered, his patience visibly thinning. 'Control yourself.'

Harper kept his expression blank as he watched this; the exchange revealed fractures in their newly reformed alliance as Mitchell's hatred for Brennan was overriding discipline, while Victor was prioritising procedure over his family's vendetta. Harper filed the observation away, as it could be potential leverage for later.

Klein interrupted, placing a radio on the table.

'Our team reached the maintenance shed, but it's empty. No sign of anyone.'

'They can't have gone far,' Victor said. 'Hunt them down. Every exit from the property is to be secured.'

'Already done,' Klein confirmed. 'And I've dispatched teams to likely hiding locations on the way back to town.'

Victor turned his attention back to Harper.

'Seriously, what was your plan here?' he asked. 'Three men against an army? Some teenagers outside with firecrackers? Even with my son siding with you, there's no way that would have worked.'

'Depends what the end goal was,' Harper shrugged. 'I owed Mike. Wanted to see this through personally.'

As Klein laughed at this, Mitchell stepped closer to his father.

'I want to see Brennan now. You promised me justice for our family.'

'You'll have it,' Victor snapped, patience finally breaking. 'But there are priorities, Mitchell. Security first, vengeance later.'

'I've waited three years since Moira—'

'*And you can wait three more minutes!*' Victor cut him off. 'Control yourself and remember your place!'

Before this could continue, though, a guard entered, interrupting the family tension.

'Sir, we've got a situation. Deputies at the main gate demanding access. Sheriff's department vehicles.'

Klein frowned.

'Santos knows not to bother us.'

'Not Santos,' the guard clarified. 'Different deputies. They're saying they have arrest warrants for Deputy Klein and Judge Whitcomb.'

The room's atmosphere shifted instantly. Victor turned to Klein with cold fury.

'You said you had control of all local personnel!'

'I do…' Klein insisted, genuine confusion evident, but then paused, staring at Harper for a long moment.

'What did you do?' he hissed.

'How well do you think you know me?' Harper asked, relaxing his shoulders. 'You must have looked into me, right? You've seen how I work, what I do.'

'You're a lone wolf,' Klein frowned. 'But you're not stupid…'

Once more, he paused, his eyes narrowing.

'There you go,' Harper smiled, watching Klein's expression. 'You're realising there's more going on here, aren't you?'

He looked around the room.

'Mister Daggett's right,' he said. 'The three men outside, the three men inside – well, two, really – we'd never be able to take you down. But I knew we could at least get to you. And, once we'd done so, we could delay you.'

'Delay for what?' Klein frowned.

'For Joy and Sarah to mobilise the town,' Harper smiled. 'And for the town to come right here. I mean, it's not quite torches and pitchforks, but it's enough.'

'Bullshit. Secure them,' Klein instructed the guard who'd taken Harper's things, pointing at Harper and Terry. 'We'll deal with him once we're clear. And I want those children found outside before they blow up more shit.'

'What about the deputies outside?' Whitcomb asked. 'How do we know they're not legit?'

'Screw them!' Klein shouted, looking at Victor Daggett. 'He's screwing with us, delaying us. We need to get moving now.'

Daggett nodded and, motioning for his son to come with him, he left the room, Klein and Whitcomb following. Now alone, Harper and Terry faced the three guards left with them.

'Nice weather for it,' Harper said mildly.

'For what?' one guard asked, frowning, just as the lights flickered. A brief surge. Two seconds, maybe less. All three glanced up.

Harper moved; a sharp pivot. The side of his hand slammed into the nearest guard's throat, driving him back into the wall, choking for air. The man reached for his weapon — but before he could, Harper delivered a vicious uppercut to the chin, and he went down.

The second guard lunged, but Terry intercepted, slamming into him with full force. They hit the ground hard, grappling. The guard threw a punch – Terry took it, then drove a fist into the man's jaw, then a second into his throat. The body jerked once, then stilled.

The third tried to run.

Harper caught him by the collar and wrenched him backwards, dragging him off balance before driving a knee into his spine. The man hit the desk face-first, and didn't move again.

Three guards down. Fast. Brutal.

Harper stripped them of weapons, radios, and access cards. The weapons were standard police issue 9mm Glock 17s and Harper checked the magazine; fifteen rounds plus one chambered. There was also a combat knife in a sheath, and Harper quickly slid it onto his belt.

Adequate but not optimal, he thought, tossing a Glock to Terry who caught it, scowling.

'Still prefer my bow,' he said, walking to the table and picking it up. 'Want your gun back?'

'I'll use these,' Harper said as he pulled the magazines out of the spare Glocks, pocketing them just in case. He did however retrieve his pocketknife. 'Nice work there.'

'I roughhouse with linebackers when I'm with my boys,' Terry grinned. 'If I can hold my own with them, I can take out that pussy right there.'

'How long do you think Chris and Luis can keep the guards busy out there?'

'They didn't seem that bright,' Terry smiled. 'As long as they have uniforms and a flashing light—'

He paused as the floor trembled, and a low, heavy vibration rolled through the walls. Lights flickered again, steadied.

'What was that?' he asked.

Harper moved to the window.

'Perimeter breach. Eastern section,' he replied, considering what had been said earlier. 'I think your sons just met up with some of Blüdridge's best.'

Crouching beside the first fallen guard, Harper checked the radio, confirming it was operational before securing it to his belt. As he did so, though, there was a crackle of static.

'We got the boy!'

Harper froze, listening as Whitcomb's voice answered.

'The others?'

'No, he led us away. But with him, we'll get them.'

'Excellent. Bring him back.'

Harper wanted to scream, but chose instead to count to five, calming himself. He'd always planned for something like this; Mitchell was a complication, and he'd expected the man to turn at one point, which was precisely why he hadn't filled him in on the full plan, but he'd not expected them to retaliate so quickly.

Or was this the case?

Harper groaned. Jake hadn't been happy about running backup; he'd wanted to face Klein himself. *What if this was some kind of Quixotic attempt to do so?*

He leant back over his guard, slapping him back to consciousness.

'What's the plan here?' he asked, ramming the Glock against the terrified man's temple.

'Helicopter on roof,' the guard whispered. 'Same one they came in. They'll leave the moment we're breached.'

'Brennan?'

'Two doors down, back exit,' the guard nodded at the door Harper had seen Brennan taken out of. 'They'll have locked him and gone. He's battered, tired and restrained.'

Harper considered this, smiled, and then butt-stroked the guard with his Glock.

Rising, he walked over to the table, taking the Hellcat, reloading it with 9mm rounds from a spare magazine, before heading to the other exit. As he did so, he stopped; the body of Ray Halvorsen stared glassily up at him.

You bloody fool.

There were no words that could be said; Harper looked at Terry, and the two men headed to find Brennan.

THEY FOUND HIM EXACTLY WHERE THE GUARD HAD SAID, AND after opening the door with one of the access keys, Harper faced an angry Sean Brennan, ready to charge, but straightening up as he saw his rescuers.

'You?' he asked as Harper pulled out his pocketknife, freeing him. 'Never thought I'd see you again.'

'You're as surprised as I am,' Harper smiled. 'When did they get you?'

'Whitcomb told me he had a proposal,' Sean Brennan spat. 'Didn't realise the proposal was to feckin' screw me over.'

Harper pulled out Doyle's Hellcat, passing it over. Brennan recognised it, looking up at him, narrowing his eyes.

'I gave this gun as a gift to a friend,' he said. 'Where the hell did you find it?'

'Mitchell Daggett gave it to me for tonight,' Harper lied. 'It was part of his arsenal – I didn't realise he'd taken it from your man.'

'Mitchell Daggett needs to feckin' die,' Brennan checked the magazine. 'He's never shut up about that bitch since she was taken care of. So, what's the plan?

Harper knew exactly what his plan for Sean Brennan was; he wasn't going to tell him right now, though.

'Events are unfolding in Blüdridge that'll change the balance of power,' he said with a dark, humourless smile. 'Daggett's time is ending. Those who position themselves appropriately now will find opportunities in what follows.'

Brennan raised a bloodstained eyebrow, recognising the same words he'd spoken to Harper days earlier.

'You're suggesting I choose a side,' he replied flatly.

'I'm suggesting that neutrality is a luxury few can afford in times of transition,' Harper, like Brennan had before, countered. 'I think it's hunting season for Daggetts, don't you?'

28

DAY OF RECKONING

After Brennan left them, Harper and Terry carried on down the south corridor, pausing as a second impact followed, stronger than the first. Dust descended from the ceiling, items rattling on shelves and desk surfaces. An alarm activated – different from standard security alerts, more urgent in its pattern. The facility had transformed into a conflict zone – security personnel rushing to defensive positions, evacuation procedures accelerating as Victor Daggett's operation collapsed into chaos.

'We need to split up,' Harper decided as they reached the south stairwell. 'Get to your sons before you get hurt.'

'That ain't your call,' Terry said. 'I'm good here.'

'I need to go to the roof and save Jake,' Harper replied. 'It's going to be hard work.'

'Save Jake from Klein, or save Jake from himself?' Terry asked.

'Either,' Harper looked around, planning his exit. 'He's got his father's knife still – he might be itching to use it.'

'Then stop talking and start moving, yeah? I got your

back,' Terry ordered as another explosion rocked the facility, closer than the previous impacts. The stairwell trembled, dust and debris cascading from above. Harper carried on up the stairs while Terry stayed back for the moment, doing his best to ignore the explosions, wondering what the hell was being used out there. Harper paused to retrieve a fallen semi auto shotgun, quickly checking the weapon - Fully loaded, safety engaged, operable condition. Superior to the sidearm for the close-quarter combat likely ahead.

The stairwell remained clear as Harper continued his ascent, the sounds of conflict echoing from multiple directions. However, as he reached the midpoint between floors, the stairwell door above crashed open. Harper pressed against the wall, shotgun ready as figures emerged – Victor Daggett flanked by two security guards, all armed and moving.

'Secure the landing pad,' Victor was instructing. 'Essential personnel only.'

Harper remained motionless as they carried on past his position, entirely focused on their extraction route. Victor Daggett appeared controlled despite the circumstances, even as his facility collapsed around him.

Once they passed, Harper continued upward, reaching the roof access door, hoping Terry had the presence of mind to stay hidden while they passed by. Through the reinforced glass panel, he observed the landing pad – a helicopter warming up, rotors already at operational speed, preparing for immediate departure. Beside the aircraft, two familiar figures directed operations.

Whitcomb and Klein.

The deputy supervised loading of equipment – precise, prioritised, professional despite chaotic circumstances, as

Harper checked the roof access door; it was locked as expected, electronic security of some kind. He had some access cards, but he wasn't sure if any of the guards had the level he needed here, plus he'd take valuable seconds, minutes even, trying to get through a door Daggett wanted secured. Which also meant more guards arriving soon.

The shotgun offered a more direct solution.

He positioned himself, took aim at the lock, and fired. The door burst open, the sound lost beneath the facility's alarm systems, currently drowned out by the helicopter sounds from above. Harper moved through, emerging onto the roof where the wind whipped across the open space.

There, standing near the edge, stood Klein. The deputy wasn't alone; Jake was held beside him, the boy's hands at his sides, Klein's hand firmly gripping his shoulder. The deputy's expression showed neither panic nor concern, just professional assessment as he registered Harper's arrival.

'I was wondering when you'd find us,' Klein said, his voice carrying across the rooftop with remarkable calm. 'Though I admit, I expected you sooner.'

Harper advanced slowly; shotgun ready but not aimed directly at Klein – not while the deputy stood so close to Jake.

'The little scamp thought he'd escape us,' Whitcomb said now, standing beside Klein with a smile. 'He lasted five minutes. So much for "chip off the old block", eh?'

'Let him go,' Harper called. 'This is between us.'

There was a commotion outside – gunshots and screams. A moment later, a battered and bleeding Sean Brennan appeared in the doorway, Hellcat in his hand.

Bollocks. He was supposed to be a distraction elsewhere. And how the hell did he get past Terry?

'I have an objection to your premature departure,' he said, slurring his words, the pain and tiredness finally hitting him as he raised the Hellcat in his hands. Whitcomb moved away from the helicopter, realising this was a situation he couldn't handle.

Klein's grip tightened on Jake's shoulder as he assessed the deteriorating scenario, his eyes coldly calculating despite the chaos.

'You're too late, Brennan,' he called over the rotor noise, edging towards the helicopter with Jake still firmly in his grasp. 'It's over. We're leaving.'

'Nothing's over until I say it is,' Brennan replied, blood trickling from his split lip as he advanced. 'For generations, the Daggetts stole from my family, before kicking us back to Ireland. Well I'm not my weak-ass forefathers, shying from a fight, and I'm not letting you and that prick Victor fly away with what's owed to us.'

Harper maintained his position, shotgun ready but with his focus divided between Klein with Jake, and the approaching Brennan. The wind whipped across the rooftop, the helicopter's rotors throwing grit and debris in swirling patterns across the landing pad.

'Where is he, anyway?' Brennan demanded, scanning the rooftop. 'Too much of a coward to face me himself?'

'Right here, Sean,' a fresh voice cut through the chaos, and all heads turned as Victor Daggett emerged from the far side of the roof. His silver hair whipped in the rotor wash, face set in grim determination, a large frame revolver in his hand.

Whitcomb, seeing salvation, quickly made his way over to Victor, standing behind the armed arrival. The judge's movement however triggered something in Brennan – rage breaking through as he raised his weapon towards Whitcomb—

Another figure burst through the door behind Brennan. Mitchell Daggett charged onto the roof, and his eyes locked not on Harper or Klein, but directly on Brennan.

'This ends now!' Mitchell shouted; all calculation gone from his voice.

Brennan pivoted, hatred transforming his face.

'The prodigal son! Come to watch Daddy's empire burn?'

Mitchell didn't slow, didn't hesitate – just charged directly at Brennan with reckless abandon. The movement caught everyone by surprise, including Brennan himself, as Mitchell collided with the Irishman at full speed, driving them both towards the roof's edge.

'Mitchell!' Victor's shout carried genuine fear and Harper used the distraction to move, as at the roof's edge Mitchell and Brennan locked in mutual destruction – neither yielding, neither retreating. Their momentum carried them to the precipice, boots slipping on rain-slicked concrete.

'No one walks away from this,' Mitchell snarled, fingers locked around Brennan's throat. 'What did you do to Moira?'

'Do you really want to know?' Brennan replied, and it almost looked as if he was enjoying himself.

'You owe me that!'

'I owe you shite! Just like I owed my *snitch bitch* cousin a slow death for what she did, siding with scum like you! But if you want, I'll tell you!' Brennan replied, a bloody smile spreading across his face as he grabbed Mitchell's own throat and twisted, deliberately overbalancing them both. 'I gave her to my men, shot her in the face and *fed her to the feckin' pigs!*'

'*Bastard!*' Mitchell screamed as he squeezed hard, the momentum still pulling him forward.

Victor lunged forward, hand outstretched towards his son, but it was too late. Mitchell Daggett and Sean Brennan, enemies by name and nature toppled over the edge of the building together, their figures silhouetted against the sky for one brief moment before disappearing into the darkness below.

The sound of their impact came seconds later – distant but final.

Victor Daggett stood frozen at the edge; face transformed by something Harper had never expected to see there: genuine grief. In that moment, he wasn't a crime boss or corrupt businessman, just a father who had watched his son die.

The helicopter's engines whined louder as the pilot prepared for immediate take off, deciding the last place he wanted to be was here. Klein, recovering from the shock, dragged Jake towards the aircraft.

'It's over, Victor!' Klein called. 'We need to move now!'

But Victor Daggett remained at the edge, staring into the darkness below where his son and oldest enemy had fallen. Something had broken in him – the calculation and control that had defined him now replaced by hollow emptiness.

Harper raised the shotgun, sighting on Klein as the deputy reached the helicopter's open door.

'Let the boy go,' Harper shouted over the rotor noise. 'Or you don't leave this roof alive.'

Klein's hand moved from Jake's shoulder to the back of his neck, tightening just enough to make his control clear.

'What's your play here, Klein?' Harper asked. 'Use the boy as a hostage?

Something flickered in Klein's expression – the first crack in his professional composure.

'Your goddamned interference has caused certain... improvisations.'

There was a groan of anguish behind, and Harper glanced quickly to see that Victor Daggett had collapsed to the roof, the pistol now on the ground beside him. Meanwhile, Whitcomb was choosing not to stay, running for the far stairwell. He likely thought himself safe, but with luck, he'd run straight into Terry and his compound bow.

Not literally though, Harper hoped.

Jake remained still beneath Klein's grip; his eyes locked on Harper. No fear now, just calculating attention. So much like Mike it was painful to see.

'It's over, Klein,' Harper repeated, taking another step forward. 'Your only play now is surrender.'

'Is that what you thought during your time in the special forces?' Klein asked suddenly. 'The times your team was compromised, routes blocked, assets burned? Did you surrender then, Captain Harper?'

Using his former rank and the specific knowledge of his service history caught Harper momentarily off-guard, but he shook it off quickly.

'Different circumstances,' Harper replied. 'Different stakes.'

Jake's eyes hadn't left Harper's face. Something in his expression shifted subtly, and Harper recognised the look immediately.

'You won't shoot me,' Klein said. 'Not while I have the boy. You prioritise his safety above all other objectives. It's what brought you here, after all. Concern for Mike Colton's family.'

'Don't do it. You'll regret it for the rest of your life,' Harper said, softer now.

'You think I care about his life?' Klein almost laughed.

'I wasn't talking to you,' Harper replied. 'I was talking to Jake. Didn't you think it was strange how he was so easily caught?'

Jake moved with startling speed – driving his shoulder directly into Klein's shoulder while twisting away from the deputy's grip. The motion caught Klein momentarily off-balance, his hand instinctively reaching to stabilise himself rather than restrain Jake, dropping his own weapon—

The moment was enough. Jake's hand now held his father's Gerber Strongarm, and before Klein could react, he rammed it into the deputy's side. However he'd mis-angled the thrust, and it wasn't as deep as it could be, likely glancing off a rib as Klein threw Jake to the floor, while the helicopter pilot, finally tiring of whatever story was unfolded – or more likely deciding this wasn't worth a jail term – lifted off. Klein screamed at him impotently, realising his way off the roof was now removed as the helicopter flew off into the dull, morning rain.

He sighed, pulled out the blade, straightened, and turned back to face Harper.

'You still don't understand what you've walked into, Harper,' he said, almost sadly.

'Maybe not,' Harper replied, dropping the shotgun and pulling out the combat blade he'd taken from the guard. 'But it ends with you.'

Judge Whitcomb had always been a lucky bastard, and right now his luck was keeping true. Granted, his way out was gone, but he was already texting the pilot, telling him to get off the roof and meet him out in the clearing. If he found himself facing anyone from Blüdridge, he'd just claim innocence, say he was an unwilling pawn, and even if he was arrested, so what? He wouldn't see a day of jail time.

However, as he paused in the entranceway to finish the text, there was a *shunk* noise as an arrow – a *bloody arrow* – slammed into the wall beside him.

Looking up, Whitcomb raised his hands as he faced Terry, nocking another arrow to his compound bow.

Judge Whitcomb frowned.

'You know, I know everyone in Blüdridge,' he said conversationally. 'But I don't recognise you. Why is that?'

Terry smiled.

'Because I ain't from your goddamned town,' he replied.

'I think we can discuss this—' Whitcomb gave the warmest smile he could as he started to talk his way out of this but then flinched back as the wall beside him exploded with the impact of a rifle round. '—what the hell was that?'

'That'll be Sarah Colton, and her husband's HK .308 rifle,' Terry grinned. 'Be grateful for small mercies; she was probably aiming for your thick skull. Now drop the phone and get on the floor, hands behind your head.'

Staring out into the open, wondering if the Widow Colton truly was out there, Judge Whitcomb decided not to risk it, and dropped to the floor.

For a heartbeat, neither man moved on the roof.

The moment stretched between them, time seeming to slow as Harper calculated angles, distances, probabilities. Across the rooftop, Jake remained still, sensing that any sudden move might spark utter carnage. Even Victor Daggett didn't flinch – though that might've been because he was physically incapable, still staring off the roof.

Then Harper moved.

He closed the distance in a blur, boots slamming against the tarred surface. Klein reacted fast, raising in a smooth, practised motion. The blade caught the light – thick, full-tang steel, made for combat and worse.

Harper ducked under the first slash, closing the gap as Klein twisted his body to keep distance, wincing as it tore at his knife wound. Not that this gave Harper an advantage, with his own broken ribs and lacerated shoulders, all this did was even the odds a little. Harper wasn't fast – not any more – but he was relentless. He drove into Klein with raw force, both of them smashing into the edge of the roof.

Klein struck low with the knife, aiming for Harper's ribs. Harper twisted just enough to catch the blade along his side – shallow, but hot with pain. His own knife came up – a basic, no-frills thing with a rubber grip and budget steel – and he slashed hard towards Klein's face.

Klein pulled back, the tip grazing across his cheekbone. Blood welled instantly as he answered with a vicious knee to Harper's injured ribs. The pain was blinding – a white-hot explosion through Harper's chest – but even though he dropped the knife; he didn't fall. Instead, he stepped in, grabbed Klein's wrist mid-swing, and drove his forehead into the deputy's face with savage force.

Cartilage crunched. Blood sprayed.

Klein staggered back, but didn't drop the Gerber. Harper,

now unarmed, followed with a brutal punch to Klein's side. Klein screamed, his knife hand faltering. Harper rammed a shoulder into him.

'For Mike,' Harper growled, driving a second savage strike into his gut.

Klein doubled over, coughing, but brought the knife back up, swinging wide. The blade missed Harper and arced dangerously close to Jake, who now ducked and bolted, dragging the half-comatose Daggett with him.

Harper caught Klein's wrist again, twisting hard. The deputy fought back with surprising strength, landing an elbow that split Harper's lip. Blood filled Harper's mouth as they grappled, each straining for control of the blade.

Klein drove forward, using momentum and weight, forcing Harper towards the roof's edge.

'You're dead,' Klein hissed through bloodied teeth.

Harper stopped resisting. Instead, he dropped his weight and pivoted, gripping Klein's belt and twisting hard. The deputy's own momentum carried him forward, and he slammed into the rooftop guttering, breath forced from his lungs as he scrambled for balance – knife slipping from his fingers, forgotten as he grabbed for anything to hold on to.

Harper didn't hesitate. He drove forward with everything he had left, slamming into Klein and sending him over the edge.

'Wait!' Klein gasped, panic overriding control. 'We can deal!'

'No deals,' Harper said as he pushed back with final, brutal anger. Klein's expression twisted into pure terror as he overbalanced – one hand shooting out, catching Harper's jacket in desperation. For a moment, he hung there, suspended over empty space, hundreds of feet below.

Their eyes locked. All pretence gone, just raw fear in Klein's face.

'Please,' he whispered.

Harper stared into the eyes of Mike's killer and felt nothing.

'You, Daggett, Brennan. You're all cancers to the town,' he said. 'You need to go join them.'

'What about Whitcomb?' Klein pleaded. 'I can help.'

'Like you helped kill Mike?' Harper reached down to the roof, Klein still scrambling to hold his jacket and picked up Klein's own weapon; the one that killed Sheriff Mills, the one that killed Ray Halvorsen. 'Nah, I'm good. Oh, by the way? Mike says *fuck you.*'

Two shots thundered across the rooftop. Klein jerked as both rounds tore through his chest. His fingers went slack, releasing Harper's jacket as life drained from his eyes, falling without sound, his body tumbling through the air before hitting the ground below with a dull, final thud.

Harper stepped back from the roof's edge; gun still raised as he confirmed Klein was no longer a threat. Only then did he turn towards Jake, who watched from the doorway.

'You okay?' Harper asked.

Jake nodded, still staring at the edge of the roof, as if expecting Klein to pop back up, not as dead as believed. Harper felt the weight of accumulated injuries asserting themselves – his shoulder bleeding freely, ribs grinding with each breath, fresh cuts and bruises forming across his body; the aftermath of violence settling into his flesh like an unwelcome guest.

'Is he dead?' Jake asked.

'Yes,' Harper confirmed, seeing no benefit in softening reality for a boy who'd already experienced too much of it.

He looked around.

'Victor Daggett?'

Jake pointed into the stairwell where, sat against the wall was the weeping form of Victor Daggett. Harper knew that he should have felt some kind of sorrow for the man, but it was proving very hard to do so.

'Whitcomb?'

Jake shrugged, and Harper grimaced.

'Well, hopefully we'll find a way to get him.'

'And the town?'

'Will survive,' Harper said as they carried on through the now quiet plant. 'Though not as it was.'

As they reached the main entrance, Harper spotted movement on the access road – not sheriff's department cruisers but unmarked SUVs with government plates.

'Federal agents,' Harper explained to Jake, noting the boy's tension. 'Looks like the evidence got through.'

He stopped as he saw Terry leaning against a car, bow in hand.

'You got out,' Harper smiled, but it was more a comment than surprise. 'I thought you were supposed to be following me up, had my back and all that?'

'Got distracted by this,' Terry said, opening the back of the car up where, hogtied and gagged was Judge Whitcomb. 'Couldn't remember if you'd asked for a corrupt judge for Christmas or not.'

The lead SUV stopped thirty yards away, agents exiting from both sides. Their weapons remained ready but not aimed directly, which was promising; cautious protocol rather than immediate threat assessment meant they weren't here to fight.

'Identify yourselves,' the lead agent called.

'Liam Harper and Jake Colton,' Harper replied, keeping his hands visible. 'This is Terry – I'm sorry, Terry, I never asked your surname.'

'Terry Raymond,' Terry smiled. 'I got you a Judge Whitcomb in the car.'

'Victor Daggett is on the top floor, and Sean Brennan, Mitchell Daggett and Deputy Klein are all out back, having fallen from the roof,' Harper added. 'Although the latter of those was already dead when he hit the ground. Self-defence.'

'And the people out here?'

'Townsfolk from Blüdridge, fighting for what's theirs.'

The lead agent approached; credentials extended.

'Special Agent Davis, FBI. We received documentation regarding criminal operations in Blüdridge. Multiple federal violations, evidence of corruption extending through local law enforcement, videos that were... troubling.'

'Took your time.'

'Yeah, well, the evidence missed my inbox,' Davis admitted sheepishly. 'Let's just say it was an administrative error.'

Or, rather, a paid-off asset in your department, Harper thought to himself, but didn't speak it aloud.

'The evidence is accurate,' he confirmed. 'Along with additional material in the conference room that Whitcomb wasn't able to squirrel away. Have a good look around, guys.'

Harper felt Jake's presence beside him, the boy quiet but watchful, processing everything with his father's analytical mind. The truth had been exposed, justice for Mike secured.

What came next would be choices rather than obligations – possibilities rather than necessities.

Harper reached into his pocket, fingers finding the small river stone he'd carried since training, its smooth surface cool against his skin.

For luck, he'd always told himself. But perhaps it had always been something more – a reminder that erosion could reshape even the hardest substances given sufficient time and pressure.

'Jake!'

The sound came from the east, and Harper turned to see Sarah run towards her son, HK on a combat sling, tears running down her face. Behind her, Luis, Chris, Jenkins and Terry's two boys, Zach and Connor followed cautiously, the latter two embracing their father as he walked over.

'You convinced the town,' Harper said, and it wasn't a question. It was a statement of fact, a task he knew she would have done, and done easily. 'You got them to fight.'

'Not all, but enough,' Luis replied as Sarah embraced Jake hard. 'You should have heard her, though. It was like the ghosts of Blood Ridge demanded us to remember who we were.'

Sarah looked back up at Harper and nodded thanks as she ruffled Jake's hair. She didn't need to speak. She knew what'd happened, even without seeing Klein's body.

The day of reckoning had arrived.

29

FULL CIRCLE

Sunset painted "Blood Ridge" in fading gold as Harper stood at the church window, watching as federal agents continued their systematic dismantling of Blüdridge's corrupt infrastructure. Three days had passed since Klein's death at the coal plant, and now the town still breathed – stunned, uncertain, but alive.

Father Jonathan moved beside him; hands clasped behind his back. The priest's face showed exhaustion but something else too – tentative hope, perhaps.

'The last of Brennan's men left this morning,' he said quietly. 'Packed up whatever wasn't seized and disappeared north.'

'And Daggett's organisation?'

'In federal custody or scattered to the wind.' Father Jonathan's mouth tightened into a thin line. 'Victor Daggett and Judge Whitcomb were transferred to federal facilities yesterday. Preliminary hearings scheduled for next month.'

Harper nodded, watching a group of agents examining

documents outside what had once been Daggett Financial Services. Evidence bags were carried to unmarked vehicles.

'The church has become something of a town centre,' Father Jonathan continued. 'People gathering, sharing information, offering support. Even those who never attended services before.'

'Communities adapt when systems fail,' Harper observed.

'They do indeed.' The priest studied Harper's profile. 'Your injuries?'

'Healing,' Harper replied simply. His ribs still protested with each deep breath, but the pain had dulled to a manageable ache.

Outside, Harper spotted Sarah and Jake crossing the street towards the church, accompanied by Luis. Jake walked with new confidence, shoulders straighter than when Harper had first arrived for Mike's funeral. Something had hardened in him – not innocence lost but purpose found. Harper was just happy he hadn't lost too much innocence on that roof – killing Klein would have been a step too far.

The church door opened inwards, and Joy appeared carrying a tray of sandwiches and coffee. Her silver-streaked hair was pulled back in its familiar neat bun, but weariness lined her face.

'Thought you all might need this,' she said, setting the tray on a nearby table. 'Been feeding half the town since this started.'

'Appreciated,' Father Jonathan said, taking a cup.

Joy's eyes found Harper's.

'Didn't think you'd still be here. Figured you for the type to disappear once the shooting stopped.'

'Almost gone,' Harper replied with a hint of a smile.

Joy studied him with the same shrewd assessment she'd shown during their first meeting at the diner.

'Stay safe,' she finally said. 'Some jobs need finishing properly.'

There was something in the way she said this, and Harper smiled as through the door and behind her, looking abashed at being spotted was Terry.

It looked like other people had jobs to finish, too.

Sarah, Jake and Luis entered the church, bringing with them the sounds of the street – federal agents coordinating operations, townspeople exchanging information, a community reorienting itself after catastrophic change.

'Harper,' Sarah greeted him warmly. 'Agent Davis says the garage will be released tomorrow.'

'Good news,' Harper replied.

Luis stepped forward; his arm still bandaged but healing.

'We've been making plans. Sarah's offered me the manager position. Going to rebuild it the way Mike wanted. Klein torched it bad, but we can fix it up real fast.'

'He'd approve,' Harper said. 'Though I owe you a new work shirt. Borrowed one when I had to bandage my ribs with my one.'

Luis laughed.

'Small price for what you did. I'll order a dozen, all with the logo on – you can take your pick next time you pass through. You know, when you come to help out in the main bay.'

Before Harper could answer, Jenkins from the hardware store entered, carrying rolled blueprints under his arm. The shopkeeper looked exhausted but determined, the same expression worn by many in Blüdridge now.

'Found these in the town archives,' Jenkins announced, spreading the plans across a pew. 'Original settlement maps from 1864, before the battle that gave us our name.'

Everyone gathered around, studying the yellowed documents. The town's layout appeared familiar yet different – simpler, more orderly, unmarked by the divisions that would define it in later years.

'Union and Confederate troops met right there,' Jenkins said, pointing to the ridge. 'But the real bloodshed was in town. Neighbour against neighbour, brother against brother. Some families never spoke again.'

'History that keeps repeating,' Father Jonathan observed quietly.

'Maybe not any more,' Joy said. 'Those families – Daggett, Brennan – they're finished here.'

'Blood feuds don't die easily,' Jenkins countered. 'This town's seen violence cycle through generations. And families that leave always seem to come back to continue fighting. Just look at Sean Brennan.'

'Cycles can be broken,' Harper said.

The group fell silent, considering the implications. The town had a chance now – perhaps its first in generations – to redefine itself beyond corruption and division.

'Well,' Joy said finally, her practical nature reasserting itself, 'history won't rewrite itself while we stand here. Drink your coffee before it gets cold.'

The conversation shifted as they shared the meal, discussing reconstruction plans, community needs, steps towards a new Blüdridge. Harper listened more than he spoke, watching these people – recent strangers, now connected to him through crisis – begin the strenuous work of rebuilding.

AS EVENING APPROACHED, THE CHURCH GRADUALLY EMPTIED. Federal agents retreated to temporary headquarters, townspeople returned to homes or businesses, life finding tentative new rhythms.

Harper found Terry outside, staring up at the ridge that dominated the eastern horizon. The older man looked thoughtful, his weathered face showing the weight of recent events.

'Heading back to Hagerstown?' Harper asked, joining him.

Terry shook his head.

'Going back to my gas station. My sons want me to stay with them, but...'

He shrugged.

'Running don't solve anything. Learned that much watching this town.'

Harper nodded, understanding the decision.

'Long drive ahead.'

'Worth it,' Terry replied. 'Place is mine. Built it from nothing. Not giving it up because some thugs think I should.'

'They might come back,' Harper warned.

Terry smiled thinly.

'Let them. I've got a compound bow and damn good aim. And my boys promised to check in more often. Also, I'm an honorary member of this town now, and I've been told they look after their own, so I might be calling on that favour.'

They stood in companionable silence, watching the sun sink lower towards the western horizon.

'And Joy?' Harper asked with a smile.

'I've promised to come visit,' Terry smiled. 'Neither of us

are spring chickens. Who knows, maybe she'll be the one that convinces me to sell up and move on. She's a hell of a woman.'

One of the FBI SUVs drove past, pausing the conversation.

'You in trouble with them?' Terry asked, nodding at it.

'No,' Harper shook his head. 'Santos and the others are all trying to save their skins, so they've all confessed as to how Klein killed Mike, Mills, and Ray. Whitcomb's giving up everything else. All they can have me for is civil unrest, I think. And as I sorted them one of their largest drug busts and helped take down two criminal organisations – three, if you count Whitcomb – I think I'm safe.'

There was a long moment of silence.

'What about you?' Terry finally asked. 'Sticking around?'

Harper considered the question. The debt that had brought him to Blüdridge was paid – justice for Mike secured; his killers facing consequences. What remained now were choices rather than obligations.

'Time to move on,' he said.

'Road's calling?' Terry nodded his understanding.

'Something like that,' Harper agreed. 'Though I've got another debt to settle first.'

There was movement to the side, and Harper glanced around to see Sarah approaching, clipboard in hand, Jake following her.

'There you are,' she smiled. 'We're finalising volunteer schedules for the garage renovation...'

She studied his expression.

'You're leaving.'

It wasn't a question. Harper nodded, and disappointment flickered across Sarah's face, but she nodded acceptance.

'You've done more than enough. We can handle it from here.'

'I know you can,' Harper said.

'Where will you go?' Jake asked.

'Not sure yet,' Harper admitted. 'The road has its own ideas sometimes. But I'm on a quest of my own, something connected to my own father. This has just pressed on me to see that through, too.'

The boy hesitated, then extended his hand formally.

'Thank you. For what you did for Dad.'

Harper shook his hand, struck again by how much the boy resembled Mike – not just physically, but in his direct gaze, his straightforward manner.

'Your father was a good man. Worth fighting for.'

AS DUSK SETTLED OVER BLÜDRIDGE, HARPER MADE HIS farewells, promising to return someday – but he knew in his heart this was more a possibility rather than a commitment. The Bonneville waited in the church parking lot, ready for whatever journey came next, checked over extensively to remove any further trackers or modifications.

Harper left Blüdridge at first light, the Bonneville's engine echoing against buildings still sleeping in pre-dawn stillness. The town looked different now – wounds visible but healing, facades stripped away to reveal foundations that might, with care, support something honest.

And that was enough for Harper.

NIGHT HAD FALLEN OVER *TERRY'S AUTO & GAS*. THE fluorescent lights cast harsh pools of illumination across the forecourt, revealing the worn concrete and carefully maintained pumps. Terry wiped his hands on a shop rag as he finished checking inventory, satisfaction clear in his weathered face, even with a couple of days off.

The station stood quiet now, isolated on this stretch of rural highway where traffic grew sparse after dark. In fact, Terry was about to close up shop for the day when headlights swept across the forecourt. Three vehicles pulled in, positioning themselves in a formation that immediately set off warning bells in his mind.

This wasn't the approach of customers seeking fuel or repairs.

Seven men emerged, spreading out with deliberate movements as they approached. Their leader – a stocky bloke with a shaved head, his arms covered in faded tattoos – stepped forward, his face twisted in a sneer that Terry recognised immediately. The same men who'd threatened that woman, Nadine, days ago, now returned with reinforcements.

'Remember us, old man?' the leader called, voice carrying across the forecourt. 'Saw you ran away for a few days. Should have stayed gone. We got some unfinished business.'

Terry straightened, setting the shop rag aside.

'Station's closed. Come back tomorrow if you need fuel.'

The man laughed, an ugly sound.

'We don't need fuel. We need compensation.'

'Compensation?' Terry repeated.

'That woman who left here with a fixed car instead of paying us?' One of the other men said, stepping forward. 'Cost us eight hundred dollars, plus the rest.'

'And now we hear that limey bastard on the motorcycle is

connected to you,' the bald leader added, anger visible in every line of his body. 'So you're paying double – for the woman *and* for him.'

'Not happening,' Terry replied calmly. 'I suggest you leave while you still can.'

The men fanned out, creating a semicircle that pushed Terry back against the pump island. The shorter one produced a knife, the blade catching the fluorescent light. Two others pulled out what looked like tyre irons from beneath their jackets.

'Last chance, old man,' the tall one warned, his voice dropping to a threatening growl. 'Pay up, or things get ugly. Real ugly.'

He leant close.

'*Please* let things get ugly, yeah? I've wanted to kick your ass since—'

'You boys picked the wrong gas station,' Terry interrupted, his voice more calm than he felt.

'Really?' The leader looked around theatrically. 'Don't see nobody here but us and you. Seven against one. Not great odds.'

'He said you picked the wrong station.'

The voice came from the darkness beyond the forecourt's harsh illumination. The men turned sharply, momentarily confused by the unexpected interruption.

A figure emerged from the shadows, moving with calm, deliberate steps into the pool of light. The bald leader's eyes widened in recognition – it was the same Brit motorcyclist from days before, the one who had interfered with their scam.

'You!' he sputtered, anger mixing with surprise. 'What the hell are you doing here?'

'Finishing what we started,' Harper replied, his voice carrying easily across the suddenly quiet forecourt. 'Didn't think we'd forgot about you, did you?'

Beside the leader, the shorter man stepped forward, fury contorting his features.

'You cost us good money, you British prick. And now you're gonna pay for it.'

'Actually,' Harper said, continuing his advance, 'I think you'll find *I'm* not the one who's going to be paying tonight.'

'There's seven of us and two of you,' the tall man sneered, regaining his composure. 'Bad odds, limey.'

'You sure about that?' Terry asked, a smile spreading across his weathered face. As if on cue, the garage bay door rolled up completely and Terry's sons emerged, their massive frames filling the doorway, both carrying themselves with the calm confidence of men who knew how to handle trouble, shotguns in their hands.

Simultaneously, headlights swept across the forecourt as a new vehicle pulled into the station. The door of a familiar pickup opened, revealing Jenkins from the hardware store, while from behind emerged Chris and Luis. All carried shotguns as well.

The tow-truck leader's sneer collapsed as he reassessed the situation. Equal odds now, with firearms entering the equation.

'What the hell is this?' he demanded, taking an involuntary step back.

'This,' Harper replied, stepping close enough that the man could see the scar above his eyebrow, 'is an *intervention*. It's what happens when you pick the wrong people to threaten.'

'You trying to start a war?' the leader asked, his voice less confident now.

'Just finishing one actually,' Harper replied, his voice dropping to a dangerous whisper. 'Here's how this works. You leave now. You don't come back. Not to this station, not to this road, not to anywhere Terry or his sons might see you. Ever.'

He paused, letting his next words carry quiet menace.

'Or I'll demonstrate exactly what happened to the last group of men who thought numbers alone made them untouchable.'

'Oh yeah? And where was that?' The leader spoke with a rapidly failing bravado.

'Blood Ridge.'

It was said as two words, the intention clear, and something in Harper's eyes – a cold certainty born of experience with violence – made the man swallow visibly. He'd heard the news reports, and the rumours of what happened in Maryland had travelled back here as well.

The stranger on a motorcycle who took down two criminal empires.

He glanced from Harper to Terry's sons, to the shotguns, back to Harper.

'This isn't over,' he muttered, but the threat sounded hollow even to his own ears.

'Oh, I think it is,' Harper said. 'In fact, I'm counting on you trying something stupid right now. Been a long ride, and I could use the chance to blow off some steam.'

The challenge hung in the night air, a promise rather than a boast.

The leader made his decision, gesturing to his companions.

'Fine,' he muttered. 'This place is crap, anyway. We won't go where we're not wanted.'

'And we won't see you again?'

The leader paused, licked his lips nervously, and tried to smile.

'Hey, it's only eight hundred bucks,' he said. 'What's that between friends?'

'Good answer,' Harper said while the tow-truck team retreated to their vehicles, casting final glares of impotent fury before engines roared to life and they sped away from the station.

The forecourt now quiet again, Terry approached, clapping a hand on Harper's shoulder.

'Remind me never to play you at poker,' he said.

Harper smiled, a genuine expression that erased the cold threat of moments before.

'Just paying debts, Terry,' he said. 'That's all any of us can do.'

VICTOR DAGGETT HADN'T EXPECTED THE VISITOR. SINCE arriving at the Federal Penitentiary, Daggett had been treated almost like a superstar; the name wasn't just known in Blüdridge, after all, the Daggetts were known across the Tri-County lines, and there were enough associates and employees of his behind bars to provide him security and a pleasant existence until the authorities decided what they wanted to do with him.

He didn't really care, if he was being honest. His son was dead, killed by a vengeance that he had helped stoke the flames of, and Whitcomb, the judge that had organised it all was now in witness protection. Daggett wanted nothing more than to find him, to gain revenge for the chaos Whitcomb had sown, and so he had kept to himself for the last week, only speaking to his lawyer when requested while waiting for information that seemed very hard to come by.

So, learning that a complete stranger wanted to speak to him had proven to be quite a surprise.

There was no glass wall, no phones to speak through; when you were Victor Daggett, the guards would arrange a personal meeting. And so it was in the outside yard, the inmates taken inside, that Victor Daggett saw the man who wanted to speak to him. He was maybe late sixties, muscled with short salt-and-pepper hair and an expensive suit that put his entire wardrobe to shame. He bore the look and positioning of career military – but nobody got *that* rich off career military.

'Thanks for meeting me, Mister Daggett,' the stranger said. 'My name's Mason Carrick.'

He held out a hand, shaking Victor's with a firm handshake. It wasn't any kind of power play; the man was simply that strong, that sure of himself. For all the years that Daggett had been the leader, one of the most feared men in Blüdridge, for the first time in a long while, he felt nervous.

'I understand you can help me?' Victor asked.

Mason Carrick smiled, sitting down on one of the benches to the side of the open space, leaning back with a casualness that most people didn't have in such a location.

'We can find your judge for you,' he went on, as if it was the simplest thing in the world. 'I've got contacts in all forms of law enforcement. Give me a week and I'll know who he is now, what he's saying… and then you can tell us what you'd like to do to him.'

Victor Daggett nodded.

'And in return?' he asked, raising an eyebrow. 'Things like this never come cheap, after all.'

'Nothing more than information,' Mason replied, 'in particular about the young man that's caused you such concern recently.'

'What, Harper?' Daggett raised an eyebrow. 'Whatever you're offering, I think you'll find I've got first dibs on that son of a—'

'Actually, Mister Daggett, I'm afraid you don't,' Mason leant forwards now, his eyes narrowing as his voice lowered. 'You see, Liam Harper and I have known each other for a very long time. And ever since his daddy's death, he's been a bit of a thorn in my side. I was hoping you could give me information about why he was passing through your shithole of a town.'

'Nothing more than a funeral of a friend,' Daggett replied. 'Although I think he's following his father's wishes somehow.'

'As I just said, his daddy's dead.'

'I know,' Daggett continued, 'but I got the impression he's got a whole list of things that he has to fix. His exact words were that he was "travelling across America with a notebook of his father's sins, fixing them before he could finish", if you understand what the hell that means.'

'I do indeed,' Mason said, waving for the guard, indicating the meeting was over. 'Thank you for that. We'll sort your judge for you. You'll hear from us soon.'

'Who the hell are you?' Daggett asked as the guards walked over.

'We're *Aegis*, the security company you *should* have hired,' Mason smiled, still sitting as Victor Daggett, confused, was walked back to his cell.

Left alone in the yard, Mason Carrick leant back, steepling his fingers together.

'So, little Liam's travelling across America with a notebook of his father's sins?' he murmured to himself. 'Well, that's *very* interesting.'

Want the next Liam Harper Thriller? CLICK HERE on digital, or turn the page...

Liam Harper will return in his next thriller

TRACK SHIFT

Order Now at Amazon:

mybook.to/trackshift

Released 17th November, 2025

Gain up-to-the-moment information on the release by signing up to our VIP Reader's Club!

Join at http://bit.ly/jackgatlandVIP

ABOUT THE AUTHOR

Jack Gatland is the pen name of *#1 New York Times Bestselling Author* Tony Lee, who has been writing in all media for thirty-five years, including comics, graphic novels, middle grade books, audio drama, TV and film for *DC Comics, Marvel, BBC, ITV, Random House, Penguin USA, Hachette* and a ton of other publishers and broadcasters.

These have included licences such as ***Doctor Who, Spider Man, X-Men, Star Trek, Battlestar Galactica, MacGyver,*** BBC's ***Doctors, Wallace and Gromit*** and ***Shrek***, as well as work created with musicians such as ***Ozzy Osbourne, Joe Satriani, Beartooth, Pantera, Megadeth, Iron Maiden*** and ***Bruce Dickinson.***

As Tony, he's toured the world talking to reluctant readers with his 'Change The Channel' school tours, and lectures on screenwriting, story craft and comic scripting for festivals and conferences such as *Raindance* in London and *Author Nation, The Global Publishing Summit* and *20Books* globally.

A Freeman of the City of London and an introvert West Londoner by heart, he lives with his wife Tracy, just outside London.

Feel free to follow Jack on all his social media by clicking on the links below. Over time these can be places where we can engage, discuss Declan, Ellie, Liam, Tom and others, and put the world to rights.

www.jackgatland.com
www.hoodemanmedia.com

Visit Jack's Reader's Group Page
(Mainly for fans to discuss his books):
https://www.facebook.com/groups/jackgatland

Subscribe to Jack's Readers List:
https://bit.ly/jackgatlandVIP

www.facebook.com/jackgatlandbooks
www.twitter.com/jackgatlandbook
ww.instagram.com/jackgatland

Want more books by Jack Gatland? Turn the page...

Printed in Dunstable, United Kingdom

76984334R00234